Contemporary
West Coast
Stories

Contemporary

West Coast

Stories

Edited by

C. Michael Curtis
Senior Editor, *The Atlantic*

The
Globe
Pequot
Press

Old Saybrook, Connecticut

"Fireworks" from *Rock Springs* by Richard Ford. Copyright © 1987 by Richard Ford. Reprinted with permission of Grove/Atlantic Monthly Press.

"Death Valley" by Joyce Carol Oates. Copyright © 1991 by The Ontario Review, Inc. Reprinted with the permission of John Hawkins Agency. First published in *Esquire*.

"The Other Miller" by Tobias Wolff. Copyright © 1986 by Tobias Wolff. Reprinted with permission of International Creative Management, Inc. First published in *The Atlantic*.

"Two Kinds" from *The Joy Luck Club* by Amy Tan. Copyright © 1989 by Amy Tan. Reprinted with permission of The Putnam Publishing Group. First published in *The Atlantic*.

"Where We Are Now" from *Emperor of the Air* by Ethan Canin. Copyright © 1988 by Ethan Canin. Reprinted with permission of Houghton Mifflin Company. All rights reserved. First published in *The Atlantic*.

"I Don't Believe This" by Merrill Joan Gerber. Copyright © 1986 by Merrill Joan Gerber. Reprinted with permission of the author. First published in *The Atlantic*.

"Edie: A Life" by Harriet Doerr. Copyright © 1988 by Harriet Doerr. Reprinted with permission of the author. First published in *EPOCH*.

"Brief Lives in California" from *Desires* by John L'Heureux. Copyright © 1984 by John L'Heureux. Reprinted with permission of the author.

"Yellow Flags" by Charles Eastman. Copyright © 1992 by Charles Eastman. Reprinted with permission of the author. First published in *The Atlantic*.

"The Jungle of Injustice" by Nora Johnson. Copyright © 1980 by Nora Johnson. Reprinted with permission of the author. First published in *The Atlantic*.

"The Women Who Walk" from *The Women Who Walk and Other Stories* by Nancy Huddleston Packer. Copyright © 1989 by Nancy Huddleston Packer. Reprinted with permission of Louisiana State University Press. First published in *Southwest Review*.

"I-80" from *Night Driving* by Peter Behrens. Copyright © 1987 by Peter Behrens. Reprinted with permission of the author.

"The Scriptwriter" from *St. Augustine's Pigeon* by Evan Connell. Copyright © by Evan Connell. Reprinted with permission of Harold Matson, Inc.

"The Indians Don't Need Me Any More" from *Impossible Appetites* by James Fetler. Copyright © 1980 by James Fetler. Reprinted with permission of the University of Iowa Press.

"Heart" by Neil McMahon. Copyright © 1979 by Neil McMahon. Reprinted with permission of the author. First published in *The Atlantic*.

"Short Rounds with the Champ" from *Yours, and Mine* by Judith Rascoe. Copyright © 1969, 1970, 1971, 1972, 1973 by Judith Rascoe. Reprinted with permission of Little, Brown and Company.

"Mendocino" by Ann Packer. Copyright © 1988 by Ann Packer. Reprinted with permission of the author. First published in *The New Yorker*.

"Twilight on the El Camino" by Leslee Becker. Copyright © 1987 by Leslee Becker. Reprinted with permission of the author.

"Aquarius Obscured" by Robert Stone. Copyright © 1974 by Robert Stone. Reprinted with permission of Donadio & Ashworth, Inc. First published in *The American Review*.

"Camelot" from *A Hole in the Language* by Marly Swick. Copyright © 1990 by Marly Swick. Reprinted with permission of the University of Iowa Press.

Copyright © 1993 by C. Michael Curtis

Library of Congress Cataloging-in-Publication Data

Contemporary west coast stories / edited by C. Michael Curtis. — 1st ed.
        p.   cm.
    ISBN 1-56440-245-2
    1. Short stories, American—Pacific Coast (U.S.) 2. American fiction—20th century. 3. Pacific Coast (U.S.)—Fiction.
PS569.C66   1993
813'.0108979--dc20   93-14426
                                                              CIP

Manufactured in the United States of America
First Edition/First Printing

For Catherine Steiner-Adair,
who helped me to understand
how life stories work,
and how they can evolve

CONTENTS

INTRODUCTION

C. Michael Curtis

The first time I visited the West Coast, in the late 1960s, I was traveling with a group of political reporters on a trip through urban ghettos. We spent our one night in Los Angeles in a motel on the outskirts of Watts. My room, as I remember it, was hung with thick drapes, decorated with vibrant colors, and equipped with a sunken bathtub, at the foot of my bed. I knew instantly that most of what I'd heard about California was true, and I hardly dared think about what I would discover next.

I've been to the West Coast many times since, visiting writers and universities as far north as Puget Sound and as far south as San Diego; I've taught and lectured at Stanford, at UC San Diego, at the University of Oregon, and at writers' conferences at Tacoma, Berkeley, Palm Springs, and elsewhere. None of this makes me an expert on West Coast mores or quirkiness; even less does it entitle me to write confidently about how a "West Coast story" is predictably different from its East Coast counterpart. On the other hand, I've lived and worked for thirty years in Boston, Massachusetts, sharing those years with men and women who I eventually learned had settled here after having been raised in Iowa, or Georgia, or New Jersey, or—as in the case of at least two of us here at *The Atlantic*—in Arkansas. No doubt the western coastal states profit from the same admixture of native born and transients.

Even so, West Coast stories, superficially at least, do seem different. For one thing, a lot of what happens in these stories happens outside. And why not. The sun is shining, the fields are full of lettuce and avocados, and a warm breeze works its way inland from the bountiful Pacific. In West Coast stories nothing happens in the upper floors of skyscrapers because you don't find skyscrapers. Or even very tall buildings. Just about everything happens on the first floor, or in the yard, or on the beach, or in cars. And all that easy access to nature encourages domestic wanderlust, or so one would guess. A good many West Coast stories, though certainly not all, are about second wives or husbands, or other deep though not necessarily felicitous attachments.

West Coast writers describe characters who tend to be what they are, rather than extensions of childhood trauma. Their mistakes, which aren't so different from those of their East Coast peers, are somehow more willful, more children of the moment. They are not the actions of victims weighted down by years of parental neglect or abuse, but seem more spontaneous, weak-minded, impulsive, sometimes relentless—but always knowing, deliberate, even when catastrophic.

The film industry affects the culture of West Coast storytellers, no doubt because it is the pot of gold so many of them covet, or quietly resent. And because the film industry places such a premium on celebrity, on personal magnetism, on the rapid ebbing and flowing of careers, on physical beauty, all of these themes, and matters related to them, work their way into West Coast stories.

So does Stanford University, though covertly. Unlike eastern writers, who either identify themselves as former Harvard students or make sure you know they weren't and wouldn't have it any other way, West Coast writers say almost nothing about university life and certainly nothing about the alma mater so many of them share. The just retired and past directors of the Stanford Writing Program, Nancy Packer and John L'Heureux, are represented in this collection. So are a great many writers who studied in that program, including James Fetler, Robert Stone, Tobias Wolff, Neil McMahon, Leslee Becker, Peter Behrens, Harriet Doerr, Merrill Joan Gerber, and perhaps others. Typically, however, West Coast writers don't write about academic life. You find more truck drivers than college professors in their stories, as if their hearts, collectively, belonged to the open road, to surprises, to what W. H. Auden might have called the "[un]rehearsed response."

West Coast writers care about physicality, about spiritual variousness, about oneness with nature, and, of course, about the more universal themes: kindness, courage, generosity, forbearance, and discovery. The sins they write about tend to cut deeply, and while West Coast writers are rarely psychological in an obvious and learned way, they write with a great respect for the permanence and gravity of moral choice.

West Coast writers care very little about news, perhaps because they're outside so much they miss the evening news shows. This is in certain ways ironic, since a West Coast person knows who won the late ball games; indeed, to a West Coast person, they *aren't* late ball games. Instead of going to bed worried about the late results, as easterners do, westerners retire contented, fully informed, anxious only about things like greens fees, the absence of a workable urban transit system, and irrigation rights. Perhaps because so much of the news is available during the supper hour, it tends to be taken for granted. Many years may pass before it is fully understood. That may explain, in the stories in this collection, an unwavering interest in the Kennedy assassination and its aftermath.

Eight of the stories originally appeared in *The Atlantic;* ten more are by writers whose work *The Atlantic* has published. That is among the reasons they appear in this collection. They are like old friends— the stories or the writers, or both. Some of the writers began their lives in California; others merely studied there or established careers that have kept them there. In at least one or two cases, Joyce Carol Oates being a good example, setting is everything.

Running through all of these stories, however, to greater or lesser extent, are one or more of a set of overlapping themes: the imminence of natural forces, of ocean, forest, or eucalyptus grove; a yearning for adventure and the certainty of retribution; the fathomlessness of love; the dignity of sorrow; the weight of moral truth. Whether they make a case for lives that are uniquely western remains to be seen. That they make a case for lives lived in awareness, triumph, or great sadness is beyond question.

Contemporary

West Coast

Stories

FIREWORKS

Richard Ford

Eddie Starling sat at the kitchen table at noon reading through the newspaper. Outside in the street some neighborhood kids were shooting off firecrackers. The Fourth of July was a day away, and every few minutes there was a lot of noisy popping followed by a hiss, then a huge boom loud enough to bring down an airplane. It was giving him the jitters, and he wished some parent would go out and haul the kids inside.

Starling had been out of work six months—one entire selling season and part of the next. He had sold real estate, and had never been off work any length of time in his life. Though he had begun to wonder, after a certain period of not working, if you couldn't simply forget *how* to work, forget the particulars, lose the reasons for it. And once that happened, it could become possible never to hold another job as long as you lived. To become a statistic: the chronically unemployed. The thought worried him.

Outside in the street he heard what sounded like kids' noises again. They were up to something suspicious, and he stood up to look out just when the phone rang.

"What's new on the home front?" Lois's voice said. Lois had gone back to work tending bar near the airport and always tried to call up in good spirits.

"Status quo. Hot." Starling walked to the window, holding the receiver, and peered out. In the middle of the street some kids he'd never seen before were getting ready to blow up a tin can using an enormous firecracker. "Some kids are outside blowing up something."

"Anything good in the paper?"

"Nothing promising."

"Well," Lois said. "Just be patient, hon. I know it's hot. Listen, Eddie, do you remember those priests who were always setting fire to themselves on TV? Exactly when were they? We were trying to remember here. Was it '68 or '72? Nobody could remember to save their life."

"Sixty-eight was Kennedy," Starling said. "They weren't just setting themselves on fire for TV, though. They were in Asia."

"Okay. But when was Vietnam exactly?"

The kids lit the firecracker under the can and went running away down the street, laughing. For a moment Starling stared directly at the can, but just then a young woman came out of the house across the street. As she stepped into her yard the can went *boom*, and the woman leaped back and put her hands into her hair.

"Christ, what was that!" Lois said. "It sounded like a bomb."

"It was those kids."

"The scamps," Lois said. "I guess they're hot, too, though."

The woman was very thin—too thin to be healthy, Starling thought. She was in her twenties and had on dull yellow shorts and no shoes. She walked out into the street and yelled something vicious at the kids, who were far down the street now. Starling knew nothing more about her than he did about anybody else in the neighborhood. The name on the mailbox had been taped over before he and Lois had moved in. A man lived with the woman and worked on his car in the garage late at night.

The woman walked slowly back across her little yard to her house. At the top step she turned and looked at Starling's house. He stared at her, and the woman went inside and closed the door.

"Eddie, take a guess who's here," Lois said.

"Who's where?"

"In the bar. One wild guess."

"Arthur Godfrey," Starling said.

"Arthur Godfrey. That's great," Lois said. "No, it's Louie. He just waltzed in the door. Isn't that amazing?"

Louie Reiner was Lois's previous husband. Starling and Reiner had been business acquaintances of a sort before Lois came along, and had co-brokered some office property at the tail end of the boom.

Reiner had been in real estate then, along with everybody else. Reiner and Lois had stayed married six weeks, then they had gone over to Reno and gotten an annulment. A year later, Lois married Starling. That had all been in '76, and Lois didn't talk about it or about Reiner anymore. Louie had disappeared somewhere—he'd heard Europe. He didn't feel like he had anything against Louie now, though he wasn't particularly happy he was around.

"Just take a guess what Louie's doing?" Lois said. Water had started to run where Lois was.

"Who knows. Washing dishes. How should I know?"

Lois repeated what Starling said and some people laughed. He heard Louie's voice saying, "Well *excuuuse* me."

"Seriously, Ed. Louie's an extraditer." Lois laughed. Hah.

"What's that mean?" Starling said.

"It means he travels the breadth of the country bringing people back here so they can go to jail. He just brought a man back from Montana who'd done nothing more than pass a forty-seven-dollar bad check, which doesn't seem worth it to me. Louie isn't in uniform, but he's got a gun and a little beeper."

"What's he doing there?" Starling said.

"His girlfriend's coming in at the airport from Florida," Lois said. "He's a lot fatter than he used to be, too, though he wouldn't like me to say that, would you, Louie?" Starling heard Reiner say *Excuuuse me* again. "Do you want to talk to him?"

"I'm busy right now."

"Busy doing what, eating lunch? You're not busy."

"I'm fixing dinner," Starling lied.

"Talk to Louie, Eddie."

Starling wanted to hang up. He wished Reiner would go back to wherever he came from.

"Helloooo dere," Reiner said.

"Who left your cage open, Reiner?"

"Come on down here and have a drink, Starling, and I'll tell you all about it. I've seen the world since I saw you. Italy, France, the islands. You know what an Italian girl puts behind her ears to make herself more attractive?"

"I don't want to know," Starling said.

"That's not what Lois says." Reiner laughed a horse laugh.

"I'm busy. Some other time, maybe."

"Sure you are," Reiner said. "Listen, Eddie, get off your face and come down here. I'll tell you how we can both retire in six months. Honest to God. This is not real estate."

"I already retired," Starling said. "Didn't Lois tell you?"

"Yeah, she told me a lot of things," Reiner said.

He could hear Lois say, "Please don't be a nerd, Eddie. Who needs nerds?" Some people laughed again.

"I shouldn't even be talking about this on the phone. It's that hot." Reiner's voice fell to a whisper. He was covering the mouthpiece of the receiver, Starling thought. "These are Italian rugs, Starling. I swear to God. From the neck of the sheep, the neck only. You only get tips on things like this in law enforcement."

"I told you. I'm retired. I retired early," Starling said.

"Eddie, am I going to have to come out there and arrest you?"

"Try it," Starling said. "I'll beat the shit out of you, then laugh about it."

He heard Reiner put the phone down and say something he couldn't make out. Then he heard Reiner shout, "Stay on your face then, cluck!"

Lois came on the line again. "Baby, why don't you come down here?" A blender started in the background, and a big cheer went up. "We're all adults. Have a Tanqueray on Louie. He's on all-expenses. There might be something to this. Louie's always got ideas."

"Reiner's just got ideas about you. Not me." He heard Reiner say to Lois to tell him—Starling—to forget it. "Tell Reiner to piss up a rope."

"Try to be nice," Lois said. "Louie's being nice. Eddie—"

Starling hung up.

When he worked, Starling had sold business properties—commercial lots and office buildings. He had studied that in college, and when he got out he was offered a good job. People would always need a place to go to work, was his thinking. He liked the professional environment, the atmosphere of money being made, and for a while he had done very well. He and Lois had rented a nice, sunny apartment in an older part of town by a park. They bought furniture and didn't save money. While Starling worked, Lois kept house, took care of plants and fish and attended a night class for her degree in history. They had no children, and didn't expect any. They liked the size of the town and the stores, knew shopkeepers' names and where the streets led. It was a life they could like, and better than they both could've guessed would come their way.

Then interest rates had gone sky-high, and suddenly no one wanted commercial property. Everything was rent. Starling rented space in malls and in professional buildings and in empty shops downtown where older businesses had moved out and leather stores, health-food and copy shops moved in. It was a holding action, Starling thought, until people wanted to spend again.

Then he had lost his job. One morning, his boss at the agency asked him back to his private office along with a fat woman named Beverley who'd been there longer than Starling had. His boss told them he was closing down and wanted to tell them first because they'd been there the longest, and he wanted them to have a chance for the other jobs. Starling remembered feeling dazed when he heard the bad news, but he remembered thanking the boss, wishing him good luck, then comforting Beverley, who went to pieces in the outer office. He had gone home and told Lois, and they had gone out to dinner at a Greek restaurant that night, and gotten good and drunk.

As it turned out, though, there weren't any other jobs to get. He visited the other agencies and talked to salesmen he knew, but all of his friends were terrified of being laid off themselves and wouldn't say much. After a month, he heard that his boss hadn't closed the agency down, but had simply hired two new people to take his and Beverley's places. When he called to ask about it the boss apologized, then claimed to have an important call on another line.

In six weeks Starling had still not found a job, and when the money ran out and they couldn't pay the rent, he and Lois sublet the apartment to two nurses who worked at a hospital, and got out. Lois found an ad in the *Pennysaver* that said, "No Rent for Responsible Couple—House Sit Opportunity." And they moved in that day.

The house was a ranchette in a tract of small, insignificant houses on fenced-in postage-stamp lots down on the plain of the Sacramento River, out from town. The owner was an Air Force sergeant who had been stationed in Japan, and the house was decorated with Oriental tastes: wind chimes and fat, naked women stitched over silk, a red enamel couch in the living room, rice-paper lanterns on the patio. There was an old pony in the back, from when the owner had been married with kids, and a couple of wrecked cars in the carport. All the people who lived on the street, Starling noticed, were younger than the two of them. More than a few were in the Air Force and fought loud, regular arguments, and came and went at all hours. There was always a door slamming after midnight, then a car starting up and racing away into the night. Starling had never thought he'd find himself living in such a place.

He stacked the dishes, put the grounds in the newspaper and emptied all the wastebaskets into a plastic bag. He intended to take the garbage for a ride. Everybody in the subdivision either drove their garbage to a dump several miles away or toured the convenience stores and shopping malls until they found a dumpster no one was watching. Once a black woman had run out of a convenience store and cursed at him for ditching his garbage in her dumpster, and since then he'd waited till dark. This afternoon, though, he needed to get out of the house, as though with the heat and talking to Reiner there wasn't enough air inside to breathe.

He had the garbage set out the back door when the phone rang again. Sometimes car dealers called during lunch, wanting to talk to the Air Force sergeant, and Starling had learned not to answer until after one, when car salesmen all left for lunch. This time it might be Lois again, wanting him to come by the bar to see Reiner, and he didn't want to answer. Only he didn't want Lois going off somewhere, and he didn't want Reiner coming over. Reiner would think the house with the pony was a comedy act.

Starling picked up the phone. "All right, what is it?"

An unfamiliar voice said, "Dad? Is that you?"

"No dads here, Reiner," Starling said.

"Dad," the voice said again, "it's Jeff."

A woman's voice came on the line. "I have a collect call to anyone from a Jeff. Will you pay for the call?"

"Wrong number," Starling said. He couldn't be sure it wasn't Reiner still.

"Dad," the voice said. It was a teenager's voice, a worried voice.

"We're in awful trouble here, Dad. They've got Margie in jail."

"No, I can't help," Starling said. "I'm sorry. I can't help you."

"This party says you've got the wrong number, Jeff," the operator said.

"I know my own father's voice, don't I? Dad, for God's sake. This is serious. We're in trouble."

"I don't know any Jeffs," Starling said. "It's just the wrong number."

Starling could hear whoever was on the line hit something against the phone very hard, then say, "Shit! This isn't happening, I can't believe this is happening." The voice said something to someone else who was wherever he was. Possibly a policeman.

"It's the wrong number," the operator said. "I'm very sorry."

"Me too," Starling said. "I'm sorry."

"Would you like to try another number now, Jeff?" the operator asked.

"Dad, *please* accept. Please, my God. *Please.*"

"Excuse the ring, sir," the operator said, and the line was disconnected.

Starling put down the phone and stared out the window. The three boys who had blown up the tin can were walking past, eyeing his house. They were going for more fireworks. The torn can lay in the street, and the woman across the way was watching them from her picture window, pointing them out to a man in an undershirt who didn't look like the man who worked on his car at night. He wondered if the woman was married or divorced. If she had children, where were they? He wondered who it was who had called—the sergeant's kids were all too young. He wondered what kind of trouble Jeff was in, and where was he? He should've accepted the charges, said a word of consolation, or given some advice since the kid had seemed at wit's end. He'd been in trouble in his life. He was in trouble now, in fact, but he hadn't been any help.

He drove toward town and cruised the lot at the King's Hat Drive-Inn, took a look in at the Super-Duper, then drove behind a truck stop. The garbage was with him in the hot front seat and already smelled bad despite the plastic. It was at the Super-Duper that the black woman had yelled at him and threatened to turn his garbage over to the police. Starling stopped back at the Super-Duper, parked at the side of the lot by the dumpster and went inside, leaving the garbage in the driver's seat. A different black woman was inside. He bought some breakfast cereal, a bag of frozen macaroni and a bottle of hot sauce, then went back out to the car. Another car had driven in and parked beside his, and the driver, a woman, was sitting in view of the dumpster, waiting for someone who had gone inside. The woman might be another Super-Duper employee, Starling thought, or possibly the wife of someone in the back he hadn't noticed.

He got in his car and drove straight out to a campground beside the Sacramento River, less than a mile from the house. He had come here and picnicked once with Lois, though the campground was empty now, all the loops and tables deserted. He pulled up beside a big green campground dumpster and heaved his garbage in without getting out of the car. Beyond the dumpster, through some eucalyptus trees, he could see the big brown river sliding swiftly by, pieces of yellow foam swirling in and out of the dark eddies. It was a treacherous river, he thought, full of perils. Each year someone drowned, and there were currents running deep beneath the surface. No one in his right mind would think of swimming in it, no matter how hot it got.

As he drove out he passed two motorcycles with Oregon plates, parked at the far end of the campground, and two hippies with long hair sitting on a rock, smoking. The hippies watched him when he drove by and didn't bother hiding their dope. Two young women were coming out of the bushes nearby, wearing bathing suits, and one of the hippies gave Starling the black power salute and grinned. Starling drove back out to the highway.

The hippies reminded him of San Francisco. His mother, Irma, had lived there with her last husband, Rex, who'd had money. When he was in community college Starling had lived there with them for six months, before moving with his first wife across the bay to Alameda near the airport. They had been hippies of a certain kind themselves then and had smoked dope occasionally. Jan, his first wife, had had an abortion in a student apartment right on the campus. Abortions were not easy to get then, and they'd had to call Honolulu to get a name out in Castroville. They had been married six months, and Starling's mother had had to lend them money she'd gotten from Rex.

When the abortionist came, he brought a little metal box with him, like a fishing-tackle box. They sat in the living room of the student apartment and talked about this and that, and drank beer. The man was named Dr. Carson. He told them he was being prosecuted at that very moment and was losing his license for doing this very thing—performing abortions—but that people needed help. He had three children of his own, he said, and Starling wondered if he ever performed abortions on his own wife. Dr. Carson said it would cost $400, and he could do it the next night, but needed all cash. Before he left he opened his metal box. There was nothing in it but fishing gear: a Pflueger reel, some monofilament line, several red-and-white Jitterbug lures. They had all three laughed. You couldn't be too cautious, Dr. Carson said. They all liked each other and acted like they could be friends in happier days.

The next night Dr. Carson came with a metal box that looked exactly the same as the one before, green with a silver handle. He went into the bedroom with Jan and closed the door while Starling sat in the living room, watched TV and drank beer. It was Christmastime and Andy Williams was on, singing carols with a man in a bear suit. After a while a loud whirring noise, like an expensive blender, came out of the bedroom. It continued for a while, then stopped, then started. Starling became nervous. Dr. Carson, he knew, was mixing up his little baby, and Jan was feeling excruciating pain but wasn't making noise. Starling felt sick then with fear and guilt and helplessness. And with love. It was the first time he knew he knew what real love was, his love for his wife and for all the things he valued in his life but could so easily lose.

Later, Dr. Carson came out and said everything would be fine. He smiled and shook Starling's hand and called him Ted, which was the phony name Starling had given him. Starling paid him the money in hundreds, and when Dr. Carson drove off, Starling stood out on the tiny balcony and waved. The doctor blinked his headlights, and in the distance Starling could see a small private plane settling down to the airport in the dark, its red taillight blinking like a wishing star.

Starling wondered where the hell Jan was now, or Dr. Carson, fifteen years later. Jan had gotten peritonitis and almost died after that, and when she got well she wasn't interested in being married to Eddie Starling anymore. She seemed very disappointed. Three months later she had gone to Japan, where she'd had a pen pal since high school, someone named Haruki. For a while she wrote Starling letters, then stopped. Maybe, he thought, she had moved back down to L.A. with her mother. He wished his own mother was alive still, and he could call her up. He was thirty-nine years old, though, and he knew it wouldn't help.

Starling drove along the river for a few miles until the wide veg-etable and cantaloupe fields opened out, and the horizon extended a long way in the heat to a hazy wind line of Lombardy poplars. High, slat-sided trucks sat stationed against the white skyline, and men were picking in the near fields and beyond in long, dense crews. Mexicans, Starling thought, transients who worked for nothing. It was a depress-ing thought. There was nothing they could do to help themselves, but it was still depressing, and Starling pulled across the road and turned back toward town.

He drove out toward the airport, along the strip where it was mostly franchises and consignment lots and little shopping plazas, some of which he had once found the tenants for. All along the way, people had put up fireworks stands for the Fourth of July, red-white-and-blue banners fluttering on the breeze. Some of these people undoubtedly lived out where he and Lois lived now, in the same subdi-vision. That would mean something, he thought, if one day you found yourself looking out at the world going past from inside a fireworks stand. Things would've gotten far out of hand when that time came, there was no arguing it.

He thought about driving past the apartment to see if the nurses who sublet it were keeping up the little yard. The nurses, Jeri and Madeline, were two big dykes with men's haircuts and baggy clothes. They were friendly types, and in the real estate business dykes were considered A-1s—good tenants. They paid their rent, kept quiet, maintained property in good order, and held a firm stake in the status quo. They were like a married couple, was the business reasoning. Thinking about Jeri and Madeline, he drove past the light where their turn was, then just decided to keep driving.

There was nothing to do now, Starling thought, but drive out to the bar. The afternoon shift meant no one came in until Lois was almost ready to leave, and sometimes they could have the bar to them-selves. Reiner would be gone by now and it would be cool inside, and he and Lois could have a quiet drink together, toast better cards on the next deal. They had had good times doing nothing but sitting talking.

Lois was leaning over the jukebox across from the bar when Starling came in. Mel, the owner, took afternoons off, and the place was empty. A dark-green bar light shone over everything, and the room was cool.

He was glad to see Lois. She had on tight black slacks and a frilly white top and looked jaunty. Lois was a jaunty woman to begin with, and he was happy he'd come.

He had met Lois in a bar called the AmVets down in Rio Vista. It was before she and Louie Reiner became a twosome, and when he saw her in a bar now it always made him think of things then. That had been a high time, and when they talked about it Lois liked to say, "Some people are just meant to experience the highest moments of their lives in bars."

Starling sat on a bar stool.

"I hope you came down here to dance with your wife," Lois said, still leaning over the jukebox. She punched a selection and turned around, smiling. "I figured you'd waltz in here pretty soon." Lois came by and patted him on the cheek. "I went ahead and punched in all your favorites."

"Let's have a drink first," Starling said. "I've got an edge that needs a drink."

"Drink first, dance second," Lois said and went behind the bar and got down the bottle of Tanqueray.

"Mel wouldn't mind," Starling said.

"Mary-had-a-little-lamb," Lois said while she poured a glassful. She looked up at Starling and smiled. "It's five o'clock someplace on the planet. Here's to old Mel."

"And some better luck," Starling said, taking a big first drink of gin and letting it trickle down his throat as slowly as he could.

Lois had been drinking already, he was sure, with Reiner. That wasn't the best he could have hoped for, but it could be worse. She and Reiner could be shacked up in a motel, or on their way to Reno or the Bahamas. Reiner was gone, and that was a blessing, and he wasn't going to let Reiner cast a shadow on things.

"Poor old Lou," Lois said and came around the bar with a pink drink she'd poured out of the blender.

"Poor Lou what?" Starling said.

Lois sat down beside him on a bar stool and lit a cigarette. "Oh, his stomach's all shot and he's got an ulcer. He said he worries too much." She blew out the match and stared at it. "You want to hear what he drinks?"

"Who cares what a dope like Reiner drinks out of a glass," Starling said.

Lois looked at him, then stared at the mirror behind the bar. The smoky mirror showed two people sitting at a bar alone. A slow country tune started to play, a tune Starling liked, and he liked the way—with the gin around it—it seemed to ease him away from his own troubles. "So tell me what Reiner drinks," he said.

"Wodka," Lois said matter-of-factly. "That's the way he says it. Wodka. Like Russian. Wodka with coconut milk—a Hawaiian Russian. He says it's for his stomach, which he says is better though it's still a wreck. He's a walking pharmacy. And he's gotten a lot fatter, too, and his eyes bulge, and he wears a full Cleveland now. I don't know." Lois shook her head and smoked her cigarette. "He's got a cute girlfriend, though, this Jackie, from Del Rio Beach. She looks like Little Bo Peep."

Starling tried to picture Reiner. Louie Reiner had been a large, handsome man at one time, with thick eyebrows and penetrating black eyes. A sharp dresser. He was sorry to hear Reiner was fat and bug-eyed and wore a leisure suit. It was bad luck if that was the way you looked to the world.

"How was it, seeing Louie? Was it nice?" He stared at himself in the smoky mirror. He hadn't gotten fat, thank God.

"No," Lois said and dragged on her cigarette. "*He* was nice. Grown-up and what have you. But *it* wasn't nice. He didn't look healthy, and he still talked the same baloney, which was all before Jackie arrived, naturally."

"All what baloney?"

"You know that stuff, Eddie. Everybody makes *themselves* happy or unhappy. You don't leave one woman for another woman, you do it for yourself. If you can't make it with one, make it with all of them—that baloney he was always full of. Take the tour. Go big casino. That stuff. Reiner stuff."

"Reiner's big casino, all right," Starling said. "I guess he wanted you to go off with him."

"Oh sure. He said he was off to Miami next week to arrest some poor soul. He said I ought to go, and we could stay at the Fontainebleau or the Eden Roc or one of those sharp places."

"What about me?" Starling said. "Did I come? Or did I stay here? What about little Jackie?"

"Louie didn't mention either one of you, isn't that funny? I guess it slipped his mind." Lois smiled and put her arm on Starling's arm. "It's just baloney, Eddie. Trashy talk."

"I wish he was here now," Starling said. "I'd use a beer bottle on him."

"I know it, hon. But you should've heard what this little girlfriend said. It was a riot. She's a real Ripley's."

"She'd need to be," Starling said.

"Really. She said if Louie ran around on her she was going to sleep with a black man. She said she already had one picked out. She really knew how to work Louie. She said Louie had a house full of these cheap Italian carpets, and nobody to sell them to. That was his big deal he needed a partner for, by the way—not a very big market over here, I guess. She said Louie was thinking of selling them in Idaho. Good luck with that, I said. She said—and this would've made you laugh, Eddie, it would've truly—she said it's a doggy-dog world out there. Doggy-dog. She was real cute. When she said that, Louie got down on the floor and barked like a dog. He dropped his pistol out of his whatever-you-call-it, his scabbard, and his beeper"—Lois was laughing—"he was like a big animal down on the floor of the bar."

"I'm sorry I missed it."

"Louie can be funny," Lois said.

"Maybe you should've married him, then."

"I *did* marry him."

"Too bad you didn't stay married to him instead of me. I don't have a beeper."

"I like what you have got, though, sweetheart." She squeezed his arm. "Nobody would love me like you do, you know I think that. Reiner was just my mistake, but I can laugh at him today because I don't have to live with him. You're such a big mamma's boy, you don't want anybody to have any fun."

"I'd like to have a little fun," Starling said. "Let's go where there's some fun."

Lois leaned and kissed him on the cheek. "You smell awfully nice." She smiled at him. "Come on and dance with me, Ed. Justice demands that you dance with me. You have that light step. It's nice when you do."

Lois walked out onto the little dance floor and took Starling's hand. He stood close to her and they danced to the slow music on the jukebox, holding together the way they had when he'd first known her. He felt a little drunk. A buzz improved a thing, he thought, made a good moment out of nothing.

"You're a natural dancer, Eddie," Lois said softly. "Remember us dancing at Powell's on the beach, with everybody watching us?"

"You like having men think about you?" Starling said.

"Oh, sure. I guess." Lois's cheek was against his cheek. "It makes me feel like I'm in a movie, sometimes, you know? Everybody does that, don't they?"

"I never do."

"Don't you ever wonder what your ex thinks about you? Old Jan. That was a long time ago, I guess."

"Bygones are bygones to me," Starling said. "I don't think about it."

"You're such a literal, Eddie. You get lost in the lonely crowd, I think sometimes. That's why I want to be nice and make you happy." She held him close to her so that her hard, flat hips were next to his. "Isn't this nice? It's nice to dance with you."

Starling saw now that the bar was decorated with red, white, and blue crêpe paper—features he'd missed. Little curlicues and ribbons and stars hung from the dark rafters and down off the shaded green bar lights and the beer signs and the framed pictures behind the back bar. This was festive, he thought. Lois had fixed it, it showed her hand. Before long a crowd would be in, the lights would go up and shine out, the music would be turned up loud. It would be a good time. "That's nice," Starling said.

"I just love this," Lois said. Her head was on his shoulder. "I just love this so much."

On the highway toward home, Starling passed the hippies he had seen at the campground. They were heading in now, the women on the rear seats, the men driving fast, leaning as if the wind blew them back.

In town, a big fireworks display staged by a shopping mall was beginning. Catherine wheels and star bursts and blue-and-pink sprays were going off in the twilight. Cars were stopped along the road, and people with children sat on their hoods, drinking beer and watching the sky. It was nearly dark and rain had begun to threaten.

"Everything's moved out to the malls now," Lois said, "including the fireworks." She had been dozing and now she leaned against her door, staring back toward the lights.

"I wouldn't care to work in one," Starling said, driving.

Lois said nothing.

"You know what I was just thinking about?" she said after a while.

"Tell me," Starling said.

"Your mother," Lois said. "Your mother was a sweet old lady, you know that? I liked her very much. I remember she and I would go to the mall and buy her a blouse. Just some blouse she could've bought in Bullock's in San Francisco, but she wanted to buy it here to be sweet and special." Lois smiled about it. "Remember when we bought fireworks?"

Starling's mother had liked fireworks. She liked to hear them pop so she could laugh. Starling remembered having fireworks one year in the time since he'd been married to Lois. When was that? he thought. A time lost now.

"Remember she held the little teenies right in her fingers and let them go off? That tickled her so much."

"That was her trick," Eddie said. "Rex taught her that."

"I guess he did," Lois said. "But you know, I don't blame you, really, for being such a mamma's boy, Eddie. Not with *your* mamma—unlike mine, for instance. She's why you're as nice as you are."

"I'm selfish," Starling said. "I always have been. I'm capable of lying, stealing, cheating."

Lois patted him on the shoulder. "You're generous, though, too."

Rain was starting in big drops that looked like snow on the windshield. Lights from their subdivision glowed out under the lowered sky ahead.

"This weird thing happened today," Starling said. "I can't quit thinking about it."

Lois slid over by him. She put her head on his shoulder and her hand inside his thigh. "I knew something had happened, Eddie. You can't hide anything. The truth is just on you."

"There's no truth to *this*," Starling said. "Just the phone rang when I was leaving, and it was this kid, Jeff. He was in some kind of mess. I didn't know who he was, but he thought I was his father. He wanted me to accept charges."

"You didn't, did you?"

Starling looked toward the subdivision. "No. I should have, though. It's on my mind now that I should've helped him. I'd just finished talking to Reiner."

"He might've been in Rangoon, for Christ's sake," Lois said. "Or Helsinki. You don't know where he was. It could've cost you five hundred dollars, then you couldn't have helped him anyway. You were smart, is what I think."

"It wouldn't matter, though. I could've given him some advice. He said somebody was in jail. It's just on my mind now, it'll go away."

"Get a good job and then accept charges from Istanbul," Lois said and smiled.

"I just wonder who he was," Starling said. "For some reason I thought he was over in Reno—isn't that odd? Just a voice."

"It'd be worse if he *was* in Reno," Lois said. "Are you sorry you don't have one of your own?" Lois looked over at him strangely.

"One what?"

"A son. Or, you know. Didn't you tell me you almost had one? There was something about that, with Jan."

"That was a long time ago," Starling said. "We were idiots."

"Some people claim they make your life hold together better, though," Lois said. "You know?"

"Not if you're broke they don't," Starling said. "All they do is make you sorry."

"Well, we'll just float on through life together, then, how's that?" Lois put her hand high on his leg. "No blues today, hon, okay?"

They were at the little dirt street where the ranchette was, at the far end. A fireworks hut had been built in the front yard of the first small house, a chain of bright yellow bulbs strung across the front. An elderly woman was standing in the hut, her face expressionless. She had on a sweater and was holding a little black poodle. All the fireworks but a few Roman candles had been sold off the shelves.

"I never thought I'd live where people sold fireworks right in their front yards," Lois said and faced front. Starling peered into the lighted hut. The rain was coming down in a slow drizzle, and water shone off the oiled street. He felt the urge to gesture to the woman, but didn't. "You could just about say we lived in a place where you wouldn't want to live if you could help it. Funny, isn't it? That just happens to you." Lois laughed.

"I guess it's funny," Starling said. "It's true."

"What'd you dream up for dinner, Eddie? I've built up a hunger all of a sudden."

"I forgot about it," Starling said. "There's some macaroni."

"Whatever," Lois said. "It's fine."

Starling pulled into the gravel driveway. He could see the pony standing out in the dark where the fenced weed lot extended to the side of the house. The pony looked like a ghost, its white eyes unmoving in the rain.

"Tell me something," Starling said. "If I ask you something, will you tell me?"

"If there's something to tell," Lois said. "Sometimes there isn't anything, you know. But go ahead."

"What happened with you and Reiner?" he said. "All that Reno stuff. I never asked you about that. But I want to know."

"That's easy," Lois said and smiled at him in the dark car. "I just realized I didn't love Reiner, that's all. Period. I realized I loved you, and I didn't want to be married to somebody I didn't love. I wanted to be married to you. It isn't all that complicated or important." Lois put her arms around his neck and hugged him hard. "Don't be cloudy now, sweet. You've just had some odd luck is all. Things'll get better. You'll get back. Let me make you happy. Let me show you something to be happy, baby doll." Lois slid across the seat against the door and went down into her purse. Starling could hear wind chimes in the rain. "Let me just show you," Lois said.

Starling couldn't see. Lois opened the door out into the drizzle, turned her back to him and struck a match. He could see it brighten. And then there was a sparkling and hissing, and then a brighter one, and Starling smelled the harsh burning and the smell of rain together. Then Lois closed the door and danced out before the car into the rain with the sparklers, waving her arms round in the air, smiling widely and making swirls and patterns and star-falls for him that were brilliant and illuminated the night and the bright rain and the little dark house behind her and, for a moment, caught the world and stopped it, as though something sudden and perfect had come to earth in a furious glowing for him and for him alone—Eddie Starling—and only he could watch and listen. And only he would be there, waiting, when the light was finally gone.

DEATH VALLEY

Joyce Carol Oates

The colors of winter here were dun, a bleached brown, layers of rich cobalt blue. The light fell vertical, sharp as a knife. And there was the wind.

He observed as she shaded her eyes, which were not strong eyes, against the glare. "That looks like water," she said brightly. "Or ice."

"Those are salt flats."

"What?"

"Salt. Salt flats."

"It *looks* like ice."

Her tone was lightly combative. As if sexual banter were her primary mode of discourse.

She said, "I was always wondering about the name. Since I was a little girl."

"The name?"

"Death Valley. It's something you hear about, or see in the movies. The old movies. You know: 'Death Valley.' You sort of wonder."

It was then he realized how young she was. Twenty years younger than he, by a generous estimate. At that age you can still reasonably think death is romance.

It was their second day. He had rented a car, a classy-looking metallic-gray BMW, and driven her out into the desert. She'd never seen the desert, she said; she'd never seen Death Valley. There was an air of mild reproach in her voice, as if he, or others like him, had cheated her of a vision that was her due.

In the big casino, where they'd met, there were no clocks on the walls because the principle of time did not apply. Nor did the principle of day and night apply. Like the interior of a great head, he thought. And even in the desert where the winter light fell sharp and straight and blinding it didn't seem like day, exactly, but like something else.

She was saying, persisting, hair blowing prettily across her face, "Are you sure that isn't water, *really?* It looks so much like water."

"Taste it and see."

In the casino at Caesar's, at the craps table he always played at Caesar's, he'd said, smiling, "Pray for me, sweetheart," turning to her as if he'd known absolutely she would be there, or someone very like her. Not a hooker but a small-town girl, a secretary or a beauty salon worker, here in Vegas for a three-day weekend with a girlfriend from the office or the beauty salon, come to play the slots and to test her luck. With her hair cascading in shiny synthetic-looking curls halfway down her back, and her eyes like an owl's with makeup, and glossed lips, wasn't she there to bring him good luck? Her or someone like her.

At craps the play is fast and nerved up and choppy like a wind-whipped sea whose waves crash in one direction, then in another, and then in another. Pray for me honey, he'd said, and twenty minutes later walked away with $14,683, not the very most he'd ever won in Vegas but the most he'd won in a long time. The girl, whose name was Linda, pressed her hand against her heart, saying it was going like crazy from all the excitement; how could people *do* such things, take such risks? He kissed her solemnly on the cheek and thanked her. His lips were cold.

She hadn't prayed for him, she said. She'd had her fingers crossed but she hadn't prayed because God is God no matter who you are or think you are; God is a wrathful God you best did not provoke.

She rolled her almost-pretty owl's eyes as if she knew, as if she'd had a personal run-in with God.

"It's just your special luck," she said, drawing her fingers slowly across his sleeve.

"You think I'm a lucky man?" he said happily.

"I *know* you're a lucky man: I just saw."

He kissed her on the lips, smelling her sweet sharp perfume, and through it he saw the bargain-rate motel room she and her girlfriend were renting for the weekend, the beaverboard walls, the stained venetian blinds pulled against the sun, the window air conditioner with its amiable guttural rumble. The girlfriend had a date for the night but Linda was alone. The kind of girl, baby fat in her cheeks, a little pinch of it under her chin, who wouldn't be alone for long and surely knew it.

But she surprised him, the quickness with which she framed his face in her hands, a dozen bracelets jingling, and kissed him, lightly, on the lips, like a woman in a movie when the music comes up.

"Well," he said, smiling his wide white happy smile, his sort of surprised smile, "I guess I *am* a lucky man."

Linda was the kind of girl too, in bright blurry makeup and highlighted ashy hair, chunky legs shaved so smooth they gave off a kind of sheen, like pewter, who has carried with her in secret since the age of sixteen a razor blade sharp as on the day of its purchase, never once used. It is likely to be wrapped in several turns of Kleenex placed carefully against the bottom of her leather shoulder bag. No one knows it is there, and often she too forgets.

An older woman, a friend, advised her to carry the razor blade with her at all times, if not on her actual person (which would be tricky) then within reach. The logic is, If you never have to use it you're in luck, right? If you have to use it and you have it, you're in luck, right? So how can you lose?

So sometimes without knowing what she does her fingers seek out the blade, the shape of the blade, neatly wrapped in its several turns of Kleenex, pressed, there, flat against the bottom of her bag. He guessed it was probably like that.

It was their second day, the first day after their first night; driving out from Vegas into the desert she'd laid her head sleepily against his shoulder, as if she had a right. Perfectly manicured pink-lacquered nails on his thigh, digging lightly into his sharp-pressed chino pants. He told her with the air of one imparting a secret that he drove out into the desert as often as he could, not just to get away from Vegas but to be alone. To listen, he said, to the wind.

"Is it always so windy?" she asked.

"And I like the quiet."

"The *quiet?* But it goes on," she said, her reedy childlike voice beginning to falter, "such a long way."

He'd stopped the car, thinking this was a good place. Back a lane leading off the tourists' loop road, where no one was likely to come. Just this side of Furnace Creek one turn beyond a turnoff for a deserted mine where he'd brought another girl a few months back. There was a dreamy illusion they were the only visitors in this part of Death Valley today, but maybe it wasn't an illusion.

She'd said back in the room she was crazy about him, but now she was holding herself just a little off; he sensed it and liked it, that edge between them, not just the loneliness of the place but the sun did it, the starkness, the sudden wonder why you are here and why with this person, some stranger you hardly know and whose actual name you could not swear to.

"Is that tumbleweed?" she was asking. "I always wondered what tumbleweed was."

"It's something like tumbleweed," he said, "some kind of vegetation that dries out, tumbles in the wind, scatters its seeds that way. It's a weed."

"Everything's a weed, isn't it, in a place like this?"

He laughed; she had him there. "Everything's a weed," he conceded.

She had a way of surprising him now and then. He liked her; he really did. "You have named the secret of the universe," he said, smiling. *"Everything's a weed."*

He was laughing, and then suddenly he was coughing. She asked was he all right and he said yes, then started in laughing again, or maybe it was coughing. In a kind of paroxysm, like sex. But not always shared, like sex. Not always something you want to see, in others. Like sex.

"Lie down, honey, let's try it here."

He spoke half seriously but teasing too so that she could take it that way if she wanted. Behind the purple-tinted glasses her eyes widened in alarm. She said, "Here? I'd rather go back to Vegas."

He laughed and wiped his mouth with a tissue. He was excited but couldn't keep from yawning; his eyes flooded with tears. "I thought you were a big growed-up girl," he said, winking. He saw that his watch had stopped almost exactly at twelve noon.

She decided he was teasing, maybe he was teasing; she laughed and walked off a little, saying it was a shame she'd left her camera behind, wouldn't you know it, Death Valley and she'd left her camera behind. You could see she was trying. Squinting at these mountains that were not Kodacolor mountains with dazzling snowy peaks but just rock formations lifting out of the earth, weirdly striated.

The striations of the brain, out there. Terrible to see if you saw them.

Vegetation that looked like it was actually mineral.

Rocks, crumbled earth. Dun-colored bleached-looking dead-looking earth.

And the dunes, and the sand in ripples like washboards. And the wind.

She said, licking her lips, uneasy because he'd been silent for so long, hands in his chino pockets, not following her with his eyes as she strolled about, in her tank-top jersey blouse with the spaghetti straps to show she wasn't wearing a bra and the black-and-white striped miniskirt that fitted her hips snug and sweet, as if to set her off the way, say, a model is set off against a dull dun-colored background. "I suppose many people have died out here—pioneers, I mean—crossing the desert? In the old days?"

"I wouldn't doubt it," he said.

"The Donner party—the people who had to eat one another's flesh in order to survive—didn't they cross Death Valley?"

"I don't believe so."

"I thought that was their name. I saw a television show about them once."

"That was the name but I don't think the Donners crossed Death Valley. I think it was Idaho. Somewhere in Idaho."

"It was just heartbreaking, the television show. Once you got to know them, the men and women and the little kids, your heart just went out to them. My God! Turning cannibal!" she spoke vehemently, gesturing with both hands. The wind blew thinly through her hair. "Our ancestors endured so much, it's a miracle we came into being at all."

She looked at him; he was smiling. She shaded her eyes against him and said, "OK, what's up? Did I say something stupid, or what?"

"You said something wonderful."

"Yeah? What?"

"'It's a miracle we came into being at all.'"

"Yeah?"

"Yeah."

"Just something, you know, nice. I don't like to talk about it, actually."

"But is it strong, is it sweet, is it a little painful, what *is* it? I'm just curious. What women feel."

"I don't like to talk about it actually."

"Why not?"

"I—"

"You said you were married, once. When—when was it?—you were nineteen."

"What's that got to do with it?"

"You're not a kid."

"No. I guess I'm not a kid." She cut her eyes at him, meaning to shift the subject. "You'd maybe prefer a kid?"

"As I said, I'm just curious. How long the sensation lasts, for instance, afterward. Minutes? Hours?"

"Oh, I don't know, you know," she said, shy again, not looking at him, a blush starting up from her neck. "A long time sometimes, hours sometimes. I guess it depends."

"On what?"

"How strong it was in the beginning."

"If you love the guy a lot—or don't, much—does that affect the orgasm too?"

"I guess so."

"But don't you *know?*"

She stood mute and resisting, her face, beneath the heavy pancake makeup, decidedly pink. "I guess I don't. I guess it's something that just . . . happens."

"The orgasm, you mean. Can't you say the word?"

She stood smiling, staring at their feet. Sandals with just enough heel to make it unwise for her to have worn them, out here. And if she'd have to run, and kick the shoes off, the sand would be like liquid fire against her feet.

Her purse too, the shoulder bag, left behind in the car. She'd never get to it in time.

"Say it," he said, bending a little to look in her face. Teasing. "Can't you say it? Orgasm."

She laughed nervously, and shook her head, and said, "It makes me feel funny. I don't like it, you looking at me so close."

"Why does it embarrass you?"

"I don't know. I'm not embarrassed."

"A big girl like you."

"I'm not embarrassed, I don't *like* it."

"You look embarrassed. But very sweet too."

"Well."

"You know you're a great-looking girl, don't you? Where did you say you were from? Oh, yes; you and your girlfriend, from Nebraska."

Her face crinkled in childish dislike.

He said, quickly, with an air of apology, "No, I mean Columbus, Ohio. You and two girlfriends from Columbus, Ohio." He was teasing, poking her with a forefinger. In the plumb resilient flesh just below her breasts. "The big weekend in Vegas. Right? First time in Vegas, right? And last night you won a hundred and twenty dollars at the slots, you were telling me. Two separate jackpots."

There was a silence. She said, quietly, "I think I'd sort of like to go back now, to Las Vegas. This place is kind of weird."

"I thought you wanted to see the countryside. The 'natural rock formations.'"

"It makes me feel . . . sort of strange, here. Like it's a dream or something."

"A dream of yours or a dream of the landscape?"

She peered at him, suspicious. "What's that mean?"

"What?"

"What you just asked me?"

"*You* were saying it, honey, not me. That it's like a dream here. Where anything can happen."

She laughed again, not exactly frightened yet but on the edge of it. He was thinking how her mouth was her cunt actually, the fat lips glossed up the way they were. The night before he'd taken a wad of toilet paper and was a little rough playing daddy, scolding her to keep it light—he was careful to keep it light—wiping the lipstick off, the apricot makeup, layers of pancake makeup and grainy powder that had caked over her young skin. Without the makeup her skin was doughy and a little coarse but he preferred it to the other. If there was anything he loathed it was female makeup smeared on him, the madman look of lipstick around his mouth, enlarging his mouth.

He kissed her, and whispered some things in her ear, and she slapped at him and said they'd better go back to the car, at least. And he kissed her again, forcing her mouth open, how wet it was, but not really warm, and how he felt, in that instant, the power flow down from his torso into his belly and loins, the first time he'd felt it that day. Last night, he must have felt it too but couldn't remember, he'd been too drunk.

He was thinking, those years he'd worked out every day, lifting weights, keeping himself in condition, he'd had that feeling a lot: you walk in someplace where no one knows you but they glance up in acknowledgment of you, in approval or even admiration, and that does it: sets you up for the rest of the day.

She didn't like him roughhousing; she said, little-girl hurt, "You got the wrong idea about me, mister," and he said, smiling, "You've got an ass, don't you? You've got a cunt. You *are* a cunt. So where's the 'wrong idea'?" But now he'd gone a little too far too fast and she was hurt and beginning to be frightened. Seeing her face he was repentant at once, saying he was sorry, damned sorry. Wouldn't hurt her for the world.

She went ahead of him to the car, swaying a little in the sandals like a drunken woman. He caught up to her, kissed her, apologized another time. He yawned; moisture flooded his eyes. In the car they drank from the bottle he'd brought along, good strong smooth delicious Jim Beam, my pal Jim Beam, don't go anywhere without him. He talked about getting married, it was time for him to settle down, Jesus, it was past the time, he had a hunch he should consolidate his luck and he should do it right now. She lay with her head against his shoulder, just a little uneasy against his shoulder, and he asked if she'd ever heard of the poet Rilke, the great German poet Rilke, and she said she'd maybe heard of the name but couldn't swear to it. Guardedly she said she didn't read much poetry now; used to read it, had to memorize it, back in high school. He was feeling good so he recited what he could remember of one of the *Duino Elegies,* the words pushing through in their startling order which he had not known he still knew, but of course there were only snatches, shreds. *"And that is how I have cherished you—deep inside / the mirror, where you put yourself, far away / from all the world. Why have you come like this / and so denied yourself. . . ."*

His voice trailed off, he sensed her embarrassment, they sat for a while without speaking. Except for the wind it was absolutely silent, but you stopped hearing the wind after a while.

She said, clearing her throat, "It's funny: in the shade it's sort of chilly, but in the sun, out there, it's so hot."

In that instant he hated her. He was very happy. He said, "It's winter, sweetheart. After all."

She was preparing to cry but holding back, thinking was he the kind of man who feels sorry when you cry or was he the kind of man who gets really angry. So he warned her, "I'm getting just a little impatient, honey," and that quieted her fast. He got her into the back of the BMW, and they kissed awhile, he called her honey and sweetheart and said how crazy he was about her, his good luck talisman dropped from the sky. She was still stiff, scared, but he unzipped his trousers anyway, closed his fingers around the nape of her neck; she began to say, "No, hey, no, I don't want to, not here," whimpering like a child, and he said, "Here's as good as anywhere, cunt," so that quieted her, and she did it, she went through with it, in the back seat of the rented car awkward as kids playing in some cramped secret place.

And he drifted off thinking of how wild it would be, how no one could stop it from happening; this is the one who's going to lean over quick to get her purse from the front seat and take out the razor blade and unwrap it while his eyes are shut and his face all slack and dreamy like the bones had melted . . . and then she'll bring the blade's edge against his neck, where the big blue artery is throbbing. And there's an immediate explosion of blood and his eyes are open now and he's screaming, he's clutching at his throat with his fingers as if to close the wound, just with his fingers, and she scrambles out of the car, running stumbling in the sand, screaming, How do you like it? How do you like it? Filthy shit-eating bastard, how do you like it?—running until she's out of the range of his cries. Until the cries subside.

Then she waits, her heart pounding hard, so scared she's begun to leak in her panties. But at the same time there's a part of her brain reasoning, I'm safe here, what can he do to me here? He can't do anything now.

And she's thinking too, Anything I did to him, it's been done before by somebody to somebody, not once but many times.

She thinks, shivering, There is that consolation.

When she returns to the BMW, she sees his body on the ground a few yards from the car where he fell, must have tried to crawl a little, though there is nowhere his crawling could have taken him. She sees he isn't breathing, must be dead; and so much blood in the sand, soaked up in the sand, and in the back seat of the car, horrible to see. She tries not to look but has to get the car keys from his pocket, his trousers around his ankles, unzipped, and his jockey shorts open, everything looking so tender and exposed like veins on the outside of the body, and soaked too with blood. The wild thought comes to her, How will they take photographs of him for the papers, lying the way he is, how will they manage to show it on the television news?

Sweet, sweet Linda. God, how sweet.

Back in Vegas, he dropped her off at her motel, said he'd call her around nine, and she said, "Oh, sure, I'm gonna hang around here all night in this shithole and wait for you to call, that's great, thanks a lot, mister," and he said, "If I say I'm going to call I'm going to call, why are you so angry? Nine P.M. sharp, or a little after," and she got out of the car, moving stiffly, as if her joints ached; then she leaned in the window, face puffy and mouth bruised-looking. "Fuck you, mister," she said, "in no uncertain terms."

He sat in the car, the engine idling, and watched her walk away and had to give her credit: she didn't once glance back. Holding herself with dignity in that wrinkled miniskirt that barely covered her thighs, walking as steady as she could manage in the tacky fake-leather sandals, as if it mattered, and she mattered, which actually scared him a little—that evidence of the difference between them when he hadn't believed there could be much.

THE OTHER MILLER

Tobias Wolff

For two days now Miller has been standing in the rain with the rest of Bravo Company, waiting for some men from another company to blunder down the logging road where Bravo waits in ambush. When this happens, if this happens, Miller will stick his head out of the hole he is hiding in and shoot off all his blank ammunition in the direction of the road. So will everyone else in Bravo Company. Then they will climb out of their holes and get on some trucks and go home, back to the base.

This is the plan.

Miller has no faith in it. He has never yet seen a plan that worked, and this one won't either. He can tell. For one thing, the lieutenant who thought up the plan has been staying away a lot—"doing recon," he claims, but that's a lie. How can you do recon if you don't know where the enemy is? Miller's foxhole has about a foot of water in it. He has to stand on little shelves he's been digging out of the walls, but the soil is sandy and the shelves keep collapsing. That means his boots are wet. Plus his cigarettes are wet. Plus he broke the bridge on his molars the first night out, while chewing up one of the lollipops he'd brought along for energy. It drives him crazy the way the broken bridge lifts and grates when he pushes it with his tongue, but last night he lost his willpower and now he can't keep his tongue away from it.

When he thinks of the other company, the one they're supposed to ambush, Miller sees a column of dry, well-fed men marching farther and farther away from the hole where he stands waiting for them. He sees them moving easily under light packs. He sees them stopping for a smoke break, stretching out on fragrant beds of pine needles under the trees, the murmur of their voices growing more and more faint as one by one they drift into sleep.

It's the truth, by God. Miller knows it like he knows he's going to catch a cold, because that's his luck. If he were in the other company then they'd be the ones standing in holes.

Miller's tongue does something to the bridge, and a surge of pain shoots through him. He snaps up straight, eyes burning, teeth clenched against the yell in his throat. He fights it back and glares around him at the other men. The few he can see look stunned and ashen-faced. Of the rest he can make out only their poncho hoods. The poncho hoods stick out of the ground like bullet-shaped rocks.

At this moment, his mind swept clean by pain, Miller can hear the tapping of raindrops on his own poncho. Then he hears the pitchy whine of an engine. A jeep is splashing along the road, slipping from side to side and throwing up thick gouts of mud behind it. The jeep itself is caked with mud. It skids to a stop in front of Bravo Company's position, and the horn beeps twice.

Miller glances around to see what the others are doing. Nobody has moved. They're all just standing in their holes.

The horn beeps again.

A short figure in a poncho emerges from a clump of trees farther up the road. Miller can tell it's the first sergeant by how little he is, so little that the poncho hangs almost to his ankles. The first sergeant walks slowly toward the jeep, big blobs of mud all around his boots. When he gets to the jeep, he leans his head inside; he pulls it out again a moment later. He looks down at the road. He kicks at one of the tires in a thoughtful way. Then he looks up and shouts Miller's name.

Miller keeps watching him. Not until the first sergeant shouts his name again does Miller begin the hard work of hoisting himself out of the foxhole. The other men turn their ashen faces up at him as he trudges past their heads.

"Come here, boy," the first sergeant says. He walks a little distance from the jeep and waves Miller over.

Miller follows him. Something is wrong. Miller can tell, because the first sergeant called him "boy," instead of "shitbird." Already he feels a burning in his left side, where his ulcer is.

The first sergeant stares down the road. "Here's the thing," he begins. He stops and turns to Miller. "Hell's bells, I don't know. God-damn it. Listen. We got a priority here from the Red Cross. Did you know your mother was sick?"

Miller doesn't say anything. He pushes his lips tight together.

"She must have been sick, right?" When Miller remains silent the first sergeant says, "She passed away last night. I'm real sorry." The first sergeant looks sadly up at Miller, and Miller watches the sergeant's right arm beginning to rise under the poncho; then it falls to his side again. Miller can see that the first sergeant wants to give his shoulder a man-to-man kind of squeeze, but it just won't work. You can only do that if you're taller than the other fellow, or maybe the same size.

"These boys here will drive you back to base," the first sergeant says, nodding toward the jeep. "You give the Red Cross a call, and they'll take it from there. Get yourself some rest," he adds. He turns away and walks off toward the trees.

Miller retrieves his gear. One of the men he passes on his way back to the jeep says, "Hey, Miller, what's the story?"

Miller doesn't answer. He's afraid that if he opens his mouth he'll start laughing and ruin everything. He keeps his head down and his lips tight as he climbs into the back seat of the jeep, and he doesn't look up again until the company is a mile or so behind. The fat Pfc. sitting beside the driver is watching him. He says, "I'm sorry about your mother. That's a bummer."

"Maximum bummer," says the driver, another Pfc. He shoots a look over his shoulder. Miller sees his own face reflected for an instant in the driver's sunglasses.

"Had to happen someday," he mumbles, and looks down again.

Miller's hands are shaking. He puts them between his knees and stares through the snapping plastic window at the trees going past. Raindrops rattle on the canvas overhead. He is inside, and everyone else is still outside. Miller can't stop thinking about the others standing around getting rained on, and the thought makes him want to laugh and slap his leg. This is the luckiest he has ever been.

"My grandmother died last year," the driver says. "But that's not the same thing as losing your mother. I feel for you, Miller."

"Don't worry about me," Miller tells him. "I'll get along."

The fat Pfc. beside the driver says, "Look, don't feel like you have to repress just because we're here. If you want to cry or anything just go ahead. Right, Leb?"

The driver nods. "Just let it out."

"No problem," Miller says. He wishes he could set these fellows straight, so they won't feel like they have to act mournful all the way to Fort Ord. But if he tells them what happened they'll turn right around and drive him back to his foxhole.

This is what happened. Another Miller in the battalion has the same initials he's got. W. P., and this Miller is the one whose mother has died. His father passed away during the summer and Miller got that message by mistake too. So he has the lay of the land now; as soon as the first sergeant started asking about his mother, he got the entire picture.

For once, everybody else is on the outside and Miller is on the inside. Inside, on his way to a hot shower, dry clothes, a pizza, and a warm bunk. He didn't even have to do anything wrong to get here; he just did as he was told. It was their own mistake. Tomorrow he'll rest up like the first sergeant ordered him to, go on sick call about his bridge, maybe go downtown to a movie after that. Then he'll call the Red Cross. By the time they get everything straightened out it will be too late to send him back to the field. And the best thing is, the other Miller won't know. The other Miller will have a whole other day of thinking his mother is still alive. You could even say that Miller is keeping her alive for him.

The man beside the driver turns around again and studies Miller. He has little dark eyes in a round, baby-white face covered with beads of sweat. His name tag reads KAISER. Showing little square teeth like a baby's, he says, "You're really coping, Miller. Most guys pretty much lose it when they get the word."

"I would too," the driver says. "Anybody would. Or maybe I should say almost anybody. It's *human*, Kaiser."

"For sure," Kaiser says. "I'm not saying any different. That's going to be my worst day, the day my mom dies." He blinks rapidly, but not before Miller sees his little eyes mist up.

"Everybody has to go sometime," Miller says. "Sooner or later. That's my philosophy."

"Heavy," the driver says. "Really deep."

Kaiser gives him a sharp look and says, "At ease, Lebowitz."

Miller leans forward. Lebowitz is a Jewish name. That means Lebowitz must be a Jew. Miller wants to ask him why he's in the Army, but he's afraid Lebowitz might take it wrong. Instead, he says, conversationally, "You don't see too many Jewish people in the Army nowadays."

Lebowitz looks into the rearview mirror. His thick eyebrows arch over his sunglasses, and then he shakes his head and says something Miller can't make out.

"At ease, Leb," Kaiser says again. He turns to Miller and asks him where the funeral is going to be held.

"What funeral?" Miller says.

Lebowitz laughs.

"Back off," Kaiser says. "Haven't you ever heard of shock?"

Lebowitz is quiet for a moment. Then he looks into the rearview mirror again and says, "Sorry, Miller. I was out of line."

Miller shrugs. His probing tongue pushes the bridge too hard and he stiffens suddenly.

"Where did your mom live?" Kaiser asks.

"Redding," Miller says.

Kaiser nods. "Redding," he repeats. He keeps watching Miller. So does Lebowitz, glancing back and forth between the mirror and the road. Miller understands that they expected a different kind of performance from the one he's given them, more emotional and all. They have seen other personnel whose mothers died and now they have certain standards that he has failed to live up to. He looks out the window. They are driving along a ridgeline. Slices of blue flicker between the trees on the left-hand side of the road; then they hit a space without trees and Miller can see the ocean below them, clear to the horizon under a bright cloudless sky. Except for a few hazy wisps in the treetops they've left the clouds behind, back in the mountains, hanging over the soldiers there.

"Don't get me wrong," Miller says. "I'm sorry she's dead."

Kaiser says, "That's the way. Talk it out."

"It's just that I didn't know her all that well," Miller says, and after this monstrous lie a feeling of weightlessness comes over him. At first it makes him uncomfortable, but almost immediately he begins to enjoy it. From now on he can say anything.

He makes a sad face and says, "I guess I'd be more broken up and so on if she hadn't taken off on us the way she did. Right in the middle of harvest season. Just leaving us like that."

"I'm hearing a lot of anger," Kaiser tells him. "Ventilate. Own it."

Miller got that stuff from a song, but he can't remember any more. He lowers his head and looks at his boots. "Killed my dad," he says, after a time. "Died of a broken heart. Left me with five kids to raise, not to mention the farm." Miller closes his eyes. He sees a field all plowed up with the sun setting behind it, a bunch of kids coming in from the field with rakes and hoes on their shoulders. As the jeep winds down through the switchbacks he describes his hardships as the oldest child in this family. He is at the end of his story when they reach the coast highway and turn north. All at once the jeep stops rattling and swaying. They pick up speed. The tires hum on the smooth road. The rushing air whistles a single note around the radio antenna. "Anyway," Miller says, "it's been two years since I even had a letter from her."

"You should make a movie," Lebowitz says.

Miller isn't sure how to take this. He waits to hear what else Lebowitz has to say, but Lebowitz is silent. So is Kaiser, who's had his back turned to Miller for several minutes now. Both men stare at the road ahead of them. Miller can see that they have lost interest in him. He is disappointed, because he was having a fine time pulling their leg.

One thing Miller told them was true: he hasn't had a letter from his mother in two years. She wrote him a lot when he first joined the Army, at least once a week, sometimes twice, but Miller sent all her letters back unopened and after a year of this she finally gave up. She tried calling a few times but Miller wouldn't go to the telephone, so she gave that up too. Miller wants her to understand that her son is not a man to turn the other cheek. He is a serious man. Once you've crossed him, you've lost him.

Miller's mother crossed him by marrying a man she shouldn't have married: Phil Dove. Dove was a biology teacher in the high school. Miller was having trouble in the course, and his mother went to talk to Dove about it and ended up getting engaged to him. Miller tried to reason with her, but she wouldn't hear a word. You would think from the way she acted that she had landed herself a real catch instead of someone who talked with a stammer and spent his life taking crayfish apart.

Miller did everything he could to stop the marriage but his mother had blinded herself. She couldn't see what she already had, how good it was with just the two of them. How he was always there when she got home from work, with a pot of coffee already brewed. The two of them drinking their coffee together and talking about different things, or maybe not talking at all—maybe just sitting in the kitchen while the room got dark around them, until the telephone rang or the dog started whining to get out. Walking the dog around the reservoir. Coming back and eating whatever they wanted, sometimes nothing, sometimes the same dish three or four nights in a row, watching the programs they wanted to watch and going to bed when they wanted to and not because some other person wanted them to. Just being together in their own place.

Phil Dove got Miller's mother so mixed up that she forgot how good their life was. She refused to see what she was ruining. "You'll be leaving anyway," she told him. "You'll be moving on, next year or the year after"—which showed how wrong she was about Miller, because he would never have left her, not ever, not for anything. But when he said this she laughed as if she knew better, as if he wasn't serious. He was serious, though. He was serious when he promised he'd stay and he was serious when he promised he'd never speak to her again if she married Phil Dove.

She married him. Miller stayed at a motel that night and two more nights, until he ran out of money. Then he joined the Army. He knew that would get to her, because he was still a month shy of finishing high school, and because his father had been killed while serving in the Army. Not in Vietnam but in Georgia, killed in an accident. He and another man were dipping mess kits in a garbage can full of boiling water and somehow the can fell over on him. Miller was six at the time. Miller's mother hated the Army after that, not because her husband was dead—she knew about the war he was going to, she knew about snipers and booby traps and mines—but because of the way it happened. She said the Army couldn't even get a man killed in a decent fashion.

She was right, too. The Army was just as bad as she thought, and worse. You spent all your time waiting around. You lived a completely stupid existence. Miller hated every minute of it, but he found pleasure in his hatred, because he believed that his mother must know how unhappy he was. That knowledge would be a grief to her. It would not be as bad as the grief she had given him, which was spreading from his heart into his stomach and teeth and everywhere else, but it was the worst grief he had power to cause, and it would serve to keep her in mind of him.

Kaiser and Lebowitz are describing hamburgers to each other. Their idea of the perfect hamburger. Miller tries not to listen but their voices go on, and after a while he can't think of anything but beefsteak tomatoes and Gulden's mustard and steaming, onion-stuffed meat crisscrossed with black marks from the grill. He is on the point of asking them to change the subject when Kaiser turns and says, "Think you can handle some chow?"

"I don't know," Miller says. "I guess I could get something down."

"We were talking about a pit stop. But if you want to keep going, just say the word. It's your ball game. I mean, technically we're supposed to take you straight back to base."

"I could eat," Miller says.

"That's the spirit. At a time like this you've got to keep your strength up."

"I could eat," Miller says again.

Lebowitz looks up into the rearview mirror, shakes his head, and looks away again.

They take the next turnoff and drive inland to a crossroads where two gas stations face two restaurants. One of the restaurants is boarded up, so Lebowitz pulls into the parking lot of the Dairy Queen across the road. He turns the engine off and the three men sit motionless in the sudden silence that follows. It soon begins to fade. Miller hears the distant clang of metal on metal, the caw of a crow, the creak of Kaiser shifting in his seat. A dog barks in front of a rust-streaked trailer next door. A skinny white dog with yellow eyes. As it barks the dog rubs itself, one leg raised and twitching, against a sign that shows an outspread hand below the words KNOW YOUR FUTURE.

They get out of the jeep, and Miller follows Kaiser and Lebowitz across the parking lot. The air is warm and smells of oil. In the gas station across the road a pink-skinned man in a swimming suit is trying to put air in the tires of his bicycle, jerking at the hose and swearing loudly at his inability to make the pump work. Miller pushes his tongue against the broken bridge. He lifts it gently. He wonders if he should try eating a hamburger, and decides that it can't hurt as long as he is careful to chew on the other side of his mouth.

But it does hurt. After the first couple of bites Miller shoves his plate away. He rests his chin on one hand and listens to Lebowitz and Kaiser argue about whether people can actually tell the future. Lebowitz is talking about a girl he used to know who had ESP. "We'd be driving along," he says, "and out of the blue she would tell me exactly what I was thinking about. It was unbelievable."

Kaiser finishes his hamburger and takes a drink of milk. "No big deal," he says. "I could do that." He pulls Miller's hamburger over to his side of the table and takes a bite.

"Go ahead," Lebowitz says. "Try it. I'm not thinking about what you think I'm thinking about," he adds.

"Yes, you are."

"All right, now I am," Lebowitz says, "but I wasn't before."

"I wouldn't let a fortune-teller get near me," Miller says. "The way I see it, the less you know the better off you are."

"More vintage philosophy from the private stock of W. P. Miller," Lebowitz says. He looks at Kaiser, who is eating the last of Miller's hamburger. "Well, how about it? I'm up for it if you are."

Kaiser chews ruminatively. He swallows and licks his lips. "Sure," he says. "Why not? As long as Miller here doesn't mind."

"Mind what?" Miller asks.

Lebowitz stands and puts his sunglasses back on. "Don't worry about Miller. Miller's cool. Miller keeps his head when men all around him are losing theirs."

Kaiser and Miller get up from the table and follow Lebowitz outside. Lebowitz is bending down in the shade of a dumpster, wiping off his boots with a paper towel. Shiny blue flies buzz around him. "Mind what?" Miller repeats.

"We thought we'd check out the prophet," Kaiser tells him.

Lebowitz straightens up, and the three of them start across the parking lot.

"I'd actually kind of like to get going," Miller says. When they reach the jeep he stops, but Lebowitz and Kaiser walk on. "Now, listen," Miller says, and skips a little to catch up. "I have a lot to do," he says to their backs. "I want to go home."

"We know how broken up you are," Lebowitz tells him. He keeps walking.

"This shouldn't take too long," Kaiser says.

The dog barks once and then, when it sees that they really intend to come within range of its teeth, runs around the trailer. Lebowitz knocks on the door. It swings open, and there stands a round-faced woman with dark, sunken eyes and heavy lips. One of her eyes has a cast; it seems to be watching something beside her while the other looks down at the three soldiers at her door. Her hands are covered with flour. She is a gypsy, an actual gypsy. Miller has never seen a gypsy before, but he recognizes her just as he would recognize a wolf if he saw one. Her presence makes his blood pound in his veins. If he lived in this place he would come back at night with some other men, all of them yelling and waving torches, and drive her out.

"You on duty?" Lebowitz asks.

She nods, wiping her hands on her skirt. They leave chalky streaks on the bright patchwork. "All of you?" she asks.

"You bet," Kaiser says. His voice is unnaturally loud.

She nods again and turns her good eye from Lebowitz to Kaiser, and then to Miller. After she takes Miller in she smiles and rattles off a string of strange sounds, words from another language or maybe a spell, as if she expects him to understand. One of her front teeth is black.

"No," Miller says. "No, ma'am. Not me." He shakes his head.

"Come," she says, and stands aside.

Lebowitz and Kaiser mount the steps and disappear into the trailer. "Come," the woman repeats. She beckons with her white hands.

Miller backs away, still shaking his head. "Leave me alone," he tells her, and before she can answer he turns and walks away. He goes back to the jeep and sits in the driver's seat, leaving both doors open to catch the breeze. Miller feels the heat drawing the dampness out of his fatigues. He can smell the musty wet canvas overhead and the sourness of his own body. Through the windshield, covered with mud except for a pair of grimy half-circles, he watches three boys solemnly urinating against the wall of the gas station across the road.

Miller bends down to loosen his boots. Blood rushes to his face as he fights the wet laces, and his breath comes faster and faster. "Goddamn laces," he says. "Goddamn rain. Goddamn Army." He gets the laces untied and sits up, panting. He stares at the trailer. Goddamn gypsy.

He can't believe those two fools actually went inside there. Yukking it up. Playing around. That shows how stupid they are, because anybody knows that you don't play around with fortune-tellers. There is no predicting what a fortune-teller might say, and once it's said, no way to keep it from happening. Once you hear what's out there it isn't out there anymore, it's here. You might as well open your door to a murderer as to the future.

The future. Didn't everybody know enough about the future already, without digging up the details? There is only one thing you have to know about the future: everything gets worse. Once you have that, you have it all. The specifics don't bear thinking about.

Miller certainly has no intention of thinking about the specifics. He peels off his damp socks and massages his white crinkled feet. Now and then he glances up toward the trailer, where the gypsy is pronouncing fate on Kaiser and Lebowitz. Miller makes humming noises. He will not think about the future.

Because it's true—everything gets worse. One day you are sitting in front of your house, poking sticks into an anthill, hearing the chink of silverware and the voices of your mother and father in the kitchen; then, at some moment you can't even remember, one of those voices is gone. And you never hear it again. When you go from today to tomorrow you're walking into an ambush.

A new boy, Nat Pranger, joins your Little League team. He lives in a boardinghouse a couple of streets over from you. The first day you meet Nat you show him the place under the bleachers where you keep the change you steal from your mother. The next morning you remember doing this, and you push your half-eaten breakfast away and run to the ball park, blindly, your chest hurting. The change is still in its hiding place. You count it. Not a penny is missing. You kneel there in the shadows, catching your breath.

All summer you and Nat throw each other grounders and develop plans to acquire a large sailboat for use in the South Seas—that is Nat's term, "the South Seas." Then school starts, your first year of junior high, and Nat makes other friends but you don't, because something about you turns people cruel. Even the teachers. You want to have friends, you would change if you knew what it was that needed changing, but you don't know. You see Nat struggling to be loyal and you hate him for it. His kindness is worse than cruelty. By December you know exactly how things will be in June. All you can do is watch it happen.

What lies ahead doesn't bear thinking about. Already Miller has an ulcer, and his teeth are full of holes. His body is giving out on him. What will it be like when he's sixty? Or even five years from now? Miller was in a restaurant the other day and saw a fellow about his own age in a wheelchair, getting fed soup by a woman who was talking to some other people at the table. This boy's hands lay twisted in his lap like gloves dropped there; his pants had crawled halfway to his knees, showing pale, wasted legs no thicker than bones. He could barely move his head. The woman feeding him did a lousy job because she was too busy blabbing to her friends. Half the soup went over the boy's shirt. Yet his eyes were bright and watchful.

Miller thought, *That could happen to me.*

You could be going along just fine and then one day, through no fault of your own, something could get loose in your bloodstream and knock out part of your brain. Leave you like that. And if it didn't happen now, all at once, it was sure to happen slowly later on. That was the end you were bound for.

Someday Miller is going to die. He knows that, and he prides himself on knowing it when other people only pretend to know it, secretly believing that they will live forever. This is not the reason that the future is unthinkable to Miller. There is something worse than that, something not to be considered, and he will not consider it.

He will not consider it. Miller leans back against the seat and closes his eye lids, but his effort to trick himself into somnolence fails. Behind his eyes he is wide awake and fidgety with gloom, probing against his will for what he is afraid to find, until, with no surprise at all, he finds it. A simple truth. His mother is also going to die. Just like him. And there is no telling when. Miller cannot count on her to be there to come home to, and receive his pardon, when he finally decides that she has suffered enough.

Miller opens his eyes and looks at the raw shapes of the buildings across the road, their outlines lost in the grime on the windshield. He closes his eyes again. He listens to himself breathe and feels the familiar, almost muscular ache of knowing that he is beyond his mother's reach. He has put himself where she cannot see him or speak to him or touch him in that thoughtless way of hers, resting her hand on his shoulder as she stops behind his chair to ask him a question or just stand for a moment, her mind somewhere else. This was supposed to be her punishment, but somehow it has become his own. He understands that it has to stop. It is killing him.

It has to stop now, and as if he has been planning for this day all along Miller knows exactly what he will do. Instead of reporting to the Red Cross when he gets back to base, he will pack his bag and catch the first bus home. No one will blame him for this. Even when they discover the mistake they've made they still won't blame him, because it would be the natural thing for a grieving son to do. Instead of punishing him they will probably apologize for giving him a scare.

He will take the first bus home, express or not. It will be full of Mexicans and soldiers. Miller will sit by a window and drowse. Now and then he will come up from his dreams to stare out at the passing green hills and loamy plowland and the stations where the bus puts in, stations cloudy with exhaust and loud with engine roar, where the people he sees through his window will look groggily back at him as if they too have just come up from sleep. Salinas. Vacaville. Red Bluff. When he gets to Redding, Miller will hire a cab. He will ask the driver to stop at Schwartz's for a few minutes while he buys some flowers, and then he will ride on home, down Sutter and over to Serra, past the ball park, past the grade school, past the Mormon temple. Right on Belmont. Left on Park. Leaning over the seat, saying farther, farther, a little farther, that's it, that one, there.

The sound of voices behind the door as he rings the bell. Door swings open, voices hush. Who are these people? Men in suits, women wearing white gloves. Someone stammers his name, strange to him now, almost forgotten. "W-W-Wesley." A man's voice. He stands just inside the door, breathing perfume. Then the flowers are taken from his hand and laid with other flowers on the coffee table. He hears his name again. It is Phil Dove, moving toward him from across the room. He walks slowly, with his arms raised, like a blind man.

Wesley, he says. Thank God you're home.

TWO KINDS

Amy Tan

My mother believed you could be anything you wanted to be in America. You could open a restaurant. You could work for the government and get good retirement. You could buy a house with almost no money down. You could become rich. You could become instantly famous.

"Of course, you can be prodigy, too," my mother told me when I was nine. "You can be best anything. What does Auntie Lindo know? Her daughter, she is only best tricky."

America was where all my mother's hopes lay. She had come to San Francisco in 1949 after losing everything in China: her mother and father, her family home, her first husband, and two daughters, twin baby girls. But she never looked back with regret. Things could get better in so many ways.

We didn't immediately pick the right kind of prodigy. At first my mother thought I could be a Chinese Shirley Temple. We'd watch Shirley's old movies on TV as though they were training films. My mother would poke my arm and say, "*Ni kan.* You watch." And I would see Shirley tapping her feet, or singing a sailor song, or pursing her lips into a very round O while saying "Oh, my goodness."

"*Ni kan,*" my mother said, as Shirley's eyes flooded with tears. "You already know how. Don't need talent for crying!"

Soon after my mother got this idea about Shirley Temple, she took me to the beauty training school in the Mission District and put me in the hands of a student who could barely hold the scissors without shaking. Instead of getting big fat curls, I emerged with an uneven mass of crinkly black fuzz. My mother dragged me off to the bathroom and tried to wet down my hair.

"You look like Negro Chinese," she lamented, as if I had done this on purpose.

The instructor of the beauty training school had to lop off these soggy clumps to make my hair even again. "Peter Pan is very popular these days," the instructor assured my mother. I now had hair the length of a boy's, with curly bangs that hung at a slant two inches above my eyebrows. I liked the haircut, and it made me actually look forward to my future fame.

In fact, in the beginning I was just as excited as my mother, maybe even more so. I pictured this prodigy part of me as many different images, and I tried each one on for size. I was a dainty ballerina girl standing by the curtain, waiting to hear the music that would send me floating on my tiptoes. I was like the Christ child lifted out of the straw manger, crying with holy indignity. I was Cinderella stepping from her pumpkin carriage with sparkly cartoon music filling the air.

In all of my imaginings I was filled with a sense that I would soon become perfect. My mother and father would adore me. I would be beyond reproach. I would never feel the need to sulk, or to clamor for anything.

But sometimes the prodigy in me became impatient. "If you don't hurry up and get me out of here, I'm disappearing for good," it warned. "And then you'll always be nothing."

Every night after dinner my mother and I would sit at the Formica-topped kitchen table. She would present new tests, taking her examples from stories of amazing children that she had read in *Ripley's Believe It or Not* or *Good Housekeeping*, *Reader's Digest*, or any of a dozen other magazines she kept in a pile in our bathroom. My mother got these magazines from people whose houses she cleaned. And since she cleaned many houses each week, we had a great assortment. She would look through them all, searching for stories about remarkable children.

The first night she brought out a story about a three-year-old boy who knew the capitals of all the states and even of most of the European countries. A teacher was quoted as saying that the little boy could also pronounce the names of the foreign cities correctly. "What's the capital of Finland?" my mother asked me, looking at the story.

All I knew was the capital of California, because Sacramento was the name of the street we lived on in Chinatown. "Nairobi!" I guessed, saying the most foreign word I could think of. She checked to see if that might be one way to pronounce *Helsinki* before showing me the answer.

The tests got harder—multiplying numbers in my head, finding the queen of hearts in a deck of cards, trying to stand on my head without using my hands, predicting the daily temperatures in Los Angeles, New York, and London. One night I had to look at a page from the Bible for three minutes and then report everything I could remember. "Now Jehoshaphat had riches and honor in abundance and . . . that's all I remember, Ma," I said.

After seeing, once again, my mother's disappointed face, something inside me began to die. I hated the tests, the raised hopes and failed expectations. Before going to bed that night I looked in the mirror above the bathroom sink, and when I saw only my face staring back—and understood that it would always be this ordinary face—I began to cry. Such a sad, ugly girl! I made high-pitched noises like a crazed animal, trying to scratch out the face in the mirror.

And then I saw what seemed to be the prodigy side of me—a face I had never seen before. I looked at my reflection, blinking so that I could see more clearly. The girl staring back at me was angry, powerful. She and I were the same. I had new thoughts, willful thoughts—or, rather, thoughts filled with lots of won'ts. I won't let her change me, I promised myself. I won't be what I'm not.

So now when my mother presented her tests, I performed listlessly, my head propped on one arm. I pretended to be bored. And I was. I got so bored that I started counting the bellows of the foghorns out on the bay while my mother drilled me in other areas. The sound was comforting and reminded me of the cow jumping over the moon. And the next day I played a game with myself, seeing if my mother would give up on me before eight bellows. After a while I usually counted only one bellow, maybe two at most. At last she was beginning to give up hope.

Two or three months went by without any mention of my being a prodigy. And then one day my mother was watching the *Ed Sullivan*

Show on TV. The TV was old and the sound kept shorting out. Every time my mother got halfway up from the sofa to adjust the set, the sound would come back on and Sullivan would be talking. As soon as she sat down, Sullivan would go silent again. She got up—the TV broke into loud piano music. She sat down—silence. Up and down, back and forth, quiet and loud. It was like a stiff, embraceless dance between her and the TV set. Finally, she stood by the set with her hand on the sound dial.

She seemed entranced by the music, a frenzied little piano piece with a mesmerizing quality, which alternated between quick, playful passages and teasing, lilting ones.

"Ni kan," my mother said, calling me over with hurried hand gestures. "Look here."

I could see why my mother was fascinated by the music. It was being pounded out by a little Chinese girl, about nine years old, with a Peter Pan haircut. The girl had the sauciness of a Shirley Temple. She was proudly modest, like a proper Chinese child. And she also did a fancy sweep of a curtsy, so that the fluffy skirt of her white dress cascaded to the floor like the petals of a large carnation.

In spite of these warning signs, I wasn't worried. Our family had no piano and we couldn't afford to buy one, let alone reams of sheet music and piano lessons. So I could be generous in my comments when my mother bad-mouthed the little girl on TV.

"Play note right, but doesn't sound good!" my mother complained. "No singing sound."

"What are you picking on her for?" I said carelessly. "She's pretty good. Maybe she's not the best, but she's trying hard." I knew almost immediately that I would be sorry I had said that.

"Just like you," she said. "Not the best. Because you not trying." She gave a little huff as she let go of the sound dial and sat down on the sofa.

The little Chinese girl sat down also, to play an encore of "Anitra's Tanz," by Grieg. I remember the song, because later on I had to learn how to play it.

Three days after watching the *Ed Sullivan Show* my mother told me what my schedule would be for piano lessons and piano practice. She had talked to Mr. Chong, who lived on the first floor of our apartment building. Mr. Chong was a retired piano teacher, and my mother had traded housecleaning services for weekly lessons and a piano for me to practice on every day, two hours a day, from four until six.

When my mother told me this, I felt as though I had been sent to hell. I whined, and then kicked my foot a little when I couldn't stand it anymore.

"Why don't you like me the way I am?" I cried. "I'm *not* a genius! I can't even play the piano. And if I could, I wouldn't go on TV if you paid me a million dollars!"

My mother slapped me. "Who ask you to be genius?" she shouted. "Only ask you be your best. For you sake. You think I want you to be genius? Hnnh! What for! Who ask you!"

"So ungrateful," I heard her mutter in Chinese. "If she had as much talent as she has temper, she'd be famous now."

Mr. Chong, whom I secretly nicknamed Old Chong, was very strange, always tapping his fingers to the silent music of an invisible orchestra. He looked ancient in my eyes. He had lost most of the hair on the top of his head, and he wore thick glasses and had eyes that always looked tired. But he must have been younger than I thought, since he lived with his mother and was not yet married.

I met Old Lady Chong once, but that was enough. She had a peculiar smell, like a baby that had done something in its pants, and her fingers felt like a dead person's, like an old peach I once found in the back of the refrigerator; its skin just slid off the flesh when I picked it up.

I soon found out why Old Chong had retired from teaching piano. He was deaf. "Like Beethoven!" he shouted to me. "We're both listening only in our head!" And he would start to conduct his frantic silent sonatas.

Our lessons went like this. He would open the book and point to different things, explaining their purpose: "Key! Treble! Bass! No sharps or flats! So this is C major! Listen now and play after me!"

And then he would play the C scale a few times, a simple chord, and then, as if inspired by an old unreachable itch, he would gradually add more notes and running trills and a pounding bass until the music was really something quite grand.

I would play after him, the simple scale, the simple chord, and then just play some nonsense that sounded like a cat running up and down on top of garbage cans. Old Chong would smile and applaud and say, "Very good! But now you must learn to keep time!"

So that's how I discovered that Old Chong's eyes were too slow to keep up with the wrong notes I was playing. He went through the motions in half time. To help me keep rhythm, he stood behind me and pushed down on my right shoulder for every beat. He balanced pennies on top of my wrists so that I would keep them still as I slowly played scales and arpeggios. He had me curve my hand around an apple and keep that shape when playing chords. He marched stiffly to show me how to make each finger dance up and down, staccato, like an obedient little soldier.

He taught me all these things, and that was how I also learned I could be lazy and get away with mistakes, lots of mistakes. If I hit the wrong notes because I hadn't practiced enough, I never corrected myself. I just kept playing in rhythm. And Old Chong kept conducting his own private reverie.

So maybe I never really gave myself a fair chance. I did pick up the basics pretty quickly, and I might have become a good pianist at that young age. But I was so determined not to try, not to be anybody different, that I learned to play only the most ear-splitting preludes, the most discordant hymns.

Over the next year I practiced like this, dutifully in my own way. And then one day I heard my mother and her friend Lindo Jong both talking in a loud, bragging tone of voice so that others could hear. It was after church, and I was leaning against a brick wall, wearing a dress with stiff white petticoats. Auntie Lindo's daughter, Waverly, who was my age, was standing farther down the wall, about five feet away. We had grown up together and shared all the closeness of two sisters, squabbling over crayons and dolls. In other words, for the most part, we hated each other. I thought she was snotty. Waverly Jong had gained a certain amount of fame as "Chinatown's Littlest Chinese Chess Champion."

"She bring home too many trophy," Auntie Lindo lamented that Sunday. "All day she play chess. All day I have no time do nothing but dust off her winnings." She threw a scolding look at Waverly, who pretended not to see her.

"You lucky you don't have this problem," Auntie Lindo said with a sigh to my mother.

And my mother squared her shoulders and bragged: "Our problem worser than yours. If we ask Jing-mei wash dish, she hear nothing but music. It's like you can't stop this natural talent."

And right then I was determined to put a stop to her foolish pride.

A few weeks later Old Chong and my mother conspired to have me play in a talent show that was to be held in the church hall. By then my parents had saved up enough to buy me a secondhand piano, a black Wurlitzer spinet with a scarred bench. It was the showpiece of our living room.

For the talent show I was to play a piece called "Pleading Child," from Schumann's *Scenes From Childhood*. It was a simple, moody piece that sounded more difficult than it was. I was supposed to memorize the whole thing. But I dawdled over it, playing a few bars and then cheating, looking up to see what notes followed. I never really listened to what I was playing. I daydreamed about being somewhere else, about being someone else.

The part I liked to practice best was the fancy curtsy: right foot out, touch the rose on the carpet with a pointed foot, sweep to the side, bend left leg, look up, and smile.

My parents invited all the couples from their social club to witness my debut. Auntie Lindo and Uncle Tin were there. Waverly and her two older brothers had also come. The first two rows were filled with children either younger or older than I was. The littlest ones got to go first. They recited simple nursery rhymes, squawked out tunes on miniature violins, and twirled hula hoops in pink ballet tutus, and when they bowed or curtsied, the audience would sigh in unison, "*Awww*," and then clap enthusiastically.

When my turn came, I was very confident. I remember my childish excitement. It was as if I knew, without a doubt, that the prodigy side of me really did exist. I had no fear whatsoever, no nervousness. I remember thinking, This is it! This is it! I looked out over the audience, at my mother's blank face, my father's yawn, Auntie Lindo's stiff-lipped smile, Waverly's sulky expression. I had on a white dress, layered with sheets of lace, and a pink bow in my Peter Pan haircut. As I sat down, I envisioned people jumping to their feet and Ed Sullivan rushing up to introduce me to everyone on TV.

And I started to play. Everything was so beautiful. I was so caught up in how lovely I looked that I wasn't worried about how I would sound. So I was surprised when I hit the first wrong note. And then I hit another, and another. A chill started at the top of my head and began to trickle down. Yet I couldn't stop playing, as though my hands were bewitched. I kept thinking my fingers would adjust themselves back, like a train switching to the right track. I played this strange jumble through to the end, the sour notes staying with me all the way.

When I stood up, I discovered my legs were shaking. Maybe I had just been nervous, and the audience, like Old Chong, had seen me go through the right motions and had not heard anything wrong at all. I swept my right foot out, went down on my knee, looked up, and smiled. The room was quiet, except for Old Chong, who was beaming and shouting, "Bravo! Bravo! Well done!" But then I saw my mother's face, her stricken face. The audience clapped weakly, and as I walked back to my chair, with my whole face quivering as I tried not to cry, I heard a little boy whisper loudly to his mother, "That was awful," and the mother whispered back, "Well, she certainly tried."

And now I realized how many people were in the audience—the whole world, it seemed. I was aware of eyes burning into my back. I felt the shame of my mother and father as they sat stiffly through the rest of the show.

We could have escaped during intermission. Pride and some strange sense of honor must have anchored my parents to their chairs. And so we watched it all: The eighteen-year-old boy with a fake moustache who did a magic show and juggled flaming hoops while riding a unicycle. The breasted girl with white makeup who sang an aria from *Madame Butterfly* and got an honorable mention. And the eleven-year-old boy who won first prize playing a tricky violin song that sounded like a busy bee.

After the show the Hsus, the Jongs, and the St. Clairs, from the Joy Luck Club, came up to my mother and father.

"Lots of talented kids," Auntie Lindo said vaguely, smiling broadly.

"That was somethin' else," my father said, and I wondered if he was referring to me in a humorous way, or whether he even remembered what I had done.

Waverly looked at me and shrugged her shoulders. "You aren't a genius like me," she said matter-of-factly. And if I hadn't felt so bad, I would have pulled her braids and punched her stomach.

But my mother's expression was what devastated me: a quiet, blank look that said she had lost everything. I felt the same way, and everybody seemed now to be coming up, like gawkers at the scene of an accident, to see what parts were actually missing.

When we got on the bus to go home, my father was humming the busy-bee tune and my mother was silent. I kept thinking she wanted to wait until we got home before shouting at me. But when my father unlocked the door to our apartment, my mother walked in and went straight to the back, into the bedroom. No accusations. No blame. And in a way, I felt disappointed. I had been waiting for her to start shouting, so that I could shout back and cry and blame her for all my misery.

I had assumed that my talent-show fiasco meant that I would never have to play the piano again. But two days later, after school, my mother came out of the kitchen and saw me watching TV.

"Four clock," she reminded me, as if it were any other day. I was stunned, as though she were asking me to go through the talent-show torture again. I planted myself more squarely in front of the TV.

"Turn off TV," she called from the kitchen five minutes later.

I didn't budge. And then I decided. I didn't have to do what my mother said anymore. I wasn't her slave. This wasn't China. I had listened to her before, and look what happened. She was the stupid one.

She came out from the kitchen and stood in the arched entryway of the living room. "Four clock," she said once again, louder.

"I'm not going to play anymore," I said nonchalantly. "Why should I? I'm not a genius."

She stood in front of the TV. I saw that her chest was heaving up and down in an angry way.

"No!" I said, and I now felt stronger, as if my true self had finally emerged. So this was what had been inside me all along.

"No! I won't!" I screamed.

She snapped off the TV, yanked me by the arm and pulled me off the floor. She was frighteningly strong, half pulling, half carrying me toward the piano as I kicked the throw rugs under my feet. She lifted me up and onto the hard bench. I was sobbing by now, looking at her bitterly. Her chest was heaving even more and her mouth was open, smiling crazily as if she were pleased that I was crying.

"You want me to be someone that I'm not!" I sobbed. "I'll never be the kind of daughter you want me to be!"

"Only two kinds of daughters," she shouted in Chinese. "Those who are obedient and those who follow their own mind! Only one kind of daughter can live in this house. Obedient daughter!"

"Then I wish I weren't your daughter. I wish you weren't my mother," I shouted. As I said these things I got scared. It felt like worms and toads and slimy things crawling out of my chest, but it also felt good, that this awful side of me had surfaced, at last.

"Too late change this," my mother said shrilly.

And I could sense her anger rising to its breaking point. I wanted to see it spill over. And that's when I remembered the babies she had lost in China, the ones we never talked about. "Then I wish I'd never been born!" I shouted. "I wish I were dead! Like them."

It was as if I had said magic words. Alakazam!—her face went blank, her mouth closed, her arms went slack, and she backed out of the room, stunned, as if she were blowing away like a small brown leaf, thin, brittle, lifeless.

It was not the only disappointment my mother felt in me. In the years that followed, I failed her many times, each time asserting my will, my right to fall short of expectations. I didn't get straight As. I didn't become class president. I didn't get into Stanford. I dropped out of college.

Unlike my mother, I did not believe I could be anything I wanted to be. I could only be me.

And for all those years we never talked about the disaster at the recital or my terrible declarations afterward at the piano bench. Neither of us talked about it again, as if it were a betrayal that was now unspeakable. So I never found a way to ask her why she had hoped for something so large that failure was inevitable.

And even worse, I never asked her about what frightened me the most: Why had she given up hope? For after our struggle at the piano, she never mentioned my playing again. The lessons stopped. The lid to the piano was closed, shutting out the dust, my misery, and her dreams.

So she surprised me. A few years ago she offered to give me the piano, for my thirtieth birthday. I had not played in all those years. I saw the offer as a sign of forgiveness, a tremendous burden removed.

"Are you sure?" I asked shyly. "I mean, won't you and Dad miss it?"

"No, this your piano," she said firmly. "Always your piano. You only one can play."

"Well, I probably can't play anymore," I said. "It's been years."

"You pick up fast," my mother said, as if she knew this was certain. "You have natural talent. You could be genius if you want to."

"No, I couldn't."

"You just not trying," my mother said. And she was neither angry nor sad. She said it as if announcing a fact that could never be disproved. "Take it," she said.

But I didn't, at first. It was enough that she had offered it to me. And after that, every time I saw it in my parents' living room, standing in front of the bay window, it made me feel proud, as if it were a shiny trophy that I had won back.

Last week I sent a tuner over to my parents' apartment and had the piano reconditioned, for purely sentimental reasons. My mother had died a few months before, and I had been getting things in order for my father, a little bit at a time. I put the jewelry in special silk pouches. The sweaters she had knitted in yellow, pink, bright orange—all the colors I hated—I put in mothproof boxes. I found some old Chinese silk dresses, the kind with little slits up the sides. I rubbed the old silk against my skin, and then wrapped them in tissue and decided to take them home with me.

After I had the piano tuned, I opened the lid and touched the keys. It sounded even richer than I remembered. Really, it was a very good piano. Inside the bench were the same exercise notes with handwritten scales, the same secondhand music books with their covers held together with yellow tape.

I opened up the Schumann book to the dark little piece I had played at the recital. It was on the left-hand page, "Pleading Child." It looked more difficult than I remembered. I played a few bars, surprised at how easily the notes came back to me.

And for the first time, or so it seemed, I noticed the piece on the right-hand side. It was called "Perfectly Contented." I tried to play this one as well. It had a lighter melody but with the same flowing rhythm and turned out to be quite easy. "Pleading Child" was shorter but slower; "Perfectly Contented" was longer but faster. And after I had played them both a few times, I realized they were two halves of the same song.

WHERE WE ARE NOW

Ethan Canin

When I met Jodi, she was an English major at Simmons College, in Boston, and for a while after that she tried to be a stage actress. Then she tried writing a play, and when that didn't work out she thought about opening a bookstore. We've been married eleven years now, and these days she checks out books at the public library. I don't mean she reads them; I mean she works at the circulation desk.

We've been arguing lately about where we live. Our apartment is in a building with no grass or bushes, only a social room, with plastic chairs and a carpet made of Astroturf. Not many people want to throw a party on Astroturf, Jodi says. She points out other things, too: the elevator stops a foot below the floors, so you have to step up to get out; the cold water comes out rusty in the mornings; three weeks ago a man was robbed in the hallway by a kid with a bread knife. The next Sunday night Jodi rolled over in bed, turned on the light, and said, "Charlie, let's look at houses."

It was one in the morning. From the fourth floor, through the night haze, I could see part of West Hollywood, a sliver of the observatory, lights from the mansions in the canyon.

"There," I said, pointing through the window. "Houses."

"No, let's look at houses to buy."

I covered my eyes with my arm. "Lovebird," I said, "where will we find a house we can afford?"

"We can start this weekend," she said.

That night after dinner she read aloud from the real estate section. "Santa Monica," she read. "Two bedrooms, yard, half-mile to beach."

"How much?"

She looked closer at the paper. "We can look at other places."

She read to herself for a while. Then she said that prices seemed lower in some areas near the Los Angeles airport.

"How much?"

"A two-bedroom for $160,000."

I glanced at her.

"Just because we look doesn't mean we have to buy it," she said.

"There's a real estate agent involved."

"She won't mind."

"It's not honest," I said.

She closed the paper and went to the window. I watched a muscle in her neck move from side to side. "You know what it's like?" she said, looking into the street.

"I just don't want to waste the woman's time," I answered.

"It's like being married to a priest."

I knew why she said that. I'm nothing like a priest. I'm a physical education teacher in the Hollywood schools and an assistant coach—basketball and baseball. The other night I'd had a couple of other coaches over to the house. We aren't all that much alike—I'll read a biography on the weekend, listen to classical music maybe a third of the time—but I still like to have them over. We were sitting in the living room, drinking beer and talking about the future. One of the coaches has a two-year-old son at home. He didn't have a lot of money, he said, so he thought it was important to teach his kid morality. I wasn't sure he was serious, but when he finished I told a story anyway about an incident that had happened a few weeks before at school. I'd found out that a kid in a gym class I was teaching, a quiet boy and a decent student, had stolen a hat from a men's store. So I made him return it and write a letter of apology to the owner. When I told the part about how the man was so impressed with the letter that he offered the boy a job, Jodi remarked that I was lucky it hadn't turned out the other way.

"What do you mean?" I asked.

"He could have called the police," she said. "He could have thanked you for bringing the boy in and then called the police."

"I just don't think so."

"Why not? The boy could have ended up in jail."

"I just don't think so," I said. "I think most people will respond to honesty. I think that's where people like us have to lead the way."

It's an important point, I said, and took a drink of beer to take the edge off what I was saying. Too much money makes you lose sight of things, I told them. I stopped talking then, but I could have said more. All you have to do is look around: in Beverly Hills there's a restaurant where a piece of veal costs thirty dollars. I don't mind being an assistant coach at a high school, even though you hear now about the fellow who earns a hundred thousand dollars with the fitness truck that comes right to people's homes. The truck has Nautilus, and a sound system you wouldn't expect. He keeps the stars in shape that way—Kirk Douglas, the movie executives. The man with the truck doesn't live in Hollywood. He probably lives out at the beach, in Santa Monica or Malibu.

But Hollywood's fine if people don't compare it with the ideas they have. Once in a while, at a party, someone from out of town will ask me whether any children of movie stars are in my classes. Sometimes Jodi says the answer is yes but that it would violate confidentiality to reveal their names. Other times I explain that movie stars don't live in Hollywood these days, that most of them don't even work here, that Hollywood is just car washes and food joints, and that the theater with the stars' footprints out front isn't much of a theater anymore. The kids race hot rods by it on Thursday nights.

Hollywood is all right, though, I say. It's got sun and wide streets and is close to everything.

But Jodi wants to look anyway.

Next Sunday I drive, and Jodi gives directions from the map. The house is in El Segundo. While I'm parking I hear a loud noise, and a 747 flies right over our heads. I watch it come down over the freeway.

"Didn't one of them land on the road once?" I ask.

"I don't remember it," Jodi says. She looks at the map. "The house should be on this block."

"I think it was in Dallas. I think it came right down on top of a car."

I think about that for a minute. It shakes me up to see a huge plane so low. I think of the people inside the one that landed on the road—descending, watching the flaps and the ailerons, the houses and automobiles coming into view.

"The ad says there are nice trees in back," says Jodi.

She leads us to the house. It's two stories, yellow stucco walls, with a cement yard and a low wire fence along the sidewalk. The roof is tar paper. Down the front under the drainpipes are two long green stains.

"Don't worry," she says. "Just because we look doesn't mean anything." She knocks on the door and slips her arm into mine. "Maybe you can see the ocean from the bedroom windows."

She knocks again. Then she pushes the door a little, and we walk into the living room. There are quick footsteps, and a woman comes out of the hallway. "Good afternoon," she says. "Would you sign in, please?"

She points to a vinyl-covered book on the coffee table, and Jodi crosses the room and writes something in it. Then the agent hands me a sheet of paper with small type on it and a badly copied picture. I've never shopped for a house before. I see two columns of abbreviations, some numbers. It's hard to tell what the picture is of, but then I recognize the long stains under the drainpipes. I fold the sheet and put it into my pants pocket. Then I sit down on the couch and look around. The walls are light yellow, and one of them is covered with a mirror that has gold marbling in it. On the floor is a cream-colored shag rug, with a matted area near the front door where a couch or maybe a trunk once stood. Above the mantel is a painting of a blue whale.

"Do the appliances and plumbing work?" Jodi asks.

"Everything works," says the agent.

Jodi turns the ceiling light on and off. She opens and closes the door to a closet in the corner, and I glimpse a tricycle and a bag full of empty bottles. I wonder what the family does on a Sunday afternoon when buyers look at their house.

"The rooms have a nice feel," the agent says. "You know what I mean?"

"I'm not sure I do," I say.

"It's hard to explain," she says, "but you'll see."

"We understand," says Jodi.

In the marbled mirror I watch Jodi's reflection. Three windows look onto the front yard, and she unlatches and lifts each one.

"I like a careful buyer," says the agent.

"You can never be too thorough," Jodi answers. Then she adds, "We're just looking."

The agent smiles, drumming her fingers against her wrist. I know she's trying to develop a strategy. In college I learned about strategies. I worked for a while selling magazines over the phone: talk to the man if you think they want it; talk to the woman if you think they don't. I was thinking of playing ball then, semi-pro, and the magazine work was evenings. I was twenty-three years old. I thought I was just doing work until I was discovered.

"Why don't you two look around," I say now to the agent. "I'll stay here."

"Perfect," she says.

She leads Jodi into the next room. I hear a door open and shut, and then they begin talking about the floors, the walls, the ceiling. We aren't going to buy the house, and I don't like being here. When I hear the two of them walk out through the back door into the yard, I get up from the couch and go over to look at the painting above the mantel. It's an underwater view, looking below the whale as it swims toward the surface. Above, the sunny sky is broken by ripples. On the mantel is a little pile of plaster powder, and as I stand there, I realize that the painting has just recently been hung. I go back to the couch. Once on a trip up the coast I saw a whale that the tide had trapped in a lagoon. It was north of Los Angeles, along the coastal highway, in a cove sheltered by two piers of man-moved boulders. Cars were parked along the shoulder. People were setting up their cameras while the whale moved around in the lagoon, stirring up the bottom. I don't like to think about trapped animals, though, so instead I sit down and try to plan what to do tomorrow at practice. The season hasn't started yet, and we're still working on base-running—the double steal, leading from the inside of the bag. Baseball isn't a thing you think about, though; baseball *comes*. I'm an assistant coach and maybe could have been a minor league pitcher, but when I think of it I realize I know only seven or eight things about the whole game. We learn so slowly, I think.

I get up and go over to the painting again. I glance behind me. I put my head next to the wall, lift the frame a little bit, and when I look I see that behind it the plaster is stained brown from an interior leak. I take a deep breath and then put the frame back. From outside in the yard I hear the women speaking about basement storage space, and rather than listen I cross the room and enter a hallway. It smells of grease. On the wall, at waist level, are children's hand marks that go all the way to the far end. I walk down there and enter the kitchen. In it are a Formica table and four plastic chairs, everything made large by the low ceiling. I see a door in the corner, and when I cross the room and open it I'm surprised to find a stairway with brooms and mops hung above the banister. The incline is steep, and when I go up I find myself in the rear of an upstairs closet. Below me Jodi and the agent are still talking. I push through the clothes hanging in front of me and open the door.

I'm in the master bedroom now. A king-size bed stands in front of me, but something's funny about it, and when I look closer I think that it might be two single beds pushed together. It's covered by a spread. I stop for a moment to think. I don't think I'm doing anything wrong. We came here to see the house, and when people show their homes they take out everything of value so that they won't have to worry. I go to the window. Framing it is a new-looking lace curtain, pinched up in a tieback. I look out at a crab apple tree and some telephone wires and try to calculate where the ocean might be. The shadows point west, but the coastline is irregular in this area and juts in different directions. The view of the crab apple is pretty, spotted with shade and light—but then I see that in the corner behind the curtain the glass is splintered and has been taped. I lift the curtain and look at the pane. The crack spreads like a spider web. Then I walk back to the bed. I flatten my hands and slip them into the crevice between the two mattresses, and when I extend my arms the two halves come apart. I push the beds back together and sit down. Then I look into the corner, and my heart skips because I see that against the far wall, half-hidden by the open door, is an old woman in a chair.

"Excuse me," I say.

"That's all right," she says. She folds her hands. "The window cracked ten years ago."

"My wife and I are looking at the house."

"I know."

I walk to the window. "A nice view," I say, pretending to look at something in the yard. The woman doesn't say anything. I can hear water running in the pipes, some children outside. Tiny, pale apples hang among the leaves of the tree.

"You know," I say, "we're not really looking at the house to buy it."

I walk back to the bed. The skin on the woman's arms is mottled and hangs in folds. "We can't afford to buy it," I say. "I don't make enough money to buy a house and—I don't know why, but my wife wants to look at them anyway. She wants people to think we have enough money to buy a house."

The woman looks at me.

"It's crazy," I say, "but what are you going to do in that kind of situation?"

She clears her throat. "My son-in-law," she begins, "wants to sell the house so he can throw the money away." Her voice is slow, and I think she has no saliva in her mouth. "He has a friend who goes to South America and swallows everything, then comes back through customs with a plastic bag in his bowel."

She stops. I look at her. "He's selling the house to invest the money in drugs?"

"I'm glad you don't want to buy," she says.

I might have had a small career in baseball, but I've learned in the past eleven years to talk about other things. I was twenty-three the last pitch I threw. The season was over and Jodi was in the stands in a wool coat. I was about to get a college degree in physical education. I knew how to splint a broken bone and how to cut the grass on a golf green, and then I decided that to turn your life around you had to start from the inside. I had a coach in college who said he wasn't trying to teach us to be pro ballplayers; he was trying to teach us to be decent people.

When we got married, I told Jodi that no matter what happened, no matter where things went, she could always trust me. We'd been seeing each other for a year, and in that time I'd been reading books. Not baseball books. Biographies: Martin Luther King, Gandhi. To play baseball right you have to forget that you're a person; you're muscles, bone, the need for sleep and food. So when you stop, you're saved by someone else's ideas. This isn't true just for baseball players. It's true for anyone who's failed at what he loves.

A friend got me the coaching job in California, and as soon as we were married we came west. Jodi still wanted to be an actress. We rented a room in a house with six other people, and she took classes in dance in the mornings and speech in the afternoons. Los Angeles is full of actors. Sometimes at parties we counted them. After a couple of years she started writing a play, and until we moved into where we are now we used to read pieces of it out loud to our six housemates.

By then I was already a little friendly with the people at school, but when I was out of the house, even after two years in Los Angeles, I was alone. People were worried about their own lives. In college I'd spent almost all my time with another ballplayer, Mitchell Lighty, and I wasn't used to new people. A couple of years after we graduated, Mitchell left to play pro ball in Panama City, and he came out to Los Angeles on his way there. The night before his plane left, he and I went downtown to a bar on the top floor of a big hotel. We sat by a window, and after a few drinks we went out onto the balcony. The air was cool. Plants grew along the edge, ivy was woven into the railing, and birds perched among the leaves. I was amazed to see the birds resting there thirty stories up on the side of the building. When I brushed the plants the birds took off into the air, and when I leaned over to watch them, I became dizzy with the distance to the sidewalk and with the small, rectangular shapes of the cars. The birds sailed in wide circles over the street and came back to the balcony. Then Mitchell put his drink on a chair, took both my hands, and stepped up onto the railing. He stood there on the metal crossbar, his wrists locked in my hands, leaning into the air.

"For God's sake," I whispered. He leaned farther out, pulling me toward the railing. A waiter appeared at the sliding door next to us. "Take it easy," I said. "Come on down." Mitchell let go of one of my hands, kicked up one leg, and swung out over the street. His black wingtip shoe swiveled on the railing. The birds had scattered, and now they were circling, chattering angrily as he rocked. I was holding on with my pitching arm. My legs were pressed against the iron bars, and just when I began to feel the lead, just when the muscles began to shake, Mitchell jumped back onto the balcony. The waiter came through the sliding door and grabbed him, but in the years after that— the years after Mitchell got married and decided to stay in Panama City—I thought of that incident as the important moment of my life.

I don't know why. I've struck out nine men in a row and pitched to a half dozen hitters who are in the majors now, but when I think back over my life, about what I've done, not much more than that stands out.

As we lie in bed that night, Jodi reads aloud from the real estate list-ings. She uses abbreviations: BR, AC, D/D. As she goes down the page—San Marino, Santa Ana, Santa Monica—I nod occasionally or make a comment.

When I wake up later, early in the morning, the newspaper is still next to her on the bed. I can see its pale edge in the moonlight. Some-times I wake up like this, maybe from some sound in the night, and when I do, I like to lie with my eyes closed and feel the difference between the bed and the night air. I like to take stock of things. These are the moments when I'm most in love with my wife. She's next to me, and her face when she sleeps is untroubled. Women say now that they don't want to be protected, but when I watch her slow breathing, her parted lips, I think what a delicate thing a life is. I lean over and touch her mouth.

When I was in school I saw different girls, but since I've been married to Jodi I've been faithful. Except for once, a few years ago, I've almost never thought about someone else. I have a friend at school, Ed Ryan, a history teacher, who told me about the time he had an affair, and about how his marriage broke up right afterward. It wasn't a happy thing to see. She was a cocktail waitress at a bar a few blocks from school, he said. Ed told me the whole long story, about how he and the waitress had fallen in love so suddenly that he had no choice about leaving his wife. After the marriage was over, though, Ed gained fifteen or twenty pounds. One night, coming home from school, he hit a tree and wrecked his car. A few days later he came in early to work and found that all the windows in his classroom had been broken. At first I believed him when he said he thought his wife had done it, but that afternoon we were talking and I realized what had really happened.

We were in a lunch place. "You know," Ed said, "sometimes you think you know a person." He was looking into his glass. "You can sleep next to a woman, you can know the way she smiles when she's turned on, you can see in her hands when she wants to talk about something. Then you wake up one day and some signal's been exchanged—and you don't know what it is, but you think for the first time, *Maybe I don't know her.* Just something. You never know what the signal is." I looked at him then and realized that there was no cocktail waitress and that Ed had broken the windows.

I turn in bed now and look at Jodi. Then I slide the newspaper off the blanket. We know each other, I think. The time I came close to adultery was a few years ago, with a secretary at school, a temporary who worked afternoons. She was a dark girl, didn't say much, and she wore turquoise bracelets on both wrists. She kept finding reasons to come into my office, which I share with the two other coaches. It's three desks, a window, a chalkboard. One night I was there late, after everyone else had gone, and she came by to do something. It was already dark. We talked for a while, and then she took off one of her bracelets to show me. She said she wanted me to see how beautiful it was, how the turquoise changed color in dim light. She put it into my hand, and then I knew for sure what was going on. I looked at it for a long time, listening to the little sounds in the building, before I looked up.

"Charlie?" Jodi says now in the dark.

"Yes?"

"Would you do whatever I asked you to do?"

"What do you mean?"

"I mean, would you do anything in the world that I asked you to do?"

"That depends," I say.

"On what?"

"On what you asked. If you asked me to rob someone, then maybe I wouldn't."

I hear her roll over, and I know she's looking at me. "But don't you think I would have a good reason to ask you if I did?"

"Probably."

"And wouldn't you do it just because I asked?"

She turns away again and I try to think of an answer. We've already argued once today, while she was making dinner, but I don't want to lie to her. That's what we argued about earlier. She asked me what I thought of the house we looked at, and I told her the truth, that a house just wasn't important to me.

"Then what is important to you?"

I was putting the forks and knives on the table. "Leveling with other people is important to me," I answered. "And you're important to me." Then I said, "And whales."

"What?"

"Whales are important to me."

That was when it started. We didn't say much after that, so it wasn't an argument exactly. I don't know why I mentioned the whales. They're great animals, the biggest things on earth, but they're not important to me.

"What if it was something not so bad," she says now, "but still something you didn't want to do?"

"What?"

The moonlight is shining in her hair. "What if I asked you to do something that ordinarily you wouldn't do yourself—would you do it if I asked?"

"And it wasn't something so bad?"

"Right."

"Yes," I say. "Then I would do it."

"What I want you to do," she says on Wednesday, "is look at another house." We're eating dinner. "But I want them to take us seriously," she says. "I want to act as if we're really thinking of buying it, right on the verge. You know—maybe we will, maybe we won't."

I take a sip of water, look out the window. "That's ridiculous," I say. "Nobody walks in off the street and decides in an afternoon whether to buy a house."

"Maybe we've been looking at it from a distance for a long time," she says, "assessing things." She isn't eating her dinner. I cooked it, chicken, and it's steaming on her plate. "Maybe we've been waiting for the market to change."

"Why is it so important to you?"

"It just is. And you said you'd do it if it was important to me. Didn't you say that?"

"I had a conversation with the old woman in the yellow house."

"What?"

"When we looked at the other house," I say, "I went off by myself for a while. I talked with the old woman who was sitting upstairs."

"What did you say?"

"Do you remember her?"

"Yes."

"She told me that the owner was selling the house so he could use the money to smuggle drugs."

"So?"

"So," I say, "you have to be careful."

This Sunday Jodi drives. The day is bright and blue, with a breeze from the ocean, and along Santa Monica Boulevard the palm fronds are rustling. I'm in my suit. If Jodi talks to the agent about offers, I've decided I'll stay to the back, nod or shrug at questions. She parks the car on a side street and we walk around the corner and go into the lobby of one of the hotels. We sit down in cloth chairs near the entrance. A bellman carries over an ashtray on a stand and sets it between us; Jodi hands him a bill from her purse. I look at her. The bellman is the age of my father. He moves away fast, and I lean forward to get my shoulder loose in my suit. I'm not sure if the lobby chairs are only for guests, and I'm ready to get up if someone asks. Then a woman comes in and Jodi stands and introduces herself. "Charlie Gordon," I say when the woman puts out her hand. She's in a gray pinstripe skirt and a jacket with a white flower in the lapel. After she says something to Jodi, she leads us outside to the parking circle, where a car is brought around by the valet, a French car, and Jodi and I get in back. The seats are leather.

"Is the weather always this nice?" Jodi asks. We pull out onto Wilshire Boulevard.

"Almost always," the woman says. "That's another thing I love about Los Angeles—the weather. Los Angeles has the most perfect weather on earth."

We drive out toward the ocean, and as the woman moves in and out of the lines of traffic, I look around the car. It's well kept, maybe leased. No gum wrappers or old coffee cups under the seat.

"Then you're looking for a second home?" the woman says.

"My husband's business makes it necessary for us to have a home in Los Angeles."

I look at Jodi. She's sitting back in the seat, her hand resting on the armrest.

"Most of the year, of course, we'll be in Dallas."

The street is curved and long with a grass island in the middle and eucalyptus along its length, and each time the car banks, I feel the nerves firing in my gut. I look at Jodi. I look at her forehead. I look at the way her hair falls on her neck, at her breasts, and I realize, the car shifting under us, that I don't trust her.

We turn and head up a hill. The street twists, and we go in and out of the shade from a bridge of elms. I can't see anything behind the hedges.

"The neighborhood is lovely," the woman says. "We have a twenty-four-hour security patrol, and the bushes hide everything from the street. We don't have sidewalks."

"No sidewalks?" I say.

"That discourages sightseeing," says Jodi.

We turn into a driveway. It heads down between two hedges to the far end, where a gravel half-circle has been cut around the trunk of a low, spreading fig tree. We stop, the agent opens Jodi's door, and we get out and stand there, looking at the house. It's a mansion.

The walls are white. There are clay tiles on the roof, sloped eaves, hanging vines. A narrow window runs straight up from the ground. Through it I can see a staircase and a chandelier. In college once, at the end of the season, the team had a party at a mansion like this one. It had windows everywhere, panes of glass as tall as flagpoles. The fellow who owned it had played ball for a while when he was young, and then gotten out and made big money. He was in something like hair care or combs then, and at the door each of us got a leather travel kit with our name embossed and some of his products inside. At the buffet table the oranges were cut so that the peels came off like the leather on a split baseball. He showed us through the house and then brought us into the yard. He told us that after all these years the game was still inside him. We stood on the lawn. It was landscaped with shrubs and willows, but he said he had bought the place because the yard was big enough for a four-hundred-foot straightaway center field.

Now the agent leads us up the porch stairs. She rings the bell and then opens the door; inside, the light is everywhere. It streams from the windows, shines on the wood, falls in slants from every height. There are oriental carpets on the floor, plants, a piano. The agent opens her portfolio and hands us each a beige piece of paper. It's textured like a wedding invitation, and at the top, above the figures, is an ink drawing of the house. The boughs of the fig tree frame the paper. I look down at it in my hand, the way I used to look down at a baseball.

The agent motions us into the living room. From there she leads us back through a glass-walled study, wisteria and bougainvillaea hanging from the ceiling, down a hallway into the kitchen. Through the windows spread the grounds of the estate. Now is the time, I think to myself, when I should explain everything.

"I think I'll go out back," Jodi says. "You two can look around in here."

"Certainly," the agent says.

After she leaves, I pretend to look through the kitchen. I open cabinets, run the water. The tap has a charcoal filter. The agent says things about the plumbing and the foundation; I nod and then walk back into the study. She follows me.

"I know you'll find the terms agreeable," she says.

"The terms."

"And one can't surpass the house, as one can see."

"You could fit a diamond in the yard."

She smiles a little bit.

"A baseball diamond," I say. I lean forward and examine the paned windows carefully. They are newly washed, clear as air. Among them hang the vines of bougainvillaea. "But some people look at houses for other reasons."

"Of course."

"I know of a fellow who's selling his house to buy drugs in South America."

She looks down, touches the flower in her jacket.

"People don't care about an honest living anymore," I say.

She smiles and looks up at me. "They don't," she says. "You're absolutely right. One sees that everywhere now. What line of work are you in, Mr. Gordon?"

I lean against the glassed wall. Outside, violet petals are spinning down beneath the jacarandas. "We're not really from Dallas," I say.

"Oh?"

Through the window I see Jodi come out onto the lawn around the corner of the house. The grass is beautiful. It's green and long like an outfield. Jodi steps up into the middle of it and raises her hands above her head, arches her back like a dancer. She was in a play the first time I ever saw her, stretching like that, on stage in a college auditorium. I was in the audience, wearing a baseball shirt. At intermission I went home and changed my clothes so that I could introduce myself. That was twelve years ago.

"No," I say to the agent. "We're not really from Dallas. We

moved outside of Dallas a while back. We live in Highland Park now."

She nods.

"I'm an investor," I say.

"I DON'T BELIEVE THIS"

Merrill Joan Gerber

After it was all over, a final detail emerged, one so bizarre that my sister laughed crazily, holding both hands over her ears as she read the long article in the newspaper. I had brought it across the street to show to her; now that she was my neighbor, I came to see her and the boys several times a day. The article said that the crematorium to which her husband's body had been entrusted for cremation had been burning six bodies at a time and dumping most of the bone and ash into plastic garbage bags, which went directly into their dumpsters. A disgruntled employee had tattled.

"Can you imagine?" Carol said, laughing. "Even that! Oh, his poor mother! His poor *father!*" She began to cry. "I don't believe this," she said. That was what she had said on the day of the cremation, when she had sat in my back yard in a beach chair at the far end of the garden, holding on to a washcloth. I think she was prepared to cry so hard that any ordinary handkerchief would never have done. But she remained dry-eyed. When I came outside after a while, she said, "I think of his beautiful face burning, of his eyes burning." She looked up at the blank blue sky and said, "I just don't believe this. I try to think of what he was feeling when he gulped in that stinking exhaust. What could he have been thinking? I know he was blaming me."

She rattled the newspaper. "A dumpster! Oh, Bard would have

loved that. Even at the end he couldn't get it right. Nothing ever went right for him, did it? And all along I've been thinking that I won't ever be able to go in the ocean again, because his ashes are floating in it! Can you believe it? How that woman at the mortuary promised they would play Pachelbel's Canon on the little boat, how the remains would be scattered with 'dignity and taste'? His mother even came all the way down with that jar of his father's ashes that she had saved for thirty years, so father and son could be mixed together for all eternity. Plastic garbage baggies! You know," she said, looking at me, "life is just a joke, a bad joke, isn't it?"

Bard had not believed me when I'd told him that my sister was in a shelter for battered women. Afraid of *him*? Running away from *him*? The world was full of dangers from which only *he* could protect her! He had accused me of hiding her in my house. "Would I be so foolish?" I had said. "She knows it's the first place you'd look."

"You better put me in touch with her," he had said, menacingly. "You both know I can't handle this for long."

It had gone on for weeks. On the last day, he called me three times, demanding to be put in touch with her. "Do you understand me?" he shouted. "If she doesn't call here in ten minutes, I'm checking out. Do you believe me?"

"I believe you," I said. "But you know she can't call you. She can't be reached in the shelter. They don't want the women there to be manipulated by their men. They want them to have space and time to think."

"*Manipulated?*" He was incredulous. "I'm checking *out*, this is *IT*. Good-bye forever!"

He hung up. It wasn't true that Carol couldn't be reached. I had the number. Not only had I been calling her but I had also been playing tapes for her of his conversations over the phone during the past weeks. This one I hadn't taped. The tape recorder was in a different room.

"Should I call her and tell her?" I asked my husband.

"Why bother?" he said. He and the children were eating dinner; he was becoming annoyed by this continual disruption of our lives. "He calls every day and says he's killing himself and he never does. Why should this call be any different?"

Then the phone rang. It was my sister. She had a fever and bronchitis. I could barely recognize her voice.

"Could you bring me some cough syrup with codeine tomorrow?" she asked.

"Is your cough very bad?"

"No, it's not too bad, but maybe the codeine will help me get to sleep. I can't sleep here at all. I just can't sleep."

"He just called."

"Really," she said. "What a surprise!" But the sarcasm didn't hide her fear. "What this time?"

"He's going to kill himself in ten minutes unless you call him."

"So what else is new?" She made a funny sound. I was frightened of her these days. I couldn't read her thoughts. I didn't know if the sound was a cough or a sob.

"Do you want to call him?" I suggested. I was afraid to be responsible. "I know you're not supposed to."

"I don't know," she said. "I'm breaking all the rules anyway."

The rules were very strict. No contact with the batterer, no news of him, no worrying about him. Forget him. Only female relatives could call, and they were not to relay any news of him—not how sorry he was, not how desperate he was, not how he had promised to reform and never do it again, not how he was going to kill himself if she didn't come home. Once, I had called the shelter for advice, saying that I thought he was serious this time, that he was going to do it. The counselor there—a deep-voiced woman named Katherine—had said to me, very calmly, "It might just be the best thing; it might be a blessing in disguise."

My sister blew her nose. "I'll call him," she said. "I'll tell him I'm sick and to leave you alone and to leave me alone."

I hung up and sat down to try to eat my dinner. My children's faces were full of fear. I could not possibly reassure them about any of this. Then the phone rang again. It was my sister.

"Oh, God," she said. "I called him. I told him to stop bothering you, and he said, *I have to ask you one thing, just one thing. I have to know this. Do you love me?*" My sister gasped for breath. "I shouted *No*—what else could I say? That's how I *felt*. I'm so sick, this is such a nightmare; and then he just hung up. A minute later I tried to call him back to tell him that I didn't mean it, that I did love him, that I *do*, but he was gone." She began to cry. "He was gone."

"There's nothing you can do," I said. My teeth were chattering as I spoke. "He's done this before. He'll call me tomorrow morning, full of remorse for worrying you."

"I can hardly breathe," she said. "I have a high fever and the boys are going mad cooped up here." She paused to blow her nose. "I don't believe any of this. I really don't."

Afterward she moved right across the street from me. At first she rented the little house, but then it was put up for sale, and my mother and aunt found enough money to make a down payment so that she could be near me and I could take care of her till she got her strength back. I could see her bedroom window from my bedroom window— we were that close. I often thought of her trying to sleep in that house, alone there with her sons and the new, big watchdog. She told me that the dog barked at every tiny sound and frightened her when there was nothing to be frightened of. She was sorry she had got him. I could hear his barking from my house, at strange hours, often in the middle of the night.

I remember when she and I had shared a bedroom as children. We giggled every night in our beds and made our father furious. He would come in and threaten to smack us. How could he sleep, how could he go to work in the morning, if we were going to giggle all night? That made us laugh even harder. Each time he went back to his room, we would throw the quilts over our heads and laugh till we nearly suffocated. One night our father came to quiet us four times. I remember the angry hunch of his back as he walked, barefoot, back to his bedroom. When he returned for the last time, stomping like a giant, he smacked us, each once, very hard, on our upper thighs. That made us quiet. We were stunned. When he was gone, Carol turned on the light and pulled down her pajama bottoms to show me the marks of his violence. I showed her mine. Each of us had our father's hand-print, five red fingers, on the white skin of her thigh. She crept into my bed, where we clung to each other till the burning, stinging shock subsided and we could sleep.

Carol's sons, living on our quiet, adult street, complained to her that they missed the shelter. They rarely asked about their father and only occasionally said that they wished they could see their old friends and their old school. For a few weeks they had gone to a school near the shelter; all the children had had to go to school. But one day Bard had called me and told me he was trying to find the children. He said he wanted to take them out to lunch. He knew they had to be at some school. He was going to go to every school in the district and look in every classroom, ask everyone he saw if any of the children there looked like his children. He would find them. "You can't keep them from me," he said, his voice breaking. "They belong to me. They love me."

Carol had taken them out of school at once. An art therapist at the shelter held a workshop with the children every day. He was a gentle, soft-spoken man named Ned, who had the children draw domestic scenes and was never once surprised at the knives, bloody wounds, or broken windows that they drew. He gave each of them a special present, a necklace with a silver running-shoe charm, which only children at the shelter were entitled to wear. It made them special, he said. It made them part of a club to which no one else could belong.

While the children played with crayons, their mothers were indoctrinated by women who had survived, who taught the arts of survival. The essential rule was *Forget him, he's on his own, the only person you have to worry about is yourself.* A woman who was in the shelter at the same time Carol was had had her throat slashed. Her husband had cut her vocal cords. She could speak only in a grating whisper. Her husband had done it in the bathroom, with her son watching. Yet each night she sneaked out and called her husband from a nearby shopping center. She was discovered and disciplined by the administration; they threatened to put her out of the shelter if she called him again. Each woman was allowed space at the shelter for a month, while she got legal help and made new living arrangements. Hard cases were allowed to stay a little longer. She said that she was sorry, but that he was the sweetest man, and when he loved her up, it was the only time she knew heaven.

Carol felt humiliated. Once each week the women lined up and were given their food: three very small whole frozen chickens, a package of pork hot dogs, some plain-wrapped cans of baked beans, eggs, milk, margarine, white bread. The children were happy with the food. Carol's sons played in the courtyard with the other children. Carol had difficulty relating to the other mothers. One had ten children. Two had black eyes. Several were pregnant. She began to have doubts that what Bard had done had been violent enough to cause her to run away. Did mental violence or violence done to furniture really count as battering? She wondered if she had been too hard on her husband. She wondered if she had been wrong to come here. All he had done— he said so himself, in the taped conversations, dozens of times—was to break a lousy hundred-dollar table. He had broken it before, he had fixed it before. Why was this time different from any of the others? She had pushed all his buttons, that's all, and he had gotten mad, and he had pulled the table away from the wall and smashed off its legs and thrown the whole thing out in the yard. Then he had put his head through the wall, using the top of his head as a battering ram. He had knocked open a hole to the other side. Then he had bitten his youngest son on the scalp. What was so terrible about that? It was just a momentary thing. He didn't mean anything by it. When his son had begun to cry in fear and pain, hadn't he picked the child up and told him it was nothing? If she would just come home, he would never get angry again. They'd have their sweet life. They'd go to a picnic, a movie, the beach. They'd have it better than ever before. He had just started going to a new church that was helping him to become a kinder and more sensitive man. He was a better person than he had ever been; he now knew the true meaning of love. Wouldn't she come back?

One day Bard called me and said, "Hey, the cops are here. You didn't send them, did you?"

"*Me?*" I said. I turned on the tape recorder. "What did you do?"

"Nothing. I busted up some public property. Can you come down and bail me out?"

"How can I?" I said. "My children . . ."

"How can you *not?*"

I hung up and called Carol at the shelter. I said, "I think he's being arrested."

"Pick me up," she said, "and take me to the house. I have to get some things. I'm sure they'll let me out of the shelter if they know he's in jail. I'll check to make sure he's really there. I have to get us some clean clothes, and some toys for the boys. I want to get my picture albums. He threatened to burn them."

"You want to go to the house?"

"Why not? At least we know he's not going to be there. At least we know we won't find him hanging from a beam in the living room."

We stopped at a drugstore a few blocks away and called the house. No one was there. We called the jail. They said their records showed that he had been booked, but they didn't know for sure whether he'd been bailed out. "Is there any way he can bail out this fast?" Carol asked.

"Only if he uses his own credit card," the man answered.

"I *have* his credit card," Carol said to me, after she had hung up. "We're so much in debt that I had to take it away from him. Let's just hurry. I hate this! I hate sneaking into my own house this way."

I drove to the house and we held hands going up the walk. "I feel his presence here, that he's right here seeing me do this," she said, in the dusty, eerie silence of the living room. "Why do I give him so much power? It's as if he knows whatever I'm thinking, whatever I'm doing. When he was trying to find the children, I thought that he had eyes like God, that he would go directly to the school where they were and kidnap them. I had to warn them, 'If you see your father anywhere, run and hide. Don't let him get near you!' Can you imagine telling your children that about their father? Oh, God, let's hurry."

She ran from room to room, pulling open drawers, stuffing clothes in paper bags. I stood in the doorway of their bedroom, my heart pounding as I looked at their bed with its tossed covers, at the phone he used to call me. Books were everywhere on the bed—books about how to love better, how to live better; books on the occult, on meditation; books on self-hypnosis for peace of mind. Carol picked up an open book and looked at some words underlined in red. *"You can always create your own experience of life in a beautiful and enjoyable way if you keep your love turned on within you—regardless of what other people say or do,"* she read aloud. She tossed it down in disgust. "He's paying good money for these," she said. She kept blowing her nose.

"Are you crying?"

"No!" she said. "I'm allergic to all this dust."

I walked to the front door, checked the street for his car, and went into the kitchen.

"Look at this," I called to her. On the counter was a row of packages, gift-wrapped. A card was slipped under one of them. Carol opened it and read it aloud: "I have been a brute and I don't deserve you. But I can't live without you and the boys. Don't take that away from me. Try to forgive." She picked up one of the boxes and then set it down. "I don't believe this," she said. "God, where are the children's picture albums! I can't *find* them." She went running down the hall.

In the bathroom I saw the fishbowl, with the boys' two goldfish swimming in it. The water was clear. Beside it was a piece of notebook paper. Written on it in his hand were the words *Don't give up, hang on, you have the spirit within you to prevail.*

Two days later he came to my house, bailed out of jail with money his mother had wired. He banged on my front door. He had discovered that Carol had been to the house. "Did *you* take her there?" he demanded. "*You* wouldn't do that to me, would you?" He stood on the doorstep, gaunt, hands shaking.

"Was she at the house?" I asked. "I haven't been in touch with her lately."

"Please," he said, his words slurred, his hands out for help. "Look at this." He showed me his arms; the veins in his forearms were black and blue. "When I saw that Carol had been home, I took the money my mother sent me for food and bought three packets of heroin. I wanted to OD. But it was lousy stuff; it didn't kill me. It's not so easy to die, even if you want to. I'm a tough bird. But please, can't you treat me like regular old me? Can't you ask me to come in and have dinner with you? I'm not a monster. Can't anyone, *anyone,* be nice to me?"

My children were hiding at the far end of the hall, listening. "Wait here," I said. I went and got him a whole ham I had. I handed it to him where he stood on the doorstep and stepped back with distaste. Ask him in? Let my children see *this?* Who knew what a crazy man would do? He must have suspected that I knew Carol's whereabouts. Whenever I went to visit her at the shelter, I took a circuitous route, always watching in my rearview mirror for his blue car. Now I had my tear gas in my pocket; I carried it with me all the time, kept it beside my bed when I slept. I thought of the things in my kitchen: knives, electric cords, mixers, graters, elements that could become white-hot and sear off a person's flesh.

He stood there like a supplicant, palms up, eyebrows raised in hope, waiting for a sign of humanity from me. I gave him what I could—a ham, and a weak, pathetic little smile. I said, dishonestly, "Go home. Maybe I can reach her today; maybe she will call you once you get home." He ran to his car, jumped in it, sped off. I thought, coldly, *Good, I'm rid of him. For now we're safe.* I locked the door with three locks.

Later Carol found among his many notes to her one that said, "At least your sister smiled at me, the only human thing that happened in this terrible time. I always knew she loved me and was my friend."

He became more persistent. He staked out my house, not believing I wasn't hiding her. "How could I possibly hide her?" I said to him on the phone. "You know I wouldn't lie to you."

"I know you wouldn't," he said. "I trust you." But on certain days I saw his blue car parked behind a hedge a block away, saw him hunched down like a private eye, watching my front door. One day my husband drove away with my daughter beside him, and an instant later the blue car tore by. I got a look at him then, curved over the wheel, a madman, everything at stake, nothing to lose, and I felt he would kill, kidnap, hold my husband and child as hostages till he got my sister back. I cried out. As long as he lived he would search for her, and if she hid, he would plague me. He had once said to her (she told me this), "You love your family? You want them alive? Then you'd better do as I say."

On the day he broke the table, after his son's face crumpled in terror, Carol told him to leave. He ran from the house. Ten minutes later he called her and said, in a voice of a wild creature, "I'm watching some men building a house, Carol. I'm never going to build a house for you now. Do you know that?" He was panting like an animal. "And I'm coming back for you. You're going to be with me one way or the other. You know I can't go on without you."

She hung up and called me. "I think he's coming back to hurt us."

"Then get out of there," I cried, miles away and helpless. "Run!"

By the time she called me again, I had the number of the shelter for her. She was at a gas station with her children. Outside the station were two phone booths. She hid her children in one; she called the shelter from the other. I called the boys in their booth and I read to them from a book called *Silly Riddles* while she made arrangements to be taken in. She talked for almost an hour to a counselor at the shelter. All the time I was sweating and reading riddles. When it was settled, she came into her children's phone booth and we made a date to meet in forty-five minutes at Sears, so that she could buy herself some underwear and her children some blue jeans. They were still in their pajamas.

Under the bright fluorescent lights in the department store we looked at price tags, considered quality and style, while her teeth chattered. Our eyes met over the racks, and she asked me, "What do you think he's planning now?"

My husband got a restraining order to keep him from our doorstep, to keep him from dialing our number. Yet he dialed it, and I answered the phone, almost passionately, each time I heard it ringing, having run to the room where I had the tape recorder hooked up. "Why is she so afraid of me? Let her come to see me without bodyguards! What can happen? The worst I could do is kill her, and how bad could that be, compared with what we're going through now?"

I played her that tape. "You must never go back," I said. She agreed; she had to. I took clean nightgowns to her at the shelter; I took her fresh vegetables, and bread that had substance.

Bard had hired a psychic that last week, and had gone to Las Vegas to confer with him, taking along a $500 money order. When Bard got home, he sent a parcel to Las Vegas containing clothing of Carol's and a small gold ring that she often wore. A circular that Carol found later under the bed promised immediate results: *Gold has the strongest psychic power—you can work a love spell by burning a red candle and reciting "In this ring I place my spell of love to make you return to me." This will also prevent your loved one from being unfaithful.*

Carol moved in across the street from my house just before Halloween. We devised a signal so that she could call me for help if some maniac cut her phone lines. She would use the antique gas alarm our father had given to me. It was a loud wooden clacker that had been used in the war. She would open her window and spin it. I could hear it easily. I promised her that I would look out my window often and watch for suspicious shadows near the bushes under her windows. Somehow neither of us believed he was really gone. Even though she had picked up his wallet at the morgue, the wallet he'd had with him while he breathed his car's exhaust through a vacuum-cleaner hose and thought his thoughts, told himself she didn't love him and so he had to do this and do it now; even though his ashes were in the dumpster; we felt that he was still out there, still looking for her.

Her sons built a six-foot-high spider web out of heavy white yarn for a decoration and nailed it to the tree in her front yard. They built a graveyard around the tree, with wooden crosses. At their front door they rigged a noose and hung a dummy from it. The dummy, in their father's old blue sweat shirt with a hood, swung from the rope. It was still there long after Halloween, swaying in the wind.

Carol said to me, "I don't like it, but I don't want to say anything to them. I don't think they're thinking about him. I think they just made it for Halloween, and they still like to look at it."

EDIE: A LIFE

Harriet Doerr

In the middle of an April night in 1919, a plain woman named Edith Fisk, lifted from England to California on a tide of world peace, arrived at the Ransom house to raise five half-orphaned children.

A few hours later, at seven in the morning, this Edith, more widely called Edie, invited the three eldest to her room for tea. They were James, seven; Eliza, six; and Jenny, four. Being handed cups of tea, no matter how reduced by milk, made them believe that they had grown up overnight.

"Have some sugar," said Edie, and spooned it in. Moments later she said, "Have another cup." But her *h*'s went unspoken and became the first of hundreds, then thousands, which would accumulate in the corners of the house and thicken in the air like sighs.

In an adjoining room the twins, entirely responsible for their mother's death, had finished their bottles and fallen back into guiltless sleep. At the far end of the house, the widower, Thomas Ransom, who had spent the night aching for his truant wife, lay across his bed, half awake, half asleep, and dreaming.

The three children sat in silence at Edie's table. She had grizzled hair pulled up in a knot, heavy brows, high cheeks, and two long hairs in her chin. She was bony and flat, and looked starched, like the apron she had tied around her. Her teeth were large and white and even, her eyes an uncompromising blue.

She talked to the children as if they were her age, forty-one. "My father was an ostler," she told them, and they listened without comprehension. "My youngest brother died at Wipers," she said. "My nephew was gassed at Verdun."

These were places the children had never heard of. But all three of them, even Jenny, understood the word "die."

"Our mother died," said James.

Edie nodded.

"I was born, oldest of eight, in Atherleigh, a town in Devon. I've lived in five English counties," she told them, without saying what a county was. "And taken care of thirty children, a few of them best forgotten."

"Which ones?" said James.

But Edie only talked of her latest charges, the girls she had left to come to America.

"Lady Alice and Lady Anne," said Edie, and described two paragons of quietness and clean knees who lived in a castle in Kent.

Edie didn't say "castle," she said "big brick house." She didn't say "lake," she said "pond." But the children, dazzled by illustrations in *Cinderella* and *King Arthur*, assumed princesses. And after that, they assumed castle, tower, moat, lake, lily, swan.

Lady Alice was seven and Lady Anne was eight when last seen immaculately crayoning with their ankles crossed in their tower overlooking the lake.

Eliza touched Edie's arm. "What is 'gassed'?" she said.

Edie explained.

Jenny lifted her spoon for attention. "I saw Father cry," she said. "Twice."

"Oh, be quiet," said James.

With Edie, they could say anything.

After that morning, they would love tea forever, all their lives, in sitting rooms and restaurants, on terraces and balconies, at sidewalk cafés and whistle stops, even under awnings in the rain. They would drink it indiscriminately, careless of flavor, out of paper cups or Spode, with lemon, honey, milk, or cream, with spices or with rum.

Before Edie came to the Ransom house, signs of orphanhood were everywhere—in the twins' colic, in Eliza's aggravated impulse to pinch

Jenny, in the state of James's sheets every morning. Their father, recognizing symptoms of grief, brought home wrapped packages in his overcoat pockets. He gave the children a Victrola and Harry Lauder records.

"Shall we read?" he would ask in the evening, and take Edward Lear from the shelf. "There was an Old Man with a beard," read Thomas Ransom, and he and his children listened solemnly to the unaccustomed voice speaking the familiar words.

While the twins baffled everyone by episodes of weight loss and angry tears, various efforts to please were directed toward the other three. The cook baked cakes and frosted their names into the icing. The sympathetic gardener packed them into his wheelbarrow and pushed them at high speeds down sloping paths. Two aunts, the dead mother's sisters, improvised weekly outings—to the ostrich farm, the alligator farm, the lion farm, to a picnic in the mountains, a shell hunt at the beach. These contrived entertainments failed. None substituted for what was needed: the reappearance at the piano or on the stairs of a young woman with freckles, green eyes, and a ribbon around her waist.

Edie came to rescue the Ransoms through the intervention of the aunts' English friend, Cissy. When hope for joy in any degree was almost lost, Cissy wrote and produced the remedy.

The aunts brought her letter to Thomas Ransom in his study on a February afternoon. Outside the window a young sycamore, planted by his wife last year, cast its sparse shadow on a patch of grass.

Cissy wrote that all her friends lost sons and brothers in the war and she was happy she had none to offer up. Wherever one went in London wounded veterans, wearing their military medals, were performing for money. She saw a legless man in uniform playing an accordion outside Harrods. Others, on Piccadilly, had harmonicas wired in front of their faces so they could play without hands. Blind men, dressed for parade, sang in the rain for theatre queues.

And the weather, wrote Cissy. Winter seemed to be a state of life and not a season. How lucky one was to be living, untouched by it all, in America, particularly California. Oh, to wake up to sunshine every morning, to spend one's days warm and dry.

Now she arrived at the point of her letter. Did anyone they knew want Edith Fisk, who had taken care of children for twenty-five years and was personally known to Cissy? Edie intended to live near a cousin in Texas. California might be just the place.

The reading of the letter ended.

"Who is Cissy?" said Thomas Ransom, unable to foresee that within a dozen years he would marry her.

James, who had been listening at the door, heard only the first part of the letter. Long before Cissy proposed Edie, he was upstairs in his room, trying to attach a harmonica to his mouth with kite string.

Edie was there within two months. The aunts and Thomas Ransom began to witness change.

Within weeks the teasing stopped. Within months the nighttime sheets stayed dry. The twins, male and identical, fattened and pulled toys apart. Edie bestowed on each of the five equal shares of attention and concern. She hung their drawings in her room, even the ones of moles in traps and inhabited houses burning to the ground. Samples of the twins' scribblings remained on permanent display. The children's pictures eventually occupied almost all one wall and surrounded a framed photograph of Lady Alice and Lady Anne, two small, light-haired girls sitting straight-backed on dappled ponies.

"Can we have ponies?" Eliza and Jenny asked their father, but he had fallen in love with a woman named Trish and, distracted, brought home a cage of canaries instead.

Edie and the Ransom children suited each other. It seemed right to them all that she had come to braid hair, turn hems, push swings, take walks; to apply iodine to cuts and embrace the cry that followed, to pinch her fingers between the muddy rubber and the shoe. Edie stopped nightmares almost before they started. At a child's first gasp she would be in the doorway, uncombed and toothless, tying on her wrapper, a glass of water in her hand.

The older children repaid this bounty with torments of their own devising. They would rush at her in a trio, shout, "We've 'idden your 'at in the 'all," and run shrieking with laughter, out of her sight. They crept into her room at night, found the pink gums and big white teeth where they lay floating in a mug and, in a frenzy of bad manners, hid them in a hat box or behind the books.

Edie never reported these lapses of deportment to Thomas Ransom. Instead she would invoke the names and virtues of Lady Alice and Lady Anne.

"They didn't talk like roustabouts," said Edie. "They slept like angels through the night."

Between spring and fall the nonsense ceased. Edie grew into the Ransoms' lives and was accepted there, like air and water and the food they ate. From the start, the children saw her as a refuge. Flounder as they might in the choppy sea where orphans and half-orphans drown, they trusted her to save them.

Later on, when their father emerged from mourning, Edie was the mast they clung to in a squall of stepmothers.

Within a period of ten years Thomas Ransom, grasping at the outer fringe of happiness, brought three wives in close succession to the matrimonial bed he first shared with the children's now sainted mother. He chose women he believed were like her, and it was true that all three, Trish, Irene, and Cissy, were small-boned and energetic. But they were brown-eyed and, on the whole, not musical.

The first to come was Trish, nineteen years old and porcelain-skinned. Before her arrival Thomas Ransom asked the children not to come knocking at his bedroom door day and night, as they had in the past. Once she was there, other things changed. The children heard him humming at his desk in the study. They noticed that he often left in mid-morning, instead of at eight, for the office where he practiced law.

Eliza asked questions at early morning tea. "Why are they always in their room, with the door locked?"

And Jenny said, "Yes. Even before dinner."

"Don't you know anything?" said James.

Edie poured more pale tea. "Hold your cups properly. Don't spill," she told them, and the lost *h* floated into the steam rising from the pot.

Trish, at nineteen, was neither mother nor sister to the children. Given their priorities of blood and birth and previous residence, they inevitably outdistanced her. They knew to the oldest steamer trunk and the latest cookie the contents of the attic and larder. They walked oblivious across rugs stained with their spilled ink. The hall banister shone with the years of their sliding. Long ago they had enlisted the cook and the gardener as allies. Three of them remembered their mother. The other two thought they did.

Trish said good morning at noon and drove off with friends. Later she paused to say good night in a rustle of taffeta on Thomas Ransom's arm as they left for a dinner or a dance.

James made computations. "She's nine years older than I am," he said, "and eighteen years younger than Father."

"He keeps staring at her," said Eliza.

"And kissing her hand," said Jenny.

Edie opened a door on a sliver of her past. "I knew a girl once with curly red hair like that, in Atherleigh."

"What was her name?" James asked, as if for solid evidence.

Edie bit off her darning thread. She looked backward with her inward eye. Finally she said, "Lily Stiles. The day I went into service in Dorset, Lily went to work at the Rose and Plough."

"The Rose and Plough," repeated Eliza. "What's that?"

"It's a pub," said Edie, and she explained what a public house was. Immediately this establishment, with its gleaming bar and its game of darts, was elevated in the children's minds to the mysterious realm of Lady Alice and Lady Anne and set in place a stone's throw from their castle.

At home, Trish's encounters with her husband's children were brief. In passing, she waved to them all and patted the twins on their dark heads. She saw more of the three eldest on those Saturday afternoons when she took them, along with Edie, to the movies.

Together they sat in the close, expectant dark of the Rivoli Theatre, watched the shimmering curtains part, shivered to the organist's opening chords, and at the appearance of an image on the screen, cast off their everyday lives to be periled, rescued, rejected, and adored. They sat spellbound through the film, and when the words "The End" came on, rose depleted and blinking from their seats to face the hot sidewalk and full sun outside.

Trish selected the pictures, and though they occasionally included Fairbanks films and ones that starred the Gishes, these were not her favorites. She detested comedies. To avoid Harold Lloyd, they saw Rudolph Valentino in *The Sheik*. Rather than endure Buster Keaton, they went to *Gypsy Blood*, starring Alla Nazimova.

"I should speak to your father," Edie would say later on at home. But she never did. Instead, she only remarked at bedtime, "It's a nice change, going to the pictures."

Trish left at the end of two years, during which the children, according to individual predispositions, grew taller and developed the hands and feet and faces they would always keep. They learned more about words and numbers, they began to like oysters, they swam the Australian crawl. They survived crises. These included scarlet fever, which the twins contracted and recovered from, and James's near electrocution as a result of his tinkering with wires and sockets.

Eliza and Jenny, exposed to chicken pox on the same day, ran simultaneous fevers and began to scratch. Edie brought ice and invented games. She cleared the table between their beds and knotted a handkerchief into arms and legs and a smooth, round head. She made it face each invalid and bow.

"This is how my sister Frahnces likes to dahnce the fahncy dahnces," Edie said, and the knotted handkerchief waltzed and two-stepped back and forth across the table.

Mesmerized by each other, the twins made few demands. A mechanical walking bear occupied them for weeks, a wind-up train for months. They shared a rocking horse and crashed slowly into one another on tricycles.

James, at eleven, sat in headphones by the hour in front of a crystal radio set. Sometimes he invited Edie to scratch a chip of rock with wire and hear a human voice advance and recede in the distance.

"Where's he talking from?" Edie would ask, and James said, "Oak Bluff. Ten miles away."

Together they marveled.

The two aunts, after one of their frequent visits, tried to squeeze the children into categories. James is the experimenter, they agreed. Jenny, the romantic. The twins, at five, too young to pigeonhole. Eliza was the bookish one.

A single-minded child, she read while walking to school, in the car on mountain curves, on the train in tunnels, on her back on the beach at noon, in theatres under dimming lights, between the sheets by flashlight. Eliza saw all the world through thick lenses adjusted for fine print. On Saturdays, she would often desert her invited friend and choose to read by herself instead.

At these times Edie would approach the bewildered visitor. Would she like to feed the canaries? Climb into the tree house?

"We'll make tiaras," she told one abandoned guest and, taking Jenny along, led the way to the orange grove.

"We're brides," announced Jenny a few minutes later, and she and Eliza's friend, balancing circles of flowers on their heads, stalked in a barefoot procession of two through the trees.

That afternoon, Jenny, as though she had never seen it before, inquired about Edie's ring. "Are you engaged?"

"I was once," said Edie, and went on to expose another slit of her past. "To Alfred Trotter."

"Was he killed at Wipers?"

Edie shook her head. "The war came later. He worked for his father at the Rose and Plough."

In a field beyond the grove, Jenny saw a plough, ploughing roses.

"Why didn't you get married?"

Edie looked at her watch and said it was five o'clock. She brushed off her skirt and got to her feet. "I wasn't the only girl in Atherleigh."

Jenny, peering into the past, caught a glimpse of Lily Stiles behind the bar at the Rose and Plough.

After Trish left, two more years went by before the children's father brought home his third wife. This was Irene, come to transplant herself in Ransom ground. Behind her she trailed a wake of friends, men with beards and women in batik scarves, who sat about the porch with big hats between them and the sun. In a circle of wicker chairs, they discussed Cubism, Freud, Proust, and Schoenberg's twelve-tone row. They passed perfumed candies to the children.

Irene changed all the lampshades in the house from white paper to red silk, threw a Persian prayer rug over the piano, and gave the children incense sticks for Christmas. She recited poems translated from the Sanskrit and wore saris to the grocery store. In spite of efforts on both sides, Irene remained an envoy from a foreign land.

One autumn day, not long before the end of her tenure as Thomas Ransom's wife, she took Edie and all five children to a fortune teller at the county fair. A pale-eyed, wasted man sold them tickets outside Madame Zelma's tent and pointed to the curtained entrance. Crowding into the stale air of the interior, they gradually made out the fortune teller's veiled head and jeweled neck behind two lighted candelabra on a desk.

"Have a seat," said Madame.

All found places on a bench or hassocks, and rose, one by one, to approach the palmist as she beckoned them to a chair facing her.

Madame Zelma, starting with the eldest, pointed to Edie.

"I see children," said the fortune teller. She concentrated in silence for a moment. "You will cross the ocean. I see a handsome man."

Alfred Trotter, thought Jenny. Us.

Madame Zelma, having wound Edie's life backward from present to past, summoned Irene.

"I see a musical instrument," said Madame, as if she knew of Irene's guitar and the chords in minor keys that were its repertory. "Your flower is the poppy. Your fruit, the pear." The fortune teller leaned closer to Irene's hand. "Expect a change of residence soon."

Edie and the children listened.

And so the fortunes went, the three eldest's full of prizes and professions, talents and awards, happy marriages, big families, silver mines and fame.

By the time Madame Zelma reached the twins, she had little left to predict. "Long lives," was all she told them. But what more could anyone divine from the trackless palms of seven-year-olds?

By the time Cissy, the next wife, came, James's voice had changed and his sisters had bobbed their hair. The twins had joined in painting an oversized panorama, titled *After the Earthquake*. Edie hung it on her wall.

Cissy, the children's last stepmother, traveled all the way from England, like Edie. Introduced by the aunts through a letter, Thomas Ransom met her in London, rode with her in Hyde Park, drove with her to Windsor for the day, then took her boating on the upper reaches of the Thames. They were married in a registry, she for the third, he for the fourth time, and spent their honeymoon on the Isle of Skye in a long, gray drizzle.

"I can hardly wait for California," said Cissy.

Once there, she lay about in the sun until she blistered. "Darling, bring my parasol, bring my gloves," she entreated whichever child was near.

"Are the hills always this brown?" she asked, splashing rose water on her throat. "Has that stream dried up for good?"

Cissy climbed mountain paths looking for wildflowers and came back with toyon and sage. Twice a week on her horse, Sweet William, she rode trails into the countryside, flushing up rattlesnakes instead of grouse.

On national holidays which celebrated American separation from Britain, Cissy felt in some way historically at fault. On the day before Thanksgiving, she strung cranberries silently at Edie's side. On the Fourth of July they sat together holding sparklers six thousand miles from the counties where their roots, still green, were sunk in English soil.

During the dry season of the year, from April to December, the children sometimes watched Cissy as she stood at a corner of the terrace, her head turning from east to west, her eyes searching the implacable blue sky. But for what? An English bird? The smell of fog?

By now the children were half grown or more, and old enough to recognize utter misery.

"Cissy didn't know what to expect," they told each other.

"She's homesick for the Sussex downs," said Edie, releasing the *h* into space.

"Are you homesick, too, for Atherleigh?" asked Eliza.

"I am not."

"You knew what to expect," said Jenny.

Edie said, "Almost."

The children discussed with her the final departure of each stepmother.

"Well, she's gone," said James, who was usually called to help carry out bags. "Maybe we'll have some peace."

After Cissy left, he made calculations. "Between the three of them, they had six husbands," he told the others.

"And father's had four wives," said one of the twins. "Six husbands and four wives make ten," said the other.

"Ten what?" said James.

"Poor souls," said Edie.

At last the children were as tall as they would ever be. The aunts could no longer say, "How are they ever to grow up?" For here they were, reasonably bright and reasonably healthy, survivors of a world war and a great depression, durable relics of their mother's premature and irreversible defection and their father's abrupt remarriages.

They had got through it all—the removal of tonsils, the straightening of teeth, the first night at camp, the first dance, the goodbyes waved from the rear platforms of trains that, like boats crossing the Styx, carried them away to college. This is not to say they were the same children they would have been if their mother had lived. They were not among the few who can suffer anything, loss or gain, without effect. But no one could point to a Ransom child's smile or frown or sleeping habits and reasonably comment, "No mother."

Edie stayed in the Ransom house until the twins left for college. By now, Eliza and Jenny were married, James married, divorced, and remarried. Edie went to all the graduations and weddings.

On these occasions the children hurried across playing fields and lawns to reach and embrace her.

"Edie!" they said. "You came!" They introduced their fellow graduates and the persons they had married. "This is Edie. Edie, this is Bill, Terry, Peter, Joan," and were carried off in whirlwinds of friends.

As the Ransom house emptied of family, it began to expand. The bedrooms grew larger, the hall banister longer, the porch too wide for the wicker chairs. Edie took leave of the place for want of children in 1938. She was sixty years old.

She talked to Thomas Ransom in his study, where his first wife's portrait, painted in pastels, had been restored to its place on the wall facing his desk. Edie sat under the green-eyed young face, her unfaltering blue glance on her employer. Each tried to make the parting easy. It was clear, however, that they were dividing between them, top to bottom, a frail, towering structure of nineteen accumulated years, which was the time it had taken to turn five children, with their interminable questions, unfounded terrors, and destructive impulses, into mature adults who could vote, follow maps, make omelets, and reach an accord of sorts with life and death.

Thinking back over the intervening years, Thomas Ransom remembered Edie's cousin in Texas and inquired, only to find that Texas had been a disappointment, as had America itself. The cousin had returned to England twelve years ago.

"Would you like that?" he asked Edie. "To go back to England?"

She had grown used to California, she said. She had no one in Atherleigh. So, in the end, prompted by the look in his first wife's eyes, Thomas Ransom offered Edie a cottage and a pension to be hers for the rest of her life.

Edie's beach cottage was two blocks back from the sea and very small. On one wall she hung a few of the children's drawings, including the earthquake aftermath. Opposite them, by itself, she hung the framed photograph of Lady Alice and Lady Anne, fair and well-seated astride their ponies. Edie had become the repository of pets. The long-lived fish swam languidly in one corner of her sitting room, the last of the canaries molted in another.

Each Ransom child came to her house once for tea, pulling in to the curb next to a mailbox marked Edith Fisk.

"Edie, you live so far away!"

On their first Christmas apart, the children sent five cards, the next year four, then two for several years, then one, or sometimes none.

During the first September of Edie's retirement, England declared war on Germany. She knitted socks for the British troops and, on one occasion four years after she left it, returned briefly to the Ransom house. This was when the twins were killed in Europe a month apart at the age of twenty-four, one in a fighter plane over the Baltic, the other in a bomber over the Rhine. Two months later Thomas Ransom asked Edie to dispose of their things and she came back for a week to her old, now anonymous, room.

She was unprepared for the mass of articles to be dealt with. The older children had cleared away childhood possessions at the time of their marriages. But here were all the books the twins had ever read, from Dr. Doolittle to Hemingway, and all their entertainments, from a Ouija board to skis and swim fins. Years of their civilian trousers, coats, and shoes crowded the closets.

Edie first wrapped and packed the bulky objects, then folded into cartons the heaps of clothing, much of which she knew. A week was barely time enough to sort it all and reach decisions. Then, suddenly, as though it had been a matter of minutes, the boxes were packed and at the door. Edie marked each one with black crayon. Boys' Club, she printed, Children's Hospital, Red Cross, Veterans.

That afternoon, she stood for a moment with Thomas Ransom on the porch, the silent house behind them. The November air was cold and fresh, the sky cloudless.

"Lovely day," said Edie.

Thomas Ransom nodded, admiring the climate while his life thinned out.

If the three surviving children had written Edie during the years that followed, this is what she would have learned.

At thirty-five, James, instead of having become an electrical engineer or a master mechanic, was a junior partner in his father's law firm. Twice divorced and about to take a new wife, he had apparently learned nothing from Thomas Ransom, not even how to marry happily once. Each marriage had produced two children, four intended cures that failed. James's practice involved foreign corporations and he was often abroad. He moved from executive offices to board rooms and back, and made no attempt to diagnose his discontent. On vacations at home, he dismantled and reassembled heaters and fans, and wired every room of his house for sound.

Whenever he visited England, he tried, and failed, to find time to send Edie a card.

Eliza had been carried off from her research library by an archaeologist ten years older and three inches shorter than she. He took her first to Guatemala, then to Mexico, where they lived in a series of jungle huts in Chiapas and Yucatán. It was hard to find native help and the clothes Eliza washed often hung drying for days on the teeming underbrush. Her damp books, on shelves and still in boxes, began to mildew. She cooked food wrapped in leaves over a charcoal fire. On special days, like her birthday and Christmas, Eliza would stand under the thatch of her doorway and stare northwest through the rain and vegetation, in the direction of the house where she was born and first tasted tea.

Edie still lived in the house when Jenny, through a letter from her last stepmother, Cissy, met the Englishman she would marry. Thin as a pencil and pale as parchment, he had entered the local university as an exchange fellow. Jenny was immediately moved to take care of him, sew on his missing buttons, comb his sandy hair. His English speech enchanted her.

"Tell about boating at Henley," she urged him. "Tell about

climbing the Trossachs. Explain cricket." And while he described these things as fully as his inherent reserve would allow, the inflections of another voice fell across his. Jenny heard "fahncy dahnces." She heard "poor souls."

"Have you ever been to Atherleigh in Devon?" she asked him.

"That's Hatherleigh," he said.

If Jenny had written Edie, she would have said, "I love Massachusetts, I love my house, I can make scones, come and see us."

On a spring afternoon in 1948, Thomas Ransom called his children together in the same study where the aunts had read Cissy's letter of lament and recommendation. The tree his wife planted thirty years ago towered in green leaf outside the window.

The children had gathered from the outposts of the world— James from Paris, Eliza from the Mayan tropics, Jenny from snowed-in Boston. When he summoned them, they had assumed a crisis involving their father. Now they sat uneasily under the portrait of their mother, a girl years younger than themselves. Thomas Ransom offered them tea and sherry. He looked through the window at the tree.

At last he presented his news. "Edie is dying," he said. "She is in the hospital with cancer," as if cancer were a friend Edie had always longed to share a room with.

They visited her on a shining April morning, much like the one when they first met. With their first gray hairs and new lines at their eyes, they waited a moment on the hospital steps.

James took charge. "We'll go in one by one," he said.

So, as if they had rehearsed together, each of them stood alone outside the door that had a sign, No Visitors; stood there while carts of half-eaten lunches or patients prepared for surgery were wheeled past; stood and collected their childhood until a nurse noticed and said, "Go in. She wants to see you." Then, one after another, they pushed the door open, went to the high narrow bed, and said, "Edie."

She may not have known they were there. She had started to be a skeleton. Her skull was pulling her eyes in. Once they had spoken her name, there was nothing more to say. Before leaving, they touched the familiar, unrecognizable hand of shoelaces and hair ribbons and knew it, for the first time, disengaged.

After their separate visits, they assembled again on the hospital steps. It was now they remembered Lady Alice and Lady Anne.

"Where was that castle?" Eliza asked.

"In Kent," said Jenny.

All at one time, they imagined the girls in their tower after tea. Below them swans pulled lengthening reflections behind them across the smooth surface of the lake. Lady Alice sat at her rosewood desk, Lady Anne at hers. They were still seven and eight years old. They wrote on thick paper with mother-of-pearl pens dipped into ivory inkwells.

"Dear Edie," wrote Lady Alice.

"Dear Edie," wrote Lady Anne.

"I am sorry to hear you are ill," they both wrote.

Then, as if they were performing an exercise in penmanship, they copied "I am sorry" over and over in flowing script until they reached the bottom of the page. When there was no more room, they signed one letter, Alice, and the other letter, Anne.

In the midst of all this, Edie died.

BRIEF LIVES IN CALIFORNIA

John L'Heureux

Leonora started out pretty and bright.

"She could be a movie star," her mother said, "but I would never do that to my child. I would never allow a child of mine to be in the limelight. I want Leonora to be just normal."

So Leonora took ballet and tap and piano.

"Perhaps she has other gifts," the dance teacher said. "Perhaps she has a gift for music."

The piano teacher was more to the point. "She has nothing," he said. "And she's driving me crazy."

"You could be a movie star," her mother said.

In junior high Leonora was one of the first to grow breasts; the other girls resented her for that. But in high school her breasts made her popular with the boys, so she didn't care about the girls. She became a cheerleader and after every game she and the other cheerleaders crowded into the booths at Dante's and waited for the team to arrive. Then they all drank Cokes and ate cheeseburgers and grabbed at one another in the booths—nothing serious, just good fun—and made out on the way home.

In November of her senior year Leonora was parked in front of her house in Chuckie's car.

"Why won't you do it?" Chuckie asked. "Everybody does."

"I don't know," she said, miserable. "I want to, but I can't. I just can't."

"Nobody saves themselves for marriage anymore. Is that what you think you're doing?"

"I think I was meant for better things," she said, not really knowing what she meant. "I mean, I get straight A's and B's."

"Ah shit," Chuckie said. "Just put your hand here. Feel this."

"No, I was meant for better things."

"But you've got to start somewhere," Chuckie said. "Hell, I'm captain of the team."

But Leonora was already getting out of the car, feeling chosen, feeling—she searched for the word—exalted. Yes, that was it. She was meant for better things.

In the admissions office at Stanford, Leonora was a floater, somebody who hadn't yet sunk to the bottom but somebody who wouldn't get picked out of the pool unless a real Stanford freshman decided to go to Yale or somewhere. That year a lot of freshmen went to Yale and so Leonora, floating almost to the end, was admitted to Stanford.

"You could be a college professor," her mother said. "Or a famous writer. You could win the Nobel Prize, maybe."

"Dry up," Leonora said. "What do you know about it? You never even went to college."

"Oh baby," she said. "Oh sweetheart, don't be mean to your mother, Leonora. I only want what's best for you. I only want you to be happy."

"Then dry up," Leonora said.

The worst part about Stanford was that they made her take freshman English. She had been among the top thirty in high school and now she was back to writing compositions. At first she had just been a little nasty to the teacher in class, to let him know how she felt about being there. But after she had written the first assigned paper, she decided to go see him and demand an explanation. He gave it to her. He explained that it was a requirement of the university that every student demonstrate a basic competence in expository writing and that she had not, in the qualifying tests, demonstrated that. And then he handed her the corrected paper.

It was covered with little red marks—diction? antecedent? obscure, no no no—and there was a large black C at the bottom of the page.

"You gave me a C," Leonora said. "I've never had a C in my life."

"There's nothing wrong with a C," he said. "It's a perfectly acceptable grade. It's average, maybe even above average."

"You gave me a C," she said and, choking on her tears, ran from his office.

Her next two papers came back with C's on them also, so she knew he was out to get her. His name was Lockhardt and he had written a couple of novels and thought he was hot shit.

Leonora went to the ombudsman and complained that she was being discriminated against. She should not have to take freshman English in the first place, and in the second place Lockhardt was guilty of unprofessional conduct in browbeating her and making her feel inferior.

The ombudsman went to the chairman of the English department who called in Lockhardt and then called in Leonora and finally checked her papers himself. The next day he told Leonora that yes, she would have to take freshman English like all the others, that the grades Professor Lockhardt had given her seemed fair enough, that he was sorry Professor Lockhardt had made her feel inferior. He told Lockhardt for God's sake go easy on the girl, she's half-crazy, and whatever you do don't be alone with her in your office. He told the ombudsman that the problem had been settled to everyone's satisfaction and there was no need to take all this to the provost. So everyone was miserable and satisfied.

Leonora's final grade was a C, all because of that bastard Lockhardt.

Patty Hearst was wrestled, struggling, into the trunk of a car in Berkeley and the next day she was headlines in all the papers. Leonora narrowed her thin eyes and thought, Why couldn't they have taken me?

In her junior year she moved in with Horst Kammer. He was clearly one of the better things that she was meant for. He was very smart and spent a lot of time with the housemaster, so that in Horst she had not only a roommate, she had instant acceptance as well. Horst was too intellectual to be much interested in sex, but he didn't mind occasional sex with Leonora and that was enough for her.

Horst dressed in army fatigues and spent a lot of his time protesting Stanford's investments in South Africa. Leonora protested along with him and they were arrested together during the spring sit-in at Old Union. Leonora felt proud to be involved in something historical, something that mattered. There were over a hundred students arrested and they were each fined nearly two hundred dollars. Leonora's mother sent the money, and with it a note saying, "You're like Vanessa Redgrave or Jane Fonda. You're doing your part."

"God, that woman is hopeless," Leonora said.

Two photographs.

One. Leonora is home from college and all the relatives have come over for dinner. Afterwards somebody snaps an Instamatic of Leonora and her mother and father, sitting on the floor in front of the Christmas tree, surrounded by gifts. The mother and father each have an arm around Leonora and they are smiling directly into the camera. Leonora is smiling too, but she is looking off to the right of the camera, as if at the very last minute she decided the picture is not what she wants; she wants something else.

"She could be a photographer's model," her mother says, examining the picture. "She could be on all the covers."

Two. Leonora has just crested the hill on Campus Drive and is about to make the long clear descent on her new ten-speed bike. She passes two professors who are taking a noon walk, looking like anybody else, just enjoying the California spring. Leonora does not notice them, does not see that one of them is Lockhardt. She sees only the long long hill before her, and she feels the warm wind blowing through her hair. She sits high on the seat, no hands, and lifts her arms straight out from the shoulders, surrendering completely to the sun and the wind and being young and pretty, with everything, every wonderful thing ahead of her.

"Look at that girl," Lockhardt says. "God, somebody should photograph that."

In her senior year, her second year with Horst, Leonora was all showered and getting ready to go to a frat party when Horst said, "Come on, let's do it." He wasn't interested in doing it that often, so she said, "I'm all ready for the party, but if you're sure you want to . . ." "I want to," he said. "I'm up for it. Look." And so he chased her from the bedroom into the living room and then back into the bedroom where she collapsed on the bed, laughing and tickling him, and they made love. "Was it wonderful?" she said. "Was it better?" "You're terrific," he said, "you're great. Where the hell is my deodorant?"

At the party everybody drank a lot of beer and tequila sunrises and after a while they got to the subject of how often you ball your roommate. When Horst's turn came, he gave a long and funny speech about the primacy of the intellect and the transitory nature of sexuality. He described the postures you get into and he made them sound new and funny, and he said the real problem is that an hour later you're still hungry for more. He had everybody with him and he was feeling really good about his performance, you could tell, and then he paused and said, anticlimactically, "Let's face it folks, what we're dealing with here is just two mucous membranes rubbing together."

Everybody laughed and applauded and spilled beer. Horst shook his head and smiled sneakily at Leonora.

But then somebody added, "They're sebaceous membranes, actually. Get your membranes straight, Horst."

Everybody laughed even louder and Leonora laughed too and Horst saw her do it.

So he was furious and, on the way home, when Leonora leaned against his side, her head on his shoulder, Horst put his hand on her breast. He felt for the nipple and when he had it firmly between his thumb and forefinger, he twisted it suddenly and violently, pressing down with his thumbnail. Leonora screamed in pain.

"You bitch," he said. "You fucking whore. Why don't you get out of my life? You're just a nothing. You're a noose around my neck."

"No," Leonora said. "No."

Patty Hearst was arrested in an apartment in San Francisco. Her picture appeared in all the papers, laughing like crazy, her fist clenched in the revolutionary salute. She listed her occupation as "urban guerrilla." Leonora was done with all that now that she was done with Horst. And who cared about Patty Hearst anyhow?

Leonora got her diploma in June, but she had to take one more course that summer before she had enough credits to officially graduate. She signed up for creative writing, taught by "staff." But staff turned out to be that bastard Lockhardt. He didn't seem to remember her, and everybody said he was a really good teacher, and she wanted to write a novel someday, so she decided to give him another chance.

Lockhardt wasn't interested in the things that interested her. She wanted to write something different, but Lockhardt kept talking about the initiating incident and the conflict and the characters. Old stuff. She wrote a story about a shoplifter named Horst, following him from the moment he picked up a tie until the moment he got out of the store, and she wrote it completely from within his mind, what he was thinking. Lockhardt said that the reader had no way of knowing that Horst was stealing, and that she should simply say so. But she explained that she was trying to be more subtle than that. She explained that the reader was supposed to find out Horst was stealing only after the fact, after he was outside the shop, otherwise the story would be just like any other story. They argued back and forth for a long time and then Lockhardt just shrugged his shoulders and said, "Well, I guess you've accomplished what you set out to do. Congratulations." The same thing happened with her next two stories. He didn't like them, so he said the reader couldn't follow them. He couldn't seem to understand that she was trying to do something different.

And then in August she got her grade. A flat C. She went straight from the registrar's office to Lockhardt.

"I have to speak to you," she said.

"Sit down," he said. "Have a seat. But I've got to see the dean in five minutes, so if you're going to need more than that . . ."

"You gave me a C."

"Right. I hope you weren't too disappointed."

"You," she said. "You," but the words wouldn't come out.

"Well, your work was not really extraordinary. I mean, I think you'll agree that it wasn't A work."

"It was C work, I suppose. It was only average."

"There's nothing wrong with being average. Most of us are. Most of our work is average."

She stood up and walked to the door. "What do I care," she said. "I can live with a C." And she slammed the door behind her.

She came back late the next afternoon, she was not sure why, but she knew she had to tell him something. Lockhardt was at his desk, typing, his back to the open door, and Leonora stood there in the corridor watching him. Nobody else was around. She could kill him and no one would know she had done it. If she had a knife or a gun, she could do it. That bastard.

He kept on typing and she just stood there watching him, thinking. And then suddenly he turned around and gave a little shout. "My God, you scared me half to death."

Leonora just stared at him, and he stared back, looking confused and maybe frightened. Then she turned and walked away.

She had not told him what he had done to her, but she would someday. She'd let him know. She'd let him know.

Leonora moved to San Francisco to be on her own. She got a studio apartment with a fire escape that looked down onto the roof of the Jack Tarr Hotel and she applied for jobs at Gumps and at the St. Francis—they asked her "doing what?"—and she shrugged and said to hell with them, she had a Stanford education. But her money ran out eventually and she took a job at Dalton's selling books.

Nothing interesting ever happened at Dalton's, and besides you had to press sixty buttons on the computerized register every time you rang up a sale. The worst part was that everybody kept buying a novel called *The Love Hostage*, written by that bastard Lockhardt. After the first four sales, she refused to sell any more. "I'm on my break," she'd say and make the customer go to another register.

Leonora hated her job, hated the people she worked with, hated books. Somewhere there must be something different happening. Even Patty Hearst, who was a zilch, a nothing, even she had things happen to her. With a name like Patty.

One night when she had worked late, Leonora decided to take a walk. She would make something happen. She moped along Polk Street to Geary and then back, but nothing happened. There were a million or so faggots eyeing each other, but nobody eyed Leonora. She went up to her studio and had a beer and then came down again and set off deliberately in the direction of Golden Gate Park. She knew what she was doing. She could be raped. She could be murdered. Lockhardt used to talk all the time about Joyce Carol Oates characters, how they set up situations for themselves, getting trapped, getting murdered, having their pink and gray brains spilled out on the sidewalk. She liked Joyce Carol Oates. She got as far as the Panhandle and was about to turn around and go home when she realized somebody was following her. For a block, then for a second block. She could hear the heels go faster when she went faster, slow down when she did. Her heart began to beat very fast and she could feel the vein in her forehead pulsing. She wanted it to happen, whatever it was. She turned around suddenly, hands on hips, her head thrown back, ready. At once the man following her crossed the street and headed in the opposite direction. Leonora walked for another hour and then went home. Would nothing happen to her, ever?

The next day she quit her job at Dalton's. They were limiting her. They were worse than Stanford.

The Women's Support Group was having a terrible time with Leonora.

"You've got to open up to your feelings as a woman," they said.

"Men have done this to you. They've refused to let you get in touch with your feelings," they said.

"What is it you feel? What is it you want?" they said.

"I want," Leonora said, "I don't know, but I think I want to die."

"No, what do you really want?" they said.

Leonora bought a gun and a copy of *The Love Hostage* on the same day. There was no connection she could see. She wanted them, that was all. It was time.

She loaded the gun with six bullets and hid it in a Kleenex box under a lot of tissues. It was for protection in this crazy city. It was a safeguard. It was just something nice to have around.

And then she sat down to read *The Love Hostage*. From the first page she was fascinated and appalled. The dust jacket said it was a novel about a young heiress who is kidnapped and brainwashed and all the other stuff that would make you think it was about Patty Hearst. But it wasn't about Patty at all; it was about her, it was about Leonora. Lockhardt had changed things to make it look as if it were about Patty, but she knew he meant her. He described her as an ordinary girl, a normal girl, average in every way. So now he had finally done it. He had killed her.

Leonora put the gun to the side of her head and pulled the trigger. There was an awful noise and the gun leaped from her hand and she felt something wet on the side of her face. She had only grazed her scalp, but inside she was dead just the same.

On the night she was committed to Agnew Mental, Leonora had forced down the beef stew her mother served for dinner and then she had gone back to her room to lie down. Almost at once she threw up into the wastebasket by her bed and then she went to the bathroom and threw up again. Back in her room she put on Phoebe Snow's *Poetry Man*. She played the album through twice, though she was not listening. She was thinking—as she had been for these last three weeks—of Lockhardt and how he had ruined everything and how someday she would let him know. But not now. Someday.

And then, as if it were somebody else doing it, she got up and got dressed and drove to the Stanford campus. She found Lockhardt's house with no trouble at all, and it was only when she had rung the doorbell that she realized she didn't know what she was going to say. But it didn't matter; somehow she would just tell him, calmly, with no tears, that he had degraded her, humiliated her, he had ruined her life.

"Yes?"

"I want to talk to you. I want to tell you something."

"Are you a student of mine? A former student?"

And then she realized that this was not Lockhardt at all, this was a much older man with a beard and glasses. The Lockhardts, it turned out, had moved to San Francisco.

Leonora got back into her car. She was frantic now, she would have to find a phone booth and get his address. She drove to Town and Country Shopping Center and found a booth, but there was no San Francisco directory. She drove to Stanford Shopping Center, and again there was no directory. Never mind. She would drive straight to the city, she would find him, he wouldn't get away from her now. She would let him know.

Traffic on 101 was heavy and it had begun to rain. Leonora passed cars that were already doing sixty. She had to get there. She had to tell him. The words were piling up in her brain, like stones, like bullets. Bullets, yes, she should have brought the gun. She should kill the bastard. A car pulled into her lane and then began slowly to brake.

Leonora braked too, but not fast enough. Her car fishtailed and, with a short crunching sound, it smashed the side of a Volkswagen. She tore on ahead, though she could see in her mirror that the Volkswagen had ground to a halt, that its lights were blinking on and off. Tough. Yes, she should kill him, she thought, and she pressed her foot harder on the accelerator.

She couldn't find a parking place and so she left the car in a tow zone a block from the Jack Tarr Hotel and ran back in the rain. She found the phone booth, the directory, she opened it to the *L*'s. Lockhardt lived in North Beach. Of course he would, with all that money from *The Love Hostage*. She ran back to her car. A tow truck was backed up to it and a little bald man was kneeling down trying to attach a bar under the front bumper. "No," she shouted. "Stop it. Stop it. Stop." He stood up and looked at her, a screaming woman with her wet hair flying all around, a real crazy. "Okay, lady, okay," he said. "Okay." And then she was in her car again, tearing up Van Ness, running yellow lights, turning right on Pacific. In a few minutes she was there, at Lockhardt's blue and gray Victorian.

Leonora's head was pounding now and her back ached. She wanted to throw up, but there was nothing left to throw up. She wanted a drink. She wanted a pill. She wanted to take Lockhardt by the hair and tear the scalp off him, to expose the pink and gray brain that had written those things, that had done this to her.

She put her finger up to ring the bell, but she was shaking so much she couldn't do it. She began to beat the doorbell with her palm and then with her fist. Still the bell made no sound. She struck the door itself, with her hand, and then with her foot, and then she leaned her entire body against it, beating the door rhythmically with her fist and then with both fists, the rhythm growing faster and faster, the blows harder and harder, until there was blood on her hands and blood on the door and she heard a voice screaming that sounded like her own.

The door opened and Lockhardt, with a book in his hand, stood there looking at the young woman whose wet hair was streaked across her face, a face distorted beyond recognition by her hysteria, and he listened to the screaming, which made no sense to him until her voice broke and he could make out the words. "I am not average," she sobbed. "I am not average. I am not average."

It was nearly a half-hour before the orderlies came and took her away.

The world had gone crazy, that's just the way it was. Leonora's mother stared at the television where for days she had been watching pictures of the 911 corpses in Guyana. They had taken poison mixed with grape Kool-Aid and in five minutes they were dead. Every one of them. And Patty Hearst had been refused parole. And so had Charles Manson. And her own Leonora in that loony bin. Leonora could have been something once. She could have been . . . but nothing came to mind. It was Lockhardt's fault, Leonora was right. It was all Lockhardt's fault. Leonora's mother turned up the volume on the TV. And now somebody had shot Mayor Moscone and that Harvey Milk. It was the way you expressed yourself today, you shot somebody.

She thought of the gun hidden in the Kleenex box and suddenly it was clear to her. She got in the car and drove to North Beach. She had no trouble finding Lockhardt's house; she had been there three times since Leonora was taken away. She had just parked opposite the house and sat there and watched. But this time she went up the steep wooden stairs and rang the bell. She rang again and as she was about to ring a third time Lockhardt opened the door, laughing. She could hear other people laughing too; he must be having a party. Over his left shoulder, in the entrance hall, she could see a chandelier, a deep green wall, the corner of a picture. She couldn't make out what it was a picture of, but she could see that he was rich. He had everything. "Yes?" he said, and there was more laughter from that other room. "Yes?" he said again.

"Leonora," she said. "She could have been something."

And then she took the gun from her purse and leveled it at his chest. There were three loud shots and when his body slumped to the floor, Leonora's mother could see that the painting on the green wall was one of those newfangled things with little blocks of color, all different sizes, that really aren't the picture of anything.

YELLOW FLAGS

Charles Eastman

I remember little of my father from the time we all lived together in
Hollywood, and only a few disturbing moments from that period,
including the afternoon when he took out after another car that had in
passing splattered ours with muddy water from the gutter. He was
suddenly furious, as though he had been injured or insulted. What he
planned to do when he caught up with the offender I didn't know, but
I saw that he was all the more determined, fiercer in his pursuit, for my
mother's high-pitched objections from the passenger seat—as our car,
a Ford sedan, hit the hazardous dips of the cross streets and barreled
forward. I think I felt that my mother was overreacting, more fearful
than need be, and was feeding my father's rage, but I did not know
about alcohol then and so assumed that she saw the peril more clearly
than I, on my feet in the back seat like a charioteer and more enter-
tained than frightened.

I also remember him at a card table in the middle of the living
room on Western Avenue. The floor lamp is at his right, out of place,
pulled from behind the couch to illuminate the card game he plays
with our guests—childless, unfettered friends my parents knew from
high school. My father lifts his arm suddenly to thwart some attempt
to calm him down, make peace, and the lamp goes over with the gesture. I hear raised voices, conciliatory, then pandering, before an
abrupt, intimidated silence. The room is tipped upside down in the
spilled light.

Here again it is my mother's reactions that stay more acutely with me, her keening moan of desperation, her see-what-you've-done-now despair. She, who would go to any lengths for the sake of appearances, suddenly surrendered and began wildly overstating her embarrassment, goading my father's temper, I think, and feeding his penchant for making scenes, on those card-playing nights of the Depression.

Otherwise, my father seemed to be laughing most of the time, or asleep, in the memory I have of him, in the few, brief years before the divorce. I can recall his teasing sense of well-being, his self-satisfaction, fixed on my mother, and the long, heavy hours of sudden, untimely slumber: eventless Sunday afternoons, when after some aborted pastime I was obliged to honor an uncommon, unreasonable quiet.

Then he was gone, his absence hardly noted in the abrupt change in our circumstances. My mother was at work now, and my grandmother was running the house—or the succession of houses—we shared with her and with my working aunts, sometimes my uncle, and finally, for a while, a stepfather.

And then, after several years, he was back.

He was in uniform, in the Army, a sergeant, and he was leaving town. It was early summer and I was not in school. The kids, my brother and sisters, were somewhere, I don't know where. Perhaps it was not summer vacation but Easter week.

My grandmother let him in and called my mother on the phone. The phone was in the hall, on a small, cluttered desk invariably lacking a pencil, with a chair in front of it, though my grandmother did not sit down. She wore a patterned pinafore apron, blue; it was damp from her interrupted work at the sink or at the tubs on the back porch. I can only think she was torn over how to handle this emergency.

"He's here and he wants to take Conrad to the beach," she said to my mother at her office across town. It was gloomy in the hall, as it always was when the bedroom doors were closed. My father stood in the door to the den, taller than anyone I knew, blocking light from that source, too. My grandmother did not turn the light on.

"No, he doesn't seem like it," she said.

"Could I speak to her?" my father said.

My grandmother gave him the phone. With her apron she wiped her wrists where suds had climbed when she'd dried her hands.

"I had one beer at lunch," my father said, as though my mother were being unreasonable. "A beer."

I sat down on the third step from the bottom of the narrow staircase that led to the rooms above. I knew that some higher order of things regulated my fate now, some jurisdiction where I didn't belong exclusively to my mother and my grandmother anymore, and where their preferences could be overruled. He was my father, after all, if currently underprivileged and in disgrace, and was thereby entitled to the sympathy and the subordination of my protectors, female. Still, I had the dim hope that my mother might prevail, would say a firm no, from the obstinate streak I knew she possessed.

"But I'm sober and I'll stay sober while he's with me," my father said. My grandmother swatted him with her dish towel, good-naturedly, warningly, and got back on the phone, her job to lighten things up.

"Tell her I'll behave," my father said, recognizing an ally. And then, turning to me, addressed the jury: "But I'm leaving for a while and I just thought I might like to go to the beach for once with one of my kids, for Christ's sake."

I could not hear my mother on the other end of the line and yet I have no doubt about what she said: "I'm pretty busy just now, Mama," as though she recognized my grandmother's divided loyalty and was feeling outnumbered, overruled. This was not indifference or callous disregard but simply the truth. Our welfare depended on my mother's salary now. Which we knew, my brother, my sisters, and I. Our mother's attention during the day, in our larger behalf, was owed elsewhere, even if we did not always temper our emergencies to that priority.

As she listened to my mother, my grandmother looked between my father and me. She said she was sure Edward was a good man and would take good care of me. If she looked as though she doubted her own argument, it was because she understood our conflicting feelings fully, and her heart went out to all three of us.

"But I want him to give Conrad five dollars, in case something happens—right now, in front of you, Mama, so he'll have money to get home at least, or to phone."

When my grandmother hung up and repeated this codicil to my father, he said, "For crying out loud."

At the beach it was not warm or crowded enough to be summer, and the briny smell, like laundry soap and sulfur, was caustic; the wind was blowing.

We stayed for a while in my father's borrowed car and stared at the wind-combed sand. The car belonged to a woman, I suspected. Someone who kept it clean, anyway, who had left a half-peeled roll of Life Savers on the seat. Wint-O-Green.

My father said that maybe we wouldn't go swimming after all, maybe we'd just walk along the Strand. He asked whether I wanted to see the apartment building where he and my mother honeymooned when they got married. It was called the Ocean Arms. It was right across the street; we didn't even have to leave the car. He pointed out the very room where he and my mother had stayed.

"She took the afternoon off," he said. "And I wasn't working." He was speaking of their wedding day.

They had liked the Ocean Arms for its Spanish arch over the entrance, for a living-room tapestry of dancing gypsies deep in the woods, held up by iron rings at the top, and for a wrought-iron grille over the front window, which was leaded, with sections of colored glass. (I'd heard about all this before, from my mother, from my grandmother.)

"We lived here two whole months," my father said, as though it were a lifetime and all anyone could expect of paradise. Then he reached to the heart of his nostalgia: "I had a straw hat that was really quite the thing."

My mother always spoke of him as "a dresser," as though looking for something to explain it all, to make some sense of it. Four kids.

I liked the past and didn't mind this information, but I was not as interested as I was at home in our dining room, when my mother opened her hope chest (the heavy relic of her life with my father and the one off-limits in the house which I respected) and a world before my own emerged in the form of folded scarves and strange lapel pins, beads and thick letters and flaking snapshots, and posed, tinted portrait pictures of remote and unrecollected people, people in their youth looking older than they would today, serious, formal, preliminary people, fixed in receding time and smelling of cedar. In my view the circle had closed, and my father was not entitled to his side of our history anymore; he was dealing in stolen goods when he presumed to speak of our past.

"But the sound of the sea made her nervous," he said. "She wanted things set—I understand that. I wanted things special. She'd get embarrassed by things, little things. For instance, everyone came down on Sundays because we had the beach. But only tenants could use the showers, which made your mother feel ashamed."

The building was now painted turquoise. A cardboard sign in the ground-floor front-room window read ROOMS. The wrought-iron grillwork remained, but the leaded patterns and the colored glass were gone.

"You thirsty? Want a Coca-Cola or something?"

A block from the Ocean Arms was a flat-faced market, and before it a dented red refrigerator box with cold drinks. My father opened a Hires for me on the rusty lip of the cap receptacle and went into the market counting his change; he came out with a bottle of Lucky Lager.

He tucked his sergeant's cap under his belt and put his foot up on a crate half filled with empties. He leaned his elbow on his elevated knee.

"Your mother should have come down with us today," he said. He held his beer before him thoughtfully, as though his right to it were without question, as if broken promises were inevitable.

"She doesn't like the beach," I said, feeling at once that my tone might sound too in-the-know and challenging. My mother was beautiful; she was easygoing, and could, in my experience, be persuaded in almost any direction. But she had positions, out of nowhere and seemingly on small points, and she held to them stubbornly. For example, she hated the beach. It was sandy, too far to go, too much trouble. She burned.

My father took a long swallow of beer. "I guess not," he said. "She never did."

He looked up and down the Strand. He nodded then, as though he felt some gesture were required, some conclusion. "Funny," he said. "It doesn't seem to have changed all that much."

I looked up and down the street as well, in case my opinion of the neighborhood was pertinent.

"You get good grades in school?" my father asked.

"Pretty good," I said, embarrassed for him, his remark so parental, obligatory.

"Just pretty good?"

"I guess."

My father cleared his throat, looking for the right voice, as if he hadn't intended to get businesslike but the issue was too important to ignore. "Well, work on your grades and keep them up there," he said.

In another swallow he had almost finished his beer. "What do you play? Do you play—what? Basketball?"

"They play kickball at my school," I said, feeling immediately some deep prevarication in my soul, an effort to cover up, slide by the abyss.

"You play, don't you?"

We were addressing the mystery of the ball, and I was at a terrible, threatening loss. I shook my head.

"How's that?" my father asked, baffled but concerned, squinting at me.

"I'm not very good," I said, recognizing in this admission a glaring want of character.

"Well, that's the way you get good," my father said. "By playing." He seemed relieved to have found what to say to me. "Ball."

"I don't like it," I said. I was down to the foam of my root beer.

"You should play, Conrad," my father said.

"I put out the yellow flags," I said.

"The what?"

"They tell when recess is just about over," I said. "Lunch period. And your time is running out."

My father said nothing. He might have been wondering what to say next, he might have been through with the conversation, but I felt the interrogation continuing, more pressing for his silence.

"At a quarter to one someone has to put out the yellow flags," I said. "That tells everyone if they have to go to the bathroom or clean up their area, they have fifteen minutes left."

"You do that instead of play?" my father said.

I said nothing. I might plead the importance of my charge, but I had my mother's integrity and would claim no distinction that another failed to grant me freely.

"I was a quarterback when I went to school," my father said. "That's how your mother met me."

"I've seen the picture of you," I said, envisioning the cedar-smelling staged photo of a high school celebrity that my mother had shown me from the chest in the dining room—shown me too often, too pointedly, I thought, trying to do my father justice and make sure I got the image of him that she herself had fallen for. This she did as faithfully as she sent me to Sunday school and to violin lessons, and in the same spirit—for my greater good, else she be charged with bias or neglect.

"She ever talk about me?" my father asked, and I knew that the subject had traveled beyond me, a duty stop, to the destination it was headed for all along.

I was relieved, of course, that my rank on the playground was no longer being investigated and that I'd slipped past the theosophy of ball without being further disgraced. But I felt awkward, as you do when you have mistaken someone's waving at you across a distance—when you've quickened, perhaps even brightened a little, and lifted your hand to respond—only to see that happy look spear past you to someone behind your back. You feel the fool then, and cheated, as you witness the reunion made in heaven you almost interrupted.

"She said she doesn't want me to dislike you or anything," I said. "Or hold anything against you."

He had bought a quart of whiskey, which he left in the paper bag, the bag held tightly around the neck of the bottle, and he drank as we walked along the Strand, his bathing suit wrapped up under his arm. I carried our towels, my grandmother's reminder at the last minute. I wore my bathing suit under my pants.

Then he said he was tired of walking.

We crossed the sand and sat down by the water.

He saw that the cuffs of his Army pants were filled with sand and he cursed, lightly, to himself, as though I weren't there. He opened his belt, because the buckle cut into his stomach now, doubled up as we were. He threw his cap aside. He warned me that he might fall asleep, and then he lay back and fell asleep.

A gathering of gulls had settled into the sand upwind, and occasional feathers blew against my father and stuck to his khaki, as though he had been punctured and his stuffing were coming out. Sometimes I reached to pull them off, these soft, curly innards, and sometimes I didn't.

Every few minutes the surf cracked at my back with the sound of a whip, and when I looked around, I could see a whooping spray thrash backward, like a mane over the breakers. After a while I took the bottle of whiskey by its brown neck; the bag lifted with it. It was heavy enough to be not empty yet, and smelled of khaki and cigarette smoke and moustache and neck. It was, as I knew it would be, warm when I drank, like something that should not be consumed. I put the bottle back where I found it, having tasted my father and my own stale origins.

My father ran into the water, his legs stabbing a fountain of clear fire up over his body. He awakened with the desire to swim after all, and now he vanished beneath the surf.

I went in only as far as the water wrapped my waist.

The sun had fallen to the horizon, and the surface of the water was blinding. The tide had gone out while my father slept, and the breakers were louder than ever and sudden and shallow, if not fierce. The wind had stopped, though, and the cool evening air on our shoulders made the water seem warm enough.

He came back toward me. "What's the matter?" he said. "Can't you swim?"

"I can but I don't want to," I said. I stood with one hand held up to my eyes to protect them from the glare of the sun. I could see my father only when a wave broke the reflection and cast a shadow, and then I had to stagger back as the wave hit me. I thought I might return to our towels, but a pair of dark surf fishermen had appeared on the beach, and for some reason I was reluctant to pass them.

My father, riding a wave, surfaced beside me. He lifted me up and carried me farther out, without asking, marching through the crackling edges of incoming water.

"I don't like it," I said tightly.

He held me up as a wave pulled under us; we continued out.

"Please."

"Come on."

"I don't want to."

"Just jump when they—just hold your breath and squat down."

"I—"

"Don't be a baby."

His body was slippery, and I could not hold on. I felt also some other prohibition against my clinging, some manners or taboo.

"Hold your nose!" I heard his wet laughter against my ear. "I said open your eyes for crying out loud!" His whiskey breath was like a muzzle clamped over his nostrils.

"I can't!"

"I got hold of you!"

"No!"

"This one we'll jump, and see—"

We did.

"—how easy it is?"

I felt the buoyant lift, the possibility of pleasure, trust.

"See?"

"I want to go back."

"What fun it is."

"Yeah, but."

"You'll get used to it."

My teeth were so tightly locked together that I took in no water when the wave hit and I was pushed down and torn from my father's hands. I bounced against the bottom and hit the top again almost immediately, surprised at my survival and a bit exhilarated, to find the surf suddenly still, covered with a hissing froth that moved in every direction at once. I felt myself riding it, a spinning marble racing away from the disinterested figures on the shore, the surf fishers.

But my father was gone and I had no foothold.

My neck tightened to keep my head above water, and twisted as another sudden locomotion struck me from behind, smashing me like a giant paw. I sprawled into the depths again, feet over head in a black cartwheel; my head struck sand. I fell over on my arm, on my back, and again over and upside down.

I came to the surface crying, put my feet down, and stood. I fell and crawled and staggered up the sand yelling *no* to my father, who was pursuing me, calling my name and swearing.

He stood over me, his hand on my shoulder. He was breathing loudly. I was shuddering. I felt him quivering in the cold.

"Rip, huh?" one of the surf fishers said. "I seen you out there."

The other one said, "This time of year."

We walked, dressed now, but damp and sandy underneath our clothes, through the evening light along the surf's edge, a golden dust rising from the breakers. The sun, which was out of sight, sank in the sand at our feet, the last of the moist dye of day. My father's strides were long and enthusiastic, and promised *You're going to like this place.*

"If it's still there, that is," he said. "I don't know if it's still even there."

He was thinking about my mother again.

"Even after we had moved away, we'd come back down for our dinners sometimes," he said. "To have the best steak and seafood dinners I ever ate. Do you like steak?"

"No."

"You don't like steak?"

I didn't answer.

The bar was through an arch to the right of the door from the beach. I could see a dining room in the back, with a stage at the far end, where tables and chairs were stored under fake palm fronds, beyond a bare, dusty dance floor reflecting the light of a jukebox living there in the dark, a glowing troll. The place was called The Palms and was on the Strand where the pier began; it had an L-shaped counter under a low roof around a large grill.

We took the one booth in the bar section, and when we sat down, I could see, out the windows over my father's head, the purple sky where the sun had gone. The table wiggled when I put my elbows on it.

"It's the wrong time of year," my father said.

He sighed, a blunt, naked statement of his disappointment. "Or early, maybe." Other than a man in the dining room, we were the only customers. "Me and your mother used to come here all the time."

Beyond the counter, by the grill, I could see a black man wearing a tall chef's hat, as if it were New Year's Eve or Halloween. He hit a flat bell with the palm of his hand as we sat down, as though summoning someone from the dining room, where Hawaiian music was playing.

My father said, "How are the steaks tonight, Cooky?"

The cook said, "Yes, sir, the steaks are real good." He rang the bell again, smiling vaguely at nothing.

"You wouldn't kid me, would you, Cooky?"

"The waitress will be right with you, sir, yes, sir."

My father reached to the counter for a menu, a typed page under clear plastic, ringed in black leatherette. "Do you like a New York steak?" he asked. "Or a Spenser steak, or a filet mignon, which is four dollars."

Then, "What's this here steak, Cooky, this here house steak, is that any good?"

The cook said, "Yes, sir, that's a real good steak." He rang the bell for the waitress again.

"Why don't we have two of them house steaks then," my father said, folding up the menu.

Then, "How do you like your steak? Rare? Medium?"

The cook hit the bell again, sharply. He had been listening to the radio when we came in, and now he turned it down.

"Medium rare or what?"

I looked around to the bar for the waitress. For some reason my father didn't seem to understand that we needed the waitress before our order was official.

"Or well done? Do you like your steak well done?"

"I guess so," I said.

"Or medium rare? That's the way I like mine."

"I guess," I said.

"Medium rare," my father said to the cook. "And we'll have two shrimp salads—I mean cocktails."

The waitress came in from the dining room. She was flipping pages in her pad as she approached us. "Salad with my prime rib," she said over her shoulder to the cook. My father repeated his order to her, adding french fries. "And I'll have a beer."

He said to me, "Do you like milk, or what do you have with your dinner at home—Hires root beer, or what?"

"Coca-Cola."

"Ginger ale," the waitress said, looking up as two men came in from the Strand.

"They only have ginger ale here," my father said.

"Ginger ale," I said, recognizing the new arrivals as the surf fishers we had seen earlier.

"He'll have milk," my father said to the waitress, who gave the cook a page from her pad and proceeded toward the surf fishers settling in at the counter, putting their tool kits on the floor by their feet, their poles against the wall. They ordered beers.

One of the surf fishers put a large red thermos onto the counter when the waitress had gone. "You want to fill this with more of that chowder there, Henry?" he said, moving the thermos to within reach of the cook. "Before we go."

My father was quiet, even when the waitress came back with everyone's beer. Then, suddenly, loudly, he said to the huddled backs of the fishermen, "Anytime I go out the only thing biting is the god-damn groupers."

The fishermen looked over from the counter. One nodded, the other shook his head. One was drinking his beer from the bottle, the other slowly pouring his into a tipped glass to regulate the foam. They were both hunched over, leaning as though into a fire; they were pulled from that warmth by the necessity of responding to my father, and I could see that they were eager to return to their comfort.

"And I'm not just only some Sunday fisherman either," my father said, as the waitress set two silver urns down before us. "I know fishing." The urns contained chipped ice and clear glass dishes of red sauce, chunks of pale flesh protruding, looking like carnage, something from first-aid class, civil defense.

My father was quiet for some time; then he turned back to me and our meal. He picked up the baby fork sticking out of the ice as though he were already angry at something. He wagged the fork at the backs of the men at the counter, at the cook prodding our steaks on the grill beyond.

"This last time," he said. "This last time—?"

The men looked around, but only briefly.

"This goddamn manta ray, this goddamn manta ray—?" My father's mouth was full. "Comes along and takes my line and snaps it right off."

"You got that chowder, Henry?" one of the surf fishers said, getting to his feet.

Once more my father turned back to me, finishing his shrimp cocktail. "Why aren't you eating?"

"I'm eating."

"I don't see you eating . . ."

I said nothing. I could hear the cook's radio program.

The other surf fisher got to his feet also as the waitress brought them their full thermos and their check. They finished their beers on their feet.

"Hey," my father said to the waitress, extending his empty beer bottle to her. "Buy those two men over there a drink, will ya?"

The surf fishers gave my father a sidelong look. One picked up his tool kit; the other went for their poles.

My father was getting to his feet, reaching for his wallet. "What are you drinking there, boys? Tell this lady here what you're drinking."

"Never mind, thanks," one of the surf fishers said.

"No, come on, I want to buy you one."

"We'll catch you another time, soldier," the other one said.

"If you reach low enough, eh?" my father said, sinking back to the booth again, laughing.

The cook hit the bell on his counter with his heavy fork. I could see that our steaks were ready.

The waitress brought my father another beer.

I watched our plates steaming on the counter.

The waitress lit a cigarette and leaned against a pillar in the back. She did not see our plates. She was taking a rest.

The surf fishers headed for the bar with their check. "Are those your friends?" I said when they had gone.

It was cold walking down the Strand from The Palms, back to the car, under the streetlamps painted black for the dimout, and to keep warm I took my arms out of my sleeves and folded them across my chest under my sweater. "You're going to stretch your sweater that way," my father said, annoyed at my posture. Or at something, someone—the surf fishers, maybe.

He drove slowly then, very carefully, and said nothing more until we were back in my neighborhood, on my street and parked before our house.

"I don't think I'll come in, though," he said. "Your mother's probably home by this time and—" The burglar alarm in the poultry shop at the corner rang briefly as the place was being shut up for the night.

"Well, it's her home," he said. "She's probably relaxing and everything. After a hard day's work and everything. Not looking forward to company or anything—some other time." As though I had asked him to come in and kept insisting. "You tell her I'll write her, though, soon as I know where I'm at and can make the allotment a little bit bigger."

He was quiet for a minute. "Which I think I ought to be able to do."

Then, "Do you need anything or anything?"

I said no.

"You're probably cold, so I don't want to keep you," he said.

"I'm not so cold," I said. "Now."

I returned my arms to my sweater sleeves, the damp of the beach gone. The light from the streetlamp, not painted over this far inland, filtering through the trees, made a pattern on the car, shadows shuddering in a slight breeze. "Where do you guess you'll go in the war?" I said.

"Well, they don't tell you that." I saw the hand of a drowning sailor sinking in the water, his stricken ship in the background. Somebody Talked! I felt un-American for having asked.

"You take care of your mother, though," my father said.

"I will," I said. But I was chilled at the possibilities inherent in this request, the prospect of such responsibility.

"Can you think of anything you need?" he said.

"A new notebook for school," I said. "That's twenty-nine cents. The good ones." I was grateful to have thought of something.

"Well, here's—fifty cents is all I got right now, I got to get gas."

He opened the glove compartment and studied his fuel gauge in the light it shed, though with the motor off this was pointless, wasn't it? "I really meant for you to keep that five dollars," he said. I had returned it to him, his deposit, when the bill for dinner had come and he was short. "But I don't want to take it back empty." He shut the glove compartment. "That wouldn't be nice." I wondered who she was, where, waiting impatiently, worried, the owner of the car.

We were quiet, my lap heavy with the damp towel wrapped around my bathing suit.

"I sure wish you could think of something I could do for you," my father said. "Besides a school notebook."

Then, "I mean, if there was any problem or anything that you were having."

"I can't think of any problems," I said.

"Well, I'm glad you haven't got any problems." In laughter he reached for my knee. I didn't move, but recoiled just the same. He withdrew his hand.

"Oh, hell, I know I'm going to be all right," he said. "I'm not the least bit concerned about that part of it."

Then, "What I mean is, I know I haven't shown you much in the way of being a father, Conrad." The amateur living of my parents, I thought. I thought of bad actors in the movies. "I mean, if today was the only chance I had and the last chance, well, I wouldn't want you to remember me—well, I'm just thankful, that's all, that I know you're in good hands. I'm grateful for that. And, I mean, I just hope you had a good time today, that's all."

"I had a real good time," I said.

"Well, good," he said. "That's what I wanted to hear."

"But I guess I better go in."

"Because if you ever felt like writing any letters to me sometime—" he said. "I sure would like that."

I was looking down the street, across the dancing light on the car hood. I could see my father in snapshots again, yellowed snapshots, dog-eared and chipped, in woolen trunks and a belt, leaning against the wall of the Ocean Arms with one of his friends from cards and high school, his moustache tilting with his grin. I could see what my mother saw in him, but I could smell the cedar of her hope chest, too, and I knew it was all in the past.

"And tell me about your grades in school and everything, and all your friends."

"I will," I said.

"You know, Conrad, what I wish you would do?"

"What?"

"I would take more interest in ball if I were you."

"In ball?"

"Sports."

I was silent.

"I'd let someone else take out the yellow flags."

"I can't," I said.

"Yes, you can," he said. "If you make up your mind."

"There's no one else to take them out."

"There is. That's foolishness, Conrad."

"The person who gets a hundred percent in fractions every day for a week takes out the yellow flags," I said. Then I said, "You get to leave class early and come back late."

"That's fine, but—"
"So you got to have mastery in fractions."
"Mastery?"
"—so only the highest kids."

He made no further attempt to touch me, and I got out of the car without touching him, though I felt some awkward debt in that regard.

I looked back once before I opened the door of our white-pillared house. He was still sitting there in the borrowed car, a black silhouette, a lawn between us. I could not be sure if he was looking at me. I was in shadow too. He didn't wave, I didn't.

I went into the house and closed the door.

THE JUNGLE OF INJUSTICE

Nora Johnson

Standing by the pool, Mandy Rivers was singing along with her own voice on stereophonic tape, watched and admired by her mother and her lover. She wore a black string bikini and an old felt fedora, and on her feet were cork-soled wedgies that laced up her ankles. She had long, honey-colored hair which flopped around as she sang, for she performed with a good deal of energy. She had a strong voice, and the double sound of it poured across the pool and patio and over the other pools and patios carved out of the side of the mountain. The arrangement was precarious, and during heavy rains (which always astonished the inhabitants), houses, or large sections of them, sometimes slid down the side and buried the property below. But John and Anita Rivers had propped up their notch with three tons of cement, which was the most that could be done short of moving down into the flats. It was worth it to live up here where there was always a breeze and the traffic on the freeway was only the faintest murmur, almost soothing, like white sound. Far below, under a perpetual dark golden haze, lay Hollywood.

Anita, stretched out in a lounge chair on the other side of the pool, watched her daughter fondly. Mandy had been endowed with every physical glory that Anita, at her age, had just missed having. Her legs were long and beautiful (Anita's were only long); her breasts were perfect, proportionate globes—inherited from some buxom ancestor, for Anita was flat-chested; the line of her gleaming tanned body from her half-naked behind up the curve of her back to her shoulder was an artist's dream. Her shoulders were straight, her neck was long; if her nose and mouth were a little large, that gave distinction to her face, set her apart from the hundreds of thousands of her kind, struggling up the same constantly narrowing ladder of success. She had a smile that could melt the cruelest heart, and that, along with her considerable talent as singer, dancer, and actress, plus her years of training, gave Anita hope for her in what she knew was a jungle of injustice. It was a world Anita could negotiate fairly well, and John excellently, but she feared for Mandy, who was only twenty-three, and whose dear, funny way of putting her foot in her mouth could be disastrous with the wrong person, and whose tendency to lateness could cost her a job.

Sprawled on a towel at her feet, Mandy's lover, Flash—*Flash*—smiled up at her through his aviator glasses, missing not a curve or a wiggle. He wore a small, shiny, white bikini, and he lounged alongside the pool in almost permanent appreciation of the situation he found himself in, one which Anita regarded alternately as natural and incredible. John thought Flash should be thrown the hell out, but Anita, first at Mandy's urging and then for her own reasons, kept staying his hand.

"They'll just go live in some rathole together," she told him.

"Well, then there's got to be some deadline. I'll put up with him for another week, period. Does he ever have any auditions?"

"He had one yesterday. He didn't get the job."

"Naturally not."

It was natural, inevitable, and annoying that Flash's career didn't move, but it was natural and understandable that Mandy was having a difficult time. There were a million Flashes, there was only one Mandy. To Anita, an eastern emigrant, Flash was some strange indigenous fauna. John had grown up in southern California, and didn't find anything remarkable about him, but Anita, even after twenty-five years in the southland, was still fascinated and horrified by that quality known as *laid-back*. Flash's presence in this family of achievers was disturbing; he was a lazy butterfly in a colony of ants. When they all got up at seven in the morning, John to be on the set at eight, and Anita to be in her office in the Valley, and Mandy prodded into action for a class when she had one or an early audition, Flash lazed naked on the twin bed he and Mandy shared in her room or floated in the Jacuzzi at the far end of the pool. Mandy would kiss him goodbye tenderly before jumping into her Fiat to go to dance class, and he would frequently be there when John and Anita got home. What he did in the meantime was unclear—the occasional audition, some surfing, a certain amount of hanging around the right places hoping to be noticed.

"Noticed for what?" John asked.

"Oh . . . just noticed," Anita replied. She and John were old-fashioned believers in hard work, and Anita particularly had gone to great lengths to instill this value in Mandy—not so easy in a place where success (whatever that meant) did often come for not much more than simply being noticed at the right moment.

"But it doesn't last," she had told her daughter. "The really great careers, every one, were built on dogged determination and an obsession to be better than anybody else. There is a certain rough justice, you'll see."

"But Tina Reynolds has already done two *Barettas* and a Mary Tyler Moore special and she's a no-talent screw-up."

"You can never afford to sit back and say you're better than the next girl. Assume she's better and see what you can learn from her."

Anita had learned this, as she had learned a great many things, from John. At Mandy's age, she had lived in a sleazy little two-room apartment on Vine Street with a Texas beauty-contest winner named Gardenia Vance. Anita, who had worked all her life for the things she had, never took Gardenia seriously until she got a part that Anita wanted.

"But it's crazy," she had said to John, whom she was "dating" at the time. "We aren't the same type at all. She's Mitzi Gaynor. I'm Rosalind Russell. Besides, I'm ten times as talented and I work ten times as hard."

John said, "She has something you don't, or she wouldn't have gotten the part. My advice to you is, find out what it is."

John Rivers was so serious and intelligent, so unlike the rest of the men she had met in California, that she took his advice to heart. She examined Gardenia as she lay sprawled on the couch covering her nails with hot-pink polish. She watched her panther walk as she went into the kitchen in her blue rayon negligee, flicking on the radio as she filled the basket of the percolator. She listened to Gardenia's stupefy-ingly dull phone conversations and her brainless comments on the state of the world and her flutelike soprano in the shower. She looked at Gardenia as she wandered naked around the tiny bedroom, fishing through the piles of clothing for a clean bra, digging her toes with her hot-pink nails into her marabou-trimmed mules, admiring herself in the mirror.

One day, with a dreadful sinking feeling, Anita realized what Gar-denia had—she had everything. Not only was she beautiful, but because of a certain unselfconscious detachment, she allowed you to stare at her without feeling like a voyeur. It was a trick she played on you, or a deal you made together. Every star that Anita could think of engaged you in the same complicity, or had the same self-framing quality, for it was quite unconscious. You couldn't take your eyes off her. It didn't matter that she was a moron and could hardly read a line—heroines were morons in those days. Thin-faced, intelligent girls like Anita were always the wise-cracking best friend who couldn't get a man, and they got parts only if they had a good comic talent. Girls like Gardenia became stars.

But Gardenia didn't care; after the picture came out she married somebody and went off to live in a trailer camp near Thousand Oaks. She had had very good reviews, and Anita, who had long gotten over being angry about losing the part, was now angry at her for not using what she saw as a precious gift. A couple of years later, when Gardenia came down for a visit, she told Anita that she had never believed she could be a success and wanted to get out while she was still ahead, rather than end up dead in the pool of the Chateau Marmont.

Now that treasured quality could be seen in her own daughter, as unmistakable to Anita as a caul. She watched as Mandy finished the song and dove into the pool, shoes and all, followed by Flash. Together they splashed and plunged about in a giggling effort to get Mandy's shoe-ribbons unwound from her legs and the shoes off her feet, which Flash tried to do with his perfect white teeth while Mandy, unbal-anced, ducked and sputtered. It was a Sunday afternoon and the mountainside was quiet except for other splashings in other pools and the occasional shift of gears as a car roared up the steep road. The flame trees rustled and billowing purple bougainvillea on the roof moved in the slight breeze. John, a director, was at a preview in Santa

Barbara. The moments of rest were few and dearly bought, and Anita had worked so hard for most of her life that she hardly knew what to do with them when she had them. Even now she had to make a conscious effort not to get up, go inside, and work on the script she was supposed to be revising. When the telephone rang she started to jump up, but Mandy was already out of the pool, one heavy clog still flopping from her ankle by its ribbons. Mandy opened the big glass sliding door that led into the living room and picked up the phone, turning her back to the patio and closing the glass door behind her. Anita made herself lie back again and Flash slowly swam toward her. He leaned his elbows on the side of the pool and smiled up at her.

"Want me to turn on the sprinklers, Anita?"

She shook her head and smiled musingly at him. Strangely enough she liked Flash, disapproval struggled with a little core of affection. He seemed to be entirely without guile or suspicion. If life were like her television scripts, she and Flash would sleep together, thereby destroying her marriage and her relationship with her daughter. Then he would callously go off to wreck another home. Flash was such a willing and good-natured houseguest (though the term didn't seem quite accurate) that she imagined he could be seduced, if that was what she wanted of him, out of sheer politeness, the desire not to be rude to his hostess. But Anita's hungers lay elsewhere, and Flash tried to please only by watering the garden in the late afternoon and occasionally straining the leaves and bugs off the surface of the pool, as well as being agreeable to his elders.

"Thanks, I did it before."

"You're going to have a few tomatoes out there," said Flash. He had a pleasant cowboy twang which went oddly with his bleached hair and chest-bangles. "And some more of those baby lettuces are ready."

"I don't know why I bother with that vegetable patch."

"Just one more thing to fuss with, Anita." He had her number. "I went back East last year," he went on. "Visited a guy I know in New York. Man, I was glad to get out of there. Everybody was in too much of a hurry."

"That's how they get things done."

Flash grinned and suddenly submerged. She watched the water close over him and then he surfaced again in another spot, still grinning. "You got to go with the flow, Anita."

"If John and I had gone with the flow all these years you wouldn't be splashing around in that pool."

Flash laughed. "I don't *need* this pool," he said. "I like it, but it sure isn't worth killing myself for."

Behind the door Mandy put the receiver down and went over to the bar on the other side of the room. She took a handful of ice cubes out of the plastic bucket, put them in a glass, opened a can of Fresca and poured it in. Then she took the glass to the telephone and continued talking. She sat on the back of the sofa, legs hanging down, picking with one hand at the shoe-ribbons. Finally she hung up, opened the sliding door, and came out onto the patio, where she lay down in the lounge chair next to Anita. She rested the Fresca on her satiny brown stomach, where tiny hairs marched in a delicate golden line, and closed her eyes.

Anita had grown up in Connecticut, in a place where communication was as sharp and clear as the winter air. In her parents' white clapboard house there were bulletin boards, note pads with pencils next to them, magnets on the refrigerator to hold messages, and a telephone in the small front hall where all conversations could be easily overheard. Everyone announced his or her comings and goings—"I'm going to town to get eggs, back in half an hour." "That was Jane on the phone—she's returning those books on her way to the dentist. Oh, and she said Bob Davis is coming next week, his mother's seriously ill." The conversation at dinner was mostly about what everyone had done all day—dull though it might be, it was considered to have a place simply because it had happened.

"I'm going in search of stimulating conversation," Anita had said when she left. Of course that wasn't true; she was going in search of acting jobs. But she assumed that people who did interesting things would talk about them in an interesting way. John did, about being a director, but he had said that when it came to making pictures, the single perfectly chosen action could be more telling than the best dialogue. He told her that after she had given up trying to be an actress and had decided to try her hand at script-writing.

She watched Mandy, waiting for the announcement that never came of its own accord. Then, as always, she gently pried.

"Was it anything about Bronstein?"

Bronstein held Mandy's fate in his hand: he was considering her for a part in a feature film. He was "hot," he was "top enchilada" at Fox. The mention of his name broke glass at twenty feet. The air shimmered, and Mandy said nothing for a moment. Her eyes pressed closed more tightly, and then she sighed and reached under the chair, groping around on the concrete for her pack of thin black cigarettes.

"Tomorrow," she said, without opening her eyes. Slowly she pulled one of the cigarettes out of the package and lit it, then inhaled and blew out a great lungful of smoke in a kind of sigh.

"Oh, Mandy, darling." Anita excitedly reached over and pressed her daughter's inert hand.

Flash had gotten out of the pool and now he walked over to where they were sitting, sprinkling diamond drops of water around. He bent down and kissed Mandy's silken middle.

"You feel good about that, baby?" he asked.

"Sure," Mandy said from behind her sunglasses. "I love to have my head chopped off."

The lighting in the kitchen was indirect, coming from under the cupboards, and it created a bright circle at the end of the long, dark living room. Outside the rough surface of the pool water picked up little points of light from the interior rooms, all of which opened with sliding glass doors onto the patio. There were tatami blinds for privacy, but Mandy's were open, and as Anita put the few dishes in the dishwasher she could see her daughter sprawled on the bed watching television. She had eaten alone. Flash had gone out to meet some people who "might help" and Mandy had said she was tired and didn't want dinner. Mandy's face was devoid of expression, her room a spectacular mess, and Anita was glad that fastidious John wasn't around to see it. She would pick it up later tonight, or first thing in the morning.

Anita closed the dishwasher and sat down at the butcher-block table with a cup of coffee. At the same moment Mandy flicked off the TV and walked toward the kitchen. She was wearing a white terry cloth robe, her hair untidily tied back with a ribbon, and she looked rather sleepy and cross.

"Is there anything to eat?" she asked, opening the refrigerator.

"I'll fix you something."

"Oh, I'll do it." She took out the makings of an enormous Dagwood sandwich, and Anita smiled. "God, I feel really weird. Dizzy, kind of. Maybe I'm just hungry." She piled salami, cheese, lettuce, pickles, and hard-boiled egg slices on a piece of bread and put mayonnaise on top.

"What do you have to do for the audition?" Anita asked. "Read a scene?"

"I guess so." Mandy's voice was low as she poked the monstrous sandwich together and opened a can of Fresca. Then she laughed. "Maybe I'll get laryngitis again. Remember that time in Pasadena, at that amateur night, and the time at CBS when I couldn't warble about the margarine?" Her eyes were bright as she took a huge bite of the sandwich. She chewed and then gulped some of it down. "I'll never forget Jimmy What's-his-face's expression when I opened my mouth and out came this croak."

Exasperation settled over Anita's head like a lowering cloud. "My God, Mandy. You laugh at the strangest things. Now if you're nervous, I don't blame you a bit. When I had my audition with Zanuck . . ."

Mandy's eyes glazed over. "I'm not nervous," she said. She held the monstrous sandwich in her graceful hands, one piece of lettuce dangling down between two long, lacquered nails.

"How about a glass of wine, to relax?" Anita submitted to a violent urge to get up and move around. She took out a jug of wine and poured them each a glass.

Mandy said, "It's not such a big deal."

"Jesus," Anita said, "it is *so* a big deal."

"But I mean, if there wasn't any audition on Monday, we'd all live, wouldn't we? We wouldn't just lie down and die or anything, would we? We'd keep on going to the studio and swimming in the pool and driving on the freeways, we'd eat and sleep, we might even be able to *smile*. The sun would rise and set, wouldn't it?" Mandy's voice was accusing, but her eyes were lowered. "I'll be all right, Mom. Okay? Everything'll be just *fine*."

The next morning John said, "Flash has to go."

John was a bald, fattish, serious man with sunbaked skin, full of energy and an exuberance that was a life force to the rest of them. As he finished dressing, Anita said worriedly, looking out of the bathroom, "All right. But not until after she sees Bronstein."

"Oh, is that this week? All the more reason he should go right away."

"Let him stay two more days, John."

"I don't want him here another hour."

"But she needs him somehow. He's a nice kid. He's sweet, really."

John laughed. "I told you that when he first came. But enough's enough."

Through the blinds a shadow moved. Anita went over and looked out, but no one was there. The surface of the water was ruffled by tiny breezes and a yellow towel lay in a soggy ball. Under one of the lounge chairs were a plastic glass and an ashtray full of cigarette butts. John looked over her shoulder.

"When are you going to make her pick up after herself?"

"I can't *make* her do anything. She's twenty-three."

"She's a slob," said John cheerfully, going out into the hall. "Hey, Mandy! Come and have breakfast with me!"

Anita finished dressing hurriedly and went down the hall to Mandy's room. Delicately, she knocked on the door and waited—for order, for a pretense of respectability—and to her surprise Mandy opened the door fully dressed in jeans and a plaid shirt.

"Daddy wants Flash to leave," Anita said. "I'll try to get him to change his mind."

After a slight pause Mandy said, "Never mind. It's all right."

"I'll try to talk him into a few more days."

"Oh, don't bother, Mom. Let's not hassle about it."

"But don't you want . . .?"

"Flash knows he's supposed to go, just stop worrying. Okay?"

She was elusive, this prized daughter, as hard to catch as a raindrop and as strangely, frustratingly formless. When she was small she had begged for a certain talking doll that was exhaustively advertised on television, and after Anita had driven all over Los Angeles to find it (supplies having been snapped up quickly), Mandy received it listlessly and said she wanted a rubber raft for the pool.

"Where is Flash?" Anita asked suspiciously.

"He's out somewhere." Mandy pulled a comb through her hair. She didn't invite Anita into the room, rather in the most subtle way blocked her every time she tried to move forward. Anita felt a surge of unexpected disappointment.

"Will he be back?"

"Oh sure. He wants to thank you for being so nice to him."

"I'm sorry," Anita said. "I'm sorry he can't stay."

"Mom, it's all *right!*" Mandy's tone was impatient. "I don't blame Daddy or anything. It's cool, okay?" She edged out the door and closed it behind her. "Had breakfast yet?"

Why doesn't she fight? Anita wondered, sitting at the kitchen table with her coffee, while John made them all an omelet. Her own growing up had been shaped by the violent pull away from her parents and the fighting off of their values, and so, as a matter of fact, had John's. Why was this child so different? Mandy's mouth was stretched over a piece of Granola toast while she read, with the intense preoccupation of the young, the entertainment section of the Los Angeles *Times.* Anita relaxed a little, her tight shoulders lowered. Mandy had her own style, that was all, and a more mature one than hers had been. She saved her energy for work and she worked hard. She talked less. Maybe she and John pressed her too much, she had to be allowed to become her own person. Anita looked at Mandy and asked silently, What do you want of us? Do you love us? Hate us? Can I do anything for you? And if so, won't you tell me what it is?

"How many girls are auditioning?" asked John from the stove.

"Just three," Mandy said.

"Wow. It's that close."

Mandy put down her toast. "I can't eat," she said. "I'm sorry, Daddy, I don't want any." He stood over her with the omelet pan.

"Are you all right, baby?"

"I'm fine. But I don't even want to *smell* it."

John gave Mandy's share to Anita. It was a glory of mushrooms, cottage cheese, and parsley, and she didn't want it either, but she began eating it anyway.

"Do you want me to go with you?" Anita asked.

"*No,*" Mandy said, "and for Christ's sake don't just happen to drop by."

"Is Flash going?"

Mandy's green eyes met hers. "Flash says screw the whole thing," she said, and before they could say anything, she turned and left the room.

By three o'clock Anita knew she could do no more work that day, and she left to go home. There was no way she could spy on Bronstein without looking like an ass, or without Mandy's finding out, and the frustration of the day lay curled up in the pit of her stomach in a small tight ball. She would have stayed home, had not John almost pushed her out the door. The driveway of the house was visible shortly after leaving the Hollywood freeway, and as Anita's BMW crept down the white street late that afternoon she looked through the tops of the eucalyptus trees to see who was home. John's Mercedes wasn't there, nor was Mandy's Fiat, but Flash's Mustang was.

She parked and went quickly inside. The house was dark in contrast to the glare outside, a place to hide. In the hall stood Flash's suitcase. She went down the hall to Mandy's room, which was empty and quite neat. The bookshelves were empty, the bare sheets smooth, the blinds closed.

She opened the glass door and went out onto the patio. The pool was quiet, sun-dappled turquoise, a vast, opaque eye that gave away nothing. She walked around it to the living room doors and slowly opened them. It took a moment for her eyes to adjust to the darkness, and then she saw Flash sitting on the sofa. He wore white jeans and a Hawaiian shirt knotted over his middle, and he held a can of Sprite.

"Hi," he said.

She looked at him in his gay getup—except he wasn't gay, he was her daughter's passionate lover, given to lying around in the sun with lightener in his hair. Slowly he stood up.

"Did she go to the audition?" Anita demanded.

"I haven't the faintest idea."

"Damn you," she said, "I don't believe you."

He looked at her in surprise. "Man, I can't help *what* you believe. I don't *know* where she is." She stared at him uncertainly. "Her suitcase is gone. And her drawers are empty. Go see for yourself." While she did so he took another drink from the Sprite can and lit a cigarette with John's leather table lighter.

Anita came back slowly and sat down in a chair. She felt weak and faint, and there was a dreadful pressure in her throat, the pressure of imminent tears. He wasn't kidding. Only a week ago they had all had dinner together, the four of them. She had cooked steaks outside on the grill and Flash had made the salad out of vegetables from the garden, their own tomatoes and cucumbers and parsley grown in a sandy patch on the mountainside. John had told stories and they had drunk two bottles of wine, and Mandy had laughed and laughed.

"You did it," Anita said, and her voice broke. "You never wanted her to audition with Bronstein. 'Flash says screw the whole thing.' With one eloquent sentence you destroyed everything, so she could go with the flow like the rest of you. Damn you, why did you ever come here?"

Flash, at the bar with his hand in a can of peanuts, turned and stared at her. "I didn't want her to audition? You think I'm crazy? I *pushed* her. You think I like sleeping on the beach, spending my time with losers?"

Anita said slowly, "But didn't you say . . . ?"

"I never said it. She *wanted* me to say it. She'd say, 'This thing with Bronstein is making me crazy. I can't sleep. I have pains in my chest. I'm not right for the part. If I don't get it my mother'll kill me.' I said, 'If you don't go, *I'll* kill you.' We're a good pair, Anita. We drove her right out of the house." Anita, sitting in the darkness, was silent. "Listen, there's a million like me out there. But Mandy's something special. I'd have to be *nuts* to want to stop her." He looked at her. "Oh, come on, don't cry. Kids disappear all the time. She's probably in Venice." He came over to her. "Listen, I want to thank you for putting me up all this time. You and your husband and Mandy are the first things in this town that didn't turn out *rotten*."

"I'm sorry," she said, and her voice shook. "I'm really sorry."

"Hey, nothing to be sorry about, man." He looked around the pleasant room and gave a small, involuntary sigh. "Well, I'd better split."

"Don't you want to . . . wait for her?" The abruptness of this announcement and the ease with which he was ready to depart their lives was a little startling. "Would you like a drink? I mean, she might phone. She might even come back." She turned on the lamp. "You know, she might even have *gone* to Bronstein and not want us to know."

Flash looked at her for a moment. "You're crazy," he said, matter-of-factly. He got out two glasses and began putting ice in them from the ice bucket, and then Scotch—he knew what she liked to drink. "Some cheese?" He went into the kitchen and got a piece of Brie out of the refrigerator, and put it on a plate with crackers. "It's always so damn hard to leave," he said.

The last fiery rays of the sun burned over the Pacific and across the white beach, so wide and magnificent that it made the tiny, rocky little edgings in the East seem hardly worthy of the name. The sand was dented with thousands of footprints, and a few late stragglers were gathering up towels to go home. Along the boardwalk floated the roller-skaters on their plastic skates, bending and dipping, ducking back and forth like ghostly birds in the fading light. The oldest people in sight were a pair of silver-haired, bronze-skinned gays strolling along the boardwalk, but everyone else was young and lovely limbed, children playing at dusk in some never-never land.

Mandy left her Fiat in a parking lot and walked along the boardwalk for a while, then sat down on the edge and looked out over the beach. She lit a joint and smoked it slowly, enjoying it as she enjoyed the warmth of the fading sun and the heat of the sand between her bare toes, the smell of the sea and of french fries from a fast-food stand. She felt as though the cold of the pool were being baked out of her, slowly thawing whatever it was that made her feel so hard and chilly in the daytime and so terrified at night—that sapphire coolness she dipped in again and again until she was coated all over with something she didn't understand. In a few minutes she'd get a hamburger from the stand, and some of the fries, and after she had eaten she'd go and find Liz, or Ralph and Dicky, and stay with them for a while till she got her head together. Not too long—you had to be careful about staying with people too long—it could do funny things to you, as it had to Flash. She knew that, and now she also knew the precious power of splitting.

She leaned back against one of the pilings and smiled, her eyes half closed. Somebody's radio was playing Billy Joel's "Movin' Out." The longer you stayed the harder it was to leave, the more you hated yourself for staying there, helpless and half strangled and exhausted from the effort of not telling them to shove it. When the time came to get in touch with her parents, in a few months or whatever it took, her explanation would be very simple: "You wore me out." Not that they'd have any idea what she was talking about. But possibly, if she worked on it in the months to come, by that time she'd have a better way of putting it—though it was stupid to think that at twenty-three there had to be an explanation.

She looked down the boardwalk, half expecting to see her mother barreling along in her big sunglasses, her well-cut pants, her gigantic leather handbag full of checks and credit cards, her mouth pulled into that tense smile. How had she gotten like that? She called it "drive," and said the rest of the Connecticut relatives had it too, but none of them were as bad as Anita. If that was drive, Mandy didn't want it, though she didn't know what she wanted instead—except, at the moment, to sit here and get stoned. She hadn't done it for a long time, since about three years ago when she used to smoke dope all the time to get her mother, before she had become a "serious actress."

She got up and went over to the hamburger stand and bought herself some dinner, and as she sat down to eat it she felt a little twinge of loneliness. She would sleep alone tonight, for the first time in weeks—alone on somebody's couch or in somebody's sleeping bag. It would be so easy for Flash to find her, if he wanted to. She was in this obvious place, hanging out like a sore thumb. Part of it was, probably, a test—the kind most people never dared make. She thought how strange it was that the strongest statements people made to each other were silent—acts or the absence of acts—and how you knew in some gut way what they meant before your head understood them. He might come, it was possible—just stroll along the walk in his white jeans and say, "Hey, babe, let's find some place of our own to live. I don't care if we're poor." Now that was the real fantasy, the ultimate dream.

THE WOMEN WHO WALK

Nancy Huddleston Packer

In the days right after Malcolm left her, Marian began to notice the women who walked the deserted streets near the university campus. They were a flash of color in the brilliant June sunlight at a distant intersection, a single shape thrusting through the shadows of the giant sycamores along the sidewalk. She did not at first differentiate one from another. She was too absorbed in her own suffering. Images of Malcolm that last day spun through her mind. The thin ankle over the thin knee as he sat on his luggage in the front hall. The silver lighter touched to the black cigarette. Well, Marian, he said. She pulled the car over to the curb and gave herself up to the blurring tears, the sudden thunder in her chest.

Soon, quieter, she looked around at the empty streets. Had anyone seen her? She saw in the distance a lonely figure, walking, walking.

Two weeks had passed and she had not yet told the children. She had said, "He's out of town, he's at a conference, he's giving a lecture, he'll be back." One evening as they sat in the dying sun in the patio, Joseph, who was eleven, said,

"When? When will he be back?"

A bluebird squawked in the high branches of the silver maple. "Your father . . ." she began. She felt suffocated by the heat in her throat. Molly began to cry and buried her face in Marian's lap. Joseph grew red and he ran into the house. Later that night, Marian called Malcolm at the backstreet hotel where he had taken a room. "I can't tell them," she managed to say, and quickly hung up.

Next day, Malcolm carried the children away for lunch. After that, each evening he spoke to them on the telephone. On the following Saturday, he took Joseph to a Giants game. On Sunday, he and Molly visited a horse farm in the hills. Marian longed to know what he had said, whether he had spoken of her. But they did not tell her.

Finally she asked. Molly grew somber, hooded, afraid. Joseph became moody and glared at the floor. Molly said,

"Daddy says we're not to carry tales back and forth."

"You're my children," she said.

"His too," said Joseph, "just as much as yours."

She felt an explosion and a wind and a fire, but she sat silent and staring.

The first few weeks, women she had counted as friends called her on the phone, invited her to lunch, came by to visit. From behind the living room curtain, she saw them walk up the drive, often in tennis whites, practicing an overhead slam or a low backhand as they waited for her to answer their knock. When she opened the door, their faces were grave. They sat on the sofa and put their sneakers on the coffee table and frowned and shook their heads in sympathy.

She could not speak of him. She tried to talk of other things, but all paths through her mind led back to the injustice she had suffered, of which she could not speak. The silence soon weighed too heavily on them, and their faces grew round and flat as moons, and pale. They knew they could not help her. They must leave now, they said, but they would return. They wished her well. They were her friends. She heard their tires sighing as they escaped down the street.

They were not her friends. They were the wives of his friends, the mothers of his children's friends, the neighbors who were no more than friends of his house. She had no friends. She would never be able to speak of herself, to share herself with friends. He had exiled her to an island of silence. She stood up and began to move around the room, shifting ashtrays, picking lint from the floor. She felt a restless, angry energy gathering in her.

During the summer, Marian frequently saw the woman in the large black coat walking rapidly on the outskirts of the university or the residential streets bordering the business area of the town. She thought the woman was an older faculty wife who apparently spent her leisure doing good works, carrying petitions door-to-door or collecting for the Cancer Society or the Red Cross.

The woman wore sandals and heavy dark socks, a floppy straw hat, and the black coat. The coat was shaped like a wigwam, with sloping shoulders and a wide skirt that struck her just above the ankles. Marian thought the woman wore it like a burnoose, a protection against the dog-day heat of late August and September. The woman was obviously a character, a throwback to the days when faculty and faculty wives were rather expected to be eccentric. Marian liked her, liked her independence and freedom from vanity. She kept her eyes down, as if she were afraid she might stumble as she rushed along in her waddling, slue-footed gait.

One hot day in late September as Marian waited for a stoplight, the woman in the black coat started across the street in front of the car. Marian had never seen her so close before. She was much younger than she looked from a distance, about thirty-five or so, Marian's age. And still quite pretty, with a high-bridged, delicate nose and delicate fine lips and a soft-looking pale skin. When she came even with the front of the car, she abruptly twisted her head and glanced at Marian through the windshield. As their gazes met, Marian knew that she had seen the woman before—how long ago, under what circumstances she could not recall, perhaps at a university party, a meeting, at the sandbox or the swings of the city park. She would never forget those startled pale gray eyes.

Marian waved but the woman ducked her head again and hurried on to the sidewalk. Watching her—the hunched tension of her neck and shoulders, the awkward, powerful, rushing gait—Marian felt that when they had met, they had been drawn together in one of those rare moments of intense though inexplicable intimacy. And now Marian longed to recapture the strange, treasured feeling.

She drove around the block and pulled into a driveway in the woman's path. She got out and stood leaning on the fender, waiting, smiling. The woman walked straight at her, heedless, but at the last moment, without lifting her gaze from the ground, veered clumsily aside. Marian reached out and touched her shoulder. "Wait," she said. "Don't I know you?"

The woman stopped and after a long moment lifted her head. Her gaze whipped from Marian to the sky to the trees. She pulled her coat collar up around her face. Marian said, "What is it? Can I help you?"

The woman threw back her head, like a colt shying, and opened her mouth. Marian heard the sound—distant, muted—of a strangled voice and she thought the voice said, "I'm so very cold." For an instant the woman stared at Marian, and then she lowered her head and rushed down the street.

Malcolm came late one evening to settle details. He sat in the red leather chair he had always sat in. He looked handsome, tanned, his graying hair tousled and longer than he had ever worn it. When he asked how everything was, he was charming and attentive, his smile warm and pleasing, as if she were his dinner partner. She sat on the edge of the wing chair, her knees close, her hands kneading each other, and told him the lie he wanted to hear. Yes, everything was fine. He nodded at her approvingly, no longer angry and irritated with her.

"Well, now," he began, and leaned forward. She did not want to hear it all just then, and she stood up.

"I'll get some coffee," she said. "Turkish coffee," she pleaded. He sighed and nodded.

She went into the kitchen and turned on the faucet. She waited for her heartbeat to slow. When she heard his footsteps, she busied herself with cups and saucers. He stood in the doorway and gazed around him, smiling at the wall decorated with dinner plates from different countries.

"I always liked that one," he said, pointing at a Mexican plate he had brought to her from Mexico City where he had gone for a conference. But, he hastened to assure her, she needn't worry, all he wanted were a few mementos, keepsakes that had been in his family for a long time. The tintype of his great-grandmother and of course its antique frame and the silver ladle his great-aunt had saved from the Yankees. He smiled. Everything else was hers, absolutely, he didn't want anything else. Nothing.

Nothing? she wanted to ask. Nothing? No memento, no keepsake of our fifteen years together?

"Nothing besides coffee?" she asked. "Some fruit?" She picked up an immense pineapple from the straw basket on the counter. It was just ripe, soft and yellow. He had always loved pineapples. "It's just ripe," she said. "I'll cut it for you." When he shook his head, she held it close to his face. "Smell it," she pleaded.

"I do not want to smell it, for God's sake," he said. For an instant his composure dropped away and she saw what she had remembered all these months: the rigid shoulders, the pinched mouth, the hard, irritated eyes. She could easily drag the sharp points of the pineapple across his face. She watched little specks of blood ooze from his skin, swell into a long thick ruby streamer that marked his cheek like a savage decoration. She put the pineapple down and handed him a cup of coffee. Back in the living room, he sat again in the red chair and put his feet up on the matching ottoman.

Molly and Joseph were already in bed, but when they heard his voice they ran into the living room. Joseph stood in the doorway, smiling quizzically. Molly climbed over Malcolm's legs and onto his lap. He set the coffee down and Molly burrowed under his arm, into his armpit. He stroked her hair. Marian felt an uneasiness, a tension, and then she was suddenly shaken by a yearning—to be held, to be stroked—and she felt dizzy, as if she might faint.

"Run along now," said Malcolm to the children, "and I'll see you Sunday." As the children left the room, he explained. "They're coming to my new place for lunch on Sunday. If that's all right with you?" She nodded. "Did you know I had a place? It's not exactly elegant, but I like it much better than the hotel. I like having a place of my own."

"This is yours." She slid off her chair and dropped to her knees beside him. She pressed her face against his thigh. He did not move beneath her caresses. When she looked up, she saw the prim set of his lips. She stood up.

"Now about the arrangements," he said. "Here's what I thought, but I want you to be thoroughly satisfied."

He pulled a folded-up piece of paper from his wallet. It was covered with words and figures in his neat small handwriting. She saw the words "Insurance" and "Automobile."

"You really should get a lawyer," he said. She seized upon the kindness in his voice.

"Who should I get?"

He drew one of the black cigarettes from the box. He tamped it against the back of his hand and lighted it with his silver lighter. After a moment, he said, "You've got to start making that kind of decision for yourself, you know."

"Don't you see that it's too late?" she whispered.

He stood up, tapped ashes into the ashtray, drank off the last of the coffee, gathered together his cigarettes and lighter and wallet. "You're a perfectly competent woman," he said, "as no one knows better than I. After all," he went on, smiling at her, his voice remote, jocular, false, "you managed to get me through graduate school. I don't forget that. I'll always be grateful for that."

She went to the window and stared out at the darkness. "Then how can you desert me like this?" Her voice was hoarse, choked.

"There's no point going over this again," he said in an exasperated voice. "I know it's right for both of us."

She heard his sigh, the sound of the ottoman scraping over the floor as he pushed it aside, his footsteps brushing across the rug. The sky was cloudless, moonless, starless. The leaves of the eucalyptus shivered. Dark spaces opened within her. She spoke softly to the windowpane.

"Can't you stay just tonight?"

"Now, Marian," he said, moving into the hallway.

"Just to hold me," she whispered, "in the dark, a last time."

"Good night," he called from the front door. Soon the lights of his car vanished into the dark. She stood at the window a moment longer. She felt the agitation rising, the fury, the rush of movement through her body. She felt the hardness gather in the center of her chest and she could make no sound.

The rains came early, and by the middle of November the ground was soggy. For days the sky was close in and gray. Through the autumn Marian had become aware of the woman in white, seen as a flash of light out of the corner of her eye as she drove along. The woman was probably a nurse, cutting through the campus on her way to the university hospital. She was about five nine or five ten and very very thin, like a wraith. She was swaybacked and as she walked she lifted her knees high, her feet far out in front of her, like a drum majorette on parade. The knobby joints between her long thin bones made her look even more awkward and absurd. Yet she walked without self-consciousness, head high, as if she had better thoughts to ponder than the amusement of people driving by in their big cars. This lack of vanity was one of the characteristics shared by the women who walked. That, and the vigorous, almost heedless, way they moved.

Marian had only seen the wraith—as she came to think of her—in the vicinity of the university until a drizzly Sunday afternoon in early December when she saw her on a downtown street. The children had eaten lunch with Malcolm and she had contrived to pick them up. Malcolm lived in a cottage behind a large Spanish house close by the freeway. Often she had driven past and stared down the overgrown path that ran alongside the house. Baskets of ferns and wandering Jew hung from the roof of the little dilapidated porch, and there were bright flowered curtains behind the windows. Though appealing in the way that dark, shabby little cottages sometimes are, the charm of this one seemed utterly foreign to everything she believed she knew of Malcolm's taste. He had always insisted that their house be neat, clean, sparse. Something had changed in him, and she thought that if only she could see inside the place, she might at last understand what had gone wrong between them. And so she had told him that she was going on an errand and since she didn't want the children to return to an empty house, she would pick them up.

But even before she had turned off the ignition, she saw Molly running down the path toward her, and Joseph sauntering behind. Malcolm, in a bright green sweatshirt and jeans, stood on the porch and waved to her as if she were only the mother of children visiting at his house. She was filled with shame at her scheme, and with disappointment at its failure, and then with relief.

Joseph got in the front seat. He looked sullen, moody, as he often did after the Sundays with his father. Molly climbed in back and grasped Marian's ears and said, "Giddap." Marian patted Molly's hands. And she said, "I'll bet anything you had—let's see—bologna on store-bought bread and Coke. And of course Oreos." The thought of Malcolm's providing such a dreary lunch gave her pleasure, and revving the motor she laughed aloud.

"No," said Joseph. He crossed his arms and dropped his head.

"We had chicken with some kind of orange stuff all over it," said Molly. "I didn't like it but that lady said I had to eat it since she made it special."

Joseph turned to the backseat. "You're stupid," he said. "Nobody can trust you, you're a baby."

Marian thrust her foot against the accelerator and the car jumped from the curb, bucked, almost died, caught, sped away. That lady. A woman. No one had told her there was a woman. But who would? Who did she have to tell her anything? Yet she should have known. She was the stupid one. The secrecy. The children's silence. The shabby place with its shabby charm. The ferns. The bright curtains. And behind the curtains, a woman peering out at her, perhaps laughing at her. The rejected wife. The discard. Garbage.

"I didn't mean to tell," said Molly. She patted Marian's shoulder. "I'm sorry."

Marian drove in silence, beneath the immense white oaks, past the fine old mansions, past the run-down rooming houses and flats. No life stirred. Even the downtown streets were empty. The car moved through empty gray streets. The day was cold, damp, dark. She saw a flash of shimmering white. Without thinking, she said,

"One of the walkers."

The woman strutted toward them on her long heron legs. She had on a pale pink jacket over her white dress. As the car drew near Marian saw that the jacket was short-sleeved, that it barely covered the woman's breasts, that it was loose-fitting, flimsy, crocheted. That it was a bed jacket. As Marian stared, the woman turned toward her. Her eyes were narrowed, glittering, defiant. She grinned fiercely.

"What walker?" asked Joseph. He dropped his feet from the dashboard and sat up to see. Marian pressed the accelerator and the car jerked forward and threw Joseph against the seat.

"Never mind. We passed her." Marian flushed with embarrassment. She felt she had somehow humiliated the woman in front of Joseph and Molly.

"I saw her," said Molly. "She had on pink and white. Joseph just doesn't look."

Joseph spun toward her. "You shut up, you shut up," he said. His voice trembled. Marian touched his shoulder.

"Please don't quarrel," she said.

He pulled away from her hand. "I hate you and Daddy," he shouted. "You don't care about us, you don't care what you do to us."

"Mommy didn't do it, did you?" said Molly. "It was Daddy and that lady."

"He wouldn't have just left," said Joseph. "It was her fault, too."

Hot moisture bubbled into her eyes, and shrill sounds rose into her ears. She pulled the car over to the curb. Now she would tell them. Her fault? Her fault too? Now she would unleash her suffering, she would engulf them in her anguish. She would tell them, she would tell them. She turned to Joseph. His eyelids were slightly lowered and his nose and mouth were stretched down and pinched. She twisted to see Molly.

"Don't," said Molly. "Please don't look like that. Don't cry, please don't cry. You're so ugly when you cry. Please don't."

Marian pressed her fingers into her skull. She held her neck muscles taut. She pushed out her chest and belly to make room for the expanding pressure. They were her children. They were all she now had. She must protect them from misery and pain. From herself. In the rearview mirror, she could make out in the gray distance the comic cakewalk of the woman in white, alone, in the cold.

Over the next weeks, she longed to tell Malcolm that she knew about the lady. She longed to taunt him. How typical, how trite, how sordid. He had deserted his family for the sleaziest of reasons, another woman, a younger woman, probably a graduate student. Malcolm with his dignity and pride. How comical it was. She saw herself pick up the telephone and dial his number. She heard her contemptuous yet amused voice ringing through the wires. Sleazy and comical, she heard herself say.

But she did not call him. She was afraid. His voice would be hard and irritable, and he would say hateful things to her that she could not bear to hear. She imagined his saying, I never loved you, not even at the beginning. She heard him say, I married you only so I could finish my degree. He would infect her memories with doubt and ruin the past for her. He would leave her with nothing. While he had his lady.

Through the winter months, she spent hours at a time daydreaming about Malcolm and his woman. Often, she sat at her bedroom window and watched the rain break against the pane. She believed that if she concentrated hard enough, she would be able to conjure up an image of his woman. But always as the face began to form on the film of the glass, the wind swept the image away.

One day as the outline of the eyes appeared, she leaned close to fasten the face to the windowpane. She saw her own reflection, and she saw that her eyes were more haggard than she remembered, her lips thin, her nose taut. She had grown suddenly old and ugly. She drew back from the windowpane, and as she did, her reflection began to move away from her, as if the image were running to a distant point in the street. She saw her reflection grow smaller, and smaller, and then vanish.

She jumped from the chair and rushed into the living room. She must come out of her misery. She had lost touch with the world, gone stale and sour inside herself. Her life had lost its shape. She had no purpose. She had been only marking time, waiting for relief that would never come. She had to build her life again, become a person again.

She sat down in the red chair, Malcolm's chair. No, she thought, it's my chair. She pulled the *New York Times Magazine* from the mahogany rack by the chair. The magazine was six months old. She dumped all the magazines on the floor, the *New Republic, Harper's, The New York Review.* They were all stiff and yellow with age. Malcolm's magazines. He had taken the subscriptions with him, and she had not even missed them. She had read nothing in months.

The blood rose to her head and pounded behind her eyes. She had once been an attractive, interesting woman who kept up, who could talk of anything. Yes, talk so that men listened to her and admired her and desired her. Malcolm had taken all that from her. That, too. Slowly, slowly. Over the years he had frequently said hurtful things to her—that she chattered, that she told everything in boring detail. Hurtful things that made her feel inadequate or silly and that broke her confidence. She had given up, content to let him do the talking, content with the warmth of his brilliance. To please him, she had become a cipher. And when he thought he had completed her destruction, he had deserted her.

But he was wrong: she was not destroyed. Free of him, she was ready to become the attractive woman she had once been. Everything was still there, ready to emerge from the half-life she had lived all these years. She felt that her powers were flooding back to her, washing away her fear of him, her timidity.

Exultant, triumphant, she rushed to the telephone and dialed his number at the university. But when a soft young female voice answered, she could not speak. She heard Malcolm ask, "Who is it, Teddy?" and then "Hello" into the phone. She could not remember what she had intended to say to him. A pressure began, swelled larger and larger until she feared it would explode in her chest, crash through her eardrums, shatter the delicate membrane of her nostrils and eyes. She opened her mouth to let the sounds out, but no sounds came.

Marian had often noticed the woman in the red plastic coat who walked with one hand palm up at her shoulder and the other on her hip. Her white hair was burnished to a metallic sheen and it stood high above her face like a chef's cap. She wore multicolored platform shoes with six-inch heels that threw her forward, and she took quick little mincing steps as if hurrying to catch up with her top before it fell. She was, Marian decided, probably a prostitute.

But prostitute or not, she was a human being and a woman, and a woman obviously mistreated by men. And so seeing her on a drizzly March afternoon walking with the red coat held straight-armed above the elaborate hair-do, Marian decided to give the woman a lift. She drew the car alongside the curb and leaned across the passenger seat to lower the window.

And then she noticed the sores on the woman's bare legs. Some of the sores were black holes with diameters the size of a pencil and some were raw looking with moist crusts and some were fresh, suppurating, leaving faint trails down her calves.

The woman turned. Her face was mottled and skull-like and Marian thought the flesh had already begun to rot back from the bones. Marian felt a hard spasm in her lower belly, as if a steel hand had fastened around her groin. The woman grinned then, a terrible grin of complicity, as if she had anticipated, had desired, now shared the sudden hatred Marian felt surging through her. As Marian reared back from the window and twisted the steering wheel toward the street, she heard a muffled, constricted whimpering, and she knew it was her own.

One Sunday afternoon in June, Malcolm came into the house with the children. It had been nearly a year since he had left; the divorce was final. He stood in the hallway and leaned casually against the wall. He was deeply tanned and his gray sideburns were long and bushy and somehow boyish. He seemed cheerful and lighthearted, qualities she thought he had long ago given up to his seriousness, his image of himself as a scholar. He wore his new happiness like an advertisement and he apparently expected her to rejoice with him.

He said, "I've got a plan I know you're going to like."

Her resentment was like a coagulant. As he spoke her blood and her energy ceased to flow, and she felt sullen, dull, thick.

He told her that he would take the children for July to one of the San Juan Islands off Seattle. No electricity, he exulted. No cars. No telephone. Just man against nature, with the necessities flown in, he said, laughing archly. He had never been there, of course, but—he paused no more than a heartbeat—he knew someone who had. He began to describe the island, as if he were enticing her to come along, the cliffs, the immense trees, the wild berries, the birds.

"This will be one of the best experiences of their lives," he said, "and you'll be free for a whole month."

"Free to do what?" she asked. Her tongue was thick and heavy, and her voice hardly rose to her mouth.

"See you next Sunday," he called to the children, and waving, waving, he backed out the front door.

"I'm going to have a shell collection," Molly said.

"There's a lot of driftwood," said Joseph, "so you can carve things and all."

"Teddy says the shells are beautiful and I'm going to make you a beautiful shell necklace."

"Be quiet," said Joseph.

"I've never been to an island," said Molly. "I wish you could come too."

"Yeah," said Joseph.

After her hot bath, she lay in bed in the dark, staring at the odd shapes the moon cast against the draperies. The moon on the water and the sandy beaches and the shadows of trees. The wind blew in her open window and the draperies billowed. She saw people in the moving folds. Heads. Bodies. Lovers moving against each other in the dark shadows. Malcolm and his lady. She drew her hands along her hips, squeezed her breasts between her fingers. No one would ever hold her, whisper to her in the night. For a moment she feared that she would scream out in her anguish, and she threw back the covers and sat up on the side of the bed.

If only she had someone to talk to, to whom she could tell her suffering. She thought of her parents, both dead, and of the brother she had not seen in years. The faces of girls she had been close to came to her, and one in particular who had blond hair in a Dutch boy cut and who had moved away when they were both eleven. She thought of a boy whose name she could not recall who had given her chocolates in a heart-shaped box and had kissed her clumsily on the ear. And of the boy who had loved her in high school and whom she had loved until she had met Malcolm. All these, and others she might have talked to, were gone.

She got up to close the window against the wind and she saw a light beneath Joseph's door. Molly had already deserted her, had said "Teddy" in an affectionate, accepting way. But Joseph, her first-born, suffered, too.

She went to his room. He lay prone on his bed, propped on his elbows, a book open in front of him. She said, "I want to talk to you."

He folded the book over his finger and turned over. He lay back against the headboard. The light from the bullet lamp fell across the side of his face. He looked frail and sad.

She sat down in the desk chair and dragged it closer to the bed. "You're going away," she said, "with them." She held his gaze.

"Mom, please don't," he said. His shadowed face turned away from her. "We're not supposed to talk about the other one. He never talks about you."

"Never? Has he never said anything?"

"All he ever said was he had a right to try to be happy," Joseph said in a soft, fretful, placating voice. He drew his knees up and folded his arms across them and buried his face in his arms. "Please don't talk to me, please," he said.

As he lifted his face to her, his head seemed to rise above the knees, disembodied. As she stared at him, his face grew larger and larger and whiter and whiter. It swelled toward her, a pale disc, like the moon. She got to her feet.

"Sleep well," she said.

She went to the kitchen to make sure she had turned off the oven and the burners. She checked the locks on outside doors. She listened for the sound of a forgotten sprinkler. The house was still and dark and hot. She felt dull and sluggish, and yet excited, too restless to stay inside.

She went into her bathroom and took her old flannel robe off the hook on the back of the door. She got in the car and drove over to the university lake. In the springtime, the students boated and swam and sunned at the lake, and often she and Malcolm had brought the children there to search for tadpoles and frogs. Now, in June, the lake was slowly drying into a swamp.

She sat on the dark bank and breathed in the cool night air. The moon shimmered in the puddles on the lake bottom. It was the end of Spring term and she heard the murmur of student lovers and the rustle of dry leaves. She imagined bodies touching, and the soft delicious look of desire on their mouths and in their eyes. She had known that ecstasy. She remembered the first night she and Malcolm had been together. They had been on Cape Cod. She saw them lying in a little pocket of leafy brush, protected from the wind by an overhanging cliff. She had felt nothing existed but the two of them, and nothing mattered but the act of love they performed.

And in the moonlight, sitting on the damp bank of the swampy lake, she began to cry. Her crying was a moan that returned to her as the sound of soft thunder. And then she saw movement in the shadows of the trees. The students, the lovers, were moving away from her along the shores of the lake. She had driven them away. In her groin was the pain that was like lust, like fear, like hatred. She didn't care what the lovers or anyone thought of her. Her chest swelled with sobs. They seemed to be exploding through her ribs, bursting from her armpits, ripping through her ears and eye-sockets.

She stood up. The streets were empty. She clutched her bathrobe tighter against the suddenly chilly night, and she began to walk quickly, recklessly, in the direction of the moon. As she walked, she felt the power of her thrusting stride, the rising flood of her energy, the release of her torment.

I-80

Peter Behrens

I was in a coffee shop at Elko with two brothers who'd picked me up out in the desert. On the table between us there was a dish containing little tubs of creamer.

"I hate this stuff," said Olsen, the younger, nineteen. He held one of the tubs and studied the labelling. "'Non-dairy product', that's what it says. Gives you cancer of the intestines."

"Quit your complaining," said Timothy.

"Would you drink this stuff, professor?" Olsen said.

"I have in the past," I told him. "But no, I don't think so."

Olsen was looking around for the waitress.

"Leave her be," said Timothy. He stirred creamer in his coffee and began scribbling lines on a napkin. He'd already told me he was a poet. While he jotted verses, his pencil-point made gashes in the fibrous paper. He tore the lid off a second tub of creamer, and a jet of milky white hit his brother in the face. Olsen jerked back and snapped a napkin from the steel container. He wiped his neck furiously. He was unshaven and the paper made a rasping sound.

"Bastard!"

"Sorry," said Timothy laughing. "But hey, it was an accident."

The manager squinted at us from behind the cash. A waitress with green eyes came over and stood by our table, hip cocked, balancing a tray and a plastic coffeepot. She looked like the kind of woman who'd come to you at night, pulled to your fire by a pair of blue dogs, wolfhounds. The dogs would strain and slaver but she'd remain calm, digging in her heels.

"Refill?" she asked.

"Yes," I said. "If you please."

"Fuck you, toots," Olsen said, crumpling the napkin and throwing it at her feet.

"Shut your mouth," said Timothy.

"What did he say?" she asked.

"Don't tell me to shut up, big brother," said Olsen, leaning his arm on the table and cupping his hand around his coffee mug. I noticed a star-shaped earring he wore.

"I'd be happy to shut it for you," said Timothy.

They were both of them drillers from the Wyoming rigs. I could imagine brawls Timothy would have fought and won over the writing of poetry. He was lean, the kind of animal that drags down its prey. He'd said his poetry was all about young women. He wrote at night, making Olsen sleep on the cement steps outside their trailer.

He snapped the pencil in half and dropped the pieces into his brother's coffee. Olsen shoved his mug so that it skidded across the table and smashed on the floor. I noticed the manager coming around from behind the cash. Timothy jumped up and placed his fingers around Olsen's throat. The manager pushed the green-eyed girl away and stood pointing a deer rifle at my heart.

"Get out of my place," he said.

"Let's get going," I said quickly. "Don't anyone worry, I'll pay for the coffee."

I laid some coins on the table and followed the brothers down the aisle. The manager huffed behind me, poking my shoulder with the rifle. Looking back, I saw the girl starting to clear off the table. I wanted to wave but knew the gesture would be misread, so I bit my lip and followed the brothers out into the colorless Nevada light. As we were going through the door, Olsen kicked over a *USA Today* vending machine and the manager tapped warningly on the plate glass with his Winchester.

Olsen wheeled around and ripped open his shirt so that the buttons went skittering.

"Do it to me then, big man," he screamed, thrusting out his chest.

The man on the other side of the thick glass made no move, and Olsen cackled, "What a chickenshit, what a big fat slice of bird-pie!"

The Nevada desert was full of test ranges, and as we were approaching the brothers' Falcon a flight of military jets swept overhead from the east. The planes came down quickly, dropping from the sky like stones. The brothers began to shout and wave. "F-16's," screamed Timothy. He pointed both forefingers at the planes and made a machine-gunning sound between his teeth. Olsen whooped around like an epileptic Comanche, pulling pins from imaginary hand grenades and lobbing them upwards.

The jets passed, leaving streaks of white exhaust like claw marks on the sky. The sound of the engines faded until it was just whistling, like desert wind creaking the neon signs on Nevada Boulevard. Then everything was silent except the rush of traffic.

Timothy opened the car door and I scrambled into the back. Timothy slid behind the wheel while Olsen leaned against the passenger side, drumming his fingers on the roof.

"You getting in, or do you want to walk to California?" Timothy said.

"Your kids are cretins, brother," Olsen said. "Your girls are just Wyoming whores."

Timothy stiffened as if a piece of wire had been inserted into his body.

Olsen leaned through the window. "The best home you've ever had was a rented trailer at Rock Springs," he taunted.

Timothy gripped the steering wheel so tightly the blood was pressed from his knuckles. I noticed how his head grew from his neck like a large fist.

"Your mind is a slave," Olsen said.

Timothy got out of the car, walked around it deliberately, and threw open the trunk. He lifted something out, slamming the lid. I saw he was holding a canvas seabag. Olsen's drumming ceased.

Timothy whirled the bag over his head and let go. It landed on the asphalt twenty yards away, flopping like a dead body. Olsen began slapping himself on the neck.

Jingling his keys, Timothy jumped behind the wheel and started the engine.

Olsen reached in the window and slipped an automatic pistol

from beneath the front seat. He grinned and I saw his earring sparkle. Timothy leaned over and locked the passenger door, rolling the window shut. Olsen started rapping on the glass. He moved around the car, smacking the fenders with the pistol butt.

"Let's get out of here," I told Timothy.

"Hold your horses, professor." Timothy shifted into reverse. He pressed the accelerator and the Falcon rocked backwards, grazing his brother, who skipped out of the way. We chased him across the lot, while he dodged and twisted like a matador. He managed to dart around the car and smash out the tail-lights. They broke with a splintering sound.

Timothy took aim and ran over the seabag.

Olsen leapt up on the hood and started pounding against the windshield. We swerved but he was holding on to the stem of the windshield wiper. Timothy punched the accelerator, then slammed the brakes, and Olsen tumbled off, landing on his hands and knees on the asphalt.

We started driving away. I looked back and saw Olsen scrambling to his feet. He crouched and took aim, gripping his pistol like an FBI man. I saw the thing buck and flame. Timothy hit the gas, and we went bouncing over the sidewalk, thrusting into the braking, honking Nevada Boulevard traffic.

After a couple of miles we came up beneath a big green interstate sign, "I–80 West, Reno, Sacramento," and shifted into the ramp lane, but at the last moment Timothy swerved, and the Falcon darted beneath the freeway on an underpass. On the other side of I–80, Nevada Boulevard was narrow and poor, flanked with cut-rate furniture and auto-supply stores. Timothy made a U-turn at the first break in traffic and a moment later we were speeding back to the place we'd left Olsen.

Timothy glanced over his shoulder and grinned at me. He said he comprehended all the reasons I was going to California. There was a lecherous tic in his right eye and I imagined him in the library of a great university poring over all the wrong books, noting their foul wisdom in a ledger he'd keep tucked inside his shirt.

When we saw Olsen, he was hurrying along the sidewalk with the seabag, pausing every few paces to stick out his thumb. The cars rushed past him and he kept walking. I noticed the checkered grip of the pistol poking from the waistband of his jeans. We made a U-turn and drew up to the curb. Timothy reached over to unlock the passenger door. Olsen ducked inside.

"Don't ever put a fucking piece in my car without telling me," said Timothy.

"Yeah, yeah, yeah," said Olsen, twisting around and dumping the seabag into the back seat. "Let's get out of here."

"I mean it."

"I heard you the first time," said Olsen.

I slept until we turned off the interstate highway at Winnemucca. I woke as soon as I felt gravel thumping beneath the tires.

"Where are we heading? This isn't the road to Reno."

Timothy grinned into the rearview mirror. "Ten miles north of Winnemucca is the biggest cathouse in the state."

"Why don't you let me off?" I asked.

"What's the matter, professor?" said Olsen. "Don't you like the ladies?"

"I don't like my women bought or sold," I said. If there'd been a back door I would have shoved it open and jumped.

"Well, you're with us now, professor."

The sky glittered like a steel frying pan. I could see nothing ahead but gravel mountains, and behind us a plume of pearl-grey dust.

After a few miles the road ended at a chain-link gate and a sign that said "The Hacienda." There was a guard with a sawed-off shotgun in a holster. The guard seemed reluctant to let us in until Timothy flashed credit cards. Then the guard began explaining the rules. Did we have liquor in the car? Knives? Firearms?

Timothy signed documents and we were allowed to park. There were a half-dozen mobile homes arranged around a grassy courtyard. The courtyard was bordered with white-painted stones and at the center was a scatter of lawn chairs and an aluminum flagpole.

We checked in at an air-conditioned office. The brothers stood at the desk laughing, feinting punches at each other.

"Come on, professor," said Olsen. "Loosen up."

The girls wore eye-shadow and pink gauze. They looked pale and cold, like sides of meat in a freezer. You could hardly hear anything over the roar of the air conditioning. Timothy and Olsen selected their women and disappeared.

I ran out to the parking lot but the car was locked. Peering inside I could see the butt of the pistol beneath the front seat. In one of the trailers someone was playing an opera record. The guard at the gate was watching me. I walked over to his hut and asked if there was a telephone. I said I needed a ride back to the highway.

"You from the base?" he said. He was a big Mexican with fingers missing on both hands.

"No."

"There's a bus of boys from the air base due tonight. You could get a ride back with them."

"I can't wait that long."

He looked at me suspiciously.

"What's waiting?" he said. "I'm waiting all the time. Those two you're with, they're bad company—jackals. They'll be done in half an hour. You ride out with them. I see any of you around here again, you'll have some trouble."

I used to love the desert even at its worst, if only because it ended in California. I used to love it for the solitude, but now all I find there is emptiness, and the blowing dust makes my teeth ache.

On the interstate between Winnemucca and Reno one of our front tires exploded. Timothy wrestled the car to the gravel shoulder. We got out, and they threw open the trunk and starting dragging out the jack and the spare. On the oilfields they'd learned how to use tools and they worked quickly, wrenching off the shredded tire and rolling it into a ditch. They took off their shirts and I noticed the crease separating Olsen's shoulder blades, sculpting the musculature in his back.

The desert air tasted like an old junkyard. The trunk was open and I could see my pack nestled inside. I inched closer to it, hoping to pull it out, run across the highway, and flag down a ride. As I was reaching for it I heard a rustling and looked up. Timothy was still levering down the jack and Olsen was cranking the wheel nuts tight. I saw the needle-shaped fighters travelling across the sky, launching missiles from underneath their wings. I watched the missiles trace long, pale incisions which turned pink, and started to open.

THE SCRIPTWRITER

Evan Connell

K oerner leaned against the glass wall of the booth and stared at the moonlight on Malibu beach while he listened to the telephone ringing.

Somebody picked up the receiver and a woman's voice said, "Yes?"

"Dana?"

"Who is this?"

"I'm calling Morris Reisling," he said because the woman did not sound like Dana. "Do I have the right number?"

"Who are you?"

"My name is William Koerner."

"It's you," she said. "Where are you?"

"On the highway near the ocean. Not far from the house."

He expected her to turn away from the telephone saying, "Morrie, Bill Koerner's here!" or "Morrie, guess who's calling!" And then Morris would be on the telephone asking if he remembered how to get there, saying the extra bedroom was waiting and there was a pot of chili on the stove.

"I suppose you remember how to get here," she said.

"I'll find it."

"Are you staying in Malibu, or just passing through?"

"I'm on the way to Mexico," Koerner said. It was not what he should be saying and not what Dana should have asked, though more than a year had gone by without a word from them. He wondered if they had been divorced.

"I look forward to seeing you," Dana said as though he was nothing but an acquaintance.

"How's Morrie?"

"Morris died."

Koerner blinked. Then he said: "What?"

"I told you," she answered in a flat voice. "He's dead."

"Morrie?"

"Yes, Morrie. How does that grab you?"

After a few moments Koerner said, "I didn't know."

"I realize you didn't. I'll look forward to seeing you. Goodby." Then she had hung up.

Koerner walked across the highway to his car and started driving slowly toward the house where he had spent so many nights. The house with those two people in it had meant as much as almost anything he knew, but now he did not want to see it again. Morris was dead and she had remarked 'How does that grab you?'

Several minutes later he coasted to a stop in front of another telephone booth and sat for a while without moving, but then continued on the highway and presently turned into a canyon. The night was warm and a deer sprang over the road, bursting through the headlights like an image on a movie screen. Going up the hill the lights followed a furry shape lumbering along, probably a small brown bear, which soon disappeared among the trees. Koerner put his head out the window to smell the pines. All of this he could remember and he had wanted to experience it again, but now none of it was pleasant.

Morris is dead, Morris is dead, he thought. Yet it might be a joke. They both were there when I called and Morris decided to give me a scare. Or he's working on a script and needs to know how people react to shocking news. He could do that because he uses people. He's experimented on me before, but it never hurt like this.

Dana was alone, wearing the ragged sweatshirt, dungarees and sandals. She shook hands calmly and asked what he wanted to drink. After that she sat down on the hassock where she always used to sit and listen while they talked; and she asked how he was, and Koerner wondered how soon he could leave.

"You were suspicious on the telephone," he said.

"I've become afraid of the telephone. There were so many bad calls after it happened. Anonymous obscene calls at night. I began to hate people. I can't pick up the receiver anymore without being frightened. But that doesn't concern you. I suppose you want to hear about Morris. He died a year ago September. It was in quite a few papers. Not as many as I expected, but quite a few."

Koerner remembered that Morris was overweight and at times his breathing sounded like a locomotive.

"Did he have a heart attack?"

"No."

"An accident?"

"Not an accident."

Koerner wondered if she expected him to guess again.

"Morris was murdered."

He realized that instead of being shocked he was annoyed. She had deliberately tried to shock him. Morris, who had been his friend and her husband, was dead and she had played a scene. He tried to excuse her because she had been an actress.

"Nor do I mean it figuratively," Dana said, looking at him with one eyebrow lifted.

Then he understood that she was playing not a scene but a role, and had been playing it ever since Morris died. Her questions on the telephone, the remoteness and the artifice, shaking hands instead of throwing her arms around him, forcing him to ask about what had happened.

"Morris was shot."

Koerner knew she would go on with it. He had done his part, now it was her turn. How many times had she behaved like this? Since Morris died how many friends had driven up the canyon road to the light burning above the door like a backstage entrance? Dana there to greet them with both hands outstretched, the palms turned down, perhaps, if the visitors were movie people, or if she happened to feel that way. Now she was sitting on the leather hassock as indifferently as a cat.

Suddenly she glanced up and said, "I know who did it."

Koerner hoped the exasperation he felt did not show on his face. She had resorted to acting because she had been hurt, and knowing this he knew he would not get angry, but still he wished she would stop.

"Actually there's no mystery. The man was tried for what he did and acquitted. He's walking around free today. He's a film cutter named Huggins. Poor little man. Morris was shot to death by a little film cutter. What do you think of that?"

Koerner said, "This isn't what I asked for. Please, Dana."

"It happened in a cheap motel on the beach. Morris was in bed with the film cutter's wife. It seems that Huggins suspected his wife was having an affair so he hired a private detective. The detective found them together one afternoon when Morris had told me he was going to the studio. The detective did something that is not ethical. He told Huggins exactly where they were, with the result that the man left the studio and took a taxi to the motel. He was not supposed to be in possession of a gun because he was an ex-convict, nevertheless he had one. He proceeded to kick open the door of the cottage and begin shooting. He shot Morris only once, but he shot his wife seven times. Both of them were naked. She was very fat. Isn't it amusing?"

"Not to me," Koerner said.

"I realize that."

"Dana," Koerner said, and waited until she would look at him. "Dana, for God's sake."

"You wanted to hear about it. I'm simply telling you. The man's wife died immediately. Morris lingered for nearly three weeks and for most of those three weeks I was at the hospital. He died in agony. His stomach was bloated like a sausage. I knew he was going to die. I knew before the doctors knew. I knew it even when they told me he was going to recover. Morris didn't believe them either, although he would nod his head when they told him. Do you know what he said to me one morning? He said 'It was a roll in the hay.' That's all the affair meant to him. Don't you find it amusing? People we know aren't murdered, are they? Gangsters are murdered and South American generals are murdered and occasionally a Brooklyn grocer is murdered by a boy who was trying to rob the cash register, but people you and I know aren't murdered, are they? Are they, Bill?"

Without any expression or any tears she was crying.

Koerner looked at the row of framed certificates on the brick wall above the fireplace and said, "Did he get another one?"

"Two since you were here. The one at the end is from a Brussels festival. He was killed before the awards were announced. Everything seems like such a waste."

Then she talked about it some more, and played a record of songs from a new musical comedy which was very popular, and before midnight Koerner was driving out of the canyon. He had hoped when he telephoned to find them both at home and if that had been so they would have insisted that he stay with them. He had hoped this is how it would be. Next, after learning that Morris was dead, he expected Dana would invite him to stay overnight in the guest room; but she had not offered and after a little while he would have refused. He thought then that he would stay at some place near the beach and perhaps go for a swim during the middle of the night as he and Morris used to do. But when he turned out of the canyon onto the Malibu road he did not slow down. From that house something was seeping like a poison and he felt it staining everything for miles in all directions. Whatever he looked at became disagreeable—the trees, the beach, the moonlight on the water—and the ocean wind had a foul odor.

Morris died without speaking, she had said, but he knew what was happening because he put on his glasses. Those horn-rimmed glasses, Koerner thought, mounted like a machine gun on that enormous nose. How could he meet Death without being able to see its visage? And he had died because of a lapse of taste, as well as poor judgment; died in a hospital, a setting he had used more than once in his scenarios, with a white plastic tube curling from his intestines into a pail beneath the bed, wagging his head slowly from side to side because he believed none of it.

She was sitting beside the bed when Death finally got around to his room. She had been reading a magazine when she knew Death was in, and quit reading and turned the magazine over on her lap and looked at her husband. Everything had been done for him that could be done, so with no particular surprise, and not much sorrow, she observed the meeting. She had loved him but her esteem for him disappeared when he was shot. He had been caught so stupidly. She had respected his intelligence, it had been the foundation of her love for him. They had lived together eighteen years and she had admired him even when she felt critical of things he did or said, but then one afternoon he was caught in bed with an overweight tramp in a roadside motel. He was caught like a foolish sailor. The stupidity of it disturbed her; three weeks she spent reading magazines and watching him suffer, and she began to feel insulted. She had selected as her husband a man who turned out to be a fool. She could not forgive him this. She might have forgiven his poor taste, because that was a thing men were often guilty of, but she could not forget or forgive his stupidity. She would have taken him back if he had believed he was in love with the woman, because men are easily confused; often they think they are in love when a woman knows it is only the body that absorbs them. If Morris had believed he was in love there would have been some dignity to the affair, at least there would have been that if nothing more. But he knew he was not. Or she might have overlooked it if the woman had been beautiful, but she was not. She was fat and ordinary, while he was a superior man. So she had quit reading that afternoon and dispassionately watched while Death strangled him, sorry that he was in such pain but otherwise not caring.

I never dreamed he would plot against me, she had said. I knew he plotted against other people, but not against me. Not in my wildest dreams. Not against me. As long as we were married I never once considered another man.

Then she attempted to explain something, which Koerner understood easily enough, although she was not sure she had made it clear. It was how she had observed herself, Dana, observing her husband's death. Did that make sense? Morris used to observe himself, many times she had noticed him doing it, and from him she had gotten the habit. He used it professionally. He would step out of himself and stand distinctly to one side observing Morris. In fact he made notes of his own behavior, she said, and later in one of the scenarios she would read what he had discovered about himself. Was this clear?

Yes, Koerner said, because he too had seen it.

As he was dying, Dana said, I did what he had taught me. I stood far away. I could see him suffering from where I was, and I was curious to learn what would happen next. As though my husband was the subject of a script. How could I be like that? Do you know?

She did not expect an answer. Koerner was looking at her and noticed how neatly her brown hair was parted and how carefully she had plaited it and closed the long braid hanging down her back with a rubber band.

Really, she said, it's a shame he never knew. He had such a sense of humor. He would have loved that touch of irony, and probably would have found a way to use it. He was so clever. But he was occupied with himself during those last few minutes. He didn't pay any attention to me. And there were other touches which were terribly reminiscent of his scenarios. He always employed at least one scene of violence—shots, screams, a door slammed, the sound of running feet. Imagine him doing the motel. The woman shrieking and collapsing on the bed while her husband was firing shot after shot into that enormous body. She was quite dead when the police arrived. She must have been as bloody as a Spanish crucifix. Morris would have enjoyed writing it, if he had lived. People used to say he was a genius. He wasn't, as we both know, but he was awfully smart. Isn't it amusing that he was shot to death by a nobody?

That doesn't amuse me either, Koerner had said.

Then he stood up and she walked with him to the door where they said goodby. She seemed to know he would not come back again. She was not blaming him for this. She had discovered within herself certain thoughts and feelings that she had never known existed, and no doubt the same was true of everyone.

The light still burned above the door when Koerner turned the car around and started through the canyon.

Halfway to Mexico he took one hand off the wheel, pointed a finger at the moon and said while wiggling his thumb: "Pok pok pok pok!" the way Morris used to do when reading one of his scripts aloud, as though by such a gesture he might get rid of the disgust and the oppression, but the moon would not fall into the sea.

THE INDIANS DON'T NEED ME ANYMORE

James Fetler

1

I suppose that was it: the last of my Alcatraz runs. I won't be hauling any more clothing and food to the entrenched Indians. It's a series of very long tacks from the Palo Alto yacht harbor to the Rock—a whole day's trip when the winds aren't good—and I finally had to admit as I was tying the *Wanderer* up the last time that I'm not really helping the American Indian Movement all that much with the few boxes of blankets and canned goods I've been able to buy or collect around here. Legal aid would be better, along with some solid political support. Ritchie wants a big generator. *There's the psychology to think about, too.* They've got enough blankets and Spam. And now that Nancy has finally remarried, and it's clear that my contract will not be renewed at Peninsula State, I'm ready to clean out my cottage, get rid of the hookah and the scented drip candles, and try again some other place.

I used to think all those shuttles in the sloop were a sign of my altruism at work. Social concern. But the truth is I found a great solace in watching the winds and the tides when I first started sailing last summer. Handling a tiller was good therapy, it kept my body and mind occupied and took me away from the traps I had set for myself. And having a meaningful destination made my hours on the water more rich—it was more than just sliding around. When I looked at the hull of the boat the other day I could see it's absorbed a real beating from the northwesterly winds. I'll have to unload it even though it's a bad time to sell. I can't afford it any more.

I'm going to start packing. Roll up that Harpo Marx poster tacked over my desk. That grin has been getting on my nerves. And there's something else telling me it's time to stop licking the wounds. Once again I can feel the machinery about to start grinding in me. Sparrow noticed it, too: he said I look as if I'm about to lock myself into a different position. Since the children have finally accepted their new Field & Stream dad, who will give them the discipline and care they both need and deserve, I might as well get on my feet. I've used up the bay.

2

As I was sailing away from the Indians today I had to finally admit that the life I've been trying to hammer together has left me empty and raw. I hadn't expected that. *Fulfillment* and *actualization* seemed easy enough to wrap up and take home when I had Abraham Maslow on the lectern before me, reinforced by my neatly typed notes and the formulas clearly outlined on the board. Even the pointer I swung back and forth felt authentic.

As the *Wanderer* was sailing under the Bay Bridge I found myself staring straight up at the massive steel girders, and that brought back the feel of the rigid geometry that would press against me at Peninsula State—in the classrooms, in the faculty lounge, even down by the tennis courts—and that little flash took me back to the Friday last May when I lost my cool while doing Tolstoy. Everything seemed to be pushing against me that Friday. Even the sidewalks on campus were slamming up needlessly hard against my arches. Off and on, over a period of several months, I'd been trying for one final clarification between Nancy and me, despite this new IBM man in her life who happened to hit it off beautifully with the kids, and for a short while we seemed to have worked up an actual glow between us, with the widower temporarily on the sidelines, but already I could sense the glow dying, since nothing was happening, we couldn't really change the deep core of whatever we were. *No good, no good,* I kept thinking, remembering the glow that was starting to spread out to Laura and

Alex, *already they're lightening up, not nearly so tense, no longer crying at night, but it isn't going to work, and this glow in the children is a terrible thing to see.* I had just had them over for the weekend: the zoo, Marine World, rattling cable cars out to Fisherman's Wharf, just the three of us having a ball, no apprehensive Mom snapping *Alex needs his nap!*, no griping about garbage sacks or the dog's bone on the couch—and then *wham!* as I was walking across campus and thinking back to that marvelous weekend, I found myself aching for leaves to rake, weeds to yank out of the ground, dirty dishes to wash, someone else flushing the toilet, the sounds of can openers, the slamming of doors. I was also hung over. The night before, loaded on sherry, I had driven down Hopkins Street with the headlights off. Craig's 4-wheel drive Toyota was parked in my former driveway, and all the curtains were drawn in the house. I kept reminding myself as I drove back to the cottage not to let this sort of thing happen again.

3

It was a hot Friday. I was sweating so hard in my bush jacket and turtleneck jersey that I finally wadded a couple of paper towels under my armpits, but the towels got soggy and slid down the sleeves. Sparrow and my other colleagues were ambling from class to class in their usual short-sleeved drip-dry shirts like NASA engineers, but I stuck to the turtleneck and boots I'd decided would best represent the real me, plus the other bold touches designed to impress and seduce undergrads—the torn jeans and the shades. That was part of the contract, I figured, getting the Camaro crowd turned on to Yeats and Flaubert using all the theatricals at your command, including the proper cosmetics. You had to relate.

By the time my 2 P.M. class dragged around that Friday I could feel the bad ache in my shoulders and neck. Every time I thought back to the split in my life, and the way it was bruising the kids, I would start to concoct weekend jaunts in my mind—Mendocino, Carmel, the whole family packed into the Hillman convertible along with a fictitious sheep dog I would throw in to finish the scene (Jip wasn't quite right for the part) like a Standard Oil billboard. But I could never imagine us alone, just Nancy and me. Not comfortably. Too much distance had crystallized between us, and it wouldn't thaw out. I couldn't imagine myself totally alone with her, the two of us seated at a restaurant table, a couple of menus and an ashtray between us, and this was peculiar because I know I felt jealousy and remorse, especially after Craig started coming around. It grated against me, and yet it was clear I would have to accept the brute fact that those crystals were permanently there. So would she. Shortly before moving into the cottage, I had told her, *You won't accept this until later, but the truth is you'll get nothing good out of me until after we've split. You're still young—you deserve a fresh start.*

As I walked into class I could spot a real bummer in the making. Their eyes told me, the tilt of their frames. I pushed them through ten, fifteen minutes of the Tolstoy, clutching my chest, acting out Ivan Ilyich's torment and death, everything but the actual screaming, but when I finally finished my performance they responded with a silence so solid and compressed you could haul it away in a furniture van.

I leaned against the desk: artificial pearls cast out to genuine swine. "So what's he saying—*Ivan Ilyich's life had been most simple and most ordinary, and therefore most terrible*—what does that mean?"

Their eyeballs were barely twitching. I waited. Nothing. I could see Sparrow standing outside, as though checking me out. George McManus was meditating on his thumb. A girl yawned.

I threw my stuff into the briefcase. *Zap:* there was the Toyota again, parked directly behind Nancy's green Maverick. "You're really disgusting," I said quietly and walked out, leaving them sitting there with their plywood expressions. I went to my car. *They haven't learned how to decipher the plain printed page!* I was feeling so bad I left tracks. I could hear Sparrow yelling to me. I ignored him. I had heard it all before.

The faculty lot seemed to be buckling with heat. I left the Menlo Park campus by way of El Camino Real and winced all the way into Palo Alto, the sun rubbing my eyes like a file. As soon as I approached my own turf I felt better. The tree-lined avenues felt cool, almost damp, and the elegantly decaying old houses dating back to the '80s and '90s, with their towers and panes of stained glass, the verandas and warped picket fences, were comforting: a world decomposing, waiting for the bulldozers, a dark falling-apart, a rich calm. Rows of diseased palm trees. Cast-iron sprinklers revolving on the lawns. I drove up to my cottage holding my breath. I listened: no motorcycles, no rock and roll. I relaxed.

4

The little place I'd been renting the last couple of years sat directly in back of a once-magnificent estate dating back to the founding of Stanford University. Since the end of the Korean War the big house had been gerrymandered into several small units, but the owners, an elderly couple in Burlingame, were merely sitting on the property, waiting and watching the land values climb, and so they had let the old mansion with its thick, crazy hedges and fruit trees disintegrate, one window and board at a time. When I moved into the cottage the week Nancy filed for divorce, the last of the tenants, a bachelor accountant who kept plants in his room, was in the process of moving out. *It's impossible,* he confided to me as he hauled out his flowerpots, *the plumbing doesn't work. Take a look at the roof.* The roof was full of bare patches where the shingles had come off.

So for several months the Victorian relic stood empty and dark. It was balm for my soul. I had my secluded retreat less than ten blocks away from my previous home, and Laura was able to drop by after school to visit with me whenever she felt like it. *This is your cottage, you know,* I assured her. *Most kids have only one home, you've got two, how about that. Huh?* She came around fairly often, especially at first, because she thought it was all kind of neat, but sometimes the whole situation confused her, and she'd squint at the light-blue light bulbs with the Tiffany shades, and the candles, and the hookah that set me back sixty-five bucks, and the posters of Harpo and W. C. Fields, and ask, *Dad, how come you're living like a teenager?*

But I had the lush, untended gardens all to myself, with the pigeons working their wings like propellers in the palms, and the lime trees and bougainvillea, the secluded green circles of clover and moss where I'd stretch out after work and accept the sun into my pores, Ravel drifting out of my windows like smoke. I was suffering over Nancy, of course, and over the other women who were plowing themselves through my life, creating the usual gouges and cuts. They came and they went, but invariably they came on too strong, leaving their toothbrushes, badgering me over the phone late at night, and I wasn't ready for any of that, not with my old world still heavy on my mind. I fixed the young ladies nice beef stroganoffs and bought a good water bed, but they didn't know when to quit. And the aching slid forward and back in my chest.

5

Then the free spirits moved in.

I was fixing my chicken and rice one tranquil afternoon, Casadesus filling the cottage with *Le tombeau de Couperin,* when a couple of young men in bib overalls loped into the kitchen. Could they borrow my john? They had taken out a lease on the big house and found all the toilets clogged. They used my bathroom, phoned the plumber, and went out to their VW bus. Ten minutes later they were back at my door.

Got any boards around here?

Boards?

Boards. Planks. That front lawn is awfully damp.

I went out with them. They had backed their bus, which was loaded with mattresses and food, up to the front door, and the wheels had sunk in on either side of the cement walk. I looked at the furrows gouged out by the spinning rear wheels.

I haven't got any planks.

The taller of the two pulled a rubber band from his wrist and grabbed the back of his mane and twisted it. He slipped the rubber band on. *Might as well unload. Want to give us a hand?*

I spent the next couple of hours hauling in pots and pans, sacks of flour and rice, boxes of canned goods, and of course the mattresses.

You've sure got a lot of mattresses.

Yeah.

That night I slept my best sleep in weeks, no moaning, no dreams, and I awoke the next morning with my arms aching but my head very bright. I hadn't had a single slug of sherry before hitting the sack, and it felt novel and good to wake up with a clean skull and all the headpieces fitting into place. When I glanced out the window I saw, in addition to the VW bus, a converted milk truck and an Easy Rider bike. I went outside. The milk truck had Oregon plates and was coated with dust.

When I came home from the campus that night a strange Studebaker pickup, outfitted with a wooden camper complete with a stovepipe and a kerosene lantern hanging from the doorknob, was occupying my stall in the carport, and now there were two motorcycles on the lawn. The rear wheel was off on one of the choppers, and a pockmarked kid wearing a floppy leather hat with a turkey feather was working on the chain. I parked my Hillman in the street and walked over. He glanced at me.

You happen to have a torque wrench?
No.
He resumed his tinkering.
Do you know who belongs to that truck?
What truck?
That Studebaker in the carport.
He shook his head. *Nope.*

6

Troubled in spirit, I went into the cottage, and while I was trying to grade a few papers before supper—*The Celebration of the Dionysian Principle in Hesse*—I could hear yet another set of pistons roar up to the front of the house, and then voices, this time the laughter of skinny girls, *Oh wow, out of sight!* and then an electric guitar started blatching out chord after chord from one of the rear dormer windows of the big house—no progression, no melody, just a blatching of random chords. I got up and closed all my windows.

Well. I thought about it. They were, after all, leasing the place and its grounds for hard cash, and were therefore entitled to run their commune any way they saw fit. And besides, they were healthy and young and conditioned to live in a world full of amplification and pounding exhausts.

The week before, I had just finished doing *Gatsby* at school, and it struck me just then that there were some connections between that Fitzgerald milieu—all those parties and motor excursions and teas—and the blatching of the electric guitar. I flashed myself back to my twenties and late teens, to the boarding house in New Haven where the volleyball boys raised the same banal hell every day and got predictably smashed on a few cans of beer every alternate night, and then to my basement cubicle on Chicago's North Side, where there wasn't fresh air and my only companion was an elderly muscatel freak who had lost control over his bladder, and then to the long, lonely rides on the El to my classes in Jackson Park, the solitary meals and the stark cafeterias with tiled floors and walls and all the menial jobs, one after the other, as I worked my way through the first years of graduate school, before Nancy showed up. And then I realized I was biting my lip over the free spirits in their kibbutz because I had never had anything like the contact they'd worked out for themselves, creating a network of interests in some ways not really so different from Scott Fitzgerald's golf games and midwinter proms. Faces and places and names. At their age—at the age of nineteen or twenty I'd be walking along Lake Michigan completely alone, my brain turning inward as usual, absorbed in its own processes, my loneliness following my tracks like a dog, just the surf of the lake on one side and the whine of the Outer Drive traffic on the other. The Beatles hadn't been invented. Acapulco gold didn't exist. Small wonder I found such a refuge in Nancy the moment she came on the scene in my Age of Johnson class, and that I dug into her like a clamp for eleven long years. And this explained, possibly, why I found the spontaneous gregariousness in the big house, along with the noises it brought, so unsettling. The free spirits made me think of the volleyball boys in New Haven, and the tiled cafeterias, and the muscatel freak.

7

But at any rate, the big house was silent that Friday. No blatches, no bikes. Two mongrels were lying on their sides in the middle of the alley, paws stretched out stiff, like freeway fatalities. I circled around them and parked and went into my place. I had ceased troubling my head over the portable kiln someone had tilted on its side in the bed of primroses and then apparently abandoned, or the overstuffed chair with the cigarette burns sitting under the pomegranate tree, or the empty wine jugs on the porch, the deer skulls propped up on the fence. They were simply a part of my life, like the smog hanging over the Santa Clara valley, the decanter of sherry on my desk. My folders and notes were jammed into the briefcase like wallpaper samples I was being paid to hustle. They had little connection with the slippery feel of the children as they sat face to face in the tub, my hands soaping their necks, or with the strained mouth of their mother those feverish early months when I wasn't quite sure where I'd be sleeping that night, and her whispers as we sat side by side on the steps of the back porch, the kids watching cartoons on TV, *What do you need that you can't get from me?* and her sudden stiffening as my fingers touched her elbow.

I stared out the door of the cottage. The unexpected silence had caught me off guard. My mind started picking through past memories the way a pick probes for fragments of food. I sat down at my desk. Harpo was grinning at me. My journal was lying on top of a stack of term papers, like a press. I opened it at random—any entry would do. This one went back a few years, to the period when everything was presumably still intact:

> *April 12, 1966. Again the chloroform on the tongue, nothing working between us, the rooms of the house like compartments for storing up silence. We poke at our dinner and strain to concoct dialogue, but the forks make more noise. Strangers at least have perfunctory exchange, a few ceremonial nods. Sparrow says I look terrible again. All evening I found myself hassling Laura about her Mary Poppins record, TURN IT DOWN! TURN IT DOWN! and finally I gave her a crack across the rear that set her spinning. I'd like to understand my machinery better, figure out what exactly is freezing me up and then making me boil. Poor design. Everybody gets caught. Mean irritations and lust.*

8

I heard a motorcycle drive up to the big house, then the VW bus. A bird started beating its wings inside me. I had papers to grade, work to do. Now the camper, horn honking. I slammed shut my journal and stuck it up on the shelf.

In the past, when the pressures built up, I could always drop over at Nancy's, have a cup of Sanka and play with the children and Jip for a while. Mow the lawn. Following the divorce we became tolerable friends, almost close, since we finally had something in common, and there were nights when I tortured myself over her. When I wasn't entertaining some woman, I kept pictures of Nancy on my desk. And then suddenly, before I was ready for him, her IBM admirer showed up and declared Nan off limits to me. Suddenly it was no longer possible to cruise over to Hopkins Street and ring the doorbell whenever I felt the need for that bell. I guess I had figured on keeping the whole business on ice over there, tucked away for emergency use. She finally had everything that I wanted for her, and it hurt.

I fixed myself a pan of tuna and noodles. *Forge on!* I kept telling myself. After dinner I started grading the papers, the decanter at my side. When I finished the sherry around ten I got into the car and drove to the Green Goose. I stayed there for a couple of hours.

Then I remember it's raining, but lightly, and I'm driving down Hopkins Street with my lights off, and there's that Toyota again in the driveway, and the windows are dark. I drive on, down Middlefield Avenue, and I turn up some side street and notice I can't get the wipers to work, although I keep twisting the knob back and forth, and then I feel a peculiar bump which I can't account for, and suddenly I'm chugging in second gear not on the street but up the manicured lawn of the Wesleyan Methodist Church, unable to stop, my foot sliding off the clutch pedal, and then I notice the windshield's got cracks in a number of places, and I get the car back on the street and somehow manage to navigate it home.

The next morning, when I finally struggled to get out of bed and go out to the carport, and when I saw how the front end had been flattened by some incredible flattening machine, I simply turned around and crawled back to bed. I didn't know what I'd hit. I didn't want to find out. The questions didn't come until several days later. I should've known better, of course, and reported it at once. Sparrow says the delay cost me my job. Yesterday he said, *Go join the Indians up there on the Rock.*

9

It isn't clear what exactly is happening on Alcatraz. Sparrow claims they are going to dig in permanently. *Time* says in its cover story: GOODBYE TO TONTO. It's obvious that the kind of relief they've been getting will have to give way to something more substantial. Ritchie is right. He poured me a cup of coffee from his thermos today and said, "Send us a couple of good electricians. And a big generator."

He was looking at me strangely—he seemed almost embarrassed. A Coast Guard cutter was idling a few hundred yards away. It hurt me a little to hear Ritchie talk like that, after all the heavy seas I had plowed the *Wanderer* through, and he must have noticed, because he said, "Look, you've done a great job. Everybody has done a great job." Then he leaned forward. "Mind if I say something?"

"What?" The coffee was sloshing out of the cup.

"Aren't you pushing yourself a bit hard?"

I stared at him.

He gave me the same kind of look I would sometimes lay on my students. "The first time I saw you ram that little boat into the dock, I said, *Jesus, now here is one wild character!* You remember?"

I laughed. Then I saw his expression. "What is it, Ritch?"

The boom was beginning to swing. Ritchie grabbed it. "Don't get me wrong, I'm not trying—." He shifted his weight. "You don't look very healthy."

"I feel fine."

"Look, it isn't my business, but you really look bad and it's bothering me. The others have noticed it, too. We don't want anyone jeopardizing their health. You look worse every time you come out. How much weight have you lost, anyway? That's an awfully long trip you've been making in the boat—it'd be a lot simpler to haul the stuff up to the city in your car. Drop it off at the Center. I mean you know we appreciate every sack of potatoes we get, but—you really look bad. You look like you've lost—."

"Okay, Ritchie." I handed him the cup. "You're probably right."

"It's senseless to burn yourself out. We're not hurting that bad."

"Okay, Ritch."

He kept holding the boom so it wouldn't swing out. "It's time we got moving on something more solid." He backed away. "Like a big generator. There's the psychology to think about, too."

"All right, Ritch."

As I pushed the sloop off he saluted me by shaking his fist. The sails luffed and snapped, suddenly filled with wind. I shook my fist back, but I could see that the Indians don't need me anymore.

HEART

Neil McMahon

After the fight I coughed for a long time, hunched over on a chair beside the ring while Charlie cut my hand wraps off. When he finished he stared at me with his fists on his hips. "For Christ's sake," he said. He tossed the soggy wads of gauze into a corner and he came back a minute later with a glass of water. It helped some.

A black fighter carrying an "Anaconda Job Corps" athletic bag nodded to me as he walked by. "You look real good out there," he said. He was wearing a wide-brim hat with a plume, patent leather boots that laced all the way to the knee, and a crimson satin shirt. Earlier I'd watched him knock out one of the toughest of the prison boxers, and make it look easy. When he came closer I could smell his sweat.

"You move real good," he said. He bent forward as he spoke, hands hanging at his waist. "I tole you before, you *slim*. You stay away from them big fat boys you be all right." He flipped his palms up and offered them to me. I slid my palms across them. His grin was a flash of white on his shiny, unmarked face.

"You do all right tomorrow," he said. "You jus keep movin." Then he sauntered on across the stage, jerking slightly with each step.

"A plume," Charlie said. "Ain't that one fancy nigger."

The man I'd just beaten was a three-time loser named Grosniak. "Armed robbery, grand larceny, and assault with a deadly weapon," he had recited to me proudly before the fight. He had been out only a week after his second term when he and a friend got drunk and took a Midi-Mart in Billings. The police were waiting for him when he drove up to his house. "Eight years this time," he explained. "There was bullets in the gun."

Grosniak's hair was bristly and unevenly cut and he had a wandering eye that I had kept trying to circle around. The roll of flesh above his trunks was still red from punches. He walked up and stood too close to me.

"I got to admit, you beat me fair and square," he said. "I dint think you could, but you did."

"Thanks," I said. Sweat was still running down the pale loose skin of his chest and belly, collecting in little drops on the sparse hair around his navel.

"You got a hell of a left hand," he said. "Your arms are too long for me. I couten figure out how to get inside you. But I'm gonna work on it. Maybe I'll get another shot at you sometime."

"Maybe so," I said.

"I knew you couten knock me out, though. I told you that before. You can pound on me all day, but you can't knock me out. Nobody's ever knocked me out." Dried blood and snot were streaked across his chin and dark red bubbles still sucked in and out of his nose. He was clenching and unclenching his fists. I looked away and started coughing again.

"Get dressed," Charlie said to me. "It's getting late."

"That's gonna be a good fight tomorrow between you and Gus," Grosniak said. "He hasn't lost a fight in four years. That's gonna be real good to see."

"Come on," Charlie said.

"He's had two hundred fights," Grosniak said. "He's won them all by knockouts." I stood up and Grosniak stepped grudgingly back. He was still clenching his fists and squeezing his walleye open and shut so it looked like he was winking at me. He took a step after me as I passed but Charlie shouldered him out of the way and pivoted to face him, hands quiet at his sides.

"Too bad you're not in my weight class," Grosniak said.

"Real too bad," Charlie said. "I love to watch fat boys go down, they make such a nice splat when they hit the canvas." He turned and walked on after me.

"Maybe I'll get a shot at you sometime," Grosniak called.

"Sucker," Charlie muttered. We passed through the door into the closet-sized room with a few battered lockers in it. "Why the hell didn't you take him down?"

"No need," I said. "I knew I had him."

"I guess you did have him, you could have knocked him on his ass any time after the first."

"He's just sorry," I said.

"He's a mean son of a bitch. And that doesn't have anything to do with it anyway."

"No point in hurting him," I said as I turned away. He grabbed my arm and jerked me around to face him.

"*Hurt*ing him? What the hell you think you're out there for?" I tried to pull loose but he clamped down, veins standing out on the back of a hand hard from years of working red iron.

"Boy," he said, "you better straighten up. You think that Indian's gonna give you a break if he gets you on the ropes tomorrow?" His face was tilted back and cocked to one side above his stocky body: a tight-clamped jaw, a bristly Fu Manchu worn in honor of Hurricane Carter, and a nose that had been redone in rings from Calgary to Salt Lake City. You knew from his eyes that he wanted to be kind, but understood when not to be. I hadn't knocked Grosniak out because I couldn't stand the smack of my glove against his rubbery flesh, and his look when my left came for his nose again, too quick for him to stop. In the last round, when he lumbered out with his hands at his waist trying to get enough air into his heavy body, I had hit him only to keep him away.

Charlie let go of my arm. "Get dressed," he said. "Let's get out of this place."

I pulled off the trunks and sweat-soaked cup that five other fighters had used that afternoon and bent over the sink at the end of the row of lockers. The porcelain was covered with gummy green-brown scum and matted with hair. The hot water tap wouldn't turn. I felt no pain when the water touched my face, so I knew I wasn't cut. I rinsed handfuls of it down my chest and groin and started shivering. "Charlie," I said, "did you bring a towel?"

When I turned, Gus Two Teeth, the prison heavyweight champ, was leaning in the doorway. He was still wearing his boxing trunks. A wine-colored stain of acne spread down his neck and across his thick, rounded chest and shoulders. He seemed to be looking slightly to one side of me, and when I nodded I couldn't tell if he ignored me or didn't see me. Twice that afternoon I had watched him leap in with a left hook that knocked a heavyweight off his feet. The first man got up and took the eight count. Two Teeth clubbed him back to the mat in seconds. The other man went down half a minute into the fight and stayed there.

Two Teeth pushed off the door with his shoulder and went back outside. I remembered that I was cold, and I dried my face and chest with my jeans and got dressed. When I came out, Charlie was sitting in a corner tying knots in the piece of cord he always carried. Several convicts were standing across the stage. The coach of the Anaconda Club, a three-hundred-pounder named Fletcher, had joined them. We knew him from other tournaments, and he had acted as second for both Charlie and me today. He waved when he saw us.

"Looks like Fletcher's renewing old acquaintances," Charlie said.

"Why, is he a cop or something?"

Charlie looked at me. "He did three years here," he said. "I thought you knew that."

"No," I said.

"Sure. Blew his old lady away. I remember reading about it in high school." I watched the boxers and convicts on the stage step out of Fletcher's way as he strode over to us. He was built to carry his weight—it only added to the impression of his physical power. Charlie's news did not surprise me.

Fletcher slapped me on the back, which started me coughing again. "You looked terrific out there," he said. "That Grosniak's a pretty tough old boy."

"He's a meat," Charlie said.

"Well, he's no Gus Two Teeth," said Fletcher. He turned to me. "I'll be straight with you. I don't think you can win tomorrow." He sounded cheerful. "I've seen Gus fight a lot of times. I just don't think you have the experience to take him. But if you stay away from him, maybe you can go the distance. He's a lousy trainer. Always wins because none of his fights ever go past the second. If you can keep him going, he'll get tired." He slapped me on the back again and started down the steps from the stage.

"Come on," he said. "I'll buy you guys a hot dog."

Thirty other boxers and coaches were waiting around the small concession stand the prisoners had set up at the back of the auditorium. I didn't feel like eating, but I drank most of a Coke. After a few minutes two guards came across the exercise yard.

"Everybody here?" one of them asked. He had small shoulders and wide fleshy hips, and his pistol and nightstick seemed too big for him. They clicked together as he moved. He yelled into the auditorium that this was the last call for the boxers to leave. "Anybody still here's gonna spend the night," he said. He grinned, and the convicts running the concession stand grinned too.

The guards led us across the exercise yard through the raw, windy twilight. Dead grass sprouted through cracks in the concrete where the snow had blown off. Scraps of rusty chain nets on basketball hoops tinkled in the wind. The fence around the yard was eighteen or twenty feet high, chain link topped with barbed wire, and I could see the guard towers at all four corners of the old brick building, a silhouette in the window of each.

At the end of every corridor was an iron door with an armed guard sitting on a stool behind it. After looking us over, he would press a button and the door would slide back. Nobody pushed to be first through, but nobody lagged behind. Finally we came to the last checkout point, a little booth with an iron grill across the front. The guard examined each of our hands under a fluorescent light for the stamp he had put there when we came in. I was glad I hadn't taken a shower.

It was almost dark when Charlie and I reached the outskirts of Deer Lodge and passed the last of the signs that read: "Warning—state penitentiary and mental health facility are located in this area. Do not pick up hitchhikers between these signs." From there we drove eleven flat miles through soggy hayfields to the Highway 12 turnoff at Garrison Junction. The car was warm from the heater and I cracked a window, but the wet air started me coughing again.

"You got tuberculosis or something?" Charlie said.

"Just a cold."

"We'll get you some cough syrup in town."

"Shelley's got some codeine," I said.

After a moment he said, "So you're going over to Shelley's tonight."

"I told her I would." He nodded his head slowly.

We passed an Indian woman walking alone by the road. She was old and hunched over and her ankles were thin. The wind blew her coat open as she turned to watch us, clutching a bundle under her arm. No houses were in sight.

"I think you can take that son of a bitch if you just stay away from him," Charlie said. "Don't listen to Fletcher's crap." I watched the old lady fade behind us into the dark of the Warm Springs Valley.

"That's the smallest ring I've ever been in, Charlie."

He shrugged. "That just means you have to work harder. He's tough, you don't want to go in and mix it up with him. But you got six inches' reach on him, and you're in shape."

"And he's got fifteen pounds on me and he's twice as fast. Jesus, I never saw anybody go at it like that." The high-pitched drone of the Mazda engine dropped as we climbed a small rise, and then I could see the lights of Garrison far ahead.

When we reached the outskirts of Helena, Charlie said, "Shelley's, huh?"

"Right," I said. A few minutes later we pulled up in front of the one-bedroom house she rented in the part of town called Moccasin Flats. The streets were dirt there, and what was left of her fence was always plastered with windblown paper. A cat's eyes glowed in the headlights, then disappeared into the abandoned chicken house across the road.

"About ten tomorrow, hey?" he said.

"Okay," I said. He leaned across the seat as I got out.

"You let that woman suck all the juice out of you, you ain't gonna be worth a hoot in hell tomorrow." He settled back low in his seat and looked straight ahead.

"I'll make her sleep on the couch," I said. He snorted.

"Eat some eggs in the morning," he said.

The faint smell of marijuana smoke hit me when I pushed open the door, old, as if it was in the curtains and furniture. "Don't move," she said. I turned slowly to the corner where she sat cross-legged. She stared at me, pupils dilated in the deepest blue-green eyes I had ever seen, then abruptly began working a pencil across the pad on her knees. "The conquering hero returns home," she said. The pencil zigzagged swiftly, her eyes still on my face. I tossed my bag on the couch and pulled off my coat.

"Hey," she said.

"Another time."

"But I've got to catch you in your moment of glory."

"Later," I said. My voice was sharp. The pencil bounced once on the old plank floor. She folded her hands in her lap and watched me.

"Sorry," she said. "Your face isn't smashed up for a change, so I thought maybe you won." The walls were covered with her sketches and charcoals. In what was supposed to be the dining room a table was piled with palettes and brushes soaking in cans of solution. She had just started painting seriously; I thought her drawings were still far better.

"I did." I said. I was tired but I didn't want to stop moving. "You got any beer?"

She nodded. "Okay," she said, jumping up. "The sketch can wait." She put her hands on my cheeks and turned my face both ways, then kissed me. "Tough fight?"

"No," I said. We kissed again, longer this time, then she led me into the kitchen. She took two bottles of San Miguel out of the refrigerator and laid a huge sirloin steak on the counter.

"Celebrate," she said. "Victory in the last fight of the season. If you lost you got Buckhorn and tuna fish."

"Shelley, where'd you get the money for this?"

Her eyes widened in mock surprise. "I keep telling you, I've got a sugar daddy." I snorted, but I thought of all my out-of-town construction jobs. She opened the bottles and raised hers. "To heroes," she said. There was an edge to her voice.

I took a long drink of beer, so cold it made my teeth hurt, sharp but soothing to my raw throat. "It wasn't the last fight of the season," I said.

"Christ," she said, setting the bottle down. "Don't tell me you let Charlie talk you into that stupid Golden Gloves thing."

I shook my head. "Tomorrow."

"To*mor*row?"

"This was just eliminations. I've got to go back for the finals."

She turned away. "I thought maybe we could do something tomorrow."

"If I hadn't won." After a moment she shrugged. When she turned back she was looking at me from a long way away.

"So how do you want your steak?"

I came up behind her and put my arms around her. Her body was tight and resisting. "Look, I'm sorry," I said. "I'm not too crazy about this either."

"Then why are you doing it?"

"I told you, I won." She reached out to the bottle on the counter and drew a face in the moisture that coated it. "I've got to go back and finish," I said.

"Who's going to give a damn if you don't?" I felt her shrug again. "I'll tell you who," she said. "A bunch of jerks who can't get off on anything but beating each other's brains out." She leaned back against me and stroked my hand that still rested on her belly, warm and tight under my fingers. "You hate it, don't you?" she said. Her hair smelled of lemon and it tickled my nose as she moved her head back and forth. "I mean, I guess I could even see it if you got paid."

"That's not the point," I said.

"So what is the point?" She reached up and caressed the back of my neck. "If you're trying to prove something, lover, I can think of better ways." She straightened up and I let her go. "How do you want your steak?"

"I don't care," I said. "Medium."

After dinner I took a long hot shower and stretched out on the bed. It was too short for me, so I always ended up sticking my feet through the iron posts at the end. The phlegm rose in my chest and I started coughing again. The stereo was playing quietly in the next room; I could hear the dark rhythmic chords and lonesome harmonica of *Blonde on Blonde,* and during breaks in the music, the bubbling of her water pipe.

She pushed open the bedroom door and lit the kerosene lantern on the dresser. I watched her take her earrings off, burnished copper teardrops that glowed dully in the flame light. Another night I would have asked her to leave them on.

"My God, you sound awful," she said. She half turned toward me as she slipped her shirt off.

"Do you have any more of that codeine?"

"I think so." She rummaged through a drawer and came up with a small brown bottle. The stuff was cherry-flavored, but you could tell there was something under the sweetness. Shelley put on a robe and walked down the hall to the bathroom. I watched a small dark shape move patiently, in silhouette, down the wall. It fluttered toward the candle.

A cold ache still touched the base of my nose when I remembered the Samoan at the Golden Gloves—that first jolt to my ribs, then opening my eyes to the lights that hung from the auditorium ceiling. The referee was on "three." I got up, and then got up again, seeing for the first time the rust-colored stains on the mat, trying to follow the grinning, kinky, blue-black head. But, as in the dream I had when I was younger, I could not make my arms move. There comes a moment when you realize you are not what you have thought. I drove home that night with three broken ribs and a nearly dislocated jaw. What had happened, I never wanted to happen again, but not because of the pain.

When Shelley came back she smelled of clean warm skin, scented soap, and toothpaste. She draped her robe over a chair and said, "Lie on your stomach." She straddled me and slid her cool hands up and down my back, pressing her thumbs into muscles sore from hours of tension. Later she said, "Turn over." I watched her sway above me while she kneaded my shoulders and then my chest. In the dim room her face looked dreamy, absorbed in the movement of her hands. When she leaned forward her hair brushed my skin.

After a while she rested her cheek against my belly. I stroked her hair, rounding the curve of her skull with my fingers. "What's the matter?" she whispered. It was a long time before I answered.

"That Indian's going to beat the crap out of me tomorrow," I said.

"Then why are you going?" She sat up and put her hands on my shoulders. "For God's sake, what's the *matter* with you? Ten minutes ago you're coughing like you're going to die, and now you tell me you're going to drive all the way to Deer Lodge to get beat up." She pressed me back into the bed until her face was inches from mine. "Don't go," she said. The scent of perfume was strong from the soft place where her jaw met her neck.

"Charlie's coming for me tomorrow at ten," I said. She jerked back upright.

"The hell with Charlie," she said angrily. "Some friend, always dragging you off to fight. Call him and tell him you're not going tomorrow.

We'll stay in bed all day. You're sick anyway. Tell him he can fight the damn Indian himself. Call him." I didn't move. She slid off me.

"Then I'll call him." Her feet thumped on the wooden floor.

"No," I said. I hooked my arm around her waist and pulled her back. She twisted my fingers.

"Let me go, goddamnit!" She broke free and strode across the room.

"Wait," I said. "I'll call him in the morning." She stopped, silvery white against the dark passageway.

"Promise?" she said. I hesitated. She jerked the door open.

"If I'm still coughing like this I won't go."

"Promise me," she said. "Say it."

"I promise."

"Now you're talking sense." She flopped back down on the bed and stretched across me. "Honey, when are you gonna understand, you're just not a fighter."

My hand stopped moving on her back.

"You're just not like Charlie and those others," she said. "That's okay. You don't have to be. I like you anyway."

After a while she said, "I'm sorry, I guess I shouldn't have said that." She watched me for a minute longer, then turned so that her back was snug against me. Later her breathing became regular. For a long time I listened to the ticking of the pendulum clock and explained to Gus Two Teeth and Grosniak and all the other prisoners who lay alone in their cell bunks night after night why I could not make love to this woman.

The weigh-in room was small and crowded, though not so many boxers were there the next morning. Five or six prisoners were standing by the door joking with each other and with the guards. Grosniak was there with Gus Two Teeth, who was wearing prison grays and a navy stocking cap, like a logger. They stopped talking when Charlie and I came into the room. I nodded to Grosniak but he just stared at me. Two Teeth again seemed to be looking to one side.

I took my clothes off, laid them on a bench, and wrapped a towel around myself. The man at the scale put his hand on my back to help me up the four-inch step. "What do you think it'll be?" he asked as he slid the balance weights around.

"One ninety-three," I said.

"One ninety-three on the nose," he said. "You look bigger than that." Two Teeth and the convicts laughed at something one of them said. I started to step into my jeans.

"You might as well just put your trunks on," the man at the scale called over. "The fights are almost ready to start." He watched me while I waited for Charlie to get some trunks. I wrapped the towel around me again.

Charlie came back with a cup and a pair of green trunks. I put them on. "Come on," he said. "I'll wrap your hands." When we got to the door one of the convicts was blocking it, his back to us. Charlie said, "Excuse me, pardner." The man turned and stared at us, and one by one all the other convicts turned too, and then my eyes met those of Gus Two Teeth. They were black and shiny and calm, set deep in an acne-scarred face the color of an old saddle. I had never felt so white.

Out in the gym I put my robe on and Charlie and I sat across from one another, me facing the wall. He took two rolls of thin gauze and a roll of white athletic tape from his gym bag. I watched his hands as he pried out the little piece of metal that held one of the gauze rolls together. His fingers were short and thick, his knuckles misshapen.

"Left hand," he said. I rested my left forearm on my thigh and extended the hand. With his Buck knife he cut a two-inch slit in the roll of gauze and hooked it around my thumb. He started wrapping the gauze around my wrist. After each turn he would pull it snug and say, "Okay?"

"Okay," I would say. Charlie worked slowly and carefully. Little beads of sweat were forming on the skin just below his hairline. I could see the carotid arteries pulsing in his throat. He opened his mouth slightly each time he inhaled, and his nostrils distended as he forced the air back out, making a small whistling sound. I looked over his head at the wall.

"Too tight?" he asked. I flexed my fingers.

"No," I said. I was having trouble taking deep breaths.

Someone yelled, "Let's have the flyweights and lightweights out in the auditorium." I could hear the job corps fighters get up and walk across the gym. Then it was quiet.

Charlie cut strips of tape with his knife and ran them down between my fingers. "How you feeling?" he asked.

"Okay," I said. For the first time I noticed a bald spot on top of his head. I started to tell him about it, but then decided to wait. The skin of his scalp was pinkish white, paler than the skin of his face. I could smell the morning's coffee on his breath.

Far away a bell rang.

"You get the chance," Charlie was saying, "throw your right. It's your best punch. Be careful, though, he's got a hell of a left hook. You drop that right too much, you'll set him up. Use that circling hook you worked on that kid in Lewistown that time. Use that a lot. But mostly jabs, and if you get a good clean shot, throw your right."

My throat was dry. When I swallowed there was a sour taste. "Charlie," I said.

He glanced up anxiously. "Too tight?" he said. He loosened the tape between my fingers. "That better?"

I looked into the eyes with no fear in them. "Yeah," I said. "Thanks."

When he taped my wrist he said, "Take an easy lap, just to get the blood going. Then I'll warm your hands up." I slipped the robe off and trotted slowly around the gym. Someone yelled from the door for the welterweights and middleweights, but they were all out watching the fights. I shook my arms as I jogged.

The auditorium was quiet. The middleweights were about to begin. Since there were no light-heavyweights, my fight was next. All around the ring the boxers and inmates and trainers sat or stood with their arms folded. Some of the boxers were holding trophies. Across the stage, surrounded by other convicts, Gus Two Teeth sat in a chair. He was wearing white trunks and no robe.

"Time to glove up," Charlie said. He held up a pair of ten-ounce gloves, about the size of ski mittens, still soggy from the last fight. After I got them on, he said, "Better take a couple more shots." I stood up and started throwing punches at his hands. "Come on, make 'em snap." I punched as hard as I could, but there was not much snap. Charlie let his hands down slowly. He looked at me until I met his eyes. His face was grim.

"Remember what I told you," he said.

They were all watching me as I walked to the ring, the convicts and boxers and people who had come from the outside. I glanced out over the rows of faces but I saw no one I recognized, just cowboy hats and the high-piled hair of the few women. The black fighter with the crimson shirt was nodding and grinning at me. He was wearing a black robe with white stripes instead of the red shirt, but I knew it was him. Someone slapped me on the back and started rubbing my shoulders. I turned and saw Fletcher's face, the size of a pumpkin, his fat-man sweat oozing out through the dark oily pores in his skin. He was close to me and I smelled cigarette smoke and liquor on his breath. His eyes were laughing.

"Stay in there long as you can, kid," he said. "We'll have the towel ready." Charlie climbed the three short steps to the ring ahead of me and held the ropes apart. I took the first step, the second, the third, and stopped.

I stepped through the ropes.

Behind me I heard the referee clear his throat. "Ladies and gentlemen. The feature event of today's exhibition. The heavyweight championship of this tournament." There was a pause and a rustle of paper. "From Helena, wearing green trunks, weighing one hundred and ninety-three pounds . . ." My name was called. I heard a few cheers from the audience and some more from around the ring.

"Go git him, Slim," somebody yelled.

". . . weighing two hundred and eight pounds, the defending champion of this tournament, Gus Two Teeth!" The crowd hooted and howled, and as the noise died a single male voice screamed, "Flatten that ski jump, Gus!" I heard applause and more yelling.

"Come on out here, fellows," said the referee. In the center of the ring I stood close to Gus Two Teeth. He was several inches shorter than me and several inches wider, and he had calm black shiny eyes.

The ref was a small man with neat sandy hair and a bow tie. "Punches below the belt," he was saying above a dull, steady murmur from the auditorium. "Break clean . . . either of you go down, the other goes back to his corner for the eight count . . ." The timekeeper rang the bell three quick times. "Good clean bout. Shake hands and come out fighting." Gus Two Teeth and I touched our four gloved fists together and turned back to our corners.

"Water," I said. Charlie got the squeeze bottle into my mouth in a hurry and Fletcher held the bucket up. I swished the water around and spat. The taste was still there.

"Seconds out," the timekeeper called. Charlie pulled the stool out and I held the ropes and bounced, trying to force air all the way into my lungs. I watched a man in a cowboy hat walk up the aisle of the auditorium. Halfway, he stopped and raised a fistful of popcorn to his mouth.

The bell rang. I turned and trotted out. Two Teeth was already loping around to my right, his fists held loosely in front of his chest, his face exposed. I circled with him. I was stiff and standing up too straight. My arms felt locked into position. I couldn't keep my eyes off his, but in Gus Two Teeth's eyes I saw no amusement, nor any hatred, nor fear—only a calmness that told of something I had never felt. We danced around and around that tiny square of canvas, and I felt that at any second my legs would give out under me.

He shifted his weight suddenly and I leaped back, almost against the ropes. He closed the distance and I slashed at his face and jerked to the right. His left hand stung my ear as it brushed by. In the center of the ring again, we circled. I felt him moving closer. I threw my left and it flopped out from me, a thing with no strength or bone. He made no attempt to slip or block it. A fine trickle of blood started from his nose. The skin on his face was drawn back tight over his cheekbones and I saw glints of white teeth at the corners of his mouth. I backed up, almost running, until I brushed the ropes, then threw my left, and this time, before my fist was halfway to his face, he was in the air between us. I didn't see the punch, but I remember it was like being touched with something very hot.

When I came back everything was almost the same, but I knew I had been gone. I bounced off the ropes with my forearms covering my head and bulled past him, trying to get clear enough to see. When I looked he was there and it landed on my right temple. I was in a corner, crouched, lucky to be stopping some of the punches with my elbows and gloves, because my eyes were down. I knew I had to watch his hands, but I could not make my eyes stay up.

Then a punch to the forehead really hurt me, and somehow I pulled my eyes up to the blur of brown face and brown gloves and brown body that was swirling in front of me. The right hand was coming at me again, and I ducked to my right and caught it on my glove and at that second the face came into focus, looking thoughtful, and I understood that the next punch I took would be the last. My body was twisted far to the right, my hands beside my head. I dropped my knee and drove my fist at the center of those shiny black eyes.

I felt it all the way to my shoulder. The face was gone and nobody was hitting me anymore. I came off the ropes and dropped my gloves enough to take a look. I heard a lot of yelling and the ref was dancing around with his arms out. Gus Two Teeth was across the ring, his back to me. His arms were stretched out over the ropes and he was walking slowly along them. When he rolled around to face me his mouth was open. He didn't seem to see me.

"Kill him," a voice was screaming. "Take him! Finish him!" I waited. "For Christ's sake, GO GET HIM!" I dropped my fists and bounced on my toes. Two Teeth shook his head and straightened up. The ref grabbed his wrists and tugged on his gloves. Two Teeth began to lope again, slower this time. The eyes were not quite so shiny now.

The bell rang.

Charlie was yelling at me before I was halfway to my corner. "For Christ's sake, you had him! What's the *matter* with you?" I dropped onto the stool and he pulled my mouthpiece out and shoved the bottle in. Fletcher held up the bucket but this time I missed and spat onto the pointed toe of his cowboy boot. Charlie was sprinkling water on my chest and talking hoarsely into my ear.

"He's got a glass jaw," he was saying. "He's shook up now. All you got to do is nail him one more time and then finish him off." The ten-second whistle blew. I wanted to explain, but talking was so much effort.

The next round lasted longer than I'd expected, over a minute. I felt loose and cool. I was moving well and I stung him with several jabs that got the blood flowing from his nose again. But then I planted my feet and cocked my right, and in the time it took my hand to shift three inches he was in the air. The hook dropped me to one knee. The ref had to push him back to his corner while I took the count, and at eight Two Teeth shoved by him and leaped at me again. This time I went down to a hand and a knee, and while I was getting my feet under me something smashed me on top of the head. I rolled onto my back and turned my head from side to side. When the ref reached ten he grabbed Gus Two Teeth's arm and raised it. The crowd was yelling for Two Teeth and Charlie and Fletcher were yelling at the ref and I got up and walked back to my corner. As I reached for the ropes to steady myself I heard my name called. A gloved hand touched my shoulder and I turned and looked for the last time into those black eyes, almost shy now.

"Good fight," he said. We put our arms around each other's waists and someone handed us each a trophy and took a picture.

Charlie was furious as we walked back to the car. "The son of a bitch hit you when you were down," he said. "He clubbed you on top of the head and drove you to the mat."

"It doesn't matter," I said. "He beat me anyway."

"You could have knocked him out."

"That was just a lucky punch," I said.

"You could have," he said. "You didn't go in on him when you had him." I exhaled slowly into my cupped hands.

"Whatever that takes, Charlie," I said, "I just don't think I've got it."

"Well you better learn, or you're going to keep on getting hurt." He unlocked the car door, and I turned for a last look at the old brick building. Flashes of sunlight gave it a warmer color than yesterday, but it was no place I ever wanted to spend any time.

"They still should have given you the fight," Charlie said as I got in.

"He'd still be the better fighter."

"You got a funny way of looking at it."

"I guess I do," I said. We passed some of the Anaconda boxers getting into a station wagon with Fletcher. The man with the red shirt grinned and waved and I waved back.

"Well, we start working out for the Gloves on Monday," Charlie said. "You gonna make it?" Main Street in Deer Lodge was empty and closed up tight, without a person or a spot that looked warm; no place to be on a Sunday afternoon in an early Montana spring.

"I don't know," I said. "Maybe I'll just wait a couple of weeks and try to kick this cold." I realized that I hadn't coughed in hours and I took a deep breath. There was only a slight raspiness in my throat.

"You could probably take the state easy," he said. "Only guy you'd have to beat is that Simmons from Great Falls, and he's just big and slow like that ape yesterday."

"I think maybe I'll just sit the rest of the season out, Charlie," I said. "See how I feel next fall."

"The regionals are in Vegas this year," he said. "That'd be a good trip."

"I'll think about it."

Charlie was quiet for a minute, then he said, "You know, two years ago I went up to Edmonton to fight some spade from Tacoma, and about ten seconds into the first round that little bastard sucker-punched me and knocked me right on my ass. After driving six hundred miles. I laid there and listened to the ref count and I could of got up again, but I was so disgusted I didn't even try. I thought that was it, my last fight." We passed the "End Speed Zone" sign at the edge of town and Charlie accelerated to seventy-five.

"You'll be back," he said. "It gets in your blood." He started whistling softly between his teeth, a tune I had never heard.

I put the seat back and closed my eyes. "What time is it?"

"About three."

"Run me by Shelley's, will you?" Charlie rolled the window part-way down and spat out his gum.

"If you hadn't been so busy with your old lady last night, you'd have had enough in you to finish Gus off," he said.

"That must have been it," I said.

When we turned the corner at Garrison, the clouds broke and we saw the peaks of the Flint range, high craggy masses of snow that usually stayed hidden from October to May. I had never been up there, but I'd heard about the fishing. The snow would still be deep even in mid-June, and it would be a good day's climb into the Trask Lakes. I knew I'd find pan-sized cutthroat where the streams emptied in.

SHORT ROUNDS WITH THE CHAMP

Judith Rascoe

One

Mrs. Damon got a letter from her son's teacher, saying, "He has a discipline problem." Her boy was six years old. Mrs. Damon put the letter away in her jewelry box. "If she wants me to come see her, I will," Mrs. Damon said to herself.

Two

It rained almost every day in March, Mrs. Damon's father broke his hip, and Mr. Damon had to go to Forth Worth three times. At the end of the month Mrs. Damon asked her husband if they could get a divorce. "No," he said. "You haven't thought this thing through. You don't have any grounds for a divorce. How would you like taking care of Chrissie and Bobby all by yourself? We'll drop this subject."

Three

When the roads opened in June Mr. and Mrs. Damon and Chrissie and Bobby drove up into the mountains between Bishop and Lone Pine and camped out one weekend. After lunch on Saturday Mr. Damon nailed a paper plate to a tree and showed Bobby how to shoot a twenty-two pistol. Bobby fired at the paper plate four times without hitting it. "That's the kind of gun they shot Kennedy with," Mrs. Damon said.

"Honey, that was a rifle," Mr. Damon said.

"No, the other Kennedy."

Bobby fired at the paper plate two more times, but he missed it both times.

"That's enough," Mr. Damon said.

"Please, I want to hit it just once," Bobby said.

"Some other time," Mr. Damon said. "Ammunition costs money." He loaded one bullet in the pistol, fired it, and made a hole in the paper plate. "Does your mother want to try it?"

"Mom, do you want to try it?"

"No, you take my turn."

Bobby fired again, but he didn't hit the plate.

"I think you're aiming high," Mr. Damon said.

Four

Mrs. Damon drove Chrissie and Bobby to their grandmother Damon's house in Riverside, and then she drove to Palm Springs and took a motel room. She bought a bathing suit and had her hair streaked. It was August, and the motel was half closed and almost empty. After her first swim she lay on a lounge chair to dry off. A girl in a brown silk bikini asked her to move to another chair. "That's my chair," the girl said. A little after midnight Mrs. Damon thought she heard somebody trying to get into her room. She got dressed and called Mr. Damon from a pay phone in the bar.

"Have a ball," he said. "I don't care when you come back. You come back when you're ready. Who're you with?"

"I'm by myself," she said.

"That's too bad."

When she went home she found a note that said he had gone to Houston for a meeting.

Five

After Chrissie and Bobby were back in school, Mrs. Damon went to her minister and told him her marriage was breaking up. Her minister sent her to a marriage counselor. The marriage counselor asked her to come to a group session and bring Mr. Damon. The marriage counselor and his wife conducted the group session in a duplex in

Hollywood. Mrs. Damon saw that the couches came from the Goodwill: the Goodwill had been covering all its upholstered furniture in the same plaid material that summer. There were ashtrays everywhere and a fifty-cup coffee maker. Five other couples came to the session. The oldest couple were Vera and Mike; they had also been to more sessions than anybody else. At the end of the first half hour Mike said to Mr. Damon, "I want you to go over to your wife and tell her that you love her."

"That's hard for me to do," Mr. Damon said.

"I want you to do it," Mike said.

"What are you afraid of?" Vera asked.

"What am I afraid of, honey?" Mr. Damon asked his wife. To Vera he said, "I'm not that way. It isn't my way to say what I feel."

"What do you feel?" Mike asked. "Do you love her? If you love her, tell her that."

Mr. Damon went over to Mrs. Damon and kissed her. "I love you, honey," he said.

Later in the session Mrs. Damon asked everybody, "What should I do?"

"Grow up," Vera said. "You aren't a child any more."

Mr. and Mrs. Damon didn't go back to see the marriage counselor; they didn't go to another group session.

"I'm not getting anything out of it," Mr. Damon said.

Six

Mrs. Damon fell in love with the man who taught ceramics and firing at the recreation center. For several weeks they had coffee together after class and told each other about their childhood and all the people they had been in love with. When he told her about his first wife's abortion, she told him that she once wanted to divorce her husband, and the next time Mr. Damon went out of town the man came to the house after dark and stayed all night in her room. That night she said she didn't want to have sex with him, but they went ahead anyway.

"I don't want the kids to hear," Mrs. Damon said.

"They know I'm here."

"No they don't," she said.

After that Mrs. Damon sometimes made the children take sleeping pills, and on those nights she built a fire in the fireplace. She and her boyfriend lay on the rug in front of the fire and drank wine. She was very happy.

Seven

Mr. and Mrs. Damon went to a PTA meeting to hear arguments about sex education in the schools. Just before the meeting started a teacher approached them and said that she wanted to talk to them about Bobby's discipline problem. Mr. Damon laughed and said, "You're the one that has the discipline problem. I don't have any discipline problem with him."

During the meeting a gray-haired man stood up and said, "Let's not fool ourselves. These kids know everything there is to know about sex. They know more than I know about sex. The way these girlies dress these days, they know what they're showing off. I want to make sure they don't spread the clap. If you want to know the truth I'm worried my kids are going to get the clap from one of these little whores." Several people shouted at the man to sit down and shut up. Mr. Damon walked up to the man and said, "Shut your filthy mouth." Then he punched him. The blow fell a little short. The gray-haired man burst into tears and swung first one fist and then the other, but neither touched Mr. Damon. He and Mr. Damon kept trying, and both men had to be restrained physically. The gray-haired man then said he would make a formal complaint to the police. "Do that," Mr. Damon said.

Eight

In May Mr. and Mrs. Damon decided to buy a camper, for family vacations. On Sunday afternoons they went to sales lots together and looked at new models. During the week Mrs. Damon answered newspaper ads inserted by owners who wanted to sell. One afternoon she drove all the way out to a house in Chatsworth to look at a Traveleze. Nobody was home but the owner, a middle-aged man with a scar from his hairline to his jaw, who said he was retired. "Even my dog's gone shopping," the man said. He would say something and then stop and look hard into her eyes until she said something back.

"What kind of a dog?" she asked him.

He would also pause a long time before he answered, looking hard into her eyes again.

After a while he said, "A German shepherd."

"Lots of people are afraid of those," she said.

After a while he said, "Yes they are." And then he said, "Nobody who gets to know Dusty is afraid of him. Nobody will be hurt by Dusty."

She couldn't think what to say next.

"Do you know something?" he said. "You have got the face of a little girl, but you have the eyes of a mature woman. Do you know what I'm talking about?"

"No," she said.

"I think you know what I'm talking about," he said.

"No I don't," she said.

"You can have it your way," he said.

Mrs. Damon said she wanted to look at the Traveleze, and he led her around the house to the driveway, where the Traveleze was parked in front of an old black Cadillac. The Traveleze was in very bad condition; there were hundreds of little scars and scratches, cigarette burns and dents and nicks all over the interior.

"It's been lived in," the owner said.

"It needs a lot of work, I guess," she said.

After a while he said, "You don't have to buy it," as if all along she had thought she had to.

"Come back and see us," he said. "Come back soon."

"We'll see," Mrs. Damon said.

Nine

Mrs. Damon and her boyfriend were lying in front of the fireplace, and her boyfriend said, "I wonder if I would be in love with you if I wasn't afraid of your husband. I wonder if I would come here."

Mrs. Damon replied, "I guess you wouldn't."

Ten

Mr. and Mrs. Damon and Chrissie and Bobby went on a vacation trip in their new camper. Mr. Damon taught Bobby how to cast with a real fishing rod. Mrs. Damon showed Chrissie how to pan for gold with an aluminum pie plate. At night the children slept in the camper and Mr. and Mrs. Damon slept in a tent beside it.

Mr. Damon told his wife that he wanted to try new ways of making love.

"Where did you get that idea?" she asked him.

"I read a book," he said. "Don't *resist* me."

"I don't want to resist you."

"Don't be scared. This is a perfectly natural thing. Anything is natural and good as long as you enjoy it."

Later she said, "I don't enjoy it."

Mr. Damon got angry.

"I enjoy it," he said. "Why can't you enjoy it? Relax and enjoy it. I can't enjoy it if you don't."

Eleven

When they got back home after their vacation in the mountains, Mr. Damon told Mrs. Damon that he took part in an orgy on a plane to Atlanta one night. The stewardess played with him and one of the co-pilots at the same time. There was nobody else on the plane except the crew and a couple of soldiers sleeping in tourist.

"You're crazy," Mrs. Damon said. "That never happened to you."

"It happens all the time," Mr. Damon said. "Do you like that story?"

"What do you mean?"

"Would you do that if you were a stewardess?"

"It never happened to you," Mrs. Damon said.

Twelve

Mrs. Damon woke up one morning at ten to six. When she looked at the clock on the night table and saw that the alarm was up and set for seven, she couldn't figure out what had awakened her. Finally she looked up and saw Bobby standing near the door. He was aiming his father's twenty-two pistol at her. "Put that down," she said. "You must not play with that pistol."

Mr. Damon woke up. When he saw Bobby with the pistol he said, "I'm gonna have to insist you put that gun down, fellow. That's against the rules, fellow."

Bobby said, "Ha ha, it is *not* against the rules."

He fired the pistol and the bullet missed Mr. Damon by less than two inches. It made a little hole and a stink in the moulding of the headboard.

MENDOCINO

Ann Packer

Bliss is driving north on Highway 1, looking at the crashing Pacific. She would like to pull the car over and walk along the water's edge, but there is no beach here, only cliffs jutting out over the ocean. The mountains, the road, the water—it's so gorgeous it's getting monotonous. So she begins to make small promises to herself. If Gerald starts in on the beauty of the self-sufficient life, she will allow herself a solitary one-hour walk. If Marisa invites her to join in the baking of bread or the pickling of cucumbers or the gathering of fresh-laid eggs, she will invent a friend who lives nearby with whom she has promised to have a drink. These people—her younger brother, Gerald, and his girlfriend, Marisa (his R.F.L., as he calls her, his Reason For Living, and, really, this irks Bliss as much as anything else)—live in Mendocino County, two and a half hours north of San Francisco, a mile from the coast, in a small, isolated house of their own design. It is, Bliss remembers, a nice enough house, made tacky by a pair of stained-glass windows that flank the front door—windows that Marisa made. She is, Gerald has said more than once, an *artisan*. Life for Marisa—and, now, for Gerald—is about using your hands whenever you can. Bliss has been tempted in the past to point out that your brain must contribute something to this equation, but she is determined to keep all snide remarks to herself on this visit. After all, it will be the first time she has seen them in over a year. And, too, today is the tenth anniversary of their father's suicide. She wants to be on her best behavior.

Bliss would like to think that this reunion was Gerald's idea—a peace offering of sorts—but she is sure that Marisa is behind it. Even the way Gerald asked her sounded like Marisa—didn't she think it would be nice if they could *be together* for a weekend. Until a couple of years ago—until Marisa—Gerald was a sensible man. Stodgy even, with his job working for a big accounting firm, with his careful haircuts and his fuel-efficient cars. They had a nice relationship; every four or five months Bliss would fly up from L.A. and Gerald would squire her around San Francisco, surprising her with tickets to chamber-music concerts, with dinner at out-of-the-way Asian restaurants. They would exchange work stories, and, into a second bottle of wine, confide in each other the news of their most recent failures at love. It amazes Bliss that until this moment she never once realized it was because they were failures that they talked about them. Now Gerald has his success, and it is as if the two of them had never been anything but what they are now: wary, cordial.

As Bliss turns from the coastal highway onto the road to Gerald and Marisa's property, it occurs to her that she has come empty-handed—no bottle of wine, no flowers, nothing. It would be worse if this were her first visit; she has been here once before, a year ago June, when Gerald and Marisa threw a housewarming party and she flew up for the day with Jason. But still, she ought to have something. So she makes a U-turn on the narrow road and heads back to the little store she passed a few miles back.

She didn't get a very good look at it when she drove by, and it's a disappointment. She was hoping for a little country fruit-and-vegetable place; she could have bought a dozen dusty peaches and offered them as coals to Newcastle—at least Gerald would have gotten it. She'll be lucky if this place has a head of iceberg; it might as well be a 7-Eleven.

She walks up and down the aisles, looking for something halfway suitable. The only beer they have isn't expensive enough to give some-one as a gift, and when she looks at the refrigerator section, thinking she might find some cheese, there's next to nothing there, either—just Velveeta and the kind of cream cheese that's whipped and has things added to it. She is drifting through the store, ordering herself to buy *something*, when she comes to the packaged cookies. She puts her hand out to a package, retracts it, then reaches again and picks the cookies up. They are Ideal bars—Gerald's favorite cookies when they were children. She's surprised they still make them; she hasn't seen or thought of them in years. The packaging hasn't changed a bit, though, and now she remembers Gerald hoarding whole packages of them in his room, eating them in bed at night. Their rooms shared a wall, and sometimes when she'd turned off her light and was lying wide awake in bed she could hear the cellophane crinkling.

She buys six packages. It seems a ridiculous number, as she tosses them onto the seat of the car and heads back up the road. One, maybe, or two, but six? She doesn't want to think of what Marisa will say.

It is almost dusk when Bliss turns down the long driveway leading to their house. She left L.A. at six this morning, and her shoulders ache. She should have flown and rented a car at the airport, as she and Jason did last summer, but she'd convinced herself it would be fun to drive. She thinks now that the reason she drove was to put off this moment for as long as she could.

She gets out of the car and stretches her arms over her head, bending from side to side; she hopes they have a decent bed. Then the front door opens and there is Gerald, in shorts and hiking boots and with—she can't believe it—a beard.

"The weary traveller," he says, coming down the walk to her car. "Are you dead?"

"Yes," she says, "I'm dead and I've gone to Heaven and met this man who looks so familiar to me." She reaches up and touches his beard. "This is new," she says.

"Like it?"

He is darker than she, and with the beard his face has a slightly menacing look. "It makes you look older," she says.

"Than who?"

She is about to answer with some kind of joke ("Than me, the aging spinster") when she realizes that he isn't really paying attention—he's looking back at the house.

Marisa appears, and Bliss has to admit it—she's beautiful. She is one of those tall, earthy women with frizzy hair—brown, in this case—but her size and strength are very feminine. She wears a flowered skirt and a man's sleeveless undershirt, and her arms and legs are lean, golden. Bliss can understand why Gerald is attracted to her—and attracted he is. When she joins them at Bliss's car, he puts an arm around her waist and squeezes her, as if she were the one who had just arrived.

"How are you?" Marisa asks. It sounds to Bliss like an invitation to make a long confession.

"O.K.," Bliss says. "You look great. Both of you—you look so healthy and fit."

"We are," says Marisa, and Bliss thinks, Well, the battle lines are drawn.

They go into the house, Gerald carrying her suitcase and Bliss holding the brown bag that contains the cookies. Gerald leads her to the guest room, which is in the back of the house, next to the kitchen. He sets the suitcase down and turns to her. For a moment she thinks he is going to tell her something—a secret, something he hasn't told Marisa, even something *about* Marisa—but all he says is "The bathroom's through there if you want to wash up. Come on into the kitchen whenever you're ready."

He leaves, and she realizes she's been hugging the cookies to her chest; and this would have been the perfect time to give them to him. She sits on the bed to test it, and when she finds that it's nice and firm her relief is so great it surprises her. She goes into the bathroom to splash some water on her face.

In the kitchen Marisa is chopping vegetables; Gerald is uncorking a bottle of wine. The kitchen windowsills are lined with jars of things, Bliss can't tell what—they are murky and either red or purple or green. Marisa sees her looking at them and says, "I'm so far behind on my canning."

"Don't listen to her," Gerald says. "You should see the cellar." He offers Bliss a glass of wine and she takes it, warning herself to be careful—the last thing she wants is to have to get through tomorrow with a hangover.

"Why don't you show Bliss around while I get dinner ready?" Marisa says. "Before it gets too dark." It seems to Bliss that Marisa has this—has everything—all planned out.

"Blister?" Gerald says, and she blushes with pleasure; he hasn't called her that in years.

"I'd love it."

"Bring your wine." She starts to follow him, but he turns back and looks at her feet. "Actually, do you have any other shoes? It's a bit muddy in places."

She does, but they're no more suitable for mud than these. She's suddenly very embarrassed—as if they could know what's in her suit-case, or in her closet at home: nothing rugged. "Think I'm a prima donna, do you?" she says. "What's a little mud?"

Gerald shrugs, but Marisa says, "You can't go out in those, you'll ruin them. We've had rain almost every day for the last two weeks." She goes to a closet and pulls out some rubber boots that remind Bliss of a pair she had in elementary school. "Here," Marisa says, "try these."

They're huge, probably three or four sizes too big, but Bliss slips off her sandals and steps into the boots. "O.K.," she says. "Great. Thanks."

"They're too big, aren't they?" Marisa says. "Wait, I'll get you some socks."

"Jesus, Mare, we're only going to be gone for ten minutes," Gerald says, but this doesn't seem to have any effect on Marisa; she disappears, then returns with two pairs of heavy socks for Bliss.

By the time they get outside, the light has nearly faded. Every-thing is a deep violet—the sky, the field behind the house, even Gerald's face. Bliss wishes she could tell what his expression is; is he irritated at Marisa?

"This way," he says, setting off around the house. "We've done a lot since you were here."

First he shows her the herb garden—a fenced-off square with neat little rows of more herbs than Bliss can imagine anyone wanting. He points them out, one by one, and Bliss tries to make admiring sounds. Then he launches into an explanation of how great it is to grow your own herbs, how they're useful for much more than just cooking. He bends and picks something, then holds it up to her nose. "Smell good?" he says.

It does, but she doesn't know what it is. "Mmm."

"It's rosemary," he says.

"Nice."

He looks down at the plants and scuffs at the earth with the toe of his boot. "We've been thinking," he says, but he doesn't go on.

"I wouldn't worry about it too much," Bliss says. "I do it, too, sometimes." Immediately she's sorry.

"Should I tell you this?" Gerald says. "Oh, why not. We've been thinking of having a baby."

Bliss is stunned. Not that it's so hard to imagine Gerald as a father—she's always thought he should have children. And Marisa was obviously born to have babies—the ultimate show of capability. But she realizes that in the back of her mind she's been waiting for him to go back to San Francisco, to being who he was.

"Are you?" she says finally. "Wow."

He waves the rosemary in her face. "Marisa wants to have a girl and name her Rosemary."

"Nice," Bliss says. And if it's a boy, Oregano?

They stand still in the herb garden for a little while longer, then Gerald says, "Come see the chicken coop. I built it myself."

When Gerald's tour is over, it is truly dark, the kind of clear, chilly night that's rare in Bliss's part of the state. There are so many stars out it looks like there's barely enough room for them all in the sky. She wonders whether Gerald can still identify the constellations; one winter when they were children, their father set up a telescope on the back porch, and after dinner on clear nights he'd tell them to put on their coats and they'd troop outside to look at the sky. Bliss remembers how impatient her father was with her: No, Bliss, he'd say, *that's* Taurus; I've told you before. You're not using your head. She'd look over and see her mother silhouetted in the doorway, and although she knew her mother would welcome her back inside—let Gerald do it, her mother would say, then your father will be satisfied—Bliss would stay outside, fingers getting numb, and try to remember.

When they reach the front door, Gerald stops and says, "I hope you don't mind vegetarian."

"Not at all," Bliss says. "It'll do me good to be so wholesome."

Gerald bites his lip, and she sees that this time she has offended him. "Seed to table," he says. "I know you think it's dumb or pretentious or something, but it's really important to me. It makes me feel like I'm in control of my life. Or at least part of it."

He turns to open the door. To stop him she says, "I don't think it's dumb at all," and she's surprised to find that it's true. It's the way she sometimes feels about the bookstore: she and her partner order books and the books arrive and they put them on the shelves and people buy them. "It's like the bookstore," she says.

"I'm not sure I get the connection," Gerald says. "But thanks. It matters to me that you don't condemn my life."

The directness of this unsettles her; it has always unsettled her that he can say something so revealing, so personal, and not have the saying of it undo him. It's the kind of confession that would choke her up. He stares at her for a moment, but the only reply she can think of is "Don't you ever miss eating meat?"

He laughs. "Not much. And when I do I get in the truck and drive to Santa Rosa to a place that makes a great meatball sub." He grins and opens the door, motioning her to go in ahead of him. Once they're inside, he heads for the kitchen, but she stops to take off the muddy boots. It's silly, really, but as she peels the socks down over her feet she's filled with the strangest feeling of satisfaction: Marisa may not like it—she may not even know it—but when he wants to he still eats meat.

There's a delicious, spicy smell coming from the kitchen as Bliss heads down the hall. When she gets there, though, she stops in the doorway: Gerald and Marisa are standing at the sink, talking in low tones. Marisa has pulled her hair into some kind of bun, and Gerald is running his finger up and down her neck.

"Hi," Bliss says.

They pull apart and turn to face her. "Hi," says Marisa.

"Hungry?" Gerald asks. "I'm starved."

Marisa pats his shoulder. "Lucky you," she says. "Dinner's almost ready." She smiles at Bliss.

"Almost?" he says in mock outrage.

She laughs. "It will be as soon as you get the salad out."

Bliss stands in a corner and watches as they move around the kitchen, taking things from the refrigerator and stove top and oven and putting them on the table. They don't look at each other or touch, but they're *connected* somehow—it's as if they were performing some kind of dance they'd been rehearsing for months.

They all sit, and Marisa serves their plates with rice and some kind of vegetable mixture—ratatouille, Bliss decides. They talk for a while about the things Gerald showed her—the chickens, the last of the tomatoes, the wood shop—and then Gerald asks about the bookstore. Bliss tells a story about a guy, Walter, who she hired a few weeks ago to be a cashier. He seemed perfect—he lived around the corner, said he could work extra hours whenever she wanted, even volunteered to open the store for her one morning when she had to go to the dentist. Then one night she was on her way home from having dinner with a friend and decided to stop at the store for a book. When she got there she found Walter and three of his friends sitting on the floor eating takeout pizza, passing around a fifth of vodka, and paging through bookstore books with their greasy fingers. "The thing that really got me," Bliss says, "is that when I told them to get out, they just walked off and left the pizza lying in the middle of the floor."

"That is terrible," Marisa says. Her forearms are resting on the edge of the table, and she has tightened her hands into fists. When Bliss looks at her face, she thinks she sees tears in her eyes. "People like that have no consideration."

This seems self-evident to Bliss—obviously Walter is a jerk; that's the point. "Well," she says.

But Marisa goes on. "He'll probably never learn, either. You know? He'll probably go through life trespassing on people's decency, never doing a single thing for anybody. Someday he'll marry some poor woman and ruin her life. God, that kind of thing makes me sick!"

Bliss is mortified. She looks away from Marisa's red face at Gerald; he's got such a worried look on his face that she wishes she could reach across the table and touch his arm. He looks the way he used to at the dinner table at home, toward the end, when her father was always angry at her mother. Is it not true, her father would say to her mother, that you told me you were going to finish that typing by dinner? Gerald, her father would say, what do you suppose could have happened? Do you suppose it just slipped your mother's mind that she had twenty pages to type for me today? Or do you suppose she was too God-damned busy talking to her friends at the grocery store to think of anything else? Well? Well, Gerald? Well?

Gerald looks up at Bliss, and she can see that his mind is whirling. She smiles at him—she will say the first thing that she can think of. But he beats her to it. "What kind of pizza was it?" he says.

Then he gets up and goes around behind Marisa's chair and leans down low, and when his arms reach around her, tears begin to stream from her eyes. Bliss looks down at her plate and pokes at the remains of her dinner with her fork. If this doesn't stop soon, she'll have to leave the room. When she looks up again, Gerald is staring at her, his face hard and challenging.

Finally Marisa reaches for her napkin and dabs at her face. She looks up at Bliss and says, "Sorry."

Bliss smiles and shrugs.

Gerald gives Marisa's shoulder a final pat and straightens up. Then Marisa pushes her chair back and stands, too. "Well," she says, as if nothing had happened, "are we done? I'll get going on the dishes. Why don't you two make a fire in the other room?" She carries a few things to the sink and begins to run the water. She turns back to Bliss. "I'm sorry we don't have any dessert," she says.

"We've got fruit," says Gerald. "Want a plum?"

"I'm fine," says Bliss. "It was delicious." She takes her plate to the sink and sets it down. This is not the right moment for the cookies.

The living room is sparsely furnished—just two armchairs and several large pillows on the floor.

"Sit," Gerald says, coming up behind her. He pats one of the chairs.

"Don't you guys want the chairs?" Bliss says. "I'll sit on one of those."

"Nonsense," he says.

So she sits in one of the chairs and watches him build the fire. Marisa's scene has disturbed her—does she do this kind of thing a lot?—but curious as Bliss is, she hopes Gerald won't bring it up. She doesn't really want to talk about it.

"That was a good dinner," she says.

"Thanks," he says, without turning around. He lights a match and touches the flame to some newspaper, then sits looking into the fireplace. Finally he turns to her. "Listen," he says, "let's just drop what happened in the kitchen, O.K.?"

"Of course," Bliss says. "I wasn't going to—"

"She's just a little on edge is all," Gerald says. "Having a visitor."

Bliss blushes. It wasn't *her* idea to come up here.

"I don't mean it like that," Gerald says. "She just wants you to like her."

He doesn't seem to expect a response; he turns back to the fireplace and pokes at the logs with a piece of kindling. She should say, "Oh, I do like her," but it would sound so forced; her mother used to sit on the edge of her bed at night and say, "I love you, baby," and then, after the slightest pause, "Do you love me?"

"That should catch," Gerald says, standing up. He claps his hands together to get rid of the wood dust, then sits in the other chair. "We were thrilled when it started getting cooler again. There's a guy up the road who lets me chop firewood for free."

"Just like that?"

"Well, I give him a hand when he needs it. I helped him build a new kitchen."

"How'd you learn to do all this stuff, anyway?"

"I must have a natural aptitude," Gerald says. They both laugh; he was the kind of child who, in art class, used his Popsicle sticks for abstract sculpture when everyone else was making a birdhouse.

"No, really," Bliss says.

"I wanted to," Gerald says. "That's really all it takes."

Marisa comes in from the kitchen carrying a tray. "I made some tea," she says. She offers the tray to Bliss, and Bliss thanks her and takes a mug. It smells strange, and she decides that it's some kind of herbal tea, made from their herbs. She would give anything for a cup of coffee right now.

Gerald takes a mug, and Marisa sets the tray on the floor at Gerald's feet. She pulls a pillow over and sits on it, leaning against his legs. No one says anything.

Bliss sips her tea, which tastes a little like almonds, and looks around the room for something to remark on. The walls are bare except for bunches of dried leaves—more herbs?—hanging in great clumps. There's a little stained-glass something-or-other in one of the windows, and Bliss thinks, O.K., that'll do; she's about to ask Marisa if she made it when Gerald clears his throat.

"So," he says, "ten years."

Bliss looks into her tea. It has been in the back of her mind that he might bring it up; she just hoped he wouldn't. She always thought they had a tacit agreement not to discuss it. She looks up and sees that Marisa has straightened a little, and she feels a flash of anger at her, as if she put the words into Gerald's mouth. They're both waiting for her to reply. "Yeah," she says.

"I think it was even a Friday," Gerald says.

"No," Bliss says, "it was a Wednesday." She remembers this distinctly. She was at home from college for the weekend and she'd driven back to school early on the Monday morning; then late that night her mother had called and said that her father hadn't come home, and she called again Tuesday afternoon to say he still wasn't home, so Bliss drove back; and on Wednesday morning the phone call came from the police: a chambermaid at a motel a hundred miles away had found his body. "I'm positive it was a Wednesday," Bliss says.

They are silent again. Bliss remembers driving over to the high school and waiting in the office while someone was sent to get Gerald from his class. Her old French teacher had come walking in, and her face lit up at the sight of Bliss. "What a wonderful surprise," she said. "How's school going? How are you?" Then Gerald appeared on the other side of the glass door, and for a moment, while Mlle. Barlow was still talking, Bliss looked through the glass at Gerald and realized from his expression that he had guessed why she was there.

She looks at Gerald now. She can tell that he's struggling with something—is he trying to get himself to say something more or to keep quiet?

"Remember how I wanted to go back to school the next day?" he says. "What a jerk."

"No," Bliss says, "I completely understood how you felt. I had a paper due that Friday and I kept thinking, My paper, my paper, like someone was going to be mad at me if I didn't get it done."

"And who do you suppose that someone was?" Gerald says.

"No kidding."

"It was different, though," Gerald says. "I just wanted to get out of the house."

Bliss nods. It was different and it was the same. Who didn't want to get out of the house? Even her mother kept saying she had to get to the store so she could make dinner, when all afternoon people were coming over with casseroles and stews—more food than they could eat in a week.

"Why do you think he did it?" Marisa says, and Bliss closes her eyes.

Why did he do it? This is the central question of Bliss's life. It's so central that it's no longer really a question at all, so much as a state of mind. She has made her accommodation to it: it's as much who she is as anything else—her name, her face in the mirror. She has always thought Gerald felt the same way, that there was no real answer. Now she can't help thinking that Marisa has asked the question for him, that he asked her to ask it, and the idea of the two of them going over it all—late at night, in the dark—makes Bliss want to get up and run. Leave it alone, she wants to say. Leave it *alone*. But then she opens her eyes and wonders whether she's wrong: Gerald seems surprised, almost fearful. Is he as reluctant to say anything as she is? She looks at Marisa and realizes that she's *curious*—she asked because she really wants to know.

For every answer, there's another question. *What* was he so angry about? *How* did that turn into despair? *Why* did he finally give up? Out of nowhere Bliss remembers a time when she was thirteen or fourteen and so awkward and shy about going to school dances that she wouldn't tell her mother about them until the last minute, when it was too late to buy a new dress; she'd pretend to be disappointed that she couldn't go because she didn't have anything to wear. Her father got wind of it somehow, and at five o'clock on the afternoon of the Christmas dance he offered to drive her to the shopping center; he took her from store to store, waiting patiently until she found something she liked. He was so nice about it—it was a dark-green velvet dress and he told her it was perfect because it matched her eyes and made her skin look luminous. He actually said that—"luminous." How does this fit in?

"I guess," Bliss says, "he didn't want to go on living," and although this is so much *not* an answer, Marisa nods, as if she's satisfied.

Gerald puts his hand on Marisa's shoulder and she nestles between his legs and rests her head on his knee. He starts playing with the hair that's come out of her bun, twisting it around his finger, and it comes to Bliss all at once: her brother loves this woman. The business with the boots, his confession about the meatball sub, her outburst in the kitchen—they don't mean anything; they're the tiniest of truths about these people. He loves her.

Bliss sinks back into her chair and sips her tea, which has grown cold. She looks at the fire. It's a perfect fire, really: the flames are spread evenly across the logs and leap to a dramatic peak in the center of the fireplace. She's not sure she even knows how to make a fire; isn't there some special way you have to place the logs so there's just the right amount of space between them?

"Are you tired?" Gerald says. He's smiling at her, a sad kind of smile, and although she's not tired—she feels absolutely wide awake— she nods and yawns and stands up.

"It was a long drive," she says.

Marisa moves as if to stand, and Bliss says, "No, don't." She walks over and kisses Gerald on the cheek, hesitates a moment, then leans down and kisses Marisa, too. "Good night," she says.

She lies on the bed in her room without undressing. She keeps seeing the morning with Jason when she first knew how it was going to be. They were at her apartment and they'd finished their coffee and were standing in the kitchen. She was waiting for him to suggest that they spend the day together, thinking, Say something, say something, until it was like an incantation in her mind. When he finally spoke, though, and said, "Bye, I'll call you," instead of disappointment she had felt an enormous rush of relief—a feeling, she thinks now, of things falling back into place. She doesn't know what her reason for living is, but it could never have been him. He was never her reason for anything except wearing more makeup than she felt comfortable in and pretending, for a few months, that she was part of something serious.

She changes into her nightgown and goes into the bathroom to brush her teeth. Lying on the counter, still in its wrapper, is a brand-new bar of scented soap. She's sure it wasn't there before. She picks it up and brings it to her face; through the blue paper she can smell the rich aroma of sandalwood. Marisa must have brought it in while she and Gerald were outside. It's an expensive soap, and she has a hard time imagining Marisa in one of those drugstores that call themselves pharmacies and sell imported brushes and combs one aisle over from the Maalox. She can't help feeling flattered—did Marisa buy this soap expressly for her?

She unwraps the soap and washes her face; it makes her skin feel clean and tight. Then she brushes her teeth, turns off the bathroom light, and gets into bed. Tomorrow she will give them the cookies. If Gerald's pleased by them, Marisa will be, too.

Lying in bed, still wide awake, she finds herself thinking of the last time she and Gerald had dinner alone together in San Francisco. He took her to a little Burmese place out by the park, and they pored over the menu, dismayed to find that everything sounded exactly like the Chinese food they'd had the night before. Then Bliss found a section of salads and they thought, Aha! Something new! They agreed on a dish called Lap Dap Dok; it was described as a spicy salad made of tea leaves.

It arrived at their table on a wide, shallow plate, and the waitress held it up for them to see. It was like a pinwheel: six different ingredients barely touching each other. Bliss had identified sliced chili peppers and peanuts and something that looked vaguely like chopped parsley when the waitress took a pair of spoons and mixed the whole thing together into a dark paste. Bliss helped herself to a large spoonful, then took a little bit between her chopsticks and put it in her mouth. Immediately she was horrified: it was bitter and sour and rotten-tasting all at the same time—easily the worst thing she'd ever eaten. She started to giggle, waiting for Gerald to taste it, and when he did his expression made her laugh even harder. "I wonder if this is what dung tastes like," he said, and then he turned red and started to laugh, too. Soon they were both laughing so hard that people began to look at them. She remembers now how familiar that laughter felt to her—the sick, giggly, helpless laughter of two children in a world of their own.

TWILIGHT ON THE EL CAMINO

Leslee Becker

When I first went into the business, my father told me: "Buying a car is one of the most important decisions people have to make." He sold Buicks, had his own dealership, Bahr Motors, a real showcase. On the Fourth of July, he had the whole fleet polished, and I rode with him in the parade in a black Roadmaster. I'd lob candy to kids, wave, and pretend I was a war hero.

My father owns a small wrecking yard now. He's seventy, and he tells people he's in the salvage phase of his automotive career. I work at Del's Auto Mart. I've been there eleven years and wouldn't be sticking it out if it weren't for my family. I want good things for them.

Del's got this ice-cream philosophy about cars. "Imagine you're driving down the road," he tells the new salesmen, "and you get a craving for ice cream. You got it in your mind that a vanilla cone will do, so you pull into the first place you see. Now, once you eye forty flavors and all kinds of extra concoctions, you think vanilla's going to satisfy you?"

So we give the customers trade-in deals no one can match, and all kinds of extras—tape decks, TVs, radials, turkeys, and barbecue grills.

We've got one of the biggest places on the El Camino, one you can spot a long ways off because of the revolving '54 Thunderbird perched above the banners on a tall pole. We need the Thunderbird because this strip is plastered with car places.

People tend to remember Del's television ads. His latest angle is to pass himself off as an evangelist. He appears in a red robe behind a podium, hollers about time running out, and then, as the car's wheeled in, his voice drops, just like he's in the presence of the vessel of salvation. All of us salesmen wear identical three-piece suits, flanking him as Del's Disciples.

My kids laugh whenever they see the ad, and the first time I saw myself on television, I decided I had to change things. I started on the weight first. I dieted, gave up smoking, and took up running. I imagine winning an important prize at the end of the run, and crowds of cheering people applauding, and my father right there congratulating me.

They say it helps to picture yourself as a nonsmoker, to remember the part of your life before you smoked and to project yourself into the future without seeing cigarettes. I didn't have any trouble with the early part, but as I tried to see my future, a little knot began to fist up in my stomach. It wasn't connected to cigarettes as much as to the image of myself getting farther away from the early and good part of my life, and moving into something sad and probably wrong.

Last night, I was out running and found myself noticing other people's homes—their careful lawns, the landscaping, the shape and condition of the houses. I was outside of one—a big mansion of a place—at dusk. A patch of light from one of the tall windows hit the center of the lawn just as I was approaching the house. I stopped, looked inside, and saw a family sitting at a table under a bright chandelier, a man, woman, and a little boy. That's all. But it held me, and I felt on the edge of something.

This morning I overslept, and because of all the El Camino traffic I got to work late. Del was sitting at his desk, involved on the phone. He looked at me and then his watch, but he left it at that. I got a cup of coffee, looked to see if I had any messages, and started to read the *Chronicle,* an article about a family living in their car. I showed the story to Bill, this guy who's been at Del's almost as long as I have.

"Jesus," he said. "If old Del sees that, he'll try to sell them something bigger. Is that a new suit, Charlie?"

"No, I've had it a while. I took off some weight."

"Wish I could," he said. "Maybe I should join one of those fitness centers."

"You don't need that. Just run. I feel a hundred percent better with that and giving up the cigarettes."

"Yeah," he said, like he was resigned to stay the way he was.

I got up for another cup of coffee, thought about taking a dough-nut, but didn't. I was watching the salesmen and the bookkeepers when Del came over.

"Did you call that fellow back, Charlie? The Toyota?"

"Not yet, Del."

He shook his head, went to the window, and thumbed me toward it. I looked out and saw an elderly man in a mulberry leisure suit, work boots, and a western hat.

"Hey," Del hollered across the showroom, "we've got a live one, a real lay down."

The man was inspecting a Datsun pickup. Del grinned as Bill and a couple of salesmen came to the window.

"You know what hemorrhoids and cowboy hats have in common?" Del asked.

Bill rolled his eyes and the other salesmen continued to gawk at the old man.

"Sooner or later every asshole's going to have 'em," Del answered.

The guys laughed. Then one started flipping a coin to see who'd take the man. Del yanked a wad of bills from his pocket, pulled out a twenty, put it on my desk, and smoothed it out.

"Twenty bucks says the old man's looking for . . ."

"A Chevette," one of the salesmen said.

"Whadya say, Charlie?" Del said, sticking his face close to mine.

"He's got a right to look," I said.

I walked outside and stood in the middle of the lot, hearing the plastic banners overhead, flapping. The man was looking at a Cutlass Supreme when I introduced myself. He had to lean toward me, crook-ing his head in my direction, to hear me over all the noise. He shook my hand.

"A fine automobile," he said.

"It sure is," I said. "Want to get in, get a closer look?"

"Nope," the man said, running his hand over the fender. "It's out of my league."

"We don't get many Cutlasses. People hang onto them."

"Came here with my boy. It's his first car. That's him over there, Mr. Bahr," he said, pointing to a tall, skinny kid eyeing a cherry red Mustang with a "RED HOT" sign propped in the windshield.

I knew this about the car. It had been wrecked. The bearings were blown and the suspension joints were bad, but Del had his boys restore it. They gave it a paint job, body work, and a set of new tires. It was one of Del's specials, and when one of us sells a car like that, we get something extra to sweeten up the commission, usually five or ten percent, under the table.

"Mr. Bahr, this is my son, Roger," the man said as we approached the boy. "He's at the community college, studying Computer Science. Plays basketball too."

"Play a little hoop, huh?" I said, and the kid looked at me a minute and then looked back at the car.

"Sure is flashy looking," the man said.

When I told him the price, he winced.

"Can I take it for a spin?" the kid asked me.

"Why don't you look around, son?" the man said. "You want to take your time on something like this."

"It's my car, Dad. I want to give it a test run, all right?"

"No law against that," I told him. "Just so you know what you're doing."

"I know what I'm doing," the kid said.

I got the keys, and the kid left, leaving me and the man in the lot.

"You sure do have a lot of automobiles here," the man said. "My boy knows all about them. Ford makes that car, don't they?"

"The Mustang? It's one of their best sellers."

"They're reliable," he said, like he was asking me for assurance. "I had a Ford pickup. They got a reputation."

The kid pulled into the lot, banging on the horn and beaming as he got out of the car.

"I want it, Dad."

The man started to press on the fenders to check the shocks.

"McPherson Struts," I told him.

The kid lifted the hood, and his father checked the oil stick. He stared at it, then held it close to his nose. Then he got down on his hands and knees and peered under the car. I glanced back to the showroom to see if anyone was watching, but they weren't. When the man stood up, he took off his hat and wiped his brow.

"It runs fine, Dad," the kid said, staring into the engine.

"Maybe we ought to look around some more, son. Wouldn't hurt to check around," the man said.

"Someone else will get it if I don't."

The man looked at me. "Is that right, Mr. Bahr? Are there other interested parties?"

"Well," I said, and paused a moment. "Cars move in and out of here pretty fast."

"You know anything about the previous owner?" the man asked. "Last thing I want is to get somebody else's headache."

"Last thing anybody wants," I said. "We've got records in the office, and in the glove compartment there's a maintenance log. But I'll tell you this. It's been repainted. The Mustang didn't look like this when we got it."

The man nodded and looked at me as though he appreciated getting privileged information. The kid shook his head and walked away from us.

"That's the one he wants, all right. He's got his mind made up," the man said, and walked over to his son.

"Look," I said, joining them. "Why don't you two take your time, talk things over by yourselves. I'll be inside. There's no rush."

The man thanked me, and I returned to my office. Del's twenty was still on my desk. When I saw the man and the boy heading toward the showroom, I put the twenty in my pocket. They wanted the car, they told me. The man reached into his pocket for his wallet, and started counting out cash.

"You're doing the down payment in cash?" I asked him.

"Doing the whole thing," he said.

"I can knock off a hundred then," I said, which is where I would've started dropping the price anyway if he hadn't gone for it outside. "I can give you that as sales manager," I added, looking to see if any of the other salesmen heard me. "I've been here a long time, and I can tell you it's a rare experience to see cash again. Most people think it's the buyer who gets taken, but we get bad checks, and a couple of times we've gotten stuck with stolen cars."

"Is that a fact?" the man said. Then he stood up, shook my hand, and looked directly into my eyes. "I got the one my boy wanted. It was good doing business with you, Mr. Bahr."

I smiled at the boy, and he and his father headed toward the door. "You have any trouble during the warranty period, even after, you come back and see me," I shouted.

"Del," I said. "I need to leave early. Personal business."

He didn't say a word.

"Toothache," I said. "It's been driving me nuts."

"Okay, Charlie. I'll have Bill take care of the Toyota."

"Thanks, Del," I said and got up to leave. "Oh, I meant to tell you, the kids love the new commercial. They get a real kick out of it."

"Yeah, well some son of a bitch wants it off the air. Claims it's sacrilegious."

I shook my head. "Well, it caught the bastard's attention, so it's doing the job for us."

I got into my car and headed north, and when I saw the sign for 80 East, the possibility of being somewhere else seemed the most important thing. I could go east, maybe to Ashtabula, Ohio, the place my father left during the Depression to come to California. I could take the same route he took, only in the opposite direction, and maybe, by following things back to their source, I could start all over again.

I remember when I was little how Ohio seemed like a magical place. I almost made it to Akron once. I was a semifinalist in the Soap Box Derby. I built the whole thing myself, the way you're supposed to. My father supervised to make sure I followed the rules exactly. The kid who beat me couldn't have built his machine by himself. I had a hard time not crying when I lost. Then my father gave me one of those talks that only made me madder.

"Charlie," he told me, "you only lost a race. Think of what he lost."

I started to feel very hungry, took an exit, and went into a convenience store. I loaded up with a pack of Marlboros and some snacks, and as I stood at the check-out counter, I knew the clerk and other customers were making assessments about me and my appetite. The woman ahead of me was pretty, well-dressed, tanned, with wheat-colored hair that looked professionally styled. Everything about her had an elegance that spelled money. She looked at what I laid out on the counter, and then she looked at me with a small smile.

"For my kids," I said, gesturing toward my food.

She kept staring at me. "You're one of those TV personalities, aren't you?" she asked me.

I looked away from her and faced the little bleacher of gum and candy by the register. "I've done some spots," I said.

"I thought so," she said, then took her bag and left.

She pulled away, and when I got into my car, I kept saying, "Jesus, Jesus."

I tore into a candy bar, and smoked a cigarette, which made me feel dizzy at first, and then it felt better.

On the drive back, I kept hoping Peg would be home. I rehearsed all the things I wanted to tell her.

She was baking, standing by the oven. "You're home early," she said. "Is anything wrong?"

I went to the liquor cabinet and poured myself some Scotch.

"Want me to fix you something to eat?"

"I'm not hungry," I said, sitting down at the table. "You wouldn't believe what happened to me today, Peg."

She sat down across from me, and I looked at her eyes, a particular blue that never quite comes across in pictures.

"I lied, Peg. What I really wanted to do was tell Del off, but I didn't. I told him I had a toothache. Can you believe it? A grown man making up stories to get out of work?"

She smiled and shook her head. "You're so hard on yourself, Charlie."

"It gets worse," I said, this nervous grin coming over me. "The man I sold this car to. I lied to him too." I waited for a reaction, a sign of disappointment, but she looked more confused than disappointed.

"Del had a hand in it, didn't he?" she said.

"Sure, in a way, but I'm the one who sold the car. Jesus, I even told the customer I was the sales manager."

"Is that all?" she said. When she started to get up from the table, I put my hand over hers.

"Peg, let's just sit still for a second."

She touched my face, ran her fingertips along the edge of my cheek. I closed my eyes for a moment, and we kept quiet for a while.

"God, I'm so sick of that job, Peg. I wish we could get away, a trip, do something different."

She looked at the clock. "I better go and get the kids." She kissed me on the forehead. "You stay here and relax."

After she left, I made another drink and took it and the atlas outside to the lawn chair. It would be secondary roads the whole way, I decided, to give us all the chance, especially the kids, to really see things. And my father would be with us, going over territory he hadn't seen in fifty years. I traced my finger over the route, then lay back in the chair. Some thin clouds threading the edge of the sky were starting to spool and drift toward the center.

When the kids came outside, I was feeling better. "Daddy's got a big surprise for both of you," I said, and Peg smiled with me. "We're going on a trip."

"Oh boy," Ellen said.

"On a plane?" Bobby asked.

"By car. Across the country. See," I said, pointing to the atlas.

"When?" Bobby said.

"How about Christmas?"

"That's a long way off," he said and looked up at his mother.

"Well, how about tonight? How about eating out? Wherever you want."

"Road Runner," Ellen said.

"Okay, Road Runner it is. We'll go over to your grandfather's afterwards. How about that?" I said, getting up from the chair.

"There's nothing to do over there," Bobby said.

The good feeling was wearing off by the time we reached the restaurant. We ordered a large pizza with the works, and when it came, horns and sirens went off. Everyone looked at our table for a minute, then returned to their eating. I burned the roof of my mouth, and some of the sauce dribbled onto my chin and shirt.

"How come we're going on a trip?" Bobby asked. He picked a mushroom off his pizza.

"Because," Peg said, "your father wants us all to see the country."

"We're going to Ohio," I said. "Where your grandfather's from."

"Ohio," Ellen said, making funny shapes with her lips.

"Ohio?" Bobby repeated.

After we left and got home, the kids rushed into the house as if they were glad to get away.

The TV was blaring at my father's house, and he had dozed off in his chair. I punched the set off, and he woke up and looked at me.

"Charlie, I didn't hear you come in." He turned on the light and stared at me with a puzzled expression.

I looked down at my shirt. "Took the kids out to dinner and spilled some food on me," I said.

"You ought to put some water on that before the stain sets," he said and started to get up from his chair.

"I'll get it, Dad," I said, and we both headed toward the kitchen.

I could hear water dripping below when I turned on the faucet. I opened the cabinet under the sink and saw a pan filled with water. I emptied it and took a look at the pipe.

"You should get this fixed. I could call this plumber I know for you."

He shook his head. "You know what plumbers get now? The pan'll do."

When we returned to the living room, he started picking through some mail. "I've got something to show you," he said. "Look at this."

He handed me a brochure that showed a new line of wrecking trucks. I looked at a device named "The Jaws of Life," a huge-toothed contraption for prying smashed cars open.

"This one caught my eye," he said, and pointed to a big truck filled with elaborate machinery. "Of course, it's top of the line, more than what I need."

"It's nice, Dad," I said and lit a cigarette.

"Smoking again, huh?"

"Afraid so."

"How are Peg and the kids?"

"Fine. They ask about you all the time. Want to know when you're coming over again."

"What's that?" he said, cupping his hand behind his ear.

"The kids, Peg, they want to see you again."

He nodded. "So, you went to dinner tonight, you say."

"To Road Runner. The kids love it. We had a great time."

"Good. How's the job going?"

"Real busy, Dad. I must have inherited it from you," I said, leaning toward him. "Del says I'm his number one man. I think he's going to put me in the assistant manager slot."

"I saw him on the TV, you too. Must have cost a bundle for those ads."

"He can afford it. A woman recognized me today from television. At the Quik Trip."

"Is that so? At the Quik Trip? You know, I tried some of those low cholesterol eggs, Charlie. They don't taste right. Say, they're having an antique auto show at the Cow Palace. I'll bet Bobby'd love to see those cars." He looked down at the floor and then at me. "Everything all right, Charlie?"

"I almost made a big commission today, Dad," I said.

"You always liked cars," he said, and both of us kept quiet a minute.

"This fellow came in today, would've gotten stuck with a real lemon, but I wouldn't allow it. I may have lost some money, but I came home with something else."

He nodded. "Is business falling off, Charlie?"

"No, that's not what I mean. I put my foot down, Dad," I shouted. "No more bad deals."

"Good for you, Charlie," he said, slapping his leg.

"Things are going to be different now, starting with a vacation. How'd you like to see Ashtabula again, look up some old friends?"

He pondered it a moment. "I doubt if I'd know anyone there anymore," he said, "and besides, what about my business? Who'd take care of things?"

"I don't know, but we can work something out. Look," I said, getting up. "I better be going. I'll get that pipe taken care of for you, and we'll all go to the auto show."

I went outside, saw the kitchen light go off and the TV come on. I went out back, lit a cigarette, and walked over to his salvage area. The moon was big and under its light, all the cars looked solemn and dignified. I got in behind the wheel of an old Chrysler and looked out through the cracked windshield. I slid my fingertips over the starred lace of cracks and wondered what the person felt right before he crashed.

I leaned back into the upholstery and remembered what it used to be like, lying down in a car, watching crowns of trees and squares of sky glide by when I was a kid, off for a drive, my parents in the front seat and me in the back. Sometimes I'd get carsick, and we'd stop and pull over so I could get air. My mother would take me in her lap, hold me, and tell me to find something solid to look at. I'd focus on the hood ornament or my father behind the wheel, and then I'd forget about being sick and would ride along, pretending I was on an important mission, responsible for reading the maps and the territory. When we got home, I liked believing I had led my family to safety.

I got out of the Chrysler and into my own car. The traffic on the El Camino was moving slowly from one stop to the next. Behind me, and as far ahead as I could see, was a spine of lights, giving everything a yellow flush, shiny and new-looking, like whatever was there under that glow must be worth having.

AQUARIUS OBSCURED

Robert Stone

In the house on Noe Street, Big Gene was crooning into the telephone.

"Geerat, Geeroot. Neexat, Nixoot."

He hung up and patted a tattoo atop the receiver, sounding the cymbal beat by forcing air through his molars.

"That's how the Dutch people talk," he told Alison. "Keroot. Badoot. Krackeroot."

"Who was it?"

He lay back on the corduroy cushions and vigorously scratched himself. A smile spread across this face and he wiggled with pleasure, his eyelids fluttering.

"Some no-nut fool. Easy tool. Uncool."

He lay still with his mouth open, waiting for rhyming characterizations to emerge.

"Was it for me?"

When he looked at her, his eyes were filled with tears. He shook his head sadly to indicate that her questions were obviated by his sublime indifference.

Alison cursed him.

"Don't answer the fucking phone if you don't want to talk," she said. "It might be something important."

Big Gene remained prone.

"I don't know where you get off," he said absently. "See you reverting to typical boojwa. Reverting to type. Lost your fire."

His junky mumble infuriated Alison. She snorted with exasperation.

"For Christ's sake!"

"You bring me down so bad," Gene said softly. "I don't need you. I got control, you know what I mean?"

"It's ridiculous," she told him. "Talking to you is a complete waste of time."

As she went into the next room she heard him moan, a lugubrious, falsetto coo incongruent with his bulk but utterly expressive of the man he had become. His needles had punctured him.

In the bedroom, Io was awake; her large brown eyes gazed fearfully through crib bars at the sunlit window.

"Hello, sweetie," Alison said.

Io turned solemnly toward her mother and yawned.

A person here, Alison thought, lifting her over the bars, the bean blossomed. Walks and conversation. The end of our madonna and child number. A feather of panic fluttered in her throat.

"Io," she told her daughter, "we have got to get our shit together here."

The scene was crumbling. Strong men had folded like stage flats, legality and common sense were fled. Celebration flickered.

Why me, she demanded of herself, walking Io to the potty. Why do I have to be the only one with any smarts?

On the potty, Io delivered. Alison wiped her and flushed the toilet. By training, Alison was an astronomer but she had never practiced.

Io could dress herself except for the shoes. When Alison tied them, it was apparent to her that they would shortly be too small.

"What'll we do?" she asked Io with a playful but genuinely frightened whine.

"See the fishies," Io said.

"See the fishies?" Alison stroked her chin, burlesquing a thoughtful demeanor, rubbing noses with Io to make her smile. "Good Lord."

Io drew back and nodded soberly.

"See the fishies."

At that moment, Alison recalled the fragment of an undersea

dream. Something in the dream had been particularly agreeable and its recall afforded her a happy little throb.

"Well that's what we'll do," she told Io. "We'll go to the aquarium. A capital idea."

"Yes," Io said.

Just outside Io's room, on the littered remnant of a sundeck, lived a vicious and unhygienic doberman, who had been named Buck after a dog Big Gene claimed to have once owned in Aruba. Alison opened the sliding glass door to admit it, and watched nervously as it nuzzled Io.

"Buck," Io said without enthusiasm.

Alison seized the dog by its collar and thrust it out the bedroom door before her.

In the living room, Big Gene was rising from the cushions, a cetaceous surfacing.

"Buck, my main man," he sang. "Bucky bonaroo."

"How about staying with him today?" Alison said. "I want to take Io to the aquarium."

"Not I," Gene declared. "Noo."

"Why the hell not?" Alison asked savagely.

"Cannot be."

"Shit! I can't leave him alone here, he'll wreck the place. How can I take him to the goddamn aquarium?"

Gene shrugged sleepily.

"Ain't this the night you get paid?" he asked after a moment.

"Yeah," Alison said.

In fact, Alison had been paid the night before, her employer having thrown some 80 dollars' worth of half-dollars full into her face. There had been a difference of opinion regarding Alison's performance as a danseuse, and she had spoken sharply with Mert the Manager. Mert had replied in an incredibly brutal and hostile manner, had fired her, insulted her breasts, and left her to peel coins from the soiled floor until the profile of Jack Kennedy was welded to her mind's eye. She had not mentioned the incident to Gene; the half-dollars were concealed under the rubber sheet beneath Io's mattress.

"Good," Gene said. "Because I got to see the man then."

He was looking down at Io, and Alison watched him for signs of resentment or contempt but she saw only sadness, sickness in his face. Io paid him no attention at all.

It was startling the way he had mellowed out behind smack. Witnessing it, she had almost forgiven him the punches, and she had noticed for the first time that he had rather a kind heart. But he stole and was feckless; his presence embarrassed her.

"How'm I going to take a dog to the aquarium, for Christ's sake?"

The prospect of having Buck along irritated Alison sorely. In her irritation, she decided that the thing might be more gracefully endured with the white-cross jobbers. The white-cross jobbers were synthetics manufactured by a mad chemist in Hayward. Big Gene called them IT-390 to distinguish them from IT-290 which they had turned out, upon consumption, not to be.

She took a handful from the saki jar in which they were stored and downed them with tap water.

"All right, *Buck*," she called, pronouncing the animal's name with distaste, "goddamn it." She put his leash on, sent Io ahead to the car, and pulled the reluctant dog out behind her.

With Io strapped in the passenger seat and Buck cringing under the dashboard, Alison ran Lombard Street in the outside lane, accelerating on the curves like Bondurant. Alison was a formidable and aggressive driver, and she drove hard to stay ahead of the drug's rush. When she pulled up in the aquarium's parking lot, her mouth had gone dry and the little sanctus bells of adjusted alertness had begun to tinkle. She hurried them under wind-rattled eucalyptus and up the massive steps that led to the building's Corinthian portico.

"Now where are we going to put this goddamn dog?" she asked Io. When she blinked, her eyeballs clicked. I've done it, she thought. I've swallowed it again. Vandalism.

After a moment's confused hesitation, she led Buck to one side of the entrance and secured his chain around a brass hydrant fixture with a carefully worked running clove hitch. The task brought to her recollection a freakish afternoon when she had tied Buck in front of a bar on El Camino. For the protection of passersby, she had fashioned a sign from the cardboard backing of a foolscap tablet and written on it with a green, felt-tipped pen—DO NOT TRY TO PET THIS DOG. Her last memory of the day was watching the sign blow away across the street and past the pumps of an Esso station.

Buck's vindictive howls pursued them to the oxidized-copper doors of the main entrance.

It was early morning and the aquarium was uncrowded. Liquefactious sounds ran up and down the smooth walls, child voices ricocheted from the ceiling. With Io by the hand, Alison wandered through the interior twilight, past tanks of sea horses, scorpion fish, African *Tilapia*. Pausing before an endlessly gyrating school of salmon, she saw that some of the fish were eyeless, the sockets empty and perfectly cleaned. The blind fish swam with the rest, staying in line, turning with the school.

Io appeared not to notice them.

In the next hall, Alison halted her daughter before each tank, reading from the lighted presentation the name of the animal contained, its habitat and Latin name. The child regarded all with gravity.

At the end of the East Wing was a room brighter than the rest; it was the room in which porpoises lived in tanks that were open to the sky. As Alison entered it, she experienced a curiously pleasant sensation.

"Look," she said to Io. "Dolphins."

"Dolphins?"

They walked up to the glass of the largest tank; its lower area was fouled with small handprints. Within, a solitary blue-gray beast was rounding furiously, describing gorgeous curves with figure of eights, skimming the walls at half an inch's distance. Alison's mouth opened in awe.

"An Atlantic Dolphin," she told Io in a soft, reverential voice. "From the Atlantic Ocean. On the other side of America. Where Providence is."

"And Grandpa," Io said.

"And Grandpa is in Providence, too."

For the space of several seconds, the dream feeling returned to her with an intensity that took her breath away. There had been some loving presence in it and a discovery.

She stared into the tank until the light that filtered through the churning water began to suggest the numinous. Io, perceiving that her mother was not about to move on, retraced her steps toward the halls through which they had come, and commenced seeing the fish over again. Whenever an aquarium-goer smiled at her, she looked away in terror.

Alison stood transfixed, trying to force recall. It had been something special, something important. But silly—as with dreams. She found herself laughing and then, in the next moment, numb with loss as the dream's sense faded. Her heart was racing with the drug.

God, she thought, it's all just flashes and fits. We're just out here in this shit.

With sudden horror, she realized at once that there had been another part of the dream and that it involved the fact that she and Io were just out there and that this was not a dream from which one awakened. Because one *was*, after all.

She turned anxiously to look for Io and saw the child several galleries back, standing in front of the tank where the blind fish were.

The dream had been about getting out of it, trying to come in and make it stop. In the end, when it was most terrible, she had been mercifully carried into a presence before which things had been resolved. The memory of that resolution made her want to weep.

Her eye fell on the animal in the tank; she followed its flights and charges with fascination.

There had been some sort of communication, with or without words.

A trained scientist, Alison loved logic above all else; it was her only important pleasure. If the part about one being out there was true—and it was—what then about the resolution. It seemed to her, as she watched the porpoise, that even dreamed things must have their origin in a kind of truth, that no level of the mind was capable of utterly unfounded construction. Even hallucinations—phenomena with which Alison had become drearily familiar—needed their origins in the empirically verifiable—a cast of light, a sound on the wind. Somehow, she thought, somewhere in the universe, the resolving presence must exist.

Her thoughts raced, she licked her lips to cool the sere dryness cracking them. Her heart gave a desperate leap.

"Was it you?" she asked the porpoise.

"Yes," she heard him say. "Yes, it was."

Alison burst into tears. When she had finished sobbing, she took a Kleenex from her bag, wiped her eyes, and leaned against the cool marble beside the tank.

Prepsychosis. Disorders of thought. Failure to abstract.

"This is ridiculous," she said.

From deep within, from the dreaming place, sounded a voice.

"You're here," the porpoise told her. "That's what matters now."

Nothing in the creature's manner suggested communication or even the faintest sentience. But human attitudes of engagement, Alison reminded herself, were not to be expected. To expect them was anthropocentrism—a limiting, reactionary position like ethnocentrism or sexism.

"It's very hard for me," she told the porpoise. "I can't communicate well at the best of times. And an aquarium situation is pretty weird." At a loss for further words, Alison fell back on indignation. "It must be awful for you."

"It's somewhat weird," she understood the porpoise to say. "I wouldn't call it awful."

Alison trembled.

"But . . . how can it not be awful? A conscious mind shut up in a tank with stupid people staring at you? Not," she hastened to add, "that I think I'm any better. But the way you're stuck in here with these slimy, repulsive fish."

"I don't find fish slimy and repulsive," the porpoise told her.

Mortified, Alison began to stammer an apology, but the creature cut her off.

"The only fish I see are the ones they feed me. It's people I see all day. I wonder if you can realize how *dry* you all are."

"Good Lord!" She moved closer to the tank. "You must hate us."

She became aware of laughter.

"I don't hate."

Alison's pleasure at receiving this information was tempered by a political anxiety. The beast's complacency suggested something objectionable; the suspicion clouded her mind that her interlocutor might be a mere Aquarium Porpoise, a deracinated stooge, an Uncle. . . .

The laughter sounded again.

"I'm sorry," Alison said. "My head is full of such shit."

"Our condition is profoundly different from yours. We don't require the same things. Our souls are as different from yours as our bodies are."

"I have the feeling," Alison said, "that yours are better."

"I think they are. But I'm a porpoise."

The animal in the tank darted upward, torpedo-like toward the fog-colored surface—then plunged again in a column of spinning, bubbling foam.

"You called me here, didn't you?" Alison asked. "You wanted me to come."

"In a way."

"Only in a way?"

"We communicated our presence here. A number of you might have responded. Personally, I'm satisfied that it was yourself."

"Are you?" Alison cried joyfully. She was aware that her words echoed through the great room. "You see, I asked because I've been having these dreams. Odd things have been happening to me." She paused thoughtfully. "Like I've been listening to the radio sometimes and I've heard these wild things—like just for a second. As though there's been kind of a pattern. Was it you guys?"

"Some of the time. We have our ways."

"Then," she asked breathlessly, "why me?"

"Don't you know why?" the beast asked softly.

"It must have been because you knew I would understand."

There was no response.

"It must have been because you knew how much I hate the way things are with us. Because you knew I'd listen. Because I need something so much."

"Yet," the porpoise said sternly, "you made things this way. You thought you needed them the way they are."

"It wasn't me," Alison said. "Not me. I don't need this shit."

Wide-eyed, she watched him shoot for the surface again, then dive and skim over the floor of his tank, rounding smartly at the wall.

"I love you," she declared suddenly. "I mean I feel a great love for you and I feel there is a great lovingness in you. I just know that there's something really super-important that I can learn from you."

"Are you prepared to know how it is with us?"

"Yes," Alison said. "Oh, yes. And what I can do."

"You can be free," the animal said. "You can learn to perceive in a new way."

Alison became aware of Io standing beside her, frowning up at her tears. She bent down and put her head next to the child's.

"Io, can you see the dolphin? Do you like him?"

"Yes," Io said.

Alison stood up.

"My daughter," she told her dolphin.

Io watched the animal contentedly for a while and then went to sit on a bench in the back of the hall.

"She's only three-and-a-half," Alison said. She feared that communion might be suspended on the introduction of a third party. "Do you like her?"

"We see a great many of your children," the beast replied. "I can't answer you in those terms."

Alison became anxious.

"Does that mean that you don't have *any* emotions? That you can't love?"

"Were I to answer yes or no I would deceive you either way. Let's say only that we don't make the same distinctions."

"I don't understand," Alison said. "I suppose I'm not ready to."

"As your perception changes," the porpoise told her, "many things will seem strange and unfamiliar. You must unlearn old structures of thought that have been forced on you. Much faith, much resolution will be required."

"I'll resist," Alison admitted sadly. "I know I will. I'm very skeptical and frivolous by nature. And it's all so strange and wonderful that I can't believe it."

"All doubt is the product of your animal nature. You must rise above your species. You must trust those who instruct you."

"I'll try," Alison said resolutely. "But it's so incredible! I mean for all these centuries you guys and us have been the only aware species on the planet, and now we've finally come together! It just blows my mind that here—now—for the first time . . ."

"What makes you think it's the first time?"

"Good Lord!" Alison exclaimed. "It's not the first time?"

"There were others before you, Alison. They were weak and fickle. We lost them."

Alison's heart chilled at his words.

"But hasn't it ever worked?"

"It's in the nature of your species to conceive enthusiasms and then to weary of them. Your souls are self-indulgent and your concentration feeble. None of you has ever stayed with it."

"I will," Alison cried. "I'm unique and irreplaceable, and nothing could be more important than this. Understanding, responding inside—that's my great talent. I can do it!"

"We believe you, Alison. That's why you're here."

She was flooded with her dreaming joy. She turned quickly to look for Io and saw her lying at full length on the bench staring up into the overhead lights. Near her stood a tall, long-haired young man who was watching Alison. His stare was a profane irritation and Alison forced it from her mind, but her mood turned suddenly militant.

"I know it's not important in your terms," she told the porpoise, "but it infuriates me to see you shut up like this. You must miss the open sea so much."

"I've never left it," the animal said, "and your pity is wasted on me. I am here on the business of my race."

"I guess it's the way I was brought up. I had a lousy upbringing, but some things about it were good. See, my father, he's a real asshole but he's what we call a liberal. He taught me to really hate it when somebody was oppressed. Injustice makes me want to fight. I suppose it sounds stupid and trivial to you, but that's how it is with me."

The dolphin's voice was low and soothing, infinitely kind.

"We know how it is with you. You understand nothing of your own behavior. Everything you think and do merely reflects what is known to us as a Dry Posture. Your inner life, your entire history are nothing more than these."

"Good Lord!" Alison said. "Dry Posture."

"As we work with you, you must bear this in mind. You must discover the quality of Dry Posture in all your thoughts and actions. When you have separated this quality from your soul, what remains will be the bond between us. At that point your life will truly begin."

"Dry Posture," Alison said. "Wow!"

The animal in the tank was disporting itself just below the surface; in her mounting enthusiasm Alison became increasingly frustrated by the fact that its blank, good-humored face appeared utterly oblivious to her presence. She reminded herself again that the hollow dissembling of human facial expression was beneath its nature, and welcomed the opportunity to be divested of a Dry Posture.

The silence from which the dolphin spoke became charged with music.

"In the sea lies our common origin," she heard him say. "In the sea all was once One. In the sea find your surrender—in surrender find victory, renewal, survival. Recall the sea! Recall our common heartbeat! Return to the peace of primordial consciousness!"

"Oh, how beautiful," Alison cried, her own consciousness awash in salt flumes of insight.

"Our lousy Western culture is worthless," she declared fervently. "It's rotten and sick. We've got to get back. Please," she implored the dolphin, "tell us how!"

"If you receive the knowledge," the animal told her, "your life will become one of dedication and struggle. Are you ready to undertake such striving?"

"Yes," Alison said. "Yes!"

"Are you willing to serve that force which relentlessly wills the progress of the conscious universe?"

"With all my heart!"

"Willing to surrender to that sublime destiny which your species has so fecklessly denied?"

"Oh, boy," Alison said, "I surely am."

"Excellent," said the porpoise. "It shall be your privilege to assist the indomitable will of a mighty and superior species. The natural order shall be restored. That which is strong and sound shall dominate. That which is weak and decadent shall perish and disappear."

"Right on!" Alison cried. She felt her shoulders squaring, her heels coming together.

"Millennia of usurpation shall be overturned in a final solution!"

"Yeah," Alison said. "By any means necessary."

It seemed to Alison that she detected in the porpoise's speech a foreign accent; if not a Third World accent, at least the accent of a civilization older and more together than her own.

"*So,*" the porpoise continued, "where your cities and banks, your aquaria and museums now stand, there shall be rubble only. The responsibility shall rest exclusively with humankind, for our patience has been thoroughly exhausted. What we have not achieved through striving for equitable dialogue, we shall now achieve by striving of another sort."

Alison listened in astonishment as the music's volume swelled behind her eyes.

"For it is our belief," the porpoise informed her, "that in strife, life finds its purification." His distant, euphonious voice assumed a shrill, hysterical note. "In the discipline of ruthless struggle, history is forged and the will tempered! Let the craven, the once-born, shirk the fray—we ourselves shall strike without mercy at the sniveling mass of our natural inferiors. Triumph is our destiny!"

Alison shook her head in confusion.

"Whoa," she said.

Closing her eyes for a moment, she beheld, with startling clarity, the image of a blond-bearded man wearing a white turtleneck sweater and a peaked officer's cap. His face was distended with fury; beside him loomed a gray cylindrical form which might have been a periscope. Alison opened her eyes quickly and saw the porpoise blithely coursing the walls of its tank.

"But that's not love or life or anything," she sobbed. "That's just cruelty."

"Alison, baby, don't you know it's all the same? Without cruelty you can't have love. If you're not ready to destroy someone, then you're not ready to love them. Because if you've got the knowledge— you know, like if you really have it—then if you do what you have to do that's just everybody's karma. If you have to waste somebody because the universe wills it, then it's just like the bad part of yourself that you're wasting. It's an act of love."

In the next instant, she saw the bearded man again. His drawn, evil face was bathed in a sinister, submarine light, reflected from God knew what fiendish instruments of death.

"I know what you are," Alison called out in horror. "You're a fascist!"

When the beast spoke once more, the softness was vanished from its voice.

"Your civilization has afforded us many moments of amusement. Unfortunately, it must now be irrevocably destroyed."

"Fascist!" Alison whimpered in a strangled voice. "Nazi!"

"Peace," the porpoise intoned, and the music behind him turned tranquil and low. "Here is the knowledge. You must say it daily."

Enraged now, she could detect the mocking hypocrisy in his false, mellow tones.

> *"Surrender to the Notion*
> *Of the Motion of the Ocean."*

As soon as she received the words, they occupied every cubit of her inner space, reverberating moronically, over and over. She put her hands over her ears.

"Horseshit!" she cried. "What kind of cheapo routine is that?"

The voice, she suspected suddenly, might not be that of a porpoise. It might be the man in the turtleneck. But where?

Hovering at the mouth of a celestial Black Hole, secure within the adjoining dimension? A few miles off Sausalito at periscope depth? Or—more monstrous—ingeniously reduced in size and concealed within the dolphin?

"Help," Alison called softly.

At the risk of permanent damage, she desperately engaged her linear perception. Someone might have to know.

"I'm caught up in this plot," she reported. "Either porpoises are trying to reach me with this fascist message or there's some kind of super-Nazi submarine offshore."

Exhausted, she rummaged through her knit bag for a cigarette, found one, and lit it. A momentary warp, she assured herself, inhaling deeply. A trifling skull pop, perhaps an air bubble. She smoked and trembled, avoiding the sight of the tank.

In the next moment, she became aware that the tall young man she had seen earlier had made a circuit of the hall and was standing beside her.

"Fish are groovy," the young man said.

"Wait a minute," Alison demanded. "Just wait a minute here. Was that . . . ?"

The young man displayed a woodchuck smile.

"You were really tripping on those fish, right? Are you stoned?"

He carried a camera case on a strap round his shoulder, and a black cape slung over one arm.

"I don't know what you're talking about," Alison said. She was suddenly consumed with loathing.

"No? 'Cause you looked really spaced out."

"Well, I'm not," Alison said firmly. She saw Io advancing from the bench.

The young man stood by as Io clutched her mother's floor-length skirt.

"I want to go outside now," Io said.

His pink smile expanded and he descended quickly to his haunches to address Io at her own level.

"Hiya, baby. My name's Andy."

Io had a look at Andy and attempted flight. Alison was holding one of her hands; Andy made her fast by the other.

"I've been taking pictures," he told her. "Pictures of the fishies." He pursued Io to a point behind Alison's knees. Alison pulled on Io's free hand and found herself staring down into the camera case.

"You like the fishies?" Andy insisted. "You think they're groovy?"

There were two Nikon lenses side by side in the case. Alison let Io's hand go, thrust her own into the case and plucked out a lens. While Andy was asking Io if she, Io, were shy, Alison dropped the lens into her knit bag. As Andy started up, she seized the second lens and pressed it hard against her skirt.

Back on his feet, Andy was slightly breathless.

"You wanna go smoke some dope?" he asked Alison. "I'm goin' over to the art museum and sneak some shots over there. You wanna come?"

"Actually," Alison told him, "I have a luncheon engagement."

Andy blinked. "Far out."

"Far out?" Alison asked. "I'll tell you something far out, Andy. There is a lot of really repulsive shit in this aquarium, Andy. There are some very low-level animals here and they're very frightening and unreal. But there isn't one thing in this place that is as repulsive and unreal as you are, Andy."

She heard the laughter echo and realized that it was her own. She clenched her teeth to stop it.

"You should have a tank of your own, Andy."

As she led Io toward the door, she cupped the hand that held the second lens against her hip, like a mannequin. At the end of the hall, she glanced back and saw Andy looking into the dolphin's tank. The smile on his face was dreadful.

"I like the fish," Io said, as they descended the pompous stone steps outside the entrance. "I like the lights in the fish places."

Recognizing them, Buck rushed forward on his chain, his tongue dripping. Alison untied him as quickly and calmly as she could.

"We'll come back, sweetie," she said. "We'll come back lots of times."

"Tomorrow?" the child asked.

In the parking lot, Alison looked over her shoulder. The steps were empty; there were no alarums or pursuits.

When they were in the car, she felt cold. Columns of fog were moving in from the bay. She sat motionless for a while, blew her nose, and wrapped a spare sweater that was lying on the seat around Io's shoulders.

"Mama's deluded," she explained.

CAMELOT

Marly Swick

When I wake up again, the bedroom is an indeterminate gray—it could be dawn or dusk. The bed is littered with used pink tissues like so many wilted roses on a parade float. I have been dreaming, I have a fever. A copy of *Swann's Way* lies open on the tangled bedclothes. I have been dreaming in rusty French. I have been dreaming about Sondra and Arthur. The gray is San Francisco, the fog. In my dream there was the strong aroma of garlic and leeks. I reach for one of the crumpled tissues and blow my nose. My nose can't smell anything, but the scent of the garlic and leeks lingers inside my fogged brain. According to the clock, it is dusk. At the foot of the bed, the television is on, the sound off. Footage of JFK—on the campaign trail, on a sailboat with Jackie, in the Oval Office, Dallas. Jackie in her pink suit and pillbox. For the past two days, floating in and out of consciousness, doped up on antihistamines, I have seen the same footage over and over. The shots are as familiar to me as snapshots in my own family albums, more familiar. It is the twenty-fifth anniversary of the assassination. The TV is full of Kennedy. In my drugged and feverish state, this disorients me. A time warp. Sondra and Arthur and I are eating *escargot*. At first I am repulsed, but then I start to like them. At any rate I like the idea of myself eating them: now you have eaten *escargot*. It was always like that when I was with them—as if I were remembering it all as it was happening. A slight time delay. As if it were all being beamed to me by satellite from across the ocean.

This was 1963, the year I graduated from college, the year I left home. I had grown up in a small town in western Washington state and attended the local branch of the state university, living at home with my parents and two younger brothers, majoring in French and working part-time in the library, reading Balzac and Flaubert and George Sand. My favorite book at that time was *Bonjour Tristesse*. There were not many French lit majors at Western Washington State— I had been inspired by our foreign exchange student, Brigitte, in high school—and Professor Lemaire took a special interest in me, lending me her own dog-eared copies of Marguerite Duras and Anaïs Nin. Once in a while she even invited me to accompany her to Seattle to see a French film—Renoir, Truffaut, Godard. Fortunately for me, her husband did not like subtitles. During the long drives, she would chat to me about her childhood in Paris, referring to specific streets and cafés as if I were of course familiar with them, even though she knew that I had never set foot out of the United States. Our conversations would be conducted in French. I had an uncanny, inexplicable talent for the language, as if I had been French in some previous incarnation. I was hopeless in German and only passable in Spanish. I was like one of those idiot savants. My parents thought I was crazy, wasting my time. But I didn't care. Dr. Lemaire was my champion; she believed in me. In my senior year she pulled some strings—the daughter of a close friend was an assistant professor in the Modern Languages Department at San Francisco State—and I was awarded a graduate assistantship. As a bon voyage gift, Dr. Lemaire presented me with an Edith Piaf album and a tiny flask of Bal de Versailles.

San Francisco, with its steep hills and rainbow Victorians, seemed as exotic and sophisticated as Europe. It was just before the whole hippie era transformed the city, before Haight-Ashbury and love-ins in Golden Gate Park. I rented a small room in a large apartment within walking distance to campus. My roommates were three other female graduate students—two in English and one in art history. Of the three, I was the only one who had never been to France and the only one who actually spoke French. They thought I was something of an oddity—like a deaf person majoring in music theory. A few years later, when I finally got to Paris with my husband on our way back from India, I felt let down; it had loomed too large in my imagination for too long. The usual complaints—food was expensive, the people were rude, it drizzled every day. I envied my colleagues in the dead languages who could never visit Sparta or Gaul. I was just as glad I had dropped out of graduate school.

But in the summer of 1963 it was a different story. I was walking around campus humming *La Vie en Rose* wrapped in a cloud of Bal de Versailles like a stray dog looking for a kind master. And I found one in Dr. Mignon—or Sondra, as she insisted I call her—Dr. Lemaire's friend and my boss. I was her research assistant, starting that spring. I had never called any of my professors by their first name and although it thrilled me, it also initially embarrassed and unnerved me. Those first couple of weeks I avoided addressing her by name and even when I left her notes, as I frequently did, asking her some factual question, I left off the salutation. Looking back, I can see that she was really quite young still herself—not even thirty—but at the time—I was twenty-one—she seemed impossibly sophisticated and mature. She had been to Vassar and the Sorbonne. She had been married, briefly, to a French journalist and amicably divorced. She wore chic but messy Parisian clothes—a hem sagging, a button missing—and her abundant dark hair was artfully pinned up in such a way that you held your breath waiting for it to tumble down. She wore narrow black sunglasses even on those days when the sun was tucked behind a dense blanket of fog. She made risqué puns in Franglais. She smoked Gauloises.

My first task as Sondra's research assistant was to index her just-completed book on Madame de Staël. Sitting in a windowless cubbyhole adjacent to Sondra's office, I worked day and night, checking and cross-checking, my desk piled high with hundreds and hundreds of index cards. (This was before computers hit the humanities.) Sondra was off for the summer and only showed up at the office infrequently—to rummage through her surprisingly neat files for something or to meet a colleague for lunch. To me she was always pleasant on the run. Once, on the spur of the moment, seeing me hunched over a stack of index cards, she invited me to join her for coffee at the student union, where she quizzed me girlishly about my romantic—or rather, sex—life. Since then I have met other women with this same talent for instant intimacy, but Sondra was my first. In the space of twenty minutes I told her all about Tommy Hubbard, my college beau, and the fact that I had allowed him to relieve me of my virginity as a sort of going-away gift from me to him. Sondra smoked her Gauloises and nodded her approval—I think she had been afraid I was still a virgin. For the first time, she offered me a cigarette. I took it and puffed on it, afraid to inhale.

Suddenly she looked at her watch. "*Merde!* I told Arthur I'd meet him at the DeJonge at two. Do you know Arthur?" She leapt up and plunked a couple of dollars on the table. "Art Schiffman? The poet? Teaches a couple of courses on French poetry in translation."

I shook my head. "I've heard his name."

"Well, you'll have to meet him," she said. "You'll like him. Maybe lunch at my place next week?"

I nodded casually, too thrilled to speak, and she took off in such a rush she left her dark glasses sitting on the table. I slipped them on and wore them for the rest of the afternoon.

The following Friday I finished the index two weeks ahead of our projected schedule and called Sondra to tell her it was done, *fini*. She sounded even more delighted with me than I had fantasized. *"Tu es un ange!"* she exclaimed. I demurred. In the background I could hear commotion and music. "Just a minute," she said, holding her hand over the mouthpiece. I could hear a low masculine murmur. Palms sweating, I berated myself for clumsily interrupting them in bed. Then she laughed, taking her hand off the mouthpiece, and said, "Listen. I'm just giving Arthur a cooking lesson. Leek soup and *escargot*. Why don't you come over? We've got enough food for Napoleon's army."

"Well, I don't know, if you really . . ." I stammered feebly, waiting to be convinced.

"Take a cab," she interrupted authoritatively—"we'll be waiting"—and gave me the address on Telegraph Hill.

All the way there in the cab I wished I'd had time to run home and change out of my jeans and shabby black sweater into some chic yet unassuming and incredibly flattering little number that I didn't actually own. But when I arrived at Sondra's apartment, I was pleasantly surprised to see that both Sondra and Art were wearing jeans and sweaters as well. I felt blessed that I'd not had enough time to follow my own stupid instincts. Even now, after twenty-five years, one of my worst nightmares is to arrive somewhere overdressed. Sondra kissed me on both cheeks, European-style, and led me by the hand into the kitchen, where Art was busy slicing mushrooms paper-thin with the delicate concentration of a neurosurgeon.

"Art, this is Nancy Long, my miraculous research assistant from heaven." Sondra reached up and rearranged the pins in her tumbling hair, then handed me a measuring cup full of egg yolks. "Here. Whisk these," she said.

I stared uncertainly at the gaudy yolks. Grilled cheese sandwiches were about as far as my culinary expertise extended.

"You do know how to whisk, don't you?" Art said in husky, vampy voice.

Sondra groaned. I looked blank.

"Don't tell me you've never seen *To Have and Have Not?*" he asked me. I shook my head. "Where did you say you're from?" He sliced the last mushroom and swung his sandaled feet up onto the kitchen table.

"Bellingham, Washington." (Actually I was from Nooksack.)

"Well, that explains it."

"Don't mind him," Sondra said. "He thinks anyone who grew up west of Brooklyn is a savage." She knocked his feet off the table and handed him a head of garlic. "Shut up and mince."

Art smiled at me and winked. "These French chefs are so imperious." He was short and slight with closely cropped black curls and horn-rimmed glasses. Except for his mouth, which was rather feminine and sensitive, he did not look at all like my idea of a poet. (A couple of years later, browsing in a London bookshop, I came across a new book of his—*Songs of Innocence and Guilt*—and in the jacket photo he was wearing rimless glasses, his hair cascading lyrically to his shoulders.)

At a loss for small talk, I was standing slightly apart, facing the window which had a spectacular view of the bay. The sun was sparkling on the water. Sondra and Art were bantering back and forth in the most witty and sophisticated manner about what an impossible tyrant she was, and the aroma of mushrooms sautéing in butter, garlic, and wine was wafting through the kitchen. Cool European-sounding jazz was on the stereo, like background music in some subtle, bittersweet foreign film. And that was the first time I remember having the odd sensation that I was not really there, present in the moment, so intent was I upon fixing every small detail in my memory. I had that transient feeling, the tourist's hunger to record and preserve. At the same time as I was struggling so hard to appear cool and nonchalant, I wanted desperately to whip out my camera and take snapshots.

"Here." Sondra took the whisked yolks and handed me the cookbook. "You read me the directions aloud." She pointed to the recipe for Escargot Façon du Chef. The directions were in French. I hesitated, suddenly nervous. In Washington state my French accent was a marvel, but perhaps it would sound less marvelous in San Francisco. Art was watching me with the bemused, amused expression I soon learned was characteristic of him. The ash from his cigarette toppled into the bowl of strawberries he was rinsing.

"I've been trying to think who she looks like," he said to Sondra. "Jeanne Moreau. A blond Jeanne Moreau, don't you think? The eyes and mouth."

Sondra squinted at me thoughtfully for a moment and nodded, probably more—I later realized—out of a courteous desire not to contradict Art (or Arthur, as she called him) than any sincere agreement, but at the time it was just the boost I needed. I cleared my throat and launched into a dramatic reading of Escargot Façon du Chef, rolling my *R*s and generally hamming it up in such an exaggerated fashion that they were both doubled over, gasping for breath; and I had never been quite so pleased with myself—and perhaps never will be again— as I was at that moment.

Lunch was a long, lingering affair with much wine and hilarity. I was relieved and emboldened to discover that intellectuals, professors, could act so silly and talk such lighthearted nonsense. At first I pushed my snails around on my plate, panicked and sickened at the thought of actually putting one in my mouth, but, luckily, a couple of glasses of wine in quick succession served to suppress my provincial squeamishness. After the first tentative bite, I was surprised and elated to discover that they were not in the least slimy. Art was in charge of wine. As soon as a glass was empty, he would reach over and refill it. "Nature abhors a vacuum," he'd say. When we'd drained the first bottle, he leapt up and deftly opened a second. He seemed to know his way around Sondra's kitchen, and I naturally assumed that the two of them were "an item," until about halfway through lunch, Art made a passing reference to someone named Janice, and I said, "Who's Janice?"

"My wife," Art said, as if it were no big deal, and the conversation sailed on smoothly. Stunned, I surreptitiously studied Sondra, looking for some sign of distress, but she seemed completely unperturbed. My own reaction, however, was not lost upon Sondra—nothing ever was—and when Art excused himself to go to the bathroom, Sondra patted my hand reassuringly. "Arthur and I are just good friends," she said. I nodded quickly, worried that she would think me too conventional and stodgy. "I think we'll all be good friends," she said, leaning back and lighting a Gauloise. "Don't you?"

I nodded again. My brain was fuzzed from all the wine—I wasn't used to drinking in the afternoon—and I felt close to tears, on the verge of making some embarrassingly maudlin remark, when Art reappeared with the bowl of strawberries in one hand and carton of sour cream in the other.

"I love it when my friends all get along," Sondra sighed contentedly and bit into a strawberry.

"What makes you think we're getting along?" Art said, perfectly straight-faced.

After dessert, Art and I started clearing the table, but Sondra gestured impatiently for us to stop. "Just leave it," she said. "There's something I want to show you." She hurried off toward the back of the apartment. Art flipped over the record on the stereo. I sat down rather primly on the chrome-and-leather sofa, the only piece of furniture in the room other than the floor-to-ceiling bookshelves . The room suggested someone with expensive taste and little money, unwilling to make compromises. Art sprawled on the other end of the sofa, lit a Camel, and fiddled with the venetian blinds so as to soften the glare. Squinting out the window, I could feel my brain bobbing buoyantly inside my head like the small white sailboats dotting the bay. Alone suddenly with Art, I felt a little nervous, girlish. I had not had that much experience with men except for Tommy, whom I had known since the fifth grade. We'd gone to the same orthodontist. I didn't think of Tommy so much as a man as a full-grown boy; he was not in the least bit "other." Art got up and came back with a bottle of cognac and three snifters just as Sondra reappeared, hugging a large glossy book to her chest. Her face was flushed, as if she'd been bending over searching for the book, and her hair was even more disheveled than usual. In her crimson sweater she reminded me of an overblown rose.

"This is the book on *châteaux* I promised to show you, Arthur." She sank down on the leather sofa between us and opened the book on her lap. "Arthur and Janice are planning to rent a house in France next summer," she explained to me, smiling serenely—look, Ma, no jealousy. Sitting so close to her, I caught a whiff of Joy, my favorite perfume that I never failed to spray myself with whenever I passed through a department store. Thousands of distilled rose petals. Fifty dollars an ounce. She turned a page. "A friend of my parents rented a smaller estate near this one a few years ago, near Tours. Their son and I had an affair. Every afternoon between four and five. I was supposed to be tutoring him in French. Instead we were screwing our brains out." She laughed. "His parents paid me four dollars an hour."

"And how was his French?" Art asked.

"His oral skills were excellent." She winked at me. I blushed and gulped my cognac.

"Tsk, tsk." Art leaned back and covered my ears with his hands. "You're corrupting her. Behold, she blushes."

"She's not so innocent as she looks," Sondra said. She smiled her confidante's smile. "Tell him about Tommy."

"Yes, tell him about Tommy. By all means," Art said. "I'm all ears."

"He's no one," I mumbled. "I mean, he's just someone back in Washington."

"Waiting for you?" Art splashed some more cognac in my glass.

"I guess so. He wants to get married—he wants *us* to get married and join the Peace Corps." I accidentally sloshed some cognac on my lap and rubbed it into my jeans. "He's studying mechanical engineering."

"And how about you? What do you want to do?" Art coaxed.

"I don't know," I shrugged. "Get my Ph.D. Be a French professor somewhere."

"Like Sondra here?"

I nodded. "Exactly like Sondra." I sounded so drunkenly earnest they both burst out laughing.

"We haven't found you a *château* yet," Sondra said, suddenly brisk, like a teacher steering a wayward class back on track. "How about this one? Château Villandry." She turned the page to an imposing stone castle complete with moat and mazelike formal garden.

"I don't know," Art mused. "Do you have anything a little more with-it? Maybe a split-level with a wet bar?"

The three of us sat there sated from the rich meal, sipping our brandy and joking about the pros and cons of the various *châteaux* with a kind of timeless, dazed concentration that blanked out the rest of the world. As if the apartment were surrounded by a deep wide moat. Finally Sondra closed the book and stretched, letting her head fall back against the sofa and her eyelids flutter shut. The book slid off her lap with a solemn clunk. Like obedient children, Art and I also sank back and shut our eyes—I opened my left eye just a crack to make certain that his were indeed closed. It reminded me of naptime after story hour at my kindergarten, when we would all curl up like so many little shrimp on our blankets. I was smiling, about to comment on this, when I felt Sondra's hand on my leg, lightly stroking the inside of my thigh. My muscles tensed involuntarily, a quiver of pure shock. For a split second she paused, her fingers acknowledging my sudden tension, and then continued. Just as involuntarily my muscles relaxed themselves again. I cracked my eye open wide enough to observe that Sondra's other hand was similarly stroking Art's thigh. This is weird, I said to myself, but my mental voice sounded distant and hollow. You should make some excuse and leave, the voice said, but I ignored it. Here in this room, with the quiet jazz and the sun reflecting off the bay, the voice seemed as remote and out of place as my mother's scolding me to get my elbows off the table. Sondra's fingers were flirting and playful, kittenish. I shivered in the warm sunlight. On the other end of the sofa I heard Art moan softly, dreamily. There must have been a clumsy sort of transition from sofa to bed, but I cannot remember one. In my memory it is all as fluid and natural as flowing lava, or some deftly edited foreign film. In one frame we are sitting on the sofa fully clothed and in the next—*voilà!*—we are lying on the bed, our naked bodies softly lit, needing no direction from anyone, every gesture a brilliant ad lib, a virtual masterpiece of erotic improvisation.

In the sudden quiet aftermath of the sensual explosion, that awkward moment when awkwardness returns, when you fall back into your separate selves, Sondra stretched luxuriously, lit a Gauloise, exhaled, and said, "I do so love it when my friends get along."

We nearly, as my teenage sons used to say, busted a gut laughing. I dared to reach over and flick a tiny speck of tobacco from the corner of Sondra's lip.

A few hours later, back in my little rented bedroom unable to fall asleep, I had an attack of guilt about the way I had more or less dismissed Tommy in conversation—not to mention what came later. In the middle of the night, I sat down and wrote him a long chatty letter about nothing. At the end, after only a slight hesitation, I lied and said that I missed him.

That was mid-June. For the next few months, the three of us met at Sondra's apartment usually once a week for our "French cooking lessons." I did in fact, among other things, learn to make Coq au vin, Coquilles St. Jacques, ratatouille, an excellent cheese soufflé, and bittersweet chocolate mousse. It was a shame that my husband was your basic steak-and-potatoes man. I probably could have made some other man with a more sophisticated palate very happy.

There was a Fourth of July barbecue at Art and Janice's. Sondra was away, visiting her current love, who was living in London for a year on a Fulbright. My roommates were also throwing a big bash in our scruffy little backyard, something I had actually been looking forward to—I had recently vowed to spend more time with people my own age—but I was too curious to turn down Art's invitation. I had never met Art's wife. In fact, I had never really seen Art without Sondra. The curious thing about this whole thing—or one of them—was that it was always the three of us together. I can, of course, vouch for the fact that Sondra and I never made love alone, never even spent much time alone together. And Sondra maintained that she and Arthur had never gone to bed without me—a claim that I believe, strange as it all may sound. The three of us seemed to form an equilateral triangle, some perfectly harmonious triad. At the time I was too naive to realize just how rare this was. A small-town girl at heart, I sometimes brooded over the dubious moral nature of our little *ménage à trois*, but I more or less took its success for granted.

"Just bring some beer," Art had said on the telephone. "We're having burgers. Nothing fancy." Still, Janice had obviously gone to quite a bit of trouble making homemade potato salad, cole slaw, and brownies. She was a short, bosomy woman—the kind who wears loose flannel shirts and painter's pants—sisterly, maternal—the sort of woman who grew up with lots of brothers. I liked her immediately and immediately felt at home, even though I recognized only one other person, a grad student in comp lit. Sitting in a webbed lawn chair watching Art flip hamburgers on the grill with his twin daughters, Aviva and Ariel, clinging adoringly to his pants legs, I marveled at this double life of his, and in the midst of such wholesome and attractive domesticity, I experienced another swift attack of guilt and remorse. How unhealthy and sordid those long gourmand afternoons in Sondra's darkened bedroom seemed suddenly in comparison to all this daylight and fresh air and simple American food.

When I got home that evening, I called Tommy long-distance. At first he was cool, still miffed that I had rebuffed his offer to drive down for the long weekend, pleading too much work, but gradually he warmed up, never any good at holding a grudge. He was all excited. He had gone to talk to some Peace Corps volunteers just returned from West Africa. The volunteers had shown slides and talked about what a great experience it was. They had even met President Kennedy at a White House reception. (Tommy's and my romance had blossomed the summer we both worked as eager young volunteers at the Kennedy campaign headquarters in Bellingham.) Yes, I said, it did sound wonderful. I even promised to give it some serious thought. "You know, you sound more like your old self," Tommy said. But the following Tuesday I was back at Sondra's apartment for another cooking lesson.

A few weeks later, the fall semester started. I had enrolled in Sondra's graduate seminar in Proust on Wednesday afternoons. At the first class meeting, I took my seat at the seminar table among the dozen other graduate students in a state of smug, exalted agitation. I had imagined there would be an undercurrent running between Sondra and me, significant glances in my direction, veiled innuendoes. In essence, I would know myself to have been singled out, chosen, promoted from the ranks of the other fawning grad students. But as Sondra waxed eloquent about the possible influences of Bergson, Schopenhauer, and Kierkegaard on Proust, it became more and more impossible for me to imagine her naked, her articulate tongue educating me in a completely different mode, and I began to feel like some pathetic and delusional creature. Wounded by her perfectly blank eyes devoid of any faint flicker of recognition, I had to fight my childish urge to betray her with my own telling look or remark. As the hour progressed, I grew more dejected and paranoid, interpreting much of what Sondra said as an oblique personal rebuke. I scribbled down one quote from a critic that struck me as particularly pointed: "Marcel yearns after a kind of mystical communion, with an individual, or with a group, dwelling, he believes, in a superior realm of existence separated from the vulgar herd." Distraught as I was, I should have remained silent, but something kept compelling me to speak up, and my comments or maybe my tone must have seemed a little off. I noticed some of my classmates eyeing me skeptically. Then, during the ten-minute break, Sondra called me into her office on some pretext and shut the door. "What goes on out there is purely professional. Don't take it so personally." She kissed me swiftly on both cheeks. *"Comprends?"* I nodded, delighted and ashamed of myself. After that, I was fine. Really, that's all it took. She was my teacher. I learned.

Things continued much the same all through the fall. I was busy with my studies. I socialized some with my fellow grad students in French lit. I talked to Tommy long-distance at least once a week. And, of course, there were the French cooking lessons. The weeks passed quickly. Suddenly, it seemed, it was late November. I was flying home for Thanksgiving. I was not exactly looking forward to it. I was, in fact, half-dreading this reunion with what now seemed to me to be some former life, some alias. All summer and fall I had made excuses. I had diplomatically but successfully managed to avoid seeing Tommy, to avoid making any decision, but there was no excuse possible this time. Our connection seemed to stretch thinner with every passing week, but I was still, for whatever reason, reluctant to sever it. Plus, my parents were anxious for me to be there. The family had always been together at Thanksgiving. Sondra and her Fulbright lover were meeting for a week's holiday in New York. Art and Janice and the twins were driving to her parents' house in Scottsdale. It was a hectic time, but we managed to schedule one final pre-Thanksgiving cooking lesson—a brunch this time because Sondra had an appointment to get her hair trimmed that afternoon—Friday, the day before we would all scatter in our various directions—Friday, November 22, 1963.

I got up early that morning in order to give myself plenty of time to pack before taking the bus to Telegraph Hill. It was cool and damp and quiet. Peaceful. My roommates had already left for home. I had always enjoyed packing—the geometric precision of it—and I had traveled so little that the mere sight of a suitcase still produced a childlike thrill. We were supposed to meet at Sondra's at ten o'clock. Sondra would make coffee. Art would pick up some croissants. I snapped my old Samsonite shut and straightened up my room, wanting everything to be neat and orderly upon my return.

For some reason, Art, who was notoriously late for everything, was early this particular morning. He was just hunting for a parking place in his battered MG as I got off the bus. We walked down the block and up the stairs together, chatting about nothing in particular. Art's hair was still damp from the shower—little, dark ringlets—and he was carrying a white paper bag from the bakery. The croissants smelled fresh and buttery. Suddenly I was starved. Sondra opened the door still in her red silk kimono—no pretenses here, I remember thinking. The aroma of French roast filled the apartment. A newspaper was lying on the doorstep. I bent down and handed it to Sondra. She tossed it onto a pile of unread papers on the kitchen counter. The kitchen clock, shaped like a coffee pot, said 10:02. (Just past noon in Dallas.) Sondra poured us coffee and arranged the croissants on a pretty stoneware platter.

We drifted into the living room. The phone rang. Art and I sat on the sofa, drinking and eating, while Sondra tried to cut short the conversation with whoever it was on the other end. It was a gray day outside—or maybe that's just how I see it in retrospect. Art reached over and brushed some flaky crumbs off my sweater. His hand on my breasts aroused me. There was something urgent and hurried in the atmosphere that morning—we all felt it—none of our usual languid postponement of pleasure. Sondra hung up and then, on second thought, left the receiver off the hook. We followed her into the bedroom. She had not even bothered to make the bed or change the pink flowered sheets from the last time. As she slipped off her robe and stretched out on the bed, I thought she seemed a little sad or depressed. I thought possibly she might have quarreled with Paul, her London paramour, but then again she may have just been tired. I was tired myself, having stayed up till one A.M. reading a scholarly essay on Proust that Sondra had recommended entitled "The Inhuman World of Pleasure." Sitting on the edge of the bed, I made some lame little joke about the title as I reached my arms back to unhook my bra—a black-lace extravagance I had invested in after our first cooking lesson—(a year or so later we would all abandon bras)—and Art said, "That's good. Don't move." I turned my neck slightly and was startled to see him standing there naked, focusing the lens of an expensive-looking camera. Instinctively my hands flew to my bare breasts and I looked at Sondra, waiting for her to protest. She was reclining, one pale arm flung wantonly over her head, like one of Matisse's *odalisques,* smoking the butt-end of a Gauloise she'd fished out of the overflowing ashtray beside the bed. She just smiled and gave a Gallic sort of shrug. Slowly I let my hands fall away from my breasts. Sondra bent over and kissed, one by one, the bony vertebrae of my spine. With my eyes closed I could still see the camera flashes, little stars of light in the darkened room. I thought I might die of pleasure.

It was just past eleven when we left. Sondra's hair appointment was for eleven-thirty in Union Square at a place called Rapunzel's— funny the things you remember. She was showering when Art and I took off. He offered to give me a ride home, and even though it was out of his way, I accepted. A fellow grad student was driving me to the airport at one-fifteen. Conversation was fitful and a little strained. I think we both felt a bit embarrassed—like two strangers emerging from a matinée of some porno film, blinking in the sudden dazzle of daylight. We were both tired, physically spent. As if in sympathy with our mood, the streets seemed oddly empty and subdued. Art lit a cigarette and said, "I should have a radio put in this heap." He drummed his fingers along the steering wheel. I kept thinking I would be at home by dinnertime. Sitting in the dining room eating my mother's pot roast. It seemed impossible.

When I walked up the steps to my apartment, the phone was ringing. I heard it ringing as I fumbled the keys out of my big purse, and it kept ringing as I flung open the door and raced for the kitchen. I was afraid maybe it was my ride to the airport calling to say her car had broken down or something had come up. Skidding across the linoleum, I grabbed the receiver off the wall and gasped a breathless hello.

"Where the hell have you been?" he burst out, then paused as if to collect himself. It was Tommy, but his voice sounded weird, choked. He was supposed to be meeting me at the Seattle airport, and my first thought was that he was calling to say he was sick.

"What's up?" I said, immediately launching into a long-winded, guilt-ridden excuse about where I'd been. He cut me off.

"Don't you *know?*" he said, incredulous. "Didn't you *hear?*" His voice was loud, and it suddenly dawned on me he was crying. I had never heard him cry before. My heart froze in my chest.

"What is it? What happened?"

"It's Kennedy," he said. "He's dead. He was shot and he's dead." His voice rose at the end of the sentence, as if he were not *telling* me but *asking* me something of grave importance. What flashed into my mind, oddly enough, was an image of Sondra sitting in the beauty parlor.

I caught the plane to Seattle on schedule and spent the weekend with Tommy and my family, glued to the television set, watching the president's funeral. Thanksgiving afternoon, Tommy and I went for a long drive along the coast. We held hands in the car. We didn't talk much—we never had really—but I felt closer to him. Before he had always seemed confident and competent, but now I was seeing a new, more vulnerable side of him. Kennedy had been his hero. We stopped for a beer at some roadside bar, and Tommy's eyes filled with tears as he was sitting there, not saying anything. I wanted to comfort him. I covered his hands with mine and squeezed hard. He blew his nose with a paper napkin and then excused himself for a minute. When he got back from the men's room, I could see he had splashed cold water on his face and combed his hair—pulled himself together. He ordered two more beers and then, when the waitress had gone, he asked me to marry him and join the Peace Corps. He said they were looking for people to go to India. He said if I didn't go with him, he would go without me. Outside it was pouring rain. I pictured hot dusty country-side, emaciated oxen, dark-eyed children, flies, simple meals of rice and chapatis, ascetic pallets. Long days, hard work. Ask not what your country can do for you. "Okay," I said. "Let's do it."

I never even went back to San Francisco to pick up my belongings. I was afraid. Pleading a family crisis, I asked my roommates to pack up my books and clothes and ship them up to Bellingham. Tommy offered to drive me down there to get my things, but I said no, and he did not press the issue. I think he sensed I had my reasons, reasons he was better off not knowing anything about. The thought of seeing Sondra and Art again made me feel sick. It was like aversion therapy. When I thought of being in bed with them, I would close my eyes and see Jackie in her pink suit and blood-stained nylons, that look of pure anguish on her face. By way of explanation of a sort, I sent Sondra a postcard on which I had copied out a quotation from *Remembrance of Things Past* that I'd remembered reading in "The Inhuman World of Pleasure," that essay which Sondra had so highly recommended:

The duke felt a momentary alarm. He could see the delights of the ball snatched away from him . . . now that he had been told of the death of M. d'Osmond. But he quickly recovered and flung at his two cousins a retort in which he declared, along with his determination not to forego his pleasure, his inability to assimilate the niceties of the French language: "He is dead! Surely not, it's an exaggeration, an exaggeration."

Tommy and I had a simple ceremony—close family and a few friends—low-key and subdued. After all, we all still felt as if we were in mourning. In January we left for Bangladesh, where we lived for two years. After India, we traveled for six months and then moved to Chicago, where Tommy got a job with the city—some urban development agency—and I went back to school to get a master's in elementary education, specializing in reading skills. For a few years I taught elementary school. Then I moved on to spearhead a task force on literacy. We had two sons, both of whom are away at college now. After the younger one, Rob, left for Stanford, Tommy and I divorced. Not so amicably.

I live alone and work only part-time now as a consultant on literacy programs. For the first time in twenty years, I find myself with free time on my hands. Too much time. A few weeks ago, in September, I enrolled in an adult education course on Proust taught by a retired professor emeritus from the University of Chicago. The course is taught in translation, which is just as well, because my French is so rusty. Still, my professor seems impressed by my background.

It is dark now. I am feeling a little more human, my head is clearer. The rubble of crumpled Kleenex offends my sense of order. I reach for the wastebasket, eyes glued to the silent television screen as the camera zooms in on Jackie in her black veil. Haunting. Unforgettable. A cultural touchstone. Idle cocktail-party chat. Where were *you* when Kennedy was shot? And each time, newly caught off guard, I experience the same sudden flush of shame and desire as I mumble my little lie: in the language lab, I say, listening to French tapes.

From time to time over the years, I would think of those photographs that Art took that last morning—I would picture them in my mind, shot by shot—and hope to hell that he had the good sense to burn them. But now suddenly I hope that he was foolhardy enough to lock them away somewhere safe—our own private little footnote to history. Sighing, I retrieve my copy of *Swann's Way*, which has tumbled onto the floor. Dressed in a little double-breasted coat, John-John salutes his father's casket. God. Has it really been twenty-five years already?

ABOUT THE AUTHORS

LESLEE BECKER was born in 1945 in Au Sable Forks, New York. She graduated from the Iowa Writers' Workshop, where she received a James Michener Writing Fellowship. She was a Wallace Stegner Fellow at Stanford and a Jones Lecturer in Fiction. She has had stories published in *The Atlantic, Iowa Review, New Letters, Nimrod, Prism, River Styx,* and elsewhere. She received the *Nimrod*/Katherine Anne Porter Fiction Prize and won the 1992 Pirate's Alley Faulkner Society Award for her story collection, *The Musical Lady*. She currently teaches at Colorado State University and is working on a second collection of stories.

PETER BEHRENS was born in 1954 in Montreal, where he has lived most of his life and where he attended Concordia and McGill universities. He held the Wallace Stegner Fellowship in Creative Writing at Stanford University in 1985. His stories have been published in literary journals and magazines, including *The Atlantic* and *Saturday Night*. He is now married to an American filmmaker and divides his time between Montreal and Los Angeles.

ETHAN CANIN was born in 1960 in Ann Arbor, Michigan. He attended Stanford University and the Iowa Writers' Workshop and published his first story when he was nineteen. He was the winner of a Houghton Mifflin Literary Fellowship in 1988 and received the Henfield Transatlantic Review Award in 1989 in addition to other awards and honors. He is a contributor to periodicals, including *The Atlantic*, and his fiction was anthologized in Houghton Mifflin's *Best American Short Stories* in 1985 and 1986. His novel *Blue River* was published in 1991. He is currently working on two other novels and another short story collection.

EVAN CONNELL was born in 1924 in Kansas City, Missouri. He attended Dartmouth College and the University of Kansas and followed with graduate work at Stanford, Columbia, and San Francisco State University. He is best known for his novels, *Mr. Bridge* and *Mrs. Bridge,* which were adapted as the film *Mr. and Mrs. Bridge* in 1990. He was a Guggenheim Fellow in 1963 and has written for *The Atlantic,* the *New York Times,* the *Washington Post,* the *Chicago Sun Times, The New Yorker,* the *San Francisco Chronicle,* the *Paris Review, Esquire,* and other periodicals. He currently lives in San Francisco.

HARRIET DOERR was born in 1910 in Pasadena, California. She attended Stanford University, where she completed both her undergraduate and graduate study and received a Wallace Stegner Fellowship. She was the winner of the Henfield Transatlantic Review Award for short stories in 1982 and received an NEA grant in 1983. She is a member of PEN and is a contributor of fiction to such periodicals as *The Atlantic, The New Yorker, EPOCH,* and the *Santa Monica Quarterly.* Her book, *Stones for Ibara,* will be followed this August by a second, entitled *Consider This, Señora* (Harcourt).

CHARLES EASTMAN was born in 1929 in Hollywood, California. He was raised in and around Los Angeles and attended Los Angeles City College. In addition to writing fiction, he is a screenwriter and author of plays. Considering it his job to "set people straight" about the West Coast, he's working on a series of books about Hollywood in the twenties, thirties, and forties, of which "Yellow Flags" is part. "Yellow Flags" was first published in *The Atlantic* in April 1992, and was chosen for *Prize Stores: The O. Henry Awards* for 1993. He currently lives in Manhattan Beach, California.

JAMES FETLER was born in 1931. He teaches English at Foothill College near San Francisco. He received an NEA fellowship in creative writing and was awarded the Gold Medal for Fiction by the Commonwealth Club of California. In 1980 his story "Impossible Appetites" won the Iowa Short Fiction Award. His stories have been published in *The Atlantic, Paris Review, Commentary,* and elsewhere.

RICHARD FORD was born in 1944 in Jackson, Mississippi. He currently lives in Western Montana and has been a writer since 1976. He is a member of the Writer's Guild (East) and PEN. He was a Guggenheim Fellow in 1977–78 and an NEA Fellow in 1979. His short stories have been widely anthologized and have appeared in such publications as *The New Yorker, Vanity Fair,* and *Granta.* He is the author of three novels.

MERRILL JOAN GERBER was born in 1938 in Brooklyn, New York. She attended the University of Miami and the University of Florida and followed with graduate study at Brandeis, and Stanford University, where she was a creative writing fellow in 1962–63. She has taught creative writing at California State University and the University of Redlands, and she currently lives in Sierra Madre, California, where she teaches fiction writing at Caltech. She is the author of five novels, her most recent being *The Kingdom of Brooklyn* (Longstreet, 1992), and three collections of short stories. A fourth collection, entitled *What's a Family For?,* is due out this fall. "I Don't Believe This" was first published in *The Atlantic* in October of 1984 and was chosen for inclusion in *Prize Stories: The O. Henry Doubleday Awards* in 1986.

NORA JOHNSON was born in 1933 in Hollywood, California, the daughter of Nunnally Johnson, a screenwriter, producer, and director. She has been a freelance writer since 1958, when *The World of Henry Orient* was released and then nominated for a Writer's Guild Award for film. She is a contributor of articles and stories to *The Atlantic, The New Yorker, McCall's, Mademoiselle, Sports Illustrated,* and other magazines. "The Jungle of Injustice" was first published in *The Atlantic* in October of 1980.

JOHN L'HEUREUX was born in 1934 in South Hadley, Massachusetts. He is a professor of English and former director of the creative writing program at Stanford University. He received an NEA creative writing fellowship in both 1981 and 1986. He is a contributor of fiction to periodicals, including *The Atlantic.* His most recent books are *Comedians,* a collection of short stories (Viking), and *The Shrine of Altamira,* a novel.

NEIL McMAHON was born in Chicago, Illinois, in 1949. He was a

Wallace Stegner Fellow at Stanford University, 1981–82, and currently lives in Missoula, Montana. "Heart" was first published in *The Atlantic* in August of 1979.

JOYCE CAROL OATES was born in Lockport, New York, in 1938 and graduated from Syracuse University in 1960. In addition to publishing fiction in *The Atlantic* and other magazines and journals, Oates has written many novels, collections of short stories, and poems. She has been the recipient of several awards and honors, including a National Book Award for her novel *them* and the 1990 Rea Award for the Short Story. She currently lives in Princeton, New Jersey, coedits the *Ontario Review,* and is the Roger S. Berlind Distinguished Professor in the Humanities at Princeton University. Her most recent novel, *Foxfire: Confessions of a Girl Gang,* is due to be published in August of 1993.

ANN PACKER was born in 1959 in Stanford, California, and was raised in the San Francisco Bay area. After a decade in New York and the Midwest, she is back on the West Coast, in Eugene, Oregon, where she lives with her husband and daughter. Her collection will be published in 1994 by Chronicle Books.

NANCY PACKER was born in 1925 in Washington, D.C. She recently retired as director of the Stanford Writing Program, but continues as a professor of English at Stanford University. She is a contributor to literary journals and popular magazines, including *Harper's, The Yale Review, The Kenyon Review, Reporter,* and *The Southwest Review.* Her stories have been reprinted in such anthologies as *Prize Stories: The O. Henry Awards* and *Best American Short Stories.* She lives in San Francisco.

JUDITH RASCOE was born in 1941 in San Francisco and was raised throughout the West. She studied at Harvard and Stanford University and in 1969 held a fellowship at the Stanford Writing Center. Since then she has divided her time between London, New York, and Los Angeles, writing stories and screenplays. She has been published in *The Atlantic* and elsewhere.

ROBERT STONE was born in 1937 in New York City. He attended

New York University and Stanford, where he received a Wallace Stegner Fellowship, 1962–64. He received a Guggenheim fellowship in
1971, won the National Book Award in 1975 for *Dog Soldiers,* was the
runner-up for a Pulitzer Prize for fiction in 1982 for *A Flag for Sun-
rise,* and received an NEA fellowship in 1983, in addition to other
awards and prizes. His fiction has been anthologized in such collections as *Best American Short Stories, Stanford Short Stories,
Contemporary American Writers,* and elsewhere. He is a contributor of
articles and reviews to *Harper's, Life,* and the *New York Times Book
Review.* He lives in California.

MARLY SWICK was born in 1949 in Indianapolis, Indiana. She
received her undergraduate degree from Stanford University and her
MFA from the University of Iowa. She now teaches fiction at the University of Nebraska. She has been a recipient of an NEA Grant, a James
Michener Award, and a Wisconsin Institute of Creative Writing Fellowship. Her short stories have appeared in *The Atlantic, Redbook, The
North Atlantic Review, The Iowa Review, McCall's,* and other places.

AMY TAN was born in Oakland, California, in 1952. From 1969 to
1976 she attended five colleges: Linfield College in Oregon, San Jose
City College, San Jose State University, from which she received a BA,
UC Santa Cruz, and UC Berkeley. Her first work of fiction, *The Joy
Luck Club,* was published in 1989 and became the longest running
bestseller on the *New York Times* hardcover bestseller list in 1989. It
was also a finalist for the National Book Award and the National Book
Critics Circle Award and has recently been made into a film. Her second book, *The Kitchen God's Wife,* was published in 1991 and also
reached the top of the *New York Times* hardcover bestseller list. She is
currently working on a third novel, *The Year of No Flood.* Her short
stories have appeared in *The Atlantic,* where "Two Kinds" was first
published in February of 1989, *Grand Street, Lear's, McCall's,* and
other magazines, as well as in numerous anthologies.

TOBIAS WOLFF was born in Birmingham, Alabama, in 1945 and
grew up in the Skagit River Valley of Washington State. He graduated
from Oxford University and received a Wallace Stegner fellowship to
Stanford University, where he received his master's degree in writing.

His novel, *The Barracks Thief,* was awarded the PEN/Faulkner Award for Fiction in 1985 and his memoir, *This Boy's Life,* was published in 1989. He is also the author of two short story collections, *In the Garden of the North American Martyrs* (1981) and *Back in the World* (1986). His work has appeared in anthologies and periodicals including *The Atlantic, Esquire, Vanity Fair, Antaeus,* and others. "The Other Miller" was first published in *The Atlantic* in June 1986. Wolff, with his wife and two sons, lives in Syracuse, New York, where he is a writer-in-residence at Syracuse University.